Praise for the n

Just O...

"Higgins provides an...
satisfying...
—*Pu...*

"Kristan Higgins has a writing voice that is very genuine, robust and amusing... *Just One of the Guys* abounds with charm and the true joys and pratfalls of falling in love."
—*RomanceJunkies.com*

"This story made me laugh out loud several times and tear up at the end and, best of all, it made me rush out to buy the backlist."
—*DearAuthor.com*

"A true masterpiece."
—*dee's book dish*

Catch of the Day
Winner—2008 Romance Writers of America RITA® Award

"Smart, fresh and fun! A Kristan Higgins book is not to be missed!"
—*New York Times* bestselling author Carly Phillips

"Higgins has crafted a touching story brimming with smart dialogue, sympathetic characters, an engaging narrative and the amusing, often self-deprecating observations of the heroine. It's a novel with depth and a great deal of heart."
—*RT Book Reviews,* 4½ stars, Top Pick

"Goes down sweetly. An utterly charming story!"
—*New York Times* bestselling author Gena Showalter

"When your heart needs a smile, when you want to believe in falling in love again or when you just want to read a great book, grab one by Higgins. You can't go wrong."
—*dee's book dish*
Best Book of the Year, 2007

Fools Rush In

"Where has Kristan Higgins been all my life?
Fools Rush In is a spectacular debut."
—*USA TODAY* bestselling author Elizabeth Bevarly

"Higgins reached deep into every woman's soul and showed some heavy truths in a fantastically funny and touching tale. This book is on my keeper shelf and will remain there for eternity. It will be re-read and loved for years to come."
—*dee's book dish*

"A fresh intelligent voice—Kristan Higgins is too much fun!"
Cindy Gerard, *USA TODAY* bestselling author of *To the Limit*

"Higgins is a talented writer [who] will make you want to search high and low for anything that she has written."
—*Chicklit Romance Writers*

"Outstanding! This is a story well worth reading."
—*Coffee Time Romance*

KRISTAN HIGGINS
too good to be true

DID YOU PURCHASE THIS BOOK WITHOUT A COVER?
If you did, you should be aware it is **stolen property** as it was
reported *unsold and destroyed* by a retailer. Neither the author nor the
publisher has received any payment for this book.

All the characters in this book have no existence outside the imagination
of the author, and have no relation whatsoever to anyone bearing the same
name or names. They are not even distantly inspired by any individual
known or unknown to the author, and all the incidents are pure invention.

All Rights Reserved including the right of reproduction in whole or
in part in any form. This edition is published by arrangement with
Harlequin Enterprises II B.V./S.à.r.l. The text of this publication or any
part thereof may not be reproduced or transmitted in any form or by any
means, electronic or mechanical, including photocopying, recording,
storage in an information retrieval system, or otherwise, without the
written permission of the publisher.

This book is sold subject to the condition that it shall not, by way of trade
or otherwise, be lent, resold, hired out or otherwise circulated without the
prior consent of the publisher in any form of binding or cover other than
that in which it is published and without a similar condition including this
condition being imposed on the subsequent purchaser.

MIRA is a registered trademark of Harlequin Enterprises Limited, used
under licence.

Published in Great Britain 2011.
MIRA Books, Eton House, 18-24 Paradise Road,
Richmond, Surrey, TW9 1SR

© Kristan Higgins 2009

ISBN 978 0 7783 0441 8

63-0211

MIRA's policy is to use papers that are natural, renewable and
recyclable products and made from wood grown in sustainable forests.
The logging and manufacturing processes conform to the legal
environmental regulations of the country of origin.

Printed and bound in Spain
by Litografia Rosés S.A., Barcelona

Also available from **Kristan Higgins**
and MIRA Books

JUST ONE OF THE GUYS
CATCH OF THE DAY
FOOLS RUSH IN

This book is dedicated to the memory of my grandmother, Helen Kristan, quite the loveliest woman I've ever known.

ACKNOWLEDGEMENTS

At the Maria Carvainis Agency…thanks as always to the brilliant and generous Maria Carvainis for her wisdom and guidance, and to Donna Bagdasarian and June Renschler for their enthusiasm for this book.

At my publisher, thanks to Keyren Gerlach for her gracious and intelligent input and to Tracy Farrell for her support and encouragement.

Thanks to Julie Revell Benjamin and Rose Morris, my writing buddies, and to Beth Robinson of PointSource Media, who makes my website and trailers look so great.

On the personal side, thanks to my friends and family members who listen endlessly to my ideas—Mom, Mike, Hilly, Jackie, Nana, Maryellen, Christine, Maureen and Lisa. How lucky I am to have such a family and such friends!

Thanks to my great kids, who make life so enjoyable, and especially to my honey, Terence Keenan. Words, in this case, are just not enough.

And, finally, thanks to my grandfather, Jules Kristan, a man of steadfast devotion, keen intelligence and innate and boundless goodness. The world is a better place because of your example, dearest Poppy.

*too good
 to be true*

PROLOGUE

MAKING UP A BOYFRIEND is nothing new for me. I'll come right out and admit that. Some people go window shopping for things they could never afford. Some look at online photos of resorts they'll never visit. And some people imagine that they meet a really nice guy when, in fact, they don't.

The first time it happened was in sixth grade. Recess. Heather B., Heather F. and Jessica A. were standing in their little circle of popularity. They wore lip gloss and eye shadow, had cute little pocketbooks and boyfriends. Back then, going out with a boy only meant that he might acknowledge you while passing in the hall, but still, it was a status symbol, and one that I lacked, right along with the eye shadow. Heather F. was watching her man, Joey Ames, as he put a frog down his pants for reasons clear only to sixth grade boys, and talking about how she was maybe going to break up with Joey and go out with Jason.

And suddenly, without a lot of forethought, I found myself saying that I, too, was dating someone…a boy from another town. The three popular girls turned to me with sharp and sudden interest, and I found myself talking about Tyler, who was really cute and smart and polite. An older man at fourteen. Also, his family owned a horse ranch and they wanted me to name the newest foal, and I was going to train it so that it came for my whistle and mine alone.

Surely we've all come up with a boy like that. Right? What was the harm in believing—almost—that somewhere out there, counterbalancing the frog-in-the-pants types was a boy like Tyler of the horses? It was almost like believing in God—you had to, because what was the alternative? The other girls bought it, peppered me with questions, looked at me with new respect. Heather B. even invited me to her upcoming birthday party, and I happily accepted. Of course, by then I was forced to share the sad news that Tyler's ranch had burned down and the family moved to Oregon, taking my foal, Midnight Sun, with them. Maybe the Heathers and the rest of the kids in my class guessed the truth, but I found I didn't really mind. Imagining Tyler had really felt…great, actually.

Later, when I was fifteen and we'd moved from our humble town of Mount Vernon, New York, to the much posher burg of Avon, Connecticut, where all the girls had smooth hair and very white teeth, I made up another boy. Jack, my Boyfriend Back Home. Oh, he was so handsome (as proved by the photo in my wallet, which had been carefully cut from a J.Crew catalogue). Jack's father owned a really gorgeous restaurant named Le Cirque (hey, I was fifteen). Jack and I were taking things slow…yes, we'd kissed; actually, we'd gotten to second base, but he was so respectful that that was as far as it went. We wanted to wait till we were older. Maybe we'd get preengaged, and because his family loved me so much, they wanted Jack to buy me a ring from Tiffany's, not a diamond but maybe a sapphire, kind of like Princess Diana's, but a little smaller.

Sorry to tell you, I broke up with Jack about four months into my sophomore year in order to be available to local boys. My strategy backfired…the local boys were not terribly interested. In my older sister, definitely…Margaret would pick me up once in a while when she was home from college, and boys would fall silent at the mere sight of her sharp, glamorous beauty. Even my younger sister, who was only in seventh grade at the time, already showed signs of becoming a great beauty. But I stayed unattached, wishing I'd never broken up with my fictional boyfriend, missing the warm curl of pleasure it gave me to imagine such a boy liking me.

Then came Jean-Philippe. Jean-Philippe was invented to counter an irritating, incredibly persistent boy in college. A chemistry major who, looking back, probably suffered from Asperger's syndrome, making him immune to every social nuance I threw his way. Rather than just flat out tell the boy that I didn't like him (it seemed so cruel) I'd instruct my roommate to scrawl messages and tack them to the door so all could see: "Grace—J-P called *again,* wants you to spend break in Paris. Call him *toute suite.*"

I *loved* Jean-Philippe, loved imagining that some well-dressed Frenchman had a thing for me! That he was prowling the bridges of Paris, staring sullenly into the Seine, yearning for me and sighing morosely as he ate chocolate croissants and drank good wine. Oh, I had a crush on Jean-Philippe for ages, rivaling only my love for Rhett Butler, whom I'd discovered at age thirteen and never let go.

All through my twenties, even now at age thirty, faking a boyfriend was a survival skill. Florence, one of the little old ladies at Golden Meadows Senior Village, recently offered me her nephew during the ballroom dancing class, which I help teach. "Honey, you would just love Bertie!" she chirped as I tried to get her to turn right on her alamaena. "Can I give him your number? He's a doctor. A podiatrist. So he has one tiny problem. Girls today are too picky. In my day, if you were thirty and unmarried, you were as good as dead. Just because Bertie has bosoms, so what? His mother was buxom, too, oh, she was stacked…"

Out came the imaginary boyfriend. "Oh, he sounds so nice, Flo…but I just started dating someone. Drat."

It's not just around other people, I have to admit. I use the emergency boyfriend as…well, let's say as a coping mechanism, too.

For example, a few weeks ago, I was driving home on a dark and lonely section of Connecticut's Route 9, thinking about my ex-fiancé and his new lady love, when my tire blew out. As is typical with brushes with death, a thousand thoughts were clear in my mind, even as I wrestled with the steering wheel, trying to keep the car from flipping, even as I distantly realized that voice shrieking "OhGodohGod!" was mine. First, I had nothing to wear to my funeral *(easy, easy, don't want to flip the car)*. Second, if open casket was an option, I hoped my hair wouldn't be frizzing in death as it did in life *(pull harder, pull harder, you're losing it)*. My sisters would be devastated, my parents struck dumb with sorrow, their endless sniping silenced, at least for the day *(hit the gas, just a little, it will straighten out the car)*. And God's nightgown, wouldn't Andrew be riddled with guilt! For the rest of his life, he'd always regret dumping me *(slow down gradually now, on with the flashers, good, good, we're still alive)*.

When the car was safe on the shoulder, I sat, shaking uncontrollably, my heart clattering against my ribs like a loose shutter in a hurricane. "JesusJesusthankyouJesus," I chanted, fumbling for my cell phone.

Alas, I was out of range for cell service (of course). I waited a few moments, then, resigned, did what I had to do. Got out of the car into the cold March downpour, examined my shredded tire. Opened the trunk, pulled out the jack and the spare tire. Though I'd never done this particular task before, I figured it out as other cars flew past me occasionally, further drenching me with icy spray. I pinched my hand badly enough for a blood blister, broke a nail, ruined my shoes, became filthy from the mud and axle grease.

No one stopped to help. Not one dang person. No one even tapped their brakes, for that matter. Cursing, quite irritable with the cruelty of the world and vaguely proud that I'd changed a tire, I climbed back into the car, teeth chattering, lips blue with cold, drenched and dirty. On the drive back, all I could think of was a bath, a hot toddy, *Project Runway* and flannel pajamas. Instead, I found disaster waiting for me.

Judging from the evidence, Angus, my West Highland terrier, had chewed through the child safety latch on the newly painted cabinet door, dragged out the garbage can, tipped it over and ate the iffy chicken I'd thrown out that morning. There was no *if* about it, apparently. The chicken was bad. My poor dog had then regurgitated with such force that the walls of my kitchen were splattered with doggy vomit so high that a streak of yellow-green bile smeared the face of my Fritz the Cat clock. A trail of wet excrement led to the living room, where I found Angus stretched out on the pastel-shaded Oriental rug I'd just had cleaned. My dog belched foully, barked once and wagged his tail with guilty love amid the steaming puddles of barf.

No bath. No Tim Gunn and *Project Runway*. No hot toddy.

So what does this have to do with another imaginary boyfriend? Well, as I scrubbed the carpet with bleach and water and tried to emotionally prepare Angus for the suppository the vet instructed me to give, I found myself imagining the following instead.

I was driving home when my tire blew out. I stopped, reached for my cell phone, yadda yadda ding dong, blah blah blah. But what was this? A car slowed and pulled in behind me. It was, let's see, an environmentally gentle hybrid, and ah, it had M.D. plates. A Good Samaritan in the form of a tall, rangy male in his mid- to late-thirties approached my car. He bent down. Hello! There it was…that moment when you look at someone and just…kablammy. You Just Know He's The One.

In my fantasy, I accepted the kind Samaritan's offer of help. Ten minutes later, he had secured the spare on the axle, heaved the blown tire in the trunk and handed me his business card. Wyatt Something, M.D., Department of Pediatric Surgery. Ah.

"Call me when you get home, just so I know you made it, okay?" he asked, smiling. Kablammy! He scrawled his home number on the card as I drank in the sight of his appealing dimples and long lashes.

It made cleaning up the puke a lot nicer.

Obviously, I was quite aware that my tire was not changed by the kindly and handsome doctor. I didn't tell anyone he had. Just a little healthy escapism, right? No, there was no Wyatt (I always liked the name, so authoritative and noble). Unfortunately, a guy like that was just too good to be true. I didn't go around talking about the pediatric surgeon who changed my tire, of course not. No. This was kept firmly private, just a little coping mechanism, as I said. I hadn't publicly faked a boyfriend in years.

Until recently, that is.

CHAPTER ONE

"And so with this one act, Lincoln changed the course of American history. He was one of the most despised figures in politics in his day, yet he preserved the Union and is considered the greatest president our country ever had. And possibly ever will have."

My face flushed…we'd just begun our unit on the Civil War, and it was my favorite class to teach. Alas, my seniors were in the throes of a Friday afternoon coma. Tommy Michener, my best student on most days, stared longingly at Kerry Blake, who was stretching so as to simultaneously torment Tommy with what he couldn't have and invite Hunter Graystone IV to take it. At the same time, Emma Kirk, a pretty, kindhearted girl who had the curse of being a day student and was thus excluded from the cool kids, who all boarded, looked at her desk. She had a crush on Tommy and was all too aware of his obsession with Kerry, poor kid. "So who can sum up the opposing viewpoints? Anyone?"

From outside came the sound of laughter. We all looked. Kiki Gomez, an English teacher, was holding class outside, as the day was mild and lovely. Her kids didn't look dazed and battered. Dang. I should've brought my kids outside, too.

"I'll give you a hint," I continued, looking at their blank faces. "States' rights vs. Federal control. Union vs. secession.

Freedom to govern independently vs. freedom for all people. Slaves or no slaves. Ring a bell?"

At that moment, the chimes that marked the end of the period sounded, and my lethargic students sprang into life as they bolted for the door. I tried not to take it personally. My seniors were usually more engaged, but it was Friday. The kids had been hammered with exams earlier in the week, and there was a dance tonight. I understood.

Manning Academy was the type of prep school that litters New England. Stately brick buildings with the requisite ivy, magnolia and dogwood trees, emerald soccer and lacrosse fields, and a promise that for the cost of a small house, we'd get your kids into the colleges of their choice—Princeton, Harvard, Stanford, Georgetown. The school, which was founded in the 1880s, was a little world unto itself. Many of the teachers lived on campus, but those of us who didn't, myself included, were usually as bad as the kids, eager for the last class to end each Friday afternoon so we could head for home.

Except this Friday. I'd have been more than happy to stay at school this Friday, chaperoning dances or coaching lacrosse. Or heck, cleaning the toilets for that matter. Anything other than my actual plans.

"Hi, Grace!" Kiki said, popping into my classroom.

"Hi, Kiki. Sounded like fun out there."

"We're reading *Lord of the Flies*," she informed me.

"Of course! No wonder you were laughing. Nothing like a little pig killing to brighten the day."

She grinned proudly. "So, Grace, did you find a date?"

I grimaced. "No. I didn't. It won't be pretty."

"Oh, shit," she said. "I'm so sorry."

"Well, it's not the end of the world," I murmured bravely.

"You sure about that?" Like me, Kiki was single. And no

one knew better than a single woman in her thirties that hell is going to a wedding stag. In a few hours, my cousin Kitty, who once cut my bangs down to the roots when I was sleeping over at her house, was getting married. For the third time. In a Princess Diana–style dress.

"Look, it's Eric!" Kiki blurted, pointing to my eastern window. "Oh, thank you, God!"

Eric was the guy who washed Manning Academy's windows each spring and fall. Though it was only early April, the afternoon was warm and balmy, and Eric was shirtless. He grinned at us, well aware of his beauty, sprayed and squeegeed.

"Ask him!" Kiki suggested as we stared with great appreciation.

"He's married," I said, not taking my eyes off him. Ogling Eric was about as intimate as I'd been with a man in some time.

"*Happily* married?" Kiki asked, not above wrecking a home or two to get a man.

"Yup. Adores his wife."

"I hate that," she muttered.

"I know. So unfair."

The male perfection that was Eric winked at us, blew a kiss and dragged the squeegee back and forth over the window, shoulder muscles bunching beautifully, washboard abs rippling, sunlight glinting on his hair.

"I should really get going," I said, not moving a muscle. "I have to change and stuff." The thought made my stomach cramp. "Kiki, you sure you don't know anyone I can take? Anyone? I really, really don't want to go alone."

"I don't, Grace," she sighed. "Maybe you should've hired someone, like in that Debra Messing movie."

"It's a small town. A gigolo would probably stand out.

Also, probably not that good for my reputation. 'Manning Teacher Hires Prostitute. Parents Concerned.' That kind of thing."

"What about Julian?" she asked, naming my oldest friend, who often came out with Kiki and me on our girls' nights.

"Well, my family knows him. He wouldn't pass."

"As a boyfriend, or as a straight guy?"

"Both, I guess," I said.

"Too bad. He's a great dancer, at least."

"That he is." I glanced at the clock, and the trickle of dread that had been spurting intermittently all week turned into a river. It wasn't just going stag to mean old Kitty's wedding. I'd be seeing Andrew for only the third time since we broke up, and having a date would've definitely helped.

Well. As much as I wished I could just stay home and read *Gone With the Wind* or watch a movie, I had to go. Besides, I'd been staying in a lot lately. My father, my gay best friend and my dog, though great company, probably shouldn't be the only men in my life. And there was always the microscopic chance that I'd meet someone at this very wedding.

"Maybe Eric will go," Kiki said, hustling over to the window and yanking it open. "No one has to know he's married."

"Kiki, no," I protested.

She didn't listen. "Eric, Grace has to go to a wedding tonight, and her ex-fiancé is going to be there, and she doesn't have a date. Can you go with her? Pretend to adore her and stuff?"

"Thanks anyway, but, no," I called, my face prickling with heat.

"Your ex, huh?" Eric said, wiping a pane clear.

"Yeah. May as well slit my wrists now." I smiled to show I didn't mean it.

"You sure you can't go with her?" Kiki asked.

"My wife would probably have a problem with that," Eric answered. "Sorry, Grace. Good luck."

"Thanks," I said. "It sounds worse than it is."

"Isn't she brave?" Kiki asked. Eric agreed that I was and moved on to the next window, Kiki nearly falling out the window to watch him leave. She hauled herself back in and sighed. "So you're going stag," she said in the same tone as a doctor might use when saying, *I'm sorry, it's terminal.*

"Well, I did try, Kiki," I reminded her. "Johnny who delivers my pizza is dating Garlic-and-Anchovies, if you can believe it. Brandon at the nursing home said he'd hang himself before being a wedding date. And I just found out that the cute guy at the pharmacy is only seventeen years old, and though he said he'd be happy to go, Betty the pharmacist is his mom and mentioned something about the Mann Act and predators, so I'll be going to the CVS in Farmington from now on."

"Oopsy," Kiki said.

"No big deal. I came up empty. So I'll just go alone, be noble and brave, scan the room for legs to hump and leave with a waiter. If I'm lucky." I grinned. Bravely.

Kiki laughed. "Being single sucks," she announced. "And God, being single at a wedding…" She shuddered.

"Thanks for the pep talk," I answered.

FOUR HOURS LATER, I was in hell.

The all too familiar and slightly nauseating combination of hope and despair churned in my stomach. Honestly, I thought I was doing pretty well these days. Yes, my fiancé had dumped me fifteen months ago, but I wasn't lying on the floor in fetal position, sucking my thumb. I went to work and taught my classes…very well, in my opinion. I went out socially. Granted, most of my excursions were either dancing with senior citizens or reenacting Civil War battles, but I did get out. And, yes, I would (theoretically) love to find a man—sort of an Atticus-Finch-meets-Tim-Gunn-and-looks-like-George-Clooney type.

So here I was at another wedding—the fourth family wedding since The Dumping, the fourth family wedding where I'd been dateless—gamely trying to radiate happiness so my relatives would stop pitying me and trying to fix me up with odd-looking distant cousins. At the same time, I was trying to perfect The Look—wry amusement, inner contentment and absolute comfort. Sort of a *Hello! I am perfectly fine being single at yet another wedding and am not at all desperate for a man, but if you happen to be straight, under forty-five, attractive, financially secure and morally upright, come on down!* Once I mastered The Look, I planned on splitting an atom, since they required just about the same level of skill.

But who knew? Maybe today, my eyes would lock on someone, someone who was also single and hopeful without being pathetic—let's say a pediatric surgeon, just for the sake of argument—and kablammy! We'd just know.

Unfortunately, my hair was making me look, at best, gypsy beautiful and reckless, but more probably like I was channeling Gilda Radner. Must remember to call an exorcist to see if I could have the evil demons cast out of my hair, which had been known to snap combs in half and eat hairbrushes.

Hmm. There was a cute guy. Geeky, skinny, glasses, definitely my type. Then he saw me looking and immediately groped behind him for a hand, which was attached to an arm, which was attached to a woman. He beamed at her, planted a kiss on her lips and shot a nervous look my way. *Okay, okay, no need to panic, mister,* I thought. *Message received.*

Indeed, all the men under forty seemed to be spoken for. There were several octogenarians present, one of whom was grinning at me. Hmm. Was eighty too old? Maybe I *should* go for an older man. Maybe I was wasting my time on men who still had functioning prostates and their original knees. Maybe there was something to be said for a sugar daddy. The old guy raised his bushy white eyebrows, but his pursuit of me being his sweet young thing ended abruptly as his wife elbowed him sharply and shot me a disapproving glare.

"Don't worry, Grace. It will be your turn soon," an aunt boomed in her foghorn of a voice.

"You never know, Aunt Mavis," I answered with a sweet smile. It was the eighth time tonight I'd heard such a sentiment, and I was considering having it tattooed on my forehead. *I'm not worried. It will be my turn soon.*

"Is it hard, seeing them together?" Mavis barked.

"No. Not at all," I lied, still smiling. "I'm very glad they're dating." Granted, *glad* may have been a stretch, but still. What else could I say? It was complicated.

"You're brave," Mavis pronounced. "You are one brave woman, Grace Emerson." Then she tromped off in search of someone else to torment.

"Okay, so spill," my sister Margaret demanded, plopping herself down at my table. "Are you looking for a good sharp instrument so you can hack away at your wrists? Thinking about sucking a little carbon monoxide?"

"Aw, listen to you, you big softy. Your sisterly concern brings tears to my eyes."

She grinned. "Well? Tell your big sis."

I took a long pull from my gin and tonic. "I'm getting a little tired of people saying how brave I am, like I'm some marine who jumped on a grenade. Being single isn't the worst thing in the world."

"I wish I was single all the time," Margs answered as her husband approached.

"Hey, Stuart!" I said fondly. "I didn't see you at school today." Stuart was the school psychologist at Manning and had in fact alerted me to the history department opening six years ago. He sort of lived the stereotype…oxford shirts covered by argyle vests, tasseled loafers, the required beard. A gentle, quiet man, Stuart had met Margaret in graduate school and been her devoted servant ever since.

"How are you holding up, Grace?" he asked, handing me a fresh version of my signature drink, a gin and tonic with lemon.

"I'm great, Stuart," I answered.

"Hello, Margaret, hello, Stuart!" called my aunt Reggie from the dance floor. Then she saw me and froze. "Oh, hello, Grace, don't you look pretty. And chin up, dear. You'll be dancing at your own wedding one day soon."

"Gosh, thanks, Aunt Reggie," I answered, giving my sister a significant look. Reggie gave me a sad smile and drifted away to gossip.

"I still think it's freakish," Margs said. "How Andrew and Natalie could ever… Gentle Jesus and His crown of thorns! I just cannot wrap my brain around that one. Where are they, anyway?"

"Grace, how are you? Are you just putting up a good front, honey, or are you really okay?" This from Mom who now approached our table. Dad, pushing his ancient mother in her wheelchair, trailed behind.

"She's fine, Nancy!" he barked. "Look at her! Doesn't she seem fine to you? Leave her alone! Don't talk about it."

"Shut it, Jim. I know my children, and this one's hurting. A *good* parent can tell." She gave him a meaningful and frosty look.

"Good parent? I'm a great parent," Dad snipped right back.

"I'm fine, Mom. Dad is right. I'm peachy. Hey, doesn't Kitty look great?"

"Almost as pretty as at her first wedding," Margaret said.

"Have you seen Andrew?" Mom asked. "Is it hard, honey?"

"I'm fine," I repeated. "Really. I'm great."

Mémé, my ninety-three-year-old grandmother, rattled the ice in her highball glass. "If Grace can't keep a man, all's fair in love and war."

"It's alive!" Margaret said.

Mémé ignored her, gazing at me with disparaging, rheumy eyes. "I never had trouble finding a man. Men loved me. I was quite a beauty in my day, you know."

"And you still are," I said. "Look at you! How do you do it, Mémé? You don't look a day over a hundred and ten."

"Please, Grace," my father muttered wearily. "It's gas on a fire."

"Laugh if you want, Grace. At least my fiancé never threw me over." Mémé knocked back the rest of her Manhattan and held out her glass to Dad, who took it obediently.

"You don't need a man," Mom said firmly. "No woman does." She leveled a significant look at my father.

"What is that supposed to mean?" Dad snapped.

"It means what it means," Mom said, her voice loaded.

Dad rolled his eyes. "Stuart, let's get another round, son. Grace, I stopped by your house today and you really need new windows. Margaret, nice job on the Bleeker case, honey." It was Dad's way to jam in as much into a conversation as possible, sort of get things over with so he could ignore my mother (and his). "And, Grace, don't forget about Bull Run next weekend. We're Confederates."

Dad and I belonged to Brother Against Brother, the largest

group of Civil War reenactors in three states. You've seen us...we're the weirdos who dress up for parades and stage battles in fields and at parks, shooting each other with blanks and falling in delicious agony to the ground. Despite the fact that Connecticut didn't see a whole lot of Civil War action (alas), we fanatics in Brother Against Brother ignored that inconvenient fact. Our schedule started in the early spring, when we'd stage a few local battles, then move on to the actual sites throughout the South, joining up with other reenactment groups to indulge in our passion. You'd be amazed at how many of us there were.

"Your father and those idiot battles," Mom muttered, adjusting Mémé's collar. Mémé had apparently fallen deeply asleep or died...but no, her bony chest was rising and falling. "Well, I'm not going, of course. I need to focus on my art. You're coming to the show this week, aren't you?"

Margaret and I exchanged wary looks and made noncommittal sounds. Mom's art was a subject best left untouched.

"Grace!" Mémé barked, suddenly springing back to life. "Get out there! Kitty's going to throw the bouquet! Go! Go!" She turned her wheelchair and began ramming it into my shins, as ruthless as Ramses bearing down on the fleeing Hebrew slaves.

"Mémé! Please! You're hurting me!" I yanked my legs out of the way, which didn't stop her.

"Go! You need all the help you can get!"

Mom rolled her eyes. "Leave her alone, Eleanor. Can't you see she's suffering enough? Grace, honey, you don't have to go if it makes you sad. Everyone will understand."

"I'm fine," I said loudly, running a hand over my uncontrollable hair, which had burst the bonds of bobby pins. "I'll go." Because damn it, if I didn't, it would be worse. *Poor*

Grace, look at her, she's just sitting there like a dead possum in the road, can't even get out of her chair. Besides, Mémé's chair was starting to leave marks on my dress.

Out onto the dance floor I went, as excited as Anne Boleyn on her way to the gallows. I tried to blend in with the other sheep, standing in the back where I wouldn't really have a chance of catching the bouquet. "Cat Scratch Fever" came booming over the stereo—so classy—and I couldn't suppress a snicker.

Then I saw Andrew. Looking right at me, guilty as sin. His date was nowhere in sight. My heart lurched.

I knew he was here, of course. Him coming was my idea. But seeing him, knowing he was with another woman today in their first appearance as a couple, made my hands sweat, my stomach turn to ice. Andrew Carson was, after all, the man I thought I'd marry. The man I came within three weeks of marrying. The man who left me because he fell in love with someone else.

A couple of years ago, at Cousin Kitty's second wedding, Andrew had come as my date. We'd been together for a while, and when it was bouquet toss time then, I'd gone up more or less happily, pretending to be embarrassed but with the smug contentment of a steady boyfriend. I didn't catch the bouquet, and when I left the dance floor, Andrew had slung his arm around my shoulder. "I thought you could've worked a little harder out there," he'd said, and I remembered the thrilling rush those words had caused.

Now he was here with his new girlfriend. Natalie of the long, straight, blond hair. Natalie of the legs that went on forever. Natalie the architect.

Natalie, my much adored younger sister, who was understandably lying low at this wedding.

Kitty tossed the bouquet. Her sister, my cousin Anne,

caught it as planned and rehearsed, no doubt. Torture time over. But, no. Kitty spied me, picked up her skirts and hustled over. "It will be your turn soon, Grace," she announced loudly. "You holding up okay?"

"Sure," I said. "It's déjà vu all over again, Kitty! Another spring, another one of your weddings."

"You poor thing." She gave my arm a firm squeeze, smug sympathy dripping out of her, glanced at my bangs (yes, they'd grown out in the fifteen years that had passed since she'd cut them) and went back to her groom and the three kids from her first two marriages.

THIRTY-THREE MINUTES LATER, I decided I'd been brave long enough. Kitty's reception was in full swing, and while the music was lively and my feet were itching to get out there and show the crowd what a rumba was supposed to look like, I decided to head for home. If there was a single, good-looking, financially secure, emotionally stable man here, he was hiding under a table. One quick pit stop and I'd be on my way.

I pushed open the door, took a quick and horrifying look in the mirror—even I didn't even know it was possible for my hair to frizz that much, holy guacamole, it was nearly horizontal—and started to push open a stall door when I heard a small noise. A sad noise. I peeked under the door. Nice shoes. Strappy, high heels, blue patent leather.

"Um…is everything okay?" I asked, frowning. Those shoes looked familiar.

"Grace?" came a small voice. No wonder the shoes looked familiar. My younger sister and I had bought them together, last winter.

"Nat? Honey, are you okay?"

There was a rustle of material; then my sister pushed

open the door. She tried to smile, but her clear blue eyes were wet with silvery tears. I noted her mascara didn't deign to run. She looked tragic and gorgeous, Ilsa saying goodbye to Rick at the Casablanca airport.

"What's wrong, Nat?" I asked.

"Oh, it's nothing…." Her mouth wobbled. "It's fine."

I paused. "Is it something to do with Andrew?"

Natalie's good front faltered. "Um…well…I don't think it's going to work between us," she said, her voice cracking a little, giving her away. She bit her lip and looked down.

"Why?" I asked. Relief and concern battled in my heart. Granted, it sure wouldn't kill me if Nat and Andrew didn't work out, but it wasn't like Natalie to be melodramatic. In fact, the last time I'd seen her cry was when I'd left for college twelve years ago.

"Um…it's just a bad idea," she whispered. "But it's fine."

"What happened?" I asked. The urge to strangle Andrew flared in my gut. "What did he do?"

"Nothing," she assured me hastily. "It's just…um…"

"What?" I asked again, more forcefully this time. She wouldn't look at me. Ah, dang it all. "Is it because of me, Nat?"

She didn't answer.

I sighed. "Nattie. Please answer me."

Her eyes darted at me, then dropped to the floor again. "You're not over him, are you?" she whispered. "Even though you said you were…I saw your face out there, at the bouquet toss, and oh, Grace, I'm so sorry. I should never have tried—"

"Natalie," I interrupted, "I'm over him. I am. I promise."

She gave me a look loaded with such guilt and misery and genuine anguish that the next words came out of my mouth without my being fully aware of them. "The truth is, Nat, I'm seeing someone."

Oops. Hadn't really planned on saying that, but it worked like a charm. Natalie blinked up at me, two more tears slipping down her petal-pink cheeks, hope dawning on her face, her eyes widening. "You are?" she said.

"Yes," I lied, snatching a tissue to dab her face. "For a few weeks now."

Nat's tragic expression was fading. "Why didn't you bring him tonight?" she asked.

"Oh, you know. Weddings. Everyone gets all excited if you come with someone."

"You didn't tell me," she said, a slight frown creasing her forehead.

"Well, I didn't want to say anything until I knew it would be worth mentioning." I smiled again, warming to the idea—just like old times—and this time, Nat smiled back.

"What's his name?" she asked.

I paused for the briefest second. "Wyatt," I answered, remembering my tire-changing fantasy. "He's a doctor."

CHAPTER TWO

LET ME JUST SAY THAT THE REST of the night went a lot better for everyone. Natalie towed me back to the table where the rest of our family sat, insisting that we hang out together a little, as she had been too nervous to actually speak to me yet this day.

"Grace has been seeing someone!" she announced softly, eyes shining. Margaret, who had been painfully listening to Mémé describe her nasal polyps, snapped to attention. Mom and Dad stopped mid-bicker to pelt me with questions, but I stuck with my "it's still a little early to talk about it" story. Margaret raised an eyebrow but didn't say anything. Out of the corner of my eye, I scanned for Andrew—he and Natalie had been keeping a bit of a distance from each other out of concern for my tender feelings. He wasn't in range.

"And just what does this person do for a living?" Mémé demanded. "He's not one of those impoverished teachers, is he? Your sisters managed to find jobs that pay a decent wage, Grace. I don't know why you can't."

"He's a doctor," I said, taking a sip of the gin and tonic the waiter brought over.

"What kind, Pudding?" Dad asked.

"A pediatric surgeon," I answered smoothly. Sip, sip. Hopefully, the flush on my face could be attributed to my cocktail and not lying.

"Ooh," Nat sighed, her face breaking into an angelic smile. "Oh, Grace."

"Wonderful," Dad said. "Hold on to this one, Grace."

"She doesn't need to hold on to anything, Jim," Mom snapped. "Honestly, you're her father! Do you really need to undermine her this way?" Then they were off and running in another argument. How nice that Poor Grace was finally off the list of things to worry about!

I TOOK A CAB HOME, claiming a misplaced cell phone and a pressing need to call my wonderful doctor boyfriend. I also managed to avoid speaking directly with Andrew. Pushing Natalie and Andrew out of my head à la Scarlett O'Hara—*I'll think about that tomorrow*—I focused instead on my new imaginary boyfriend. Good thing my tire had blown out a few weeks ago, or I wouldn't have been nearly so quick on my feet.

How nice it would've been if Wyatt, pediatric surgeon, were a real guy. If he'd been a good dancer, too, even if it was just a little turning box step. If he could've charmed Mémé and asked Mom about her sculptures and not cringed when she described them. If he was a golfer like Stuart and the two guys made plans for a morning on the links. If he just happened to know a little bit about the Civil War. If he occasionally broke off midsentence when he was talking because he looked at me and simply forgot what he was saying. If he was here to lead me upstairs, unzip this uncomfortable dress and shag me silly.

The cab turned onto my street and cruised to a stop. I paid the driver, got out and just stood for a minute, looking at my house. It was a teensy little three-story Victorian, tall and narrow. A few brave daffodils stood bobbing along the walk, and soon the tulip beds would erupt in pink and yellow. In

May, the lilacs along the eastern side of my house would fill the entire house with their incomparable smell. I'd spend most of the summer on my porch, reading, writing papers for various journals, watering my Boston ferns and begonias. My home. When I bought the house—correction, when Andrew and I bought it—it had been tattered and neglected. Now, it was a showplace. *My* showplace, as Andrew had left me before the new insulation was installed, before the walls were knocked down and repainted.

At the sound of my high heels on the flagstone path, Angus's head popped up in the window, making me grin... and then wobble. Apparently, I was a little buzzed, a fact underscored as I fumbled ineffectively for my keys. There. Key in door, turn. "Hello there, Angus McFangus! Mommy's home!"

My little dog raced up to me, then, too overcome by the miracle of my very being, raced around the downstairs in victory-lap style—living room, dining room, kitchen, hallway, repeat. "Did you miss Mommy?" I asked every time he whizzed past me. "Did you...miss...Mommy?" Finally, his energy expended somewhat, he brought me his victim of the night, a shredded box of tissues, which he deposited proudly at my feet.

"Thank you, Angus," I said, understanding that this was a gift. He collapsed in front of me, panting, black button eyes adoring, his back legs straight out behind him, as if he were flying, in what I thought of as his Super Dog pose. I sat down, slipped off my shoes and scratched Angus's cunning little head. "Guess what? We have a boyfriend now," I said. He licked my hand in delight, burped, then ran into the kitchen. Good idea. I'd hit the Ben & Jerry's for a little snack. Hoisting myself out of my chair, I glanced out the window and froze.

A man was creeping along the side of the house next door.

Obviously, it was dark outside, but the streetlight illuminated the man clearly as he walked slowly along the side of the house next to mine. He looked in both directions, paused, then continued on to the back of the house, climbed the back steps, slowly, tentatively, then tried the doorknob. Locked, apparently. He looked under the doormat. Nothing. Tried the doorknob again, harder.

I didn't know what to do. I'd never seen a house being broken into before. No one lived in that house, 36 Maple. I'd never even seen someone look at it in the two years I'd lived in Peterston. It was sort of a bungalow style, pretty worn down, in need of a good bit of work. I'd often wondered why no one bought it and fixed it up. Surely there was nothing inside worth stealing....

Swallowing with an audible click, I realized that, should the burglar look in my direction, he'd see me quite clearly, as my light was on and the curtains open. Reaching out slowly without taking my eyes off him, I turned off the lamp.

The suspect, as I was already calling him, then gave the door a shove with his shoulder. He repeated the action, harder this time, and I flinched as his shoulder hit the door. No go. He tried again, stepped back, then walked to a window, cupped his hands around his eyes and peered in.

This all looked very suspicious to me. Sure enough, the man tried to open the window. Again, no luck. Perhaps, yes, I'd watched too many episodes of *Law & Order,* friend to single women everywhere, but this seemed pretty cut-and-dried. A *crime* was in progress at the vacant house next door. Surely this wasn't good. What if the burglar came over here? In his two years on earth, Angus had yet to be put to the test of home protection. Ripping up shoes and rolls of toilet paper, that he had mastered. Protect me from an average-size male? Not too sure. And was the burglar average? He looked pretty brawny to me. Pretty solid.

I let the usual stream of horrific images slide through my head and acknowledged the slim odds of their actually happening. The man, who was currently trying another window, was probably not a murderer looking for a place to stash a body. He probably didn't have a million dollars' worth of heroin in his car. And I hoped quite fervently that he had no plans to chain an average-size woman in the pit in his cellar and wait for her to lose enough weight so he could use her skin to whip up a new dress, like that guy in *Silence of the Lambs*.

The burglar tried the door a second time. *Okay, pal*, I thought. *Enough is enough. Time to call the authorities.* Even if he wasn't a murderer, he clearly was looking for a house to burgle. Was that a verb? *Burgle?* It sounded funny. Granted, yes, I'd had two gin and tonics tonight (or was it three?), and drinking wasn't really a strong suit of mine, but still. No matter how I broke it down, the activity next door looked pretty damn criminal. The man disappeared around the back of the house again, still, I assumed, searching for a point of entry. What the heck. Time to put my tax dollars to use and call the cops.

"911, please state your emergency."

"Hi, how are you?" I asked.

"Do you have an emergency, ma'am?"

"Oh, well, you know, I'm not sure," I answered, squinting one eye shut to see the burglar better. No such luck; he'd disappeared around the far corner of the house. "I think the house next door to me is being robbed. I'm at 34 Maple Street, Peterston. Grace Emerson."

"One moment, please." I heard the squawk of a radio in

the background. "We have a cruiser in your area, ma'am," she said after a moment. "We'll dispatch a unit right now. What exactly can you see?"

"Um, right now, nothing. But he was…casing the joint, you know?" I said, wincing. Casing the joint? Who was I, Tony Soprano? "What I mean is, he's walking around, trying the doors and windows. No one lives there, you know."

"Thank you, ma'am. The police should be there any moment. Would you like us to stay on the line?" she asked.

"No, that's okay," I said, not wanting to seem too much of a wuss. "Thank you." I hung up, feeling vaguely heroic. A regular neighborhood watch, I was.

I couldn't see the man anymore from the kitchen, so I slipped into the dining room (oops, a little dizzy…maybe that *was* three G&Ts). Peeking out the window, I saw nothing irregular at the moment. And I didn't hear sirens, either. Where were those cops? Maybe I should've stayed on the line. What if the burglar realized there's nothing to steal over there, but then took a look over here? *I* had plenty of nice things. That sofa set me back almost two grand. My computer was state-of-the-art. And last birthday, Mom and Dad had given me that fabulous plasma screen TV.

I looked around. Sure, it was dumb, but I'd feel safer if I was…well, not armed, but something. I didn't own a handgun, God knew…not the type. I glanced at my knife block. Nah. That seemed a little over the top, even for me. Granted, I had two Springfield rifles in the attic, not to mention a bayonet, along with all my other Civil War gear, but we didn't use bullets, and I couldn't quite imagine bayoneting someone, no matter how much fun I had pretending to do just that at our battle reenactments.

Creeping into the living room, I opened the closet and surveyed my options. Hanger, ineffective. Umbrella, too lightweight. But wait. There, in the back, was my old field hockey stick from high school. I'd kept it all these years for sentimental reasons, harking back to the brief period of time when I was an athlete, and now I was glad. Not quite a weapon, but some protection nevertheless. Perfect.

Angus was now asleep on his bed, a red velvet cushion in a wicker basket, in the kitchen. He lay on his back, furry white paws in the air, his little bottom teeth locked over his uppers. He didn't look like he was going to be much help in the case of a home invasion. "Cowboy up, Angus," I whispered. "Being cute isn't everything, you know."

He sneezed, and I ducked. Did the burglar hear that? For that matter, did he hear me on the phone? I chanced a peek out the dining-room window. Still no cops. No movement from next door, either. Maybe he was gone.

Or coming over. Coming for *me*. Well, my stuff, anyway. Or me. You never knew.

Holding the field hockey stick reassured me. Maybe I'd just slip upstairs and lock myself in the attic, I thought. Sit next to those rifles, even if I didn't own bullets. Surely the police could handle the thief next door. And speaking of cops, a black-and-white cruiser glided down the street, parking right in front of the Darrens' house. Great. I was safe. I'd just tiptoe into the dining room and see if Mr. Burglar Man was in sight.

Nope. Nothing. Just the ticking of the lilac branches against the windows. Speaking of the windows, Dad was right. They did need to be replaced. I could feel a draft, and it wasn't even that windy. My heating bill had been murder this year.

Just then, a quiet knock came on the door. Ah, the cops. Who said they were never around when you needed them? Angus leaped up as if electrocuted and raced to the door, dancing happily, leaping so that all four paws left the ground, barking shrilly. *Yarp! Yarpyarpyarpyarp!* "Sh!" I told him. "Sit. Stay. Calm down, honey."

Stick still in hand, I opened the front door.

It wasn't the cops. The burglar was standing right in front of me. "Hi," he said.

I heard the stick hit him before I realized I'd moved, and then my frozen brain acknowledged all sorts of things at once—the muffled thunking of wood against human. The trembling reverberation up my arm. The stunned expression on the burglar's face as he reached up to cover his eye. My shaking legs. The slow sinking of said burglar to his knees. Angus's hysterical yapping.

"Ouch," the burglar said faintly.

"Back off," I squeaked, the hockey stick wavering. My entire body shook violently.

"Jesus, lady," he muttered, his voice more surprised than anything. Angus, snarling like an enraged lion cub, took hold of the burglar's sleeve and whipped his little head back and forth, trying to do some damage, tail wagging joyfully, body trembling at the thrill of defending his mistress.

Should I put the stick down? Wouldn't that be the prime moment for him to grab me? Wasn't that the mistake most women make just before they're tossed into the pit in the cellar and starved till their skin gets loose?

"Police! Hands in the air!"

Right! The police! Thank God! Two officers were running across my lawn.

"Hands in the air! Now!"

I obeyed, the field hockey stick slipping out of my hands, bouncing off the burglar's head and landing on the porch floor. "For Christ's sake," the burglar muttered, wincing.

Angus released the sleeve and pounced instead upon the stick, snarling and yapping with glee.

The burglar squinted up at me. The skin around his eye had already turned livid red. And oh, dear, was that blood?

"Hands on your head, pal," one of the cops said, whipping out his handcuffs.

"I don't believe this," the burglar said, obeying with (I imagined) the wearied resignation of someone who's been through this before. "What did I do?"

The first cop didn't answer, just snapped on the cuffs. "Please step inside, ma'am," the other officer said.

I finally unfroze from my hands-in-the-air position and staggered inside. Angus dragged the field hockey stick in behind me before abandoning it to zip in joyous circles around my ankles. I collapsed on the sofa, gathering my dog in my arms. He licked my chin vigorously, barked twice, then bit my hair.

"Are you Ms. Emerson?" the cop asked, tripping slightly over the field hockey stick.

I nodded, still shaking violently, my heart galloping in my chest like Seabiscuit down the final stretch.

"So what happened here?"

"I saw that man breaking into the house next door," I answered, disentangling my hair from Angus's teeth. My voice was fast and high. "Where no one lives, by the way. And so I called you guys, and then he came right up on my porch. So I hit him with a field hockey stick. I played in high school."

I sat back, swallowed and glanced out the window, taking a few deep breaths, trying not to hyperventilate. The cop gave me a moment, and I stroked Angus's rough fur, making my doggy croon with joy. Now that I thought of it, perhaps whacking the burglar wasn't quite…necessary. It occurred to me that he said "Hi." I thought he did, anyway. He said hi. Do burglars usually greet their victims? *Hi. I'd like to rob your house. Does that work for you?*

"You okay?" the cop asked. I nodded. "Did he hurt you? Threaten you?" I shook my head. "Why did you open the door, miss? That wasn't a smart thing to do." He frowned disapprovingly.

"Uh, well, I thought it was you guys. I saw your car. And, no, he didn't hurt me. He just..." *said hi.* "He looked, um...suspicious? Sort of? You know, he was creeping around that house, that's all. Creeping and looking, sort of peeking? And no one lives there. No one's lived over there since I've lived over here. And I didn't actually mean to hit him."

Well, didn't I sound smart!

The cop gave me a dubious look and wrote a few things in his little black notebook. "Have you been drinking, ma'am?" he asked.

"A little bit," I answered guiltily. "I didn't drive, of course. I was at a wedding. My cousin. She's not very nice. Anyway, I had a cocktail. A gin and tonic. Well, really more like two and a half. Possibly three?"

The cop flipped his notebook closed and sighed.

"Butch?" The second officer stuck his head in the door. "We have a problem."

"Did he run?" I blurted. "Did he escape?"

The second cop gave me a pitying look. "No, ma'am, he's sitting on your steps. We've got him cuffed, nothing for you to worry about. Butch, could you come out here a second?"

Butch left, his gun catching the light. Clutching Angus to me, I tiptoed to the living room window and pushed back the curtain (blue raw silk, very pretty). There was the burglar, still sitting on my front steps, his back to me, as Officer Butch and his partner conferred.

Now that I wasn't in mortal fear, I took a good look at him. Bed-heady brown hair, kind of appealing, really. Broad shoulders...it was a good thing I didn't get into a scuffle with him. Well, into more of a scuffle, I supposed. Burly arms, from the look of the way the fabric strained against his biceps. Then again, it could just be the pose forced on him by having his hands cuffed behind his back.

As if sensing my presence, the burglar turned toward me. I leaped back from the window, wincing. His eye was already swollen shut. Dang it. I hadn't planned on hurting him. I hadn't planned anything, really...just acted in the moment, I guess.

Officer Butch came back inside.

"Does he need some ice?" I whispered.

"He'll be fine, ma'am. He says he's staying next door, but we're gonna take him to the station and verify his story. Can you give me your contact information?"

"Sure," I answered, reciting my phone number. Then the cop's words sank in. *Staying next door*.

Which meant I just clubbed my new neighbor.

CHAPTER THREE

THE FIRST THING I DID UPON awakening was roll out of bed and squint through my hangover at the house next door. All was quiet. No sign of life. Guilt throbbed in time with my pounding head as I recalled the stunned look on the burglar's—or the not-burglar's—face. I'd have to call the police station and see what had happened. Maybe I should alert my dad, who was a lawyer. Granted, Dad handled tax law, but still. Margaret was a criminal defense lawyer. She might be a better bet.

Dang it. I wished I hadn't hit the guy. Well. Accidents happen. He *was* skulking around a house at midnight, right? What did he expect? That I'd invite him in for a coffee? Besides, maybe he was lying. Maybe "staying next door" was just his cover story. Maybe I'd just done a community service. Still, clubbing people was new to me. I hoped the guy wasn't too hurt. Or mad.

The sight of my dress, which I hadn't hung up in my furor last night, reminded me of Kitty's wedding. Of Andrew and Natalie, together. Of Wyatt, my new imaginary boyfriend. I smiled. Another fake boyfriend. I'd done it again.

You may have gotten the impression that Natalie was... well, not spoiled, but protected. You'd be right. She was universally adored by our parents, by Margs, who didn't give her love easily and, yes, even by Mémé. But especially by me. In fact, my very first clear memory in life was of Natalie. It was my fourth birthday, and Mémé was smoking a ciggie in our kitchen, ostensibly watching us while my cake baked in the oven, the warm smell of vanilla mingling not unpleasantly with her Kool Lights.

The kitchen of my childhood seemed to be an enormous place full of wonderful, unexpected treasures, but my favorite spot was the pantry, a long, dark closet with floor-to-ceiling shelves. Often would I go in and close the door behind me, eating chocolate chips from the bag in delicious silence. It was like a little house unto itself, complete with bottles of seltzer water and dog food. Marny, our cocker spaniel, would come in with me, wagging her little stump of a tail as I fed her kibbles, eating one myself once in a while. Sometimes Mom would open the door and yelp, startled to find me there, curled up next to the mixer with the dog. It always felt so safe in there.

At any rate, on my fourth birthday, Mémé was smoking, I was lurking in the pantry with Marny, sharing a box of Cheerios, when I heard the back door open. In came Mom and Dad. There was a flurry of activity...Mommy had been away for a few days, and then I heard her call my name.

"Gracie, where are you! Happy birthday, honey! We have someone who wants to meet you!"

"Where's the birthday girl?" boomed Dad. "Doesn't she want her presents?"

Suddenly aware of how much I missed my mother, I bolted from the cabinet, past Mémé's skinny, vein-bumpy legs, and charged toward my mother, who was sitting at the kitchen table, still in her coat. She was holding a baby wrapped in a soft pink blanket.

"My birthday present!" I cried in delight.

Eventually, the grown-ups explained to me that the baby

wasn't just for me, but for Margaret and everyone else, too. My present was, in fact, a stuffed animal, a dog. (Later that day, according to family lore, I put the stuffed dog in the baby's crib, delighting my parents with my generosity.) But I never got over the feeling that Natalie Rose was mine, certainly much more than she was Margaret's, a feeling that Margaret, who was seven at the time and horribly sophisticated, nurtured in order to get out of her sisterly responsibilities. "Grace, your baby needs you," she'd call when Mom asked for help spooning yogurt into Nat's mouth or changing a poopy diaper. I didn't mind. I loved being the special sister, the big sister after four long years of being bossed around or ignored by Margaret. My birthday became more about Natalie and me, our beginning, than the day I was born. No, now my birthday was much more important. The day I got Natalie.

Natalie did not fail to delight. A stunning baby, she became more beautiful as she grew, her hair silky and blond, her eyes a startling sky-blue, cheeks as soft as tulip petals, eyelashes so long they touched her silken eyebrows. Her first word was *Gissy,* which we all knew was her attempt to say my name.

As she grew, she looked up to me. Margaret, for all her gruffness and disdain, was a good sister, but more of the type to take you aside and explain how to get out of trouble or why you should leave her stuff alone. For playing, for cuddling, for company, Nat turned to me, and I was more than willing. At age four, she spent hours putting barrettes in my kinky curls, wishing aloud that her own blond waterfall of smoothness was, in her words "a beautiful brown cloud." In kindergarten, she brought me in for show-and-tell, and on Special Person's Day, you know who was at her side. When she needed help in spelling, I took over for Mom or

Dad, making up silly sentences to keep things fun. During her ballet recitals, her eyes sought me out in the audience, where I'd be beaming back at her. I called her Nattie Bumppo after the hero of *The Deerslayer,* pointing to her name in the book to show her how famous she was.

Thus went our childhood—Natalie perfect, me adoring, Margs gruff and a little above it all. Then, when Natalie was seventeen and I was in my junior year at William & Mary, I got a call from home. Natalie had been feeling crummy for a day or so. She was not one to complain, so when she finally admitted that her stomach hurt pretty badly, Mom called the doctor. Before they could get to the office, Nat's appendix ruptured. The resulting appendectomy was messy, since infected fluid had spread throughout her abdomen, and she came down with peritonitis. She spiked a fever. It didn't come down.

I was in my dorm room when Mom called me, nine hours away by car. "Get home as fast as you can, Grace," she ordered tightly. Nat had been moved to the ICU, and things weren't looking good.

My memories of that trip back home alternated between horribly vivid and completely blank. A professor drove me to Richmond International Airport. I don't remember which professor, but I can see the dusty dashboard of his car as clearly as if I were sitting in that hot vinyl front seat right now, the crack in the windshield that flowed lazily down from its source like the Mississippi bisecting the United States. I remember weeping in the plastic seat in front of my gate, my fists clenched as the airplane crept with agonizing slowness toward the terminal. I remember my friend Julian's face at the airport, his eyes wide with fear and compassion. My mother, swaying on her feet outside Natalie's cubicle in the hospital, my father, gray-faced and silent, Margaret tight and hunched in the corner near the curtain that separated Natalie from the next patient.

And I remember Natalie, lying in a bed, obscured by tubes and blankets, looking so small and alone that my heart cracked in half. I took her hand and kissed it, my tears falling on the hospital sheets. "I'm here, Nattie Bumppo," I whispered. "I'm here." She was too weak to answer, too sick even to open her eyes.

Outside, the doctor spoke in a somber murmur to my parents. "...Abscess...bacteria...kidney function...white count...not good."

"Jesus God in heaven," Margaret whispered in the corner. "Oh, shit, Grace." Our eyes met in bleak horror at the possibility we couldn't imagine. Our golden Natalie, the sweetest, kindest, loveliest girl in the world, dying.

The hours ticked past. Coffee cups came and went, Natalie's IVs were changed, her wound checked. A day crawled by. She didn't wake up. A night. Another day. She got worse. We were only allowed in for a few minutes at a time, sent off to a grim waiting room full of old magazines and bland, nubby furniture, the fluorescent lights sparing no detail of the fear on our faces.

On day four, a nurse burst into the room. "Natalie Emerson's family, come now!" she ordered.

"Oh, Jesus," my mother said, her face white as chalk. She staggered, my father caught her and half dragged her down the hall. Terrified that our sister was slipping away, Margaret and I ran ahead of our parents. It seemed to take a year to get down that hall—every step, every slap of my sneakers, every breath was punctuated with my desperate prayer. *Please. Please. Not Natalie. Please.*

I got there first. My baby sister, my birthday present, was awake, looking at us for the first time in days, smiling weakly. Margaret careened in behind me.

"Natalie!" she exploded in typical fashion. "Jesus Christ hanging on the cross, we thought you were dead!" She wheeled around and charged out to smite the nurse who'd taken a decade off of each our lives.

"Nattie," I whispered. She held out her hand to me, and you can bet that I promised then and there to make sure God knew how grateful I was to have her back.

"YOU DID WHAT?" JULIAN ASKED. We were strolling through the four-block downtown of Peterston, eating apricot danish from Lala's Bakery and sipping cappuccinos. I'd already dazzled my friend with my story of clubbing the neighbor, completely outranking his tale of having successfully cooked chicken tikka masala from scratch.

"I told her I was seeing someone. Wyatt, a pediatric surgeon." I took another bite of the still-warm pastry and groaned in pleasure.

Julian paused, his eyes wide with admiration. "Wow."

"Kind of brilliant, don't you think?"

"I do," he said. "Not only have you taken a stand against crime in your neighborhood, you've invented another boyfriend. Busy night!"

"I just wish I'd thought of it earlier," I said smugly.

Julian grinned, bent down to give Angus a piece of his pastry, then resumed walking, only to pause again in front of his place of business. Jitterbug's Dance Hall, tucked between a dry cleaner and Mario's Pizza. He peered in the windows, checking that everything was perfect within. A woman walking behind us glanced at Julian, looked away, then did a double take. I smiled fondly. My oldest friend, though he'd been a pudgy outcast when we'd first met, now resembled a clean-shaven Johnny Depp, and the woman's reaction was fairly typical. Alas, he was gay or I would have married him and borne his children long ago. Like me, Julian had been burned romantically, though even I, his oldest friend, didn't know the details of his long-ago breakup.

"So now you're Wyatt's girl," he said, resuming our stroll. "What is his last name?"

"I don't know," I said. "I haven't invented that yet."

"Well, what are we waiting for?" Julian thought a minute. "Dunn. Wyatt Dunn."

"Wyatt Dunn, M.D. I love it," I said.

Julian turned to flash a smile at the woman behind us. She turned purple in response and pretended to drop something. Happened all the time. "So what does Dr. Wyatt Dunn look like?" he asked.

"Well, he's not terribly tall...that's sort of overrated, don't you think?" Julian smiled; he was five foot ten. "Kind of lanky. Dimples. Not too good-looking but he has a really friendly face, you know? Green eyes, blond hair. Glasses, don't you think?"

Julian's smile faded. "Grace. You just described Andrew."

I choked on my cappuccino. "Did I? Crap. Okay, scratch that. Tall, dark and handsome. No glasses. Um, brown eyes." Angus barked once, affirming my taste in men.

"I'm thinking of that Croatian guy from *E.R.* Dr. Good-looking," Julian said.

"Oh, yes, I know who you mean. Perfect. Yes, that's Wyatt to a T." We laughed.

"Hey, is Kiki joining us this morning?" he asked.

"No," I said. "She met someone last night and really thinks he's The One." Julian chorused the last few words along with me. It was Kiki's habit, this falling madly in love. She excelled at finding The One, which she did often, and usually with disastrous results, becoming obsessed by the end of the first date, scaring the man away with talk of forevermore. If history repeated itself (and it usually did, as this history teacher knew quite well), she'd be crushed by this time next week, possibly with a restraining order filed against her.

So no Kiki. That was okay. Julian and I shared a love of antiques and vintage clothes. I was, after all, a history teacher, so it made sense. He was a gay man and dance instructor, so that made sense, too. Strolling along the crooked and quiet streets of Peterston, stopping in at the funky shops, the promise of leaves and flowers just around the corner, I felt happy. After a long, sloppy winter, it was good to be outside.

Peterston, Connecticut, is a small city on the Farmington River, accessible only by locals and clever tourists who excel in map-reading. Once famed for making more plow blades than any other place on God's green earth, the town had gone from desolate neglect to a scruffy charm in the past decade or so. Main Street led right down to the river, where there was a trail for walking. In fact, I could get home by walking along the Farmington, and often did. Mom and Dad lived five miles downriver in Avon, and sometimes I walked there, too.

Yes, I was content this morning. I loved Julian, I loved Angus, who trotted adorably at the end of his red-and-purple braided leash. And I loved having my family think I was in a relationship, not to mention completely over Andrew.

"Maybe I should get a new outfit or two," I mused outside of The Chic Boutique. "Now that I'm seeing a doctor and all. Something never worn by another."

"Absolutely. You'll need something nice for those hospital functions," Julian seconded immediately. We entered the store, Angus in my arms, and emerged an hour or so later, laden with bags.

"I love dating Wyatt Dunn," I said, grinning. "In fact, I may get an entire makeover. Haircut, mani, pedi…God, I haven't done that in ages. What do you think? Want to come?"

"Grace," Julian said, pausing. He took a deep breath, nodded to a passerby, then continued. "Grace, maybe we should…"

"Get lunch instead?" I suggested, petting Angus, who was licking the bag that contained my new shoes.

Julian smiled. "No, I was thinking more like maybe we should really try to meet someone. Two someones. You know. Maybe we should stop depending on each other so much and really get out there again."

I didn't answer. Julian sighed. "See, I think I might be ready. And you having a fake boyfriend, well, that's cute and all, but…maybe it's time for the real thing. Not that your fake boyfriends aren't fun, too." Julian had known me a long time.

"Right," I said, nodding slowly. The thought of dating made a light sweat break out on my back. It wasn't that I didn't want love, marriage, the whole shmere… I just hated the thought of what one had to do to get to that point.

"I will if you will," he prodded. "And just think. Maybe there is a real Wyatt Dunn out there for you. You could fall in love and then Andrew wouldn't…" His voice trailed off, and his dark eyes were apologetic. "Well. Who knows?"

"Sure. Yeah. Well." I closed my eyes briefly. Pictured Tim Gunn/Atticus Finch/Rhett Butler/George Clooney. "All right. I'll give it a shot."

"Okay. So. I'm going home to register on a dating Web site, and you do the same."

"Yes, General Jackson. Whatever you say." I saluted, he returned the gesture, kissed me on the cheek and headed for his place.

Watching my old friend walk away, I imagined with an unpleasant jolt what it would be like to have Julian as half of a happy couple. Imagined him not coming over once or twice a week, not asking me to help at his Dancin' with the Oldies class at Golden Meadows, not going shopping with me on Saturday mornings. Instead of me, some gorgeous man would be sitting in my place.

Now that would really suck. "Not that we're selfish or anything," I muttered. Angus chewed on the hem of my jeans in response. We headed for home, down the narrow path that followed the river, Angus straining on the leash and getting tangled in my bags. My dog wanted to investigate the Farmington, but it was so fat and full and loud that it would sweep him away. Red buds swelled on the swamp maples, but only a few bushes had any actual green on them. The earth was damp, the birds twittered and hopped in their annual search for a mate.

The last man I'd been in love with was Andrew, and try though I might, I couldn't remember how it had felt when we first fell in love. All my memories of him were tainted, obviously, but still…to belong to someone again, someone right this time. Really meant for me.

Julian had a point. It was time to start over. Sure, I'd tried to scare up a date for Kitty's wedding. But a relationship was different. I wanted to meet someone. I *needed* to meet someone, a man I could really love. Surely, somewhere out there, there was a man who would see me as the most beautiful creature on earth, the one who made his very heart beat, made the breath in his lungs sweet and all that sappy garbage. Someone who would help me put the final nail in the Andrew coffin.

It was time.

MY ANSWERING MACHINE LIGHT was blinking when I got home. "You have five messages," the mechanical voice announced. Wow. That was unusual for me. One each from Nat and Margaret—Nat was dying to get together and hear about Wyatt; Margaret sounded a bit more sardonic. Number three was from Mom, reminding me about her upcoming art show and suggesting I bring my lovely doctor. Number four was from Dad, giving me my assignment for next week's battle and also suggesting I bring Wyatt, as Brother Against Brother was low on Yankees.

Looked like my family had swallowed my tale of Wyatt pretty well.

The final message was from Officer Butch Martinelli of the Peterston Police Department asking me to return his call. Oh, crap. I'd almost forgotten about that. The clubbing. Beads of sweat jumped out on my forehead. I dialed the number immediately and asked for the good sergeant.

"Yes, Ms. Emerson. I have some information on the man you assaulted last night."

Assaulted. I *assaulted* someone. The guy was a burglar last night; now he was the vic. "Right," I said, my voice squeaking. "I didn't exactly assault him—more of a...misplaced act of self-defense." *Because he said hi, and we can't have that, can we?*

"He's legit," the officer continued, ignoring me. "Apparently, he just bought the house, long-distance, and the key was supposed to be left for him, but it wasn't. He was looking for it—that's why he was wandering around." The officer paused. "We kept him overnight, because we couldn't verify the story until this morning. We just released him about an hour ago."

I closed my eyes. "Um...is he okay?"

"Well, nothing's broken, though he does have quite a shiner."

"Oh, good God!" What a way to make friends! Another thought occurred to me. "Um, Officer Butch?"

"Yes?"

"If he was legit, why did you arrest him? And keep him overnight? That's kind of above and beyond the call, isn't it?"

Officer Butch didn't answer.

"Well, I guess you can do a whole bunch of things without just cause now, right?" I babbled. "Patriot Act, the death of civil liberties. Well, I mean..."

"We take 911 calls very seriously, ma'am. It appeared that you were engaged in a physical dispute with the man. We felt it was worth checking out." Disapproval dripped from his tone. "Ma'am."

"Right. Of course, Officer. Sorry. Thanks for calling."

I peered out my dining-room window toward the house next door. No signs of life. That was good, because though I clearly needed to apologize, the idea of seeing my new neighbor made me nervous. I hit him. He spent the night in jail because of me. Not exactly my best foot forward.

So, okay, I'd have to apologize. I'd make the poor man some brownies. Not just any brownies, but my Disgustingly Rich Chocolate Brownies, a sure way to soothe any wounded soul.

I opted against calling any of my family members back. They could think that I was with Wyatt, as I'd been with Julian. Except instead of parting ways, Wyatt and I had gone to the movies. Yes. We'd seen a flick, come home and were now, in fact, shagging. Then perhaps we were planning to go out for an early dinner. Which would be, I admitted, a very nice way to spend a Saturday afternoon.

"Come on, Angus, me boy-o," I said. He followed me into the kitchen and flopped on the floor, rolling on his back to watch me upside down as I got to work on those brownies. Ghirardelli's chocolate, nothing but the best for the man I sent to jail, a pound of butter, six eggs. I melted, stirred, blended, then set the timer. Spent thirty minutes checking my e-mail and responding to three parents who were protesting their kids' grades and wanting to know what their little prodigy would have to do to get an A in my class. "Work harder?" I suggested to the computer. "Think more?" I typed in a more politically correct response and hit Send.

When the brownies were done, I took them out of the oven. Looking over at the house next door, I decided that, yes, I could wait a little longer. I had papers to correct, after all. The bathroom could use a scrubbing. The brownies needed to cool, anyway. No need to race over and face the music.

Somewhere around 8:00 p.m., I woke up from where I'd dozed off over Suresh Onabi's paper on the Declaration of Independence, Angus asleep on my chest, half of a page damp and chewed in his mouth. "Down we go, boy," I said, setting him to the floor and retrieving what he'd eaten. Drat. My policy was that if *my* dog ate the homework, I'd have to assume the kid did perfectly.

Standing up, I peered out the dining-room window. There were no lights on next door. My heart seemed to be beating rather fast, my palms a little sweaty. I reminded myself that last night was simply an unfortunate misunderstanding. Surely we could all just get along. I arranged the brownies on a nice plate and took a bottle of wine from the kitchen rack, stashed Angus in the cellar so he wouldn't get out and bite the guy and headed over with my peace offerings. Brownies and wine. Breakfast of champions. What man could resist?

Walking up to 36 Maple Street was quite intimidating, really…the crumbling walkway, the broken-down house, the long grass which, who knew, could be full of snakes or something, the utter silence that hovered over the house like a malevolent, hungry animal. *Relax, Grace. Nothing to fear. Just being a good neighbor and apologizing for the head-whacking.*

The front porch of the house sagged wearily, the steps soft and rotting. Still, they supported my weight as I carefully and quietly negotiated them. I gave the front door a little knock with my elbow, as my hands were full, and waited. My heart clattered in my chest. I remembered that little…tug…I felt when I took a look at the not-burglar as he sat handcuffed on my porch…his boyish cowlick, the broad shoulders. And in that second before I hit him…he had a nice face. *Hi,* he'd said. *Hi.*

There was no answer to my feeble knock. I imagined what I most wanted to happen. That he'd open the door, and some soft music—let's make it South American guitar, shall we?—would drift out. My neighbor's face, which will sport only the slightest bruise under one eye, barely noticeable, will light in recognition. "Oh, hey, my neighbor!" he'll exclaim with a grin. I'll apologize, he'll laugh it off. The scent of roasting chicken and garlic will waft out. "Would you like to come in?" I'll agree, apologizing once more for my unfortunate mistake, which he'll simply wave off. "It could happen to anyone," he'll say. We'll chat, immediately comfortable with each other. He'll mention that he loves dogs, even hyperactive terriers with behavior issues. A glass of wine will be poured for the lovely girl next door.

See? In my mind, this guy and I were well on the way to becoming great friends, quite possibly more. Unfortunately, he didn't seem to be home right now, so he remained unaware of this pleasant fact.

I knocked again, albeit quietly, because I actually felt a little relieved that I didn't have to see him, pleasant fantasies aside. Setting my offerings in front of the door, I eased back down the rotting steps.

Now that I knew he wasn't home, I took a better look around. The streetlight gave an eerie, peachy glow to the yard. I'd never been over here before, but obviously, I'd wondered about the house. It had been neglected for a while...roof tiles were missing, and plastic covered an upstairs window. The latticework under the porch gapped like a mouthful of missing teeth.

It was a beautiful, soft night. The damp smell of distant rain filled the air, mixing with the coppery smell of the river, and far away, the song of springtime peepers graced the night. This house could be really charming, I thought, if someone restored it. Maybe my neighbor was here to do that very thing. Maybe it would become a gem.

The crumbling cement path that led from the street continued around the side of the house. No sign of the guy. However, a rake lay right across the walkway. Someone could trip over that, I thought. Trip, fall, hit head on the concrete birdbath just a few feet away, lie bleeding in the grass... Hadn't he suffered enough?

I went over and picked it up. See? Already being a great neighbor.

"Are these from you?"

The voice so startled me that I whirled around. Unfortunately, I was still holding the rake in my hand. Even more unfortunately, the wooden handle caught him right along the side of his face. He staggered back, stunned, the bottle of wine I'd just left at his door slipping from his grasp and shattering on the path with a crash. The scent of merlot drifted up around us, canceling out the smells of spring.

"Oops," I said in a strangled voice.

"Jesus Christ, lady," my new neighbor cursed, rubbing his cheek. "What is your problem?"

I winced as I looked him in the face. His eye was still

swollen, and even in the dim light, I could see the bruise. Pretty damn impressive.

"Hi," I said.

"Hi," he bit out.

"Uh, well... Welcome to the neighborhood," I squeaked. "Um... Are you...are you okay?"

"No, as a matter of fact."

"Do you need some ice?" I asked, taking a step toward him.

"No." He took a defensive step back.

"Look," I said, "I'm so, so sorry. I just came over to...well, to say I'm sorry." The irony of further wounding him while on a mission of mercy hit me, and I gave a nervous laugh, sounding remarkably like Angus when he vomited up grass.

The man said nothing, merely glared, and I found myself thinking that the beat-up look was kind of...hot. He was wearing jeans and a light-colored T-shirt, and, yes, he had very nice arms. Big, powerful, thick muscles, not the overly defined, ripped kind that smacked of too many hours at a heavily mirrored gym. No. These were blue-collar arms. Iron-worker arms. Man-who-can-fix-car arms. An image of Russell Crowe in *L.A. Confidential* flashed to mind. Remember when he's sitting in the backseat at the very end of the movie, and his jaw is wired shut and he can't talk? I found that *very* horny.

I swallowed again. "Hi. I'm Grace," I said, trying to start over. "I wanted to apologize about...last night. I'm so sorry. And of course, I'm sorry again, for all this. Very sorry." I glanced down at his feet, which were bare. "I think you're bleeding. You might've stepped in glass."

He looked down, then turned an impassive gaze to me. Call me paranoid, but he looked quite disgusted.

That was all it took. Bruised, bleeding, smelling like a wino, and the pièce de résistance, disgust. I was undeniably attracted to this guy. Heat rose to my cheeks, making me glad for the dim light.

"Well," I said slowly. "Listen. I'm really sorry. It looked like you were breaking in…that's all."

"Maybe you should be sober the next time you call the police," he returned.

My mouth fell open. "I was! I was sober." I paused. "Mostly."

"Your hair was all wild, you smelled like gin, and you hit me in the face with a walking stick. Does that sound mostly sober to you?"

Sweat broke out on my back. "It was a field hockey stick, actually, and my hair is always like that. As you can see."

He rolled his eyes. Well, the eye that wasn't swollen shut. Apparently that movement hurt, because he winced.

"It's just…you looked suspicious, that's all. I wasn't drunk. Buzzed, maybe, okay. A tiny bit, yes." I swallowed. "But it was past midnight, and you definitely didn't have a key, did you? So…you know. It looked suspicious. That's all. I'm sorry you spent the night in jail. Very, very sorry."

"Fine," he grunted.

Okay, well, that wasn't exactly as nice as my wine-drinking, South American guitar fantasy, but it was something. "So," I said, determined that we would part on good terms. "I'm sorry. I didn't catch your name."

"I didn't give it," he said, crossing his arms and staring.

Sweet. "Okay. Nice meeting you, whatever your name is. Have a good night." He still said nothing. Very carefully, I put the rake down, forced a smile, walked past the shards of broken glass, past *him*, painfully aware of my every move. The walk home, though it was only a matter of yards, felt very long. I should've cut through the yard, but there was the question of the long, snake-concealing grass.

He didn't say another word, and from the corner of my eye, I could see that he hadn't moved, either. Fine. He wasn't friendly. I wouldn't invite him to the neighborhood picnic in June. So there.

For a second, I imagined telling Andrew about this. Andrew, whose sharp sense of humor had always made me laugh, would've howled over this apology gone wrong. But no. Andrew didn't get to hear my stories anymore. To quash the Andrew image, I instead summoned to mind Wyatt Dunn. Gentle, dark-haired Wyatt, who'd have to possess a lovely sense of humor and kind, kind heart, being a children's doctor and all.

Just as had been true in the old days of my painful adolescence, the imaginary boyfriend took away some of the sting imparted by the surly neighbor whose head I'd just bruised for the second time.

And while I knew all too well that Wyatt Dunn was a fake, I also knew that someday I was going to find someone wonderful. Hopefully. Probably. Someone better than Andrew, possibly better looking than my grouchy neighbor, and just as great as Wyatt, and just thinking about this made me feel a little more chipper.

CHAPTER FOUR

ANDREW AND I HAD MET at Gettysburg—well, the reenactment of the battle here in fair Connecticut. He was assigned to be a nameless Confederate soldier, instructed to shout, "May God condemn this War of Northern Aggression!" then fall dead in the first cannon barrage. I was Colonel Buford, quiet hero of Gettysburg's first day, and my dad was General Meade. It was the biggest reenactment in three states, and there were hundreds of us (don't be so surprised, these things are very popular). That year, I was the secretary of Brother Against Brother, and before the battle, I'd been running around with a clipboard, making sure everyone was ready. Apparently, I was adorable…at least, that's what I was told later by one Andrew Chase Carson.

Eight hours after we started and when a sufficient number of bodies littered the field, Dad allowed the dead to rise, and a Confederate soldier approached me. When I pointed out that most Civil War soldiers didn't wear Nikes, the man laughed, introduced himself and asked me out for coffee. Two weeks later, I was in love.

In every way, it was the relationship I had always imagined. Andrew was wry and quiet, appealing rather than good-looking, with an infectious laugh and cheerful outlook. He was on the scrawny side, had a sweetly vulnerable neck, and I loved hugging him, the feel of his ribs creating in me the overwhelming urge to feed and protect him. Like me, he was a history buff—he was an estate attorney at a big firm in New Haven, but he'd majored in history at NYU. We liked the same food, the same movies, read the same books.

How was the sex, you ask? It was fine. Regular, hearty enough, quite enjoyable. Andrew and I found each other attractive, had mutual interests and excellent conversations. We laughed. We listened to the other's tales about work and family. We were really, really happy. I thought so, anyway.

If there was a hesitation on Andrew's part, I only noticed it in hindsight. If certain things were said with the smallest edge of uncertainty, I didn't see it. Not until later.

Natalie was at Stanford during the time of Andrew, having finished up at Georgetown the year before. Since her near-death experience, she'd become only more precious to me, and my little sister continued to delight our family with her academic achievements. My own intellect was on the vague side, not counting American history…I was good at Trivial Pursuit and able to hold my own at cocktail parties, that sort of thing. Margaret, on the other hand, was razor sharp, scary intelligent. She'd graduated second from Harvard Law and headed up the criminal defense department at the firm where my dad was a partner, making him prouder than he could say.

Nat was a blend. Softly brilliant, quietly gifted, she chose architecture, a perfect mix of art, beauty and science. I talked to her at least a couple of times a week, e-mailed her daily and visited her when she opted to stay in California for the summer. How she loved hearing about Andrew! How delighted she was that her big sister had met The One!

"What does it feel like?" she asked one night during one of our phone calls.

"How does what feel?" I said.

"Being with the love of your life, silly." I could hear the smile in her voice and grinned back.

"Oh, it's great. It's so...perfect. And easy, too, you know? We never fight, not like Mom and Dad." Being different from my parents was a clear sign that Andrew and I were on the right track.

Nat laughed. "Easy, huh? But passionate, too, right? Does your heart beat faster when he comes into the room? Do you blush when you hear his voice on the phone? Does your skin tingle when he touches you?"

I paused. "Sure." Did I feel those things? Sure, I did. Of course I did. Or I *had,* those dizzying new feelings having matured to something more...well, comfortable.

Seven months into the relationship, I moved into Andrew's apartment in West Hartford. Three weeks later, we were watching *Oz* on HBO—okay, not the most romantic show, but still, we were cuddled together on the couch, and that was nice. Andrew turned to me and said, "I think we should probably get married, don't you?"

He bought me a lovely ring. We told our families and chose Valentine's Day, six months away, as our wedding day. My parents were pleased—Andrew seemed so solid and reliable, so trustworthy. He was a corporate lawyer, very steady work, very well paid, which put to ease my father's worries that my teacher's salary would render me eventually homeless. Andrew, an only child, was doted on by his parents, and while they weren't quite as ecstatic as my parents, they were friendly enough. Margaret and he talked law, Stuart seemed to enjoy his company. Even Mémé liked him as much as she liked any human.

Only Natalie hadn't met him, stranded out there at Stanford as she was. She spoke to Andrew on the phone when I called to tell her we were engaged, but that was it.

Finally, she came home. It was Thanksgiving, and when Andrew and I arrived at the family domicile, Mom greeted us at the door in her usual flurry of complaints about how early she'd had to get up to put the "damn bird" in the oven, how she'd dry-heaved stuffing it, how useless my father was. Dad was watching a football game and ignoring Mom, Stuart was playing the piano in the living room while Margaret read.

And then Natalie came flying down the stairs, arms outstretched, and grabbed me in a huge hug. "Gissy!" she cried.

"Hey, Nattie Bumppo!" I exclaimed, squeezing her hard.

"Don't kiss me, I have a cold," she said, pulling back. Her nose was red, her skin a little dry, she was clad in sweatpants and an old cardigan belonging to our father, and yet she still managed to look more beautiful than Cinderella at the ball, her silken blond hair tied up in a high ponytail, her clear blue eyes unaccented by makeup.

Andrew took one look at her and literally dropped the pie he was holding.

Of course, the pie plate was slippery. Pyrex, you know? And Nat's face flushed that way because...well, because she had a cold, and isn't flushing and blushing part of a cold? Of course it was. Later, of course, I admitted it wasn't any slippery Pyrex. I knew the kablammy when I saw it.

Natalie and Andrew sat at opposite ends of the Thanksgiving table. When Stuart broke out the Scrabble board and asked them if they wanted to play after dinner, Andrew accepted and Natalie instantly declined. The next day, we all went bowling, and they didn't speak. Later, we went to the movies, and they sat as far away from each other as possible. They avoided going into a room if the other was there.

"So what do you think?" I asked Natalie, pretending that all was normal.

"He's great," she said, her face going nuclear once more. "Very nice."

That was good enough for me. I didn't need to hear more. Why talk about Andrew, after all? I asked her about school, congratulated her on winning an internship with Cesar Pelli and once again marveled at her perfection, her brains, her kind heart. After all, I'd always been my sister's biggest fan.

Andrew and Natalie saw each other again at Christmas, where they leaped away from the mistletoe like it was a glowing rod of uranium, and I pretended not to be disturbed. There couldn't be anything between them, because he was my fiancé and she was my baby sister. When Dad told Nat to take Andrew down the back hill on our old toboggan and neither of them could find a way to get out of it, I laughed when they crashed and rolled, becoming entangled in each other. No, no, nothing there.

Nothing, my ass.

I wasn't about to say anything. Each time the irritating little voice in my soul brought it up, usually at 3:00 a.m., I told her she was wrong. Andrew was right here with me. He loved me. I'd reach out and touch his knobby elbow, that sweet neck of his. We had something real. If Nat had a crush on him…well. Who could blame her?

My wedding was in ten weeks, then eight, then five. Invitations went out. Menu finalized. Dress altered.

And then, twenty days before our wedding, Andrew came home from work. I had a pile of tests beside me on the kitchen table, and he'd very thoughtfully brought home some Indian food. He even dished it out, spooning the fragrant sauce over the rice, just as I liked it. And then came the awful words.

"Grace…there's something we need to talk about," he said, staring at the onion *kulcha*. His voice was shaking. "You know I care about you very much."

I froze, not looking up from the exams, the words as ominous as *Sherman's in Georgia.* The moment I'd successfully avoided thinking about was upon me. Knowing I would never look at Andrew the same way, I couldn't take a normal breath. My heart thundered sickly.

He *cared* about me. I don't know about you, girls, but when a guy says *I care about you very much,* it seems to me that the shit is about to rain down. "Grace," he whispered, and I managed to look at him. As our untouched garlic naan cooled, he told me that he didn't quite know how to say this, but he couldn't marry me.

"I see," I said distantly. "I see."

"I'm so sorry, Grace," he whispered, and to his credit, his eyes filled with tears.

"Is it Natalie?" I asked, my voice quiet and unrecognizable.

His gaze dropped to the floor, his face burned red, and his hand shook as he ran it through his soft hair. "Of course not," he lied.

And that was that.

We'd just bought the house on Maple Street, though we weren't living there yet. As part of our divorce settlement or whatever you want to call it—blood money, guilt, emotional damages—he let me keep his portion of the down payment. Dad reworked my finances to tap into a few mutual funds that my grandfather had left me, reduced the size of my mortgage so I could swing it alone, and I moved in. Alone.

Natalie was wrecked when she found out. Obviously, I didn't tell her the reason for our breakup. She listened to me lie as I detailed the reasons for our breakup…*just wasn't right…not really ready…figured we should be sure.*

She asked only one quiet little question when I was done. "Did he say anything else?"

Because she must have known it wasn't me doing the breaking up. She knew me better than anyone. "No," I answered briskly. "It just...wasn't meant to be. Whatever."

Natalie had no part of this, I assured myself. It was just that I hadn't really found The One, no matter how deceptively perfect Andrew had looked, felt, seemed. Nope, I thought as I sat in my newly painted living room in my newly purchased house, power-eating brownies and watching Ken Burns's documentary on the Civil War till I just about had it memorized. Andrew just wasn't The One. Fine. I'd find The One, wherever he was, and, hey. Then the world would know what love was, goddamn it.

Natalie finished her degree and moved back East. She got a nice little apartment in New Haven and started work. We saw each other often, and I was glad. It wasn't like she was the other woman...she was my sister. The person I loved best in the world. My birthday present.

CHAPTER FIVE

ON SUNDAY, I had the misfortune of attending my mother's opening at Chimera's, a painfully progressive art gallery in West Hartford.

"What do you think, Grace? Where have you been? The show started a half hour ago. Did you bring your young man?" my mother asked, bustling up as I tried not to look directly at the artwork. Dad lurked in the back of the gallery, nursing a glass of wine, looking noticeably pained.

"Very...very, uh, detailed," I answered. "Just...lovely, Mom."

"Thank you, honey!" she cried. "Oh, someone is looking at a price tag on *Essence Number Two*. Be back in a flash."

When Natalie went off to college, my mother decided it was time to indulge her artistic side. For some reason unbeknownst to us, she decided on glassblowing. Glassblowing and the female anatomy.

The family domicile, once the artistic home only for two Audubon bird prints, a few oil paintings of the sea and a collection of porcelain cats, was now littered with girl-parts. Vulvae, uteruses, ovaries, breasts and more perched on mantels and bookshelves, end tables and the back of the toilet. Varied in color, heavy and very anatomically correct, my mother's sculptures were fuel for gossip in the Garden Club and the source of a new ulcer for Dad.

However, no one could argue with success, and to the astonishment of the rest of us, Mom's sculptures brought in a small fortune. When Andrew dumped me, Mom took me on a four-day spa cruise, courtesy of *The Unfolding* and *Milk #4*. The *Seeds of Fertility* series had paid for a little greenhouse on the side of the barn last spring, as well as a new Prius in October.

"Hey," said Margaret, joining us. "How's it going?"

"Oh, just great," I answered. "How are you?" I glanced around the gallery. "Where's Stuart?"

Margaret closed one eye and gritted her teeth, looking somewhat like Anne Bonny, she-pirate. "Stuart...Stuart's not here."

"Got that," I said. "Everything okay with you guys? I noticed you barely spoke at Kitty's wedding."

"Who knows?" Margaret answered. "I mean, really. Who the hell knows? You think you know someone...whatever."

I blinked. "What's going on, Margs?"

Margaret looked around at the voyeurs who flocked to Mom's shows and sighed. "I don't know. Marriage isn't always easy, Grace. How's that for a fortune cookie? Is there any wine here? Mom's shows are always better with a little buzz, if you know what I mean."

"Over there," I said, nodding to the refreshments table in the back of the gallery.

"Okay. Be right back."

Ahahaha. Ahahaha. Ooooh. Ahahaha. My mother's society laugh, heard only at art shows or when she was trying to impress someone, rang through the gallery. She caught my eye and winked, then shook the hand of an older man, who was cradling a glass...oh, let's see now...ew. A sculpture, let's put it that way. Another sale. Good for Mom.

"Are we still on for Bull Run?" Dad asked, coming up behind me and putting his arm around my shoulder.

"Oh, definitely, Dad." The Battle of Bull Run was one of my favorites. "Did you get your assignment?" I asked.

"I did. I'm Stonewall Jackson." Dad beamed.

"Dad! That's great! Congratulations! Where is it?"

"Litchfield," he answered. "Who are you?"

"I'm a nobody," I said mournfully. "Just some poor Confederate hack. But I do get to fire the cannon."

"That's my girl," Dad said proudly. "Hey, will you be bringing your new guy? What's his name again? By the way, your mother and I are thrilled that you're finally back on the old horse."

I paused. "Uh, thanks, Dad. I'm not sure if Wyatt can make it. I— I'll ask, though."

"Hey, Dad," Margaret said, coming up to smooch our father on the cheek. "How are the labias selling?"

"Don't get me started on your mother's artwork. Porn is what I call it." He glanced over in our mother's direction. *Ahahaha. Ahahaha. Oooh. Ahahaha.* "Damn it, she sold another one. I'll have to box that one up." Dad rolled his eyes at us and stomped off to the back of the gallery.

"So, Grace," Margaret said, "about this new guy." She glanced around to make sure that we weren't being overheard. "Are you really seeing someone, or is this another fake?"

She wasn't a criminal defense attorney for nothing. "Busted," I murmured.

"Aren't you a little old for this?" she asked, taking a slug of her wine.

I made a face. "Yes. But I found Nat in the bathroom at Kitty's wedding, writhing with guilt." Margs rolled her eyes. "So I figured I'd make it easy for her."

"Yes. Life must be easy for the princess," Margaret muttered.

"And another thing," I continued in a low voice. "I'm sick of the pity. Nat and Andrew should just get on with it, you know, and stop treating me like some crippled, balding cat who has seizures and can't keep down her food."

Margaret laughed. "Gotcha."

"The truth is," I admitted, "I think I'm ready to meet someone. I'll just pretend to be seeing someone and then, you know…find someone real."

"Cool," Margaret said with a considerable lack of enthusiasm.

"So what's going on with you and Stuart?" I asked, moving out of the way as an older woman sidled up to *LifeSource*, a sculpture of an ovary that looked to my nonmedical eye like a lumpy gray balloon.

Margaret sighed, then finished off her wine. "I don't know, Grace. I don't really want to talk about it, okay?"

"Sure," I murmured, frowning. "I do see Stuart at school, of course."

"Right. Well. You can tell him to fuck off for me."

"I…I won't be doing that. Jeez, Margs, what's wrong?" While theirs was a case of opposites attract, Margaret and Stuart had always seemed happy enough. They were childless by choice, rather well-off thanks to Margaret's endless success in court, lived in a great house in Avon, took swanky vacations to Tahiti and Liechtenstein and places like that. They'd been married for seven years, and while Margaret was not the type to coo and gloat, she'd always seemed pretty content.

"Well, crap, speaking of disastrous couples, here come Andrew and Natalie. Shit. I need a little more wine for this." She fled back to the table for another glass of cheap pinot grigio.

And there they were indeed, Andrew's fair hair a few

shades lighter than Natalie's honey-gold. Considerably more relaxed than at the wedding, when they dared not get within ten feet of each other lest I burst into sobs, they now radiated happiness. Their hands brushed as they approached, fingers giving a little caress though they stopped just short of actual hand-holding. The chemistry crackled between them. No, not just chemistry. Adoration. That's what it was. My sister's eyes were glowing, her cheeks flushed with pink, while a smile played at the corner of Andrew's mouth. Gack.

"Hey, guys!" I said merrily.

"Hi, Grace!" Natalie said, flushing brighter as she hugged me. "Is he here? Did you bring him?"

"Bring whom?" I asked.

"Wyatt, of course!" she chuckled.

"Right! Um, no, no. I think we should be dating longer than a few weeks before I bring him to one of Mom's shows! Also, he's...at the hospital." I forced a chortle. "Hi, Andrew."

"How are you, Grace?" he said, grinning, his green eyes bright.

"I'm great." I looked down at my untouched wine.

"Your hair looks gorgeous!" Nat exclaimed, reaching out to touch a lock that was for once curly and not electrocuted.

"Oh, I got a haircut this morning," I murmured. "Bought some new tamer." Had to practically sell an ovary of my own to afford it, but, yes, along with the clothes, I figured some better hair control was in order. Couldn't hurt to look my best when seeking The One, right?

"Where's Margaret?" Natalie asked, craning her swanlike neck to look around. "Margs! Over here!"

My older sister sent me a dark look as she obeyed. She and Natalie had always scraped a bit...well, it would be more fair to say that Margaret scrapped, since Natalie was too sweet to really fight with anyone. As a result, I got along better with each than they did with each other—my reward for generally being taken for granted as the poor neglected middle child.

"I just sold a uterus for three thousand dollars!" Mom exclaimed, joining our little group.

"There is no limit to the bad taste of the American people," Dad said, trailing sullenly behind her.

"Oh, shut it, Jim. Better yet, find your own damn bliss and leave mine alone."

Dad rolled his eyes.

"Congratulations, Mom, that's wonderful!" Natalie said.

"Thank you, dear. It's nice that some people in this family can be supportive of my art."

"Art," Dad snorted.

"So, Grace," Natalie said, "when can we meet Wyatt? What's his last name again?"

"Dunn," I answered easily. Margaret smiled and shook her head. "I will definitely get him up here soon."

"What does he look like?" Nat asked, reaching for my hand in girlish conspiracy.

"Well, he's pretty damn cute," I chirruped. Good thing Julian and I had gone over this. "Tall, black hair…" I tried to recall Dr. Handsome from *E.R.*, but I hadn't watched since the episode where the wild dogs got loose in the hospital, mauling patients and staffers alike. "Um, dimples, you know? Great smile." My face felt hot.

"She's blushing," Andrew commented fondly, and I felt an unexpectedly hot sliver of hatred pierce my heart. How dare he be thrilled that I'd met someone!

"He sounds wonderful," my mother declared. "Not that a man is going to make you happy, of course. Look at your father and me. Sometimes a spouse tries to suffocate your dreams, Grace. Make sure he doesn't do that. Like your father does to me."

"Who do you think pays for all your glassblowing crap, huh?" Dad retorted. "Didn't I convert the garage for your little hobby? Suffocate your dreams. I'd like to suffocate something, all right."

"God, they're adorable," Margaret said. "Who wants to mingle?"

When I finally got home from my mother's gynecological showcase, my surly neighbor was ripping shingles off his porch roof. He didn't look up as I pulled into the driveway, even though I paused after getting out of my car. Not a nice man. Not friendly, anyway. Definitely nice to look at though, I thought, as I tore my eyes off his heavily muscled arms, unwillingly grateful that it was warm out, warm enough that Surly Neighbor Man had taken off his shirt. The sun gleamed on his sweaty back as he worked. Those upper arms of his were as thick as my thighs.

For a second, I pictured those big, burly, capable arms wrapped around me. Imagined Surly Neighbor Man pressing me against his house, his muscles hard and hot as he lifted me against him, his big manly hands—

Wow, you need to get laid, came the thought, unbidden. Clearly, the pulsating showerhead wasn't doing the trick. Surly Neighbor Man, fortunately, had not noticed my lustful reverie. Hadn't noticed me at all, in fact.

I went into the house, let Angus into my fenced-in backyard to pee and dig and roll. The scream of a power saw ripped through the air. With a tight sigh, I clicked on the computer to finally follow Julian's advice. Match.com, eCommitment, eHarmony, yes, yes, yes. Time to find a man. A good man. A decent, hardworking, morally upright, good-looking guy who freakin' adored me. *Here I come, mister. Just you wait.*

After describing my wares online, I took a look at a few profiles. Guy #1—no. Too pretty. Guy #2—no. His hobbies were NASCAR and ultimate fight clubs. Guy #3—no. Too weird-looking, let's be honest. Acknowledging that perhaps my mood wasn't right for this, I corrected World War II quizzes until it was dark, stopping only to eat some of the Chinese food Julian had brought over on Thursday, then going right back to correcting, circling grammatical errors and asking for more detail in the answers. It was a common Manning complaint that Ms. Emerson was a tough grader, but hey. Kids who got an A in my classes earned it.

When I was done, I sat back and stretched. On the kitchen wall, my Fritz the Cat clock ticked loudly, tail swishing to keep the time. It was only eight o'clock, and the night stretched out in front of me. I could call Julian…no. Apparently, my best friend thought we were codependent, and while that happened to be completely true, it stung a little nonetheless. Nothing wrong with codependence, was there? Well. He e-mailed me, at least, a nice chatty note about the four men who'd been interested in his profile online, and the resultant stomach cramps he'd suffered. Poor little coward. I typed in an answer, assured him that I, too, was now available for viewing online and told him I'd see him at Golden Meadows for Dancin' with the Oldies.

With a sigh, I got up. Tomorrow was a school day. Maybe I'd wear one of my new outfits. Angus trotting at my heels, I clumped upstairs to reacquaint myself with my new clothes. In fact, I thought as I surveyed my closet, it was time to purge. Yes. One had to ask oneself when vintage became simply old. I grabbed a trash bag and started yanking. Goodbye to the sweaters with the holes in the armpits, the chiffon skirt with the burn in the back, the jeans that fit in 2002. Angus gnawed companionably on an old vinyl boot (what was I thinking?), and I let him have it.

Last week, I saw a show on this woman who was born without legs. She was a mechanic...actually, not having legs made her job easier, she said, because she could just slide under cars on the little skateboard thing she used to get around. She'd been married once, but was now dating two other guys, just enjoying herself for the time being. Her ex-husband was interviewed next, a good-looking guy, two legs, the whole nine yards. "I'd do anything to get her back, but I'm just not enough for her," he said mournfully. "I hope she finds what she's looking for."

I found myself getting a little...well, not *jealous,* exactly, but it did seem this woman had an unfair advantage in the dating world. Everyone would look at *her* and say, *Wow, what a plucky spirit. Isn't she great!* What about me? What about the two-legged among us, huh? How were we supposed to compete with *that?*

"Okay, Grace," I told myself aloud, "we're crossing the line. Let's find you a boyfriend and be done with it, shall we? Angus, move it, sweetie. Mommy has to go up to the attic with this crap, or you'll chew through it in a heartbeat, won't you? Because you're a very naughty boy, aren't you? Don't deny it. That's my toothbrush you have in your mouth. I am not blind, young man."

I dragged the trash bag full of stuff down the hall to the attic stairs. Drat. The light was out, and I didn't feel like tromping downstairs to get another. Well, I was only stashing the stuff till I could make a trip to the dump.

Up the narrow flight of stairs I went, the close, sharp smell of cedar tickling my nose. Like many Victorian homes, mine had a full-size attic, ten-foot ceilings and windows all around. Someday, I imagined, I'd put up some insulation and drywall and make this a playroom for my lovely children. I'd have a bookshelf that ran all the way around the room. An art area near the front window where the sun streamed in. A train table over there, a dress-up corner here. But for now, it held just some old pieces of furniture, a couple of boxes of Christmas ornaments and my Civil War uniforms and guns. Oh, and my wedding dress.

What does one do with a never-been-worn, tailored-just-for-you wedding dress? I couldn't just throw it out, could I? It had cost quite a bit. Granted, if I did find some flesh-and-blood version of Wyatt Dunn, maybe I'd get married, but would I want to use the dress I bought for Andrew? No, of course not. Yet there it still sat in its vacuum-packed bag, out of the sun so it wouldn't fade. I wondered if it still fit. I'd packed on a few pounds since The Dumping. Hmm. Maybe I should try it on.

Great. I was becoming Miss Havisham. Next I'd be eating rotten food and setting the clocks to twenty till nine.

Something gnawed my ankle bone. Angus. I didn't hear him come up the stairs. "Hi, little guy," I said, gathering him up and removing a sesame noodle from his little head. Apparently, he'd gotten into the Chinese food. He whined affectionately and wagged. "What's that? You love my hair? Oh, thank you, Angus McFangus. Excuse me? It's Ben & Jerry's time? Why, you little genius! You're absolutely right. What do you think? Crème Brûlée or Coffee Heath Bar?" His little tail wagged even as he bit my earlobe and tugged painfully. "Coffee Heath Bar it is, boy. Of course you can share."

I disentangled him, then turned to go, but something outside caught my eye.

A man.

Two stories below me, my grumpy, bruised neighbor was

lying on his roof, in the back where it was nearly flat. He'd put on more clothes (alas), and his white T-shirt practically glowed in the dark. Jeans. Bare feet. I could see that he was just…just lying there, hands behind his head, one knee bent, looking up at the sky.

Something contracted down low in my stomach, my skin tightened with heat. Suddenly, I could feel the blood pulsing in parts too long neglected.

Slowly, so as not to attract attention, I eased the window up a crack. The sound of springtime frogs rushed in, the smell of the river and distant rain. The damp breeze cooled my hot cheeks.

The moon was rising in the west, and my neighbor, too irritable to tell me his name, was simply lying on the roof, staring at the deep, deep blue of the night sky.

What kind of man did that?

Angus sneezed in disgust, and I jumped back from the window lest Surly Neighbor Man hear.

Suddenly, everything shifted into focus. I wanted a man. There, right next door, was a man. A *manly* man. My girl parts gave a warm squeeze.

Granted, I didn't want a fling. I wanted a husband, and not just any husband. A smart, funny, kind and moral husband. He'd love kids and animals, especially dogs. He'd work hard at some honorable, intellectual job. He'd like to cook. He'd be unceasingly cheerful. He'd adore me.

I didn't know a thing about that guy down there. Not even his name. All I knew was that I felt something—lust, let's be honest—for him. But that was a start. I hadn't felt anything for any man in a long, long time.

Tomorrow, I told myself as I closed the window, I was going to find out my neighbor's name. And I'd invite him to dinner, too.

CHAPTER SIX

"So although Sewell Point wasn't a major battle, it had the potential to greatly affect the outcome of the war. Obviously, Chesapeake Bay was a critical area for both sides. So. Ten pages on the blockade and its effects, due on Monday."

My class groaned. "Ms. Em!" Hunter Graystone protested. "That's, like, ten times what any other teacher gives."

"Oh, you poor little kittens! Want me to prop you up while you type?" I winked. "Ten pages. Twelve if you fight me."

Kerry Blake giggled. She was texting someone. "Hand it over, Kerry," I said, reaching out for her phone. It was a new model, encrusted with bling.

Kerry raised a perfectly waxed eyebrow at me. "Ms. Emerson, do you, like, *know* how much that *cost?* Like, if my father knew you *took* it, he'd be, like...totally unhappy."

"You can't use your phone in class, honey," I said for what had to be the hundredth time this month. "You'll get it back at the end of the day."

"Whatever," she muttered. Then, catching Hunter's eye, she flipped her hair back and stretched. Hunter grinned appreciatively. Tommy Michener, painfully and inexplicably in love with Kerry, froze at the display, which caused Emma Kirk to droop. Ah, young love.

Across the hall, I heard a burst of sultry laughter from Ava

Machiatelli's Classical History class. Most Manning students *loved* Ms. Machiatelli. Easy grades, false sympathy for their busy schedules resulting in very little homework, and the most shallow delving into history since...well, since Brad Pitt starred in *Troy*. But like Brad Pitt, Ava Machiatelli was beautiful and charming. Add to this her low-cut sweaters and tight skirts, and you had Marilyn Monroe teaching history. The boys lusted after her, the girls took fashion notes from her, the parents loved her since their kids all got A's. Me...not such a fan.

The chimes sounded, marking the end of the period. Manning Academy didn't have bells—too harsh for the young ears of America's wealthiest. The gentle Zen chimes had the same effect as electric shock therapy, though—my seniors lunged out of their seats toward the door. On Mondays, Civil War was the last class before lunch.

"Hang on, kids," I called. They stopped, sheeplike. They may have been, for the most part, overindulged and too sophisticated for their tender ages, but they were obedient, I had to give them that. "This weekend, Brother Against Brother is reenacting the Battle of Bull Run, also known as First Manassas, which I'm sure you know all about, since it was in your reading homework from Tuesday. Extra credit to anyone who comes, okay? E-mail me if you're interested, and I'd be happy to pick you up here."

"As if," Kerry said. "I don't need extra credit that bad."

"Thanks, Ms. Em," Hunter called. "Sounds fun."

Hunter wouldn't come, though he was one of my more polite students. His weekends were spent doing things like having dinner with Derek Jeter before a Yankees game or flying to one of his many family homes. Tommy Michener might, since he seemed to like history—his papers were always sharp and insightful—but more than likely, peer pressure would keep him home, miserably lusting after Kerry, Emma Kirk's wholesome appeal lost on him.

"Hey, Tommy?" I called.

He turned back to me. "Yeah, Ms. Em?"

I waited a beat till everyone else was gone. "Everything okay with you these days?"

He smiled a bit sadly. "Oh, yeah. Just the usual crap."

"You can do better than Kerry," I said gently.

He snorted. "That's what my dad says."

"See? Two of your favorite grown-ups agree."

"Yeah. Well, you can't pick who you fall for, can you, Ms. Em?"

I paused. "Nope. You sure can't."

Tommy left, and I gathered up my papers. History was a tough subject to teach. After all, most teenagers barely remembered what had happened last month, let alone a century and a half ago, but still. Just once, I wanted them to *feel* how history had impacted the world we lived in. Especially the Civil War, my favorite part of American history. I wanted them to understand what had been risked, to imagine the burden, the pain, the uncertainty President Lincoln must have experienced, the loss and betrayal felt by the Southerners who had seceded—

"Hello, there, Grace." Ava stood in my doorway, doing her trademark sleepy smile, followed by three slow, seductive blinks. There was one…and the second…and there was three.

"Ava! How are you?" I said, forcing a smile.

"I'm quite well, thank you." She tipped her head so that her silky hair fell to one side. "Have you heard the news?"

I hesitated. Ava, unlike myself, had her ear to the ground when it came to Manning's politics. I was one of those teachers who dreaded schmoozing with the trustees and wealthy alumni, preferring to spend my time planning classes and tutoring the kids who needed extra help. Ava, on the other hand, worked the system. Add that to the fact that I didn't live on campus (Ava had a small house at the edge of campus, and speculation was that she'd slept with the Dean of Housing to get it), and she definitely heard things.

"No, Ava. What news is that?" I asked, trying to keep my tone pleasant. Her blouse was so low-cut that I could see a Chinese symbol tattooed on her right boob. Which meant that every child who came through her classroom could see it, too.

"Dr. Eckhart's stepping down as chairman of the history department." She smiled, catlike. "I heard it from Theo. We've been seeing a lot of each other." Super. Theo Eisenbraun was the chairman of the Manning Academy board of trustees.

"Well. That's interesting," I said.

"He'll announce it later this week. Theo's already asked me to apply." Smile. Blink. Blink. And…wait for it…blink again.

"Great. Well, I have to run home for lunch. See you later."

"Too bad you don't live on campus, Grace. You'd seem so much more committed to Manning if you did."

"Thanks for caring," I said, shoving my papers into my battered leather bag. Ava's news had hit a nerve. Yes, Dr. Eckhart was old, but he'd been old for a long time. He was the one who'd hired me six years ago, the one who stood by me when a parent pressured me to raise little Peyton or Katharine's grade, the one who heartily approved of my efforts to engage my kids. I'd think he'd have told me if he was leaving. Then again, it was hard to say. Private schools were odd places, and Ava's information was usually on the money, I had to give her that.

Kiki met me outside Lehring Hall. "Hey, Grace, want to grab some lunch?"

"I can't," I said. "I have to run home before Colonial History."

"It's that dog of yours, isn't it?" she said suspiciously. Kiki was the proud owner of the mysteriously named Mr. Lucky, a diabetic Siamese cat who was blind in one eye, missing several teeth and prone to hairballs and irritable bowel syndrome.

"Well, yes, Angus was a little bound up, if you must know, and I don't want to come home tonight and find that his colon just couldn't hold on anymore."

"Dogs are so gross."

"I won't dignify that with an answer, except to say that there are double coupons for Fresh Step at Stop & Shop."

"Oh, thanks!" Kiki said. "I'm actually running low. Hey, Grace, did I tell you I met someone?"

As we walked to our cars, Kiki extolled the virtues of some guy named Bruce, who was kind, generous, soulful, funny, sexy, intelligent, hardworking and completely honest.

"And when did you meet this guy?" I asked, shifting my papers to open my car door.

"We had coffee on Saturday. Oh, Grace, I think this guy is it. I mean, I know I've said that before, but he's perfect."

I bit my tongue. "Good luck," I said, making a mental note to pencil in some conciliatory time for Kiki about ten days from now, when Bruce would more than likely have changed his phone number and my friend would be crying on my couch. "Hey, Kiki, have you heard anything about Dr. Eckhart?"

She shook her head. "Why? Did he die?"

"No," I answered. "Ava told me he's retiring."

"And Ava knows this because she slept with him?" Kiki,

like Ava, lived on campus, and they hung out together sometimes.

"Now, now."

"Well, if he is, that's great for you, Grace! Only Paul has more seniority, right? You'd apply for the job, wouldn't you?"

"It's a little early to be talking about that," I said, sidestepping the question. "I just wondered if you'd heard. See you later."

I pulled carefully out of the parking lot—Manning students tended to drive cars worth more than my annual salary, and nicking one would not be advisable—and headed through Farmington back to the twisted streets of Peterston, thinking about Dr. Eckhart. If it was true, then yes, I'd apply to be the new chairman of our department. To be honest, I thought Manning's history curriculum was too stodgy. Kids needed to feel the importance of the past, and, yes, sometimes they needed it jammed down their throats. Gently and lovingly, of course.

I pulled into my driveway and saw the true reason for my trip home, Angus's bowels not withstanding. My neighbor stood in his front yard by a power saw or some such tool. Shirtless. Shoulder muscles rippling under his skin, biceps thick and bulging...hard...golden... *Okay, Grace! That's enough!*

"Howdy, neighbor," I said, wincing as the words left my mouth.

He turned off his saw and took off the safety glasses. I winced. His eye was a mess. It was open a centimeter or two—progress from being swollen completely shut yesterday—and from what I could see, the white of his eye was quite bloodshot. A purple-and-blue bruise covered him from brow to cheekbone. *Hello, bad boy!* Yes, granted, I'd given him the bruise—actually, make that plural, because I saw a faint stripe of purplish-red along his jaw, right where I'd hit him with the rake—but still. He had all the rough and sultry appeal of Marlon Brando in *On the Waterfront*. Clive Owen in *Sin City*. Russell Crowe in everything he did.

"Hi," he said, putting his hands on his hips. The motion made his arms curve most beautifully.

"How's your eye?" I asked, trying not to stare at his broad, muscular chest.

"How does it look?" he grumbled.

Okay, so he wasn't over that. "So, listen, we got off to a bad start," I said with what I hoped was a rueful smile. From inside my house, Angus heard my voice and began barking with joy. *Yarp! Yarp! Yarp! Yarpyarpyarpyarpyarp!* "Can we start over? I'm Grace Emerson. I live next door." I swallowed and stuck out my hand.

My neighbor looked at me for a moment, then came toward me and took my hand. Oh, God. Electricity shot up my arm like I'd grabbed a downed wire. His hand was most definitely a working-man's hand. Callused, hard, warm...

"Callahan O'Shea," he said.

Ohh. Oh, wow. What a *name*. Regions of my anatomy, long neglected, made themselves known to me with a warm, rolling squeeze.

Yarpyarpyarpyarpyarp! I realized I was staring at Callahan O'Shea (sigh!) and still holding on to his hand. And he was smiling, just a little bit, softening the bad-boy look quite nicely.

"So," I said, my voice weak, letting go of his hand reluctantly. "Where'd you move from?"

"Virginia." He was staring at me. It was hard to think.

"Virginia. Huh. Where in Virginia?" I said. *Yarpyarpyarp yarpyarp!* Angus was nearly hysterical now. *Quiet, baby,* I thought. *Mommy's lusting.*

"Petersburg," he said. Not the most vociferous guy, but that was okay. Muscles like that...those eyes...well, the unbruised, unbloodshot eye...if the other one was like that, I was in for a treat.

"Petersburg," I repeated faintly, still staring. "I've been there. Quite a few Civil War battles down there. Assault on Petersburg, Old Men and Young Boys. Yup."

He didn't respond. *Yarp! Yarp! Yarp!* "So what were you doing in Petersburg?" I asked.

He folded his arms. "Three to five."

Yarpyarpyarpyarp! "Excuse me?" I asked.

"I was serving a three- to five-year sentence at Petersburg Federal Prison," he said.

It took a few beats of my heart for that to register. *Ka-bump...ka-bump...ka...* God's nightgown!

"Prison?" I squeaked. "And um...wow! Prison! Imagine that!"

He said nothing.

"So...when...when did you get out?"

"Friday."

Friday. *Friday*. He just got out of the clink! He was a criminal! And just what crime did he commit, huh? Maybe I hadn't been so far off with the pit-digging after all! And I had clubbed him! Holy Mother of God! I clubbed an ex-con and sent him to jail! Sent him to...oh, God...sent him to jail the night after he got out. Surely this would not endear me to Callahan O'Shea, Ex-Con. What if he wanted revenge?

My breath was coming in shallow gasps. Yes, I was definitely hyperventilating a bit. *Yarpyarpyarpyarpyarp!* Finally, the *flight* part of the *fight or flight* instinct kicked in.

"Wow! Listen to my dog! I better go. Bye! Have a good day! I have to...I should call my boyfriend. He's waiting for me to call. We always call at noon to check in. I should go. Bye."

I managed not to run into my house. I did, however, lock the door behind me. And dead bolt it. And check the back door. And lock that. As well as the windows. Angus raced around the house in his traditional victory laps, but I was too stunned to pay him the attention he was accustomed to.

Three to five years! In prison! I was living next to an ex-con! I almost invited him over for dinner!

I grabbed the phone and stabbed in Margaret's cell phone number. She was a lawyer. She'd tell me what to do.

"Margs, I'm living next to an ex-con! What should I do?"

"I'm on my way into court, Grace. An ex-con? What was he in for?"

"I don't know! That's why I need you."

"Well, what do you know?" she asked.

"He was in Petersburg. Virginia. Three years? Five? Three to five? What would that be for? Nothing bad, right? Nothing scary?"

"Could be anything." Margaret's voice was blithe. "People serve less time for rape and assault."

"Oh, good God!"

"Settle down, settle down. Petersburg, huh? That's a minimum security place, I'm pretty sure. Listen, Grace, I can't help you now. Call me later. Google him. Gotta go."

"Right. Google. Good idea," I said, but she'd already hung up. I jabbed on my computer, sweating. A glance out the dining-room windows revealed that Callahan O'Shea had gone back to work. The rotting steps of his front porch had been removed, the shingles mostly gone. I pictured him stabbing trash along a state highway, wearing an orange jumpsuit. Oh, shit.

"Come on," I muttered, waiting for my computer to come to life. When the Google screen came on, finally, I typed in *Callahan O'Shea* and waited. Bingo.

Callahan O'Shea, lead fiddler for the Irish folk group We Miss You, Bobby Sands, *sustained minor injuries when the band was pelted with trash Saturday at Sullivan's Pub in Limerick.*

Okay. Not my guy, probably. I scrolled down. Unfortunately, that band had quite a bit of press, recently...they were enraging crowds by playing "Rule Britannia" and the clientele wasn't taking it well.

It was then that my Internet connection, never the most reliable of creatures, decided to quit. Crap.

With another wary glance next door, I let Angus into the fenced-in backyard, then went back into my kitchen to scare up some lunch. Now that my initial shock was wearing off, I felt a little less panicky. Calling on my vast legal knowledge, obtained from many happy hours with *Law & Order,* two blood relatives who were lawyers and one ex-fiancé of the same profession, I seemed to believe that three to five in a minimum security prison wouldn't be for scary, violent, muscular men. And if he *had* done something scary...well. I'd move.

I swallowed some lunch, called Angus back in, reminded him that he was the very finest dog in the universe and not to so much as look at the big ex-con next door, and grabbed my car keys.

Callahan O'Shea was hammering something on the front porch as I approached my car. He didn't *look* scary. He looked gorgeous. Which didn't mean he wasn't dangerous, but still. Minimum security, that was reassuring. And hey. This was my house, my neighborhood. I would not be cowed. Straightening my shoulders, I decided to take a stand. "So what were you in for, Mr. O'Shea?" I called.

He straightened up, glanced at me, then jumped off the porch, scaring me a little with the quick grace of his move.

Very...predatory. Walking up to the split rail fence that divided our properties, he folded his arms again. Ooh. *Stop it, Grace.*

"What do you think I was in for?" he asked.

"Murder?" I suggested. May as well start with my worst fear.

"Please. Don't you watch *Law & Order?*"

"Assault and battery?"

"No."

"Identity theft?"

"Getting warmer."

"I have to get back to work," I snapped. He raised an eyebrow and remained silent. "You dug a pit in your basement and chained a woman there."

"Bingo. You got it, lady. Three to five for woman-chaining."

"Well, here's the thing, Callahan O'Shea. My sister's an attorney. I can ask her to dig around and uncover your sordid past—" *already did, in fact* "—or you can just come out and tell me if I need to buy a Rottweiler."

"Seemed to me like your little rat-dog did a pretty good job on his own," he said, running a hand through his sweat-dampened hair, making it stand on end.

"Angus is not a rat-dog!" I protested. "He's a purebred West Highland terrier. A gentle, loving breed."

"Yes. Gentle and loving is just what I thought when he sank his little fangs into my arm the other night."

"Oh, please. He only had your sleeve."

Mr. O'Shea extended his arm, revealing two puncture marks on his wrist.

"Damn," I muttered. "Well, fine. File a lawsuit, if a felon is allowed to do that. I'll call my sister. And the second I get back to school, I'm going to Google you."

"All the women say that," he replied. He turned back to his saw, dismissing me. I found myself checking out his ass. *Very* nice. Then I mentally slapped myself and got into my car.

RECALCITRANT CALLAHAN O'SHEA might not be too forthcoming about his sordid past, but I felt it certainly behooved me to know just what kind of criminal lived next door. As soon as my Twentieth Century sophomores were finished, I went to my tiny office and surfed the Net. This time, I was rewarded.

The *Times-Picayune* in New Orleans had the following information from two years ago.

Callahan O'Shea pleaded guilty to charges of embezzlement and was sentenced to three to five years at a minimum security facility. Tyrone Blackwell pleaded guilty to charges of larceny...

The only other hits referred to the ill-fated Irish band.

Embezzlement. Well. That wasn't so bad, was it? Not that it was good, of course...but nothing violent or scary. I wondered just how much Mr. O'Shea had taken. I wondered, too, if he was single.

No. The last thing I needed was some sort of fascination with a churlish ex-con. I was looking for someone who could go the distance. A father for my children. A man of morals and integrity who was also extremely good-looking and an excellent kisser who could hold his own at Manning functions. Sort of a modern-day General Maximus, if you will. I didn't want to waste time on Callahan O'Shea, no matter how beautiful a name he had or how good he looked without a shirt.

CHAPTER SEVEN

"VERY GOOD, MRS. SLOVANANSKI, one *two* three snap, five *six* seven pause. You got it, girl! Okay, now watch Grace and me." Julian and I did the basic salsa step twice more, me smiling gamely and swishing so my skirt twirled. Then he twirled me left, spun me back against him and dipped. "Ta-da!"

The crowd went wild, gingerly clapping their arthritic hands. It was Dancin' with the Oldies, the favorite weekly event at Golden Meadows Retirement Community, and Julian was in his element. Most weeks, I was his partner and co-teacher. Also, Mémé lived here, and though she was about as loving as the sharks who ate their young, a Puritanical familial duty had been long drilled into my skull. We were, after all, Mayflower descendants. Ignoring nasty relatives was for other, luckier groups. Plus, dancing opportunities were few and far between, and I loved to dance. Especially with Julian, who was good enough to compete.

"Does everyone have it?" Julian asked, checking our couples. "One *two* three snap…other way, Mr. B.—five *six* seven, don't forget the pause, people. Okay, let's see what we can do when the music's on! Grace, grab Mr. Creed and show him how it's done."

Mr. and Mrs. Bruno had already taken the dance floor. Their osteoporosis and artificial joints couldn't quite pull off the sensuality the salsa usually required, but they made up for it in the look on their faces...love, pure and simple, and happiness, and joy, and gratitude. It was so touching, so lovely, that I miscounted, resulting in a stumble for Mr. Creed.

"Sorry," I said, grabbing him a little more firmly. "My fault." From her chariot of doom, my grandmother made a disgusted noise. Like a lot of GM residents, she came each week to watch the dancers. Then Mrs. Slovananski cut in—she'd had her eye on Mr. Creed for some time, rumor had it—and I went over to one of the spectators as Julian carefully dipped Helen Pzorkan so as not to aggravate her weak bladder.

"Hey, Mr. Donnelly, feeling up to a turn on the dance floor?" I said to one of the many folks who came to watch, enjoying the music from eras gone by, but a little shy or stiff to venture out.

"I'd love to, Grace, but my knee isn't what it used to be," he said. "Besides, I'm not much of a dancer. I only looked good when my wife was with me, telling me what to do."

"I'm sure that's not true," I reassured him, patting his arm.

"Well," he said, looking at his feet.

"How did you and your wife meet?" I asked.

"Oh," he said, smiling, his eyes going distant. "She was the girl next door. I don't remember a day that I didn't love her. I was twelve when her family moved into the neighborhood. Twelve years old, but I made sure the other boys knew she'd be walking to school with me."

His voice was so wistful that it brought a lump to my throat. "How lucky, to meet when you were so young," I murmured.

"Yes. We were lucky," he said, smiling at the memory. "Lucky indeed."

You know, it sounded so noble and selfless, teaching a dance class to the old folks, but the truth was, this was usually the best night of my week. Most nights I spent home, correcting papers and making up tests. But on Mondays, I put on a flowing, bright-colored skirt (often with sequins, mind you) and set off to be the belle of the ball. Usually I went in early to read to some of the nonverbal patients, which always made me feel rather holy and wonderful.

"Gracie," Julian called, motioning for me. I glanced at my watch. Sure enough, it was nine o'clock, bedtime for many of the residents. Julian and I ended our sessions by putting on a little show, a dance where we'd really ham it up.

"What are we doing tonight?" I asked.

"I thought a fox-trot," he said. He changed the CD, walked to the center of the floor and held out his arms with a flourish. I stepped over to him, swishing, and extended my hand, which he took with aplomb. Our heads snapped to the audience, and we waited for the music. Ah. The Drifters, "There Goes My Baby." As we slow-slow-quick-quicked around the dance floor, Julian looked into my eyes. "I signed us up for a class."

I tipped my head as we angled our steps to avoid Mr. Carlson's walker. "What kind of class?"

"Meeting Mr. Right or something. Money-back guarantee. You owe me sixty bucks. One night only, two-hour seminar, don't have kittens, okay? It's sort of like a motivational class."

"You're serious, aren't you?" I said.

"Quiet. We need to meet people. And you're the one faking a boyfriend. Might as well date someone who can actually pick up the check."

"Fine, fine. It just sounds kind of…dumb."

"And the fake boyfriend is smart?" I didn't answer.

"We're both dumb, Grace, at least when it comes to men, or we wouldn't be hanging out together three times a week watching *Dancing with the Stars* and *Project Runway* with this as the highlight of our social calendar, would we?"

"Aren't we grouchy," I muttered.

"And correct." He twirled me swiftly out and spun me back in. "Watch it, honey, you almost stepped on my foot."

"Well, to tell you the truth, I'm meeting someone in half an hour. So there. I'm way ahead of you in the dating game."

"Well, good for you. That's a killer skirt you're wearing. Here we go, two three four, spin, slide, ta-da!"

Our dance ended, and our captive audience once again applauded. "Grace, you sure live up to your name!" cooed Dolores Barinski, one of my favorites.

"Oh, pshaw," I said, loving the compliment. The old folks, male and female, thought I was adorable, admired my young skin and bendable limbs. Of *course* it was the highlight of my social life! And it was so *romantic* here. Everyone here had a story, some hopelessly romantic tale of how they met their love. No one here had to go online and fill out forms that asked if you were a Sikh looking for a Catholic, if you found piercings a turnoff or a turn-on. No one here had to take a class to figure out how to make a man notice you.

That being said, I did have a date from one of my Web sites. eCommitment had come through. Dave, an engineer who worked in Hartford, wanted to meet me. Checking out his picture, I saw that, aside from a rather dated and conservative haircut, he was awfully cute. I e-mailed back, saying I'd love to meet for coffee. And just like that, Dave made a date. Who knew it was so easy, and why had I waited so long?

Yes, as I smooched withered cheeks and received gentle pats from soft, loving hands, I couldn't help the hope that prickled in my chest. Dave and Grace. Gracie and Dave. As early as tonight, I might meet The One. I'd go into Rex Java's, our eyes would meet, he'd slosh his coffee as he stood up to greet me, flustered and, dare I say, a little bit dazzled. One look and we'd just know. Six months from now, we'd be planning our wedding. He'd cook me breakfast on Saturday mornings, and we'd take long walks, and then, one day, when I told him I was pregnant, grateful tears would flood his eyes. Not that I was getting ahead of myself or anything.

Mémé left before the dance was over, so I didn't have to undergo the usual criticism of my technique, hair, clothing choices. I bid goodbye to Julian. "I'll call with the time and date of the class," he said, kissing my cheek.

"Okay. No stone left unturned."

"That's my girl." He winked and hefted his bag across his shoulder, waving as he left.

My hair felt a bit large, so I hit the loo to spritz on a little more frizz tamer/curl enhancer/holy water before my date with Dave. "Hi, Dave, I'm Grace," I said to my reflection. "No, no, it's natural. Oh, you love curly hair? Why, thank you, Dave!"

As I left the bathroom, I caught a glimpse of someone at the end of the hall, walking away from me. He turned left, heading for the medical wing. It was Callahan O'Shea. What was he doing here? And why was I blushing like some schoolkid who was just busted for smoking in the bathroom? And why was I still staring after him when I had a date, a real live date, hmm? With that thought in mind, I headed out to my car.

REX JAVA'S was about half-full when I got there, mostly high school kids, though none from Manning, which was in Farmington. I glanced around furtively. Dave didn't appear to be here…there was a couple in their forties in one corner, holding hands, laughing. The man took a bite of the woman's cake, and she swatted his hand, smiling. Show-offs, I thought with a smile. The whole world could see how happy they were. Over against the wall, a white-haired older man sat reading a paper. But no Dave.

I ordered a decaf cappuccino and took a seat, wondering if I should've changed out of my skirt before coming. Sipping the foam, I warned myself about getting my hopes up. Dave could be nice or he could be a jerk. Still. His picture was nice. Very promising.

"Excuse me, are you Grace?"

I looked up. It was the white-haired gentleman. He looked familiar…had he ever come to Dancin' with the Oldies? It was open to the public, after all. Possibly a Manning connection?

"Yes, I'm Grace," I said tentatively.

"I'm Dave! Nice to meet you!"

"Hi…uh…" My mouth seemed to be hanging open. "You're Dave? Dave from eCommitment?"

"Yes! Great to see you! Can I have a seat?"

"Um…I…sure," I said slowly.

Blinking rapidly, I watched as Dave sat, easing his leg out from the table. The man in front of me was sixty-five if he was a day. Possibly seventy. Thinning white hair. Lined face. Veiny hands. And was it me, or was his left eye made of glass?

"This is a cute place, isn't it?" he said, scooting his chair in and looking around. Yep. The left eye didn't move a bit. Definitely man-made.

"Yes. Um, listen, Dave," I said, trying for a friendly but puzzled smile. "Forgive me for saying this, but your photo… well, you looked so…youthful."

"Oh, that," he laughed. "Thank you. So you said you're a dog lover? Me, too. I have a golden retriever, Maddy." He leaned forward and I caught a whiff of Bengay. "You mentioned that you also have a dog?"

"Um, yes. Yes, I do. Angus. A Westie. So. When was that taken? The picture?"

Dave thought a minute. "Hmm, let's see now. I think I used the one taken just before I went to Vietnam. Do you like to eat out? I love it myself. Italian, Chinese, everything." He smiled. He had all his own teeth, I had to give him that, though most of them were yellow with nicotine stains. I tried not to wince.

"Yeah, about the photo, Dave. Listen. Maybe you should update that, don't you think?"

"I suppose," he said. "But you wouldn't have gone out with me if you knew my real age, would you?"

I paused. "That's...that's exactly my point, Dave," I said. "I really am looking for someone my own age. You said you were near forty."

"I *was* near forty!" Dave chuckled. "Once. But listen, sweetheart, there are advantages to being with an older man, and I figured you gals would be more open to them if you met me in person." He smiled broadly.

"I'm sure there are, Dave, but the thing is—"

"Oh, excuse me," he interrupted. "I really should empty this leg bag. You don't mind, do you? I was injured at Khe Sanh."

Khe Sanh. Being a history teacher, I knew quite well that Khe Sanh was one of the bloodiest battles of the Vietnam War. My shoulders slumped. "No, of course I don't mind. You go ahead."

He winked his real eye and rose, walking to the restroom with a slight limp. Great. Now I'd have to stay, because I couldn't walk out on a Purple Heart, could I? It would be unpatriotic. I couldn't just say, *Sorry, Dave, I don't date elderly wounded veterans who can't pee on their own.* That wouldn't be nice, not a bit.

So, in honor of my country, I spent another hour hearing about Dave's quest for a trophy wife, his five children by three women, the amazing AARP discount he got on his La-Z-Boy recliner and which type of catheter worked best for him.

"Well, I should get going," I said the moment I felt my duty to America had been served. "Uh, Dave, you have some very nice qualities, but I really am looking for someone closer to my own age."

"You sure you wouldn't like to go out again?" he asked, his good eye glued to my boobs as his fake eye pointed in a more northerly direction. "I find you very attractive. And you said you liked ballroom dancing, so I bet you're quite... flexible."

I suppressed a shudder. "Goodbye, Dave."

Julian's class was sounding better and better.

"No Daddy yet," I said to Angus upon my arrival back home. He didn't seem to care. "Because I'm all that you need, right?" I asked him. He barked once in affirmation, then began leaping at the back door to go out. "Yes, my darling. Sit... Sit. Stop jumping. Come on, boy, you're wrecking my skirt. Sit." He didn't. "Okay, you can go out anyway. But next time, you're sitting. Got it?" Out he raced toward the back fence.

I had one message. "Grace, Jim Emerson here," said my father's voice.

"Better known as 'Daddy,'" I said to the machine, rolling my eyes with a smile.

The message continued. "I dropped by this evening but you were out. Your windows need replacing. I'm taking care of it. Think of it as a birthday present. Your birthday was last month, wasn't it? Anyway, it's done. See you at Bull Run." The machine beeped.

I had to smile at my father's generosity. Truthfully, I made enough to pay my bills, but as a teacher, I didn't make nearly as much as the other folks in my family. Natalie probably made three times what I made, and it was only her first year in the working world. Margaret earned enough to buy a small country. Dad's family "came from money," as Mémé liked to remind us, and he made a very comfortable salary on top of that. It made him feel paternal, paying for home repairs to be done. Ideally, he'd have liked to do it himself, but he tended to injure himself around power tools, a fact he learned only after getting nineteen stitches from what he still called a "rogue" radial saw.

Returning to the living room, I sat on my couch and looked around. Maybe it was time to repaint a room, something I tended to do when down in the dumps. But no. After almost a year and a half of nonstop renovations, the house was pretty perfect. The living-room walls were a pale lavender with gleaming white trim and a Tiffany lamp in one corner. I'd bought the curved-back Victorian sofa at an auction and had it reupholstered in shades of green, blue and lavender. The dining room was pale green, centered around a walnut Mission-style table. The house wanted for nothing, except new windows. I probably needed another project. I almost envied Callahan O'Shea next door, starting from scratch.

Yarp! Yarp! Yarpyarpyarp! "Okay, what now, Angus?" I muttered, hauling myself off the couch. Opening the slider in the kitchen, I saw no sign of my furry white baby, who was usually easy to spot. *Yarp! Yarp!* I moved to the dining-room windows for a different view.

There he was. Crap. In a move he was bred for, Angus had tunneled under the fence and stood now in the yard next door, barking at someone. Three guesses as to whom. Callahan O'Shea was sitting on his stairless front porch, staring at my dog, who yapped from the yard, leaping and snapping, trying to bite the man's legs. With a sigh, I headed out the front door.

"Angus! Angus! Come, sweetie!" Not surprisingly, my dog failed to obey. Grumbling at my dog, I walked across my front yard to 36 Maple. The last thing I needed was another confrontation with the ex-con next door, but with Angus snapping and snarling at him, I didn't have much choice. "Sorry," I called. "He's afraid of men."

Callahan hopped off the porch, cut me a cynical glance. "Yes. Terrified." At those words, Angus launched himself onto Callahan's work boot, sinking his teeth into the leather and growling adorably. *Hrrrrr. Hrrrrr.* Callahan shook his foot, which detached Angus momentarily, only to have my little dog spring upon the shoe with renewed vigor.

"Angus, no! You're being very naughty. Sorry, Mr. O'Shea."

Callahan O'Shea said nothing. I bent over, grabbed my wriggling little pet by the collar and tugged, but he didn't let go of the boot. *Please, Angus, listen.* "Come on, Angus," I ground out. "Time to go inside. Bedtime. Cookie time." I tugged again, but Angus's bottom teeth were crooked and adorable, and I didn't want to dislodge any.

However, I was hunched over, my head about level with Mr. O'Shea's groin, and you know, I was starting to feel a bit warm. "Angus, release. Release, boy."

Angus wagged his tail and shook his head, the laces of

the work boot clenched in his crooked little teeth. *Hrrrrr. Hrrrrr.* "I'm sorry," I said. "He's not usually so—" I straightened up and bang! The top of my head cracked into something hard. Callahan O'Shea's chin. His teeth snapped together with an audible clack, his head jerked back. "Jesus, woman!" he exclaimed, rubbing his chin.

"Oh, God! I'm so sorry!" I exclaimed. The top of my head stung from the impact.

With a glare, he reached down and grabbed Angus by the scruff of his neck, lifted him—there was a small snap as the laces were tugged out of Angus's mouth—and handed him to me.

"You're not supposed to lift him like that," I said, petting Angus's poor neck as my dog nibbled my chin.

"He's not supposed to bite me, either," Callahan said, not smiling.

"Right." I glanced down at my dog, kissed his head. "Sorry about your, um…chin."

"Of all the injuries you've given me so far, this one hurt the least."

"Oh. That's good, then." My face actually hurt from blushing. "So. Are you going to live here, or is this an investment or what?"

He paused, obviously wondering whether I was worth the effort of an answer. "I'm flipping it."

"Oh," I answered, relieved. Angus spotted a leaf blowing across my lawn and convulsed to be put down. After a second's hesitation, I complied, relieved when he ran off to give chase. "Well. Good luck with the house. It's very cute."

"Thank you."

"Good night."

"'Night."

I took a few steps toward my house, then stopped. "By

the way," I added, turning back to my neighbor, "I did Google you and saw that you're an embezzler."

Callahan O'Shea said nothing.

"I have to say, I'm a little disappointed. Hannibal Lecter, at least he's interesting."

Callahan smiled at that, an abrupt, wicked smile that crinkled his eyes and lightened his face, and something twisted hard and hot in my stomach and seemed to surge toward my burly neighbor. That smile promised all kinds of wickedness, all sorts of heat, and I found that I was breathing rather heavily through my mouth.

And then I heard the noise, and so did Callahan O'Shea. A little pattering noise. We both looked down. Angus was back, leg lifted, peeing on the boot he'd tried to eat a few moments before.

Callahan O'Shea's smile was gone. He raised his eyes to me. "I don't know which one of you is worse," he said, then turned and headed for his house.

CHAPTER EIGHT

THIRTEEN MONTHS, TWO WEEKS and four days after Andrew called off our wedding, I thought I was doing fairly well. The summer after had been pretty rough without the daily presence of my students, but I threw myself into the house and became a gardener. When I was antsy, I tramped through the state forest behind my house, following the Farmington River miles upriver and down, getting chewed on by mosquitoes and scratched by branches, Angus leaping along beside me on his festive leash, pink tongue lapping the river, white fur spattered with mud.

I spent Fourth of July weekend at Gettysburg—the real Gettysburg, in Pennsylvania—with several thousand other reenactors, forgetting the ache in my chest for a few days in the thrill of battle. When I got back, Julian put me to work at Jitterbug's, teaching basic ballroom. Mom and Dad invited me over often, but, fearful of upsetting me, they were painfully polite to each other, and it was so tense and freakish that I found myself wishing they'd just be normal and fight. Margaret and I drove up the coast of Maine so far north that the sun didn't set till almost 10:00 p.m. We spent a few quiet days walking the shore, watching the lobster boats bob on their moorings and not talking about Andrew.

Thank God I had the house. Floors to sand, trim to paint, tag sales to attend so I could fill my little wedding cake of a home with sweet, thoughtful things that weren't associated with Andrew. A collection of St. Nicholas statues that I'd line up on the fireplace mantel come Christmas. Two brass doorknobs carved with *Public School, City of New York*. I made curtains. I painted walls. I installed light fixtures. I even went on a date or two. Well, I went on one date. That was enough to show me that I didn't want to get involved with anyone just yet.

School started, and I'd never loved my kids more. They may have had their little foibles, the overindulgences and the horrible speech patterns laden with *like* and *totally* and *whatever*, but they were so fascinating, so full of potential and the future. I lost myself in school, as I always did, watching among the resigned for the spark in one or two, the glow that told me someone connected with the past the way I had when I was a kid, that someone could *feel* how much history mattered to the present.

Christmas came and went, New Year's, too. On Valentine's Day, Julian came over armed with violent movies, Thai food and ice cream, and we laughed till our stomachs ached, both of us pretending to ignore the fact that this should've been my first anniversary and that Julian hadn't been on a date in eight years.

And my heart mended. It did. Time did its work, and Andrew faded to a dull ache that I mostly only thought about when I was lying alone in bed. Was I over him? I told myself I was.

Then, a few weeks before Kitty the Hair Cutting Cousin's wedding, Natalie and I went out for dinner. I had never told her the real reason Andrew and I had broken up. In fact, Andrew had never even said those words aloud. He didn't have to.

Natalie picked the place. She was working at Pelli Clarke

Pelli in New Haven, one of the top architectural firms in the country. She'd had to work late and suggested the Omni Hotel, which boasted a restaurant with a nice view and good drinks.

When I met her there, I was a little shocked at her transformation. Somewhere along the line, my little sister had gone from beautiful to stunning. Each time I'd seen her in grad school or at home, she'd been dressed in jeans or sweats, typical student clothing, and her long, straight, blond hair was all one length. Then, she looked like a classic American girl next door, wholesome and lovely. But when she started working for real, she invested in some clothes and a stylish haircut, started wearing a little makeup, and wow. She looked like a modern day Grace Kelly.

"Hi, Bumppo!" I said, hugging her proudly. "You look gorgeous!"

"So do you," she returned generously. "Every time I see you, I think I'd sell my soul for that hair."

"This hair is the devil's hair. Don't be silly," I said, but I was pleased. Only Natalie could be sincere about that, the sweet angel.

I ordered my standard, generic G&T, not being a really sophisticated drinker. Nat ordered a dirty martini. "What kind of vodka would you like?" the waiter asked.

"Belvedere if you've got it," she answered with a smile.

"We do. Excellent choice," he said, obviously smitten. I smiled, wondering when my little sister had learned to drink good vodka.

And so we chatted, Natalie telling me about the team she was on at Pelli, the house they were designing that would overlook the Chesapeake Bay, how much she loved her work. By comparison, I felt a little...well, a little pedestrian, I guess. Not that teaching wasn't incredibly fulfilling, because it was. I loved my kids, my subject, and I felt like Manning, with its faded brick buildings and stately trees, was part of my soul. But despite Natalie's genuine interest in hearing about how Dr. Eckhart fell asleep at the department meeting when I suggested revamping the curriculum and why it bugged me that Ava had never given so much as a B-, my news sounded pale.

It was at that moment that we heard a burst of laughter. We turned and saw a group of six or eight men just coming off the elevator into the bar, and right in front was Andrew.

I hadn't seen him since the day he dumped me, and the sight of him was like a kick in the stomach. The blood drained out of my face, then flooded back in a sickening rush. A high-pitched whine shrilled in my ear, and I was hot, then cold, then hot again. Andrew. Not very tall, not all that good-looking, still on the scrawny side, his glasses sliding down his sharp nose, his sweet, vulnerable neck.... My entire body roared at his presence, but my mind was completely blank. Andrew smiled at one of his buddies and said something, and once again, his compadres burst into laughter.

"Grace?" Natalie whispered. I didn't answer.

Then Andrew turned, saw us, and the same thing that had just happened to me happened to him. He went white, then red, his eyes grew wide. Then he forced a smile and headed our way.

"Do you want to go?" Nat asked. I turned to look at her and saw, without much surprise, that she looked, well, utterly beautiful. A rosy flush stained her cheeks, not like mine, which could grill a steak. One of her eyebrows was arched delicately in concern. Her slender hands with their neat, unpolished nails reached out to touch my hand.

"No! No, of course not. I'm fine. Hi, there, stranger!" I said, standing up.

"Grace," Andrew said, and his voice was so familiar it was like a part of me, almost.

"What a nice surprise," I said. "You remember Nat, of course."

"Of course," he said. "Hello, Natalie."

"Hi," she said in a half whisper, cutting her eyes away.

I wasn't sure why I asked Andrew to join us for a few minutes. He pretty much had to say yes. We all sat together, so civilized and pleasant it could've been high tea at Windsor Castle. Andrew gulped upon learning that Nat lived in the same city where he worked, but covered well. *Ninth Square, nice renovations over there. Oh, really, you're at Pelli, how exciting... Funny. Small world. And you, Grace? How's Manning? Kids good this year? Great. Um...are your parents well? Good, good. Margaret and Stu? Great.*

And so we sat there, Nat, Andrew, me and the four-ton elephant that was tap-dancing on the table. Andrew chattered like a nervous monkey, and though I couldn't hear over the roaring in my ears, I could see everything as clearly as if I were on some sense-enhancing drug. Natalie's hands were shaking just slightly, and to hide this fact, she'd folded them primly on the table. When she glanced at Andrew, her pupils dilated, though she was trying not to look at him at all. Above the neckline of her silky blouse, her skin was flushed, nearly blotchy. Even her lips looked redder. It was like watching the Discovery Channel's show on the science of attraction.

If Natalie was...affected, well, Andrew was terrified. His forehead was dotted with sweat, and the tips of his ears were so red they looked ready to burst into flame. His voice was faster than usual, and he made a point to smile at me often, though he couldn't seem to look me straight in the eye.

"Well," he said the minute he could escape, "I should get

back to my workmates there. Um, Grace…you…you look great. Wonderful to see you." He gave me a fast hug, and I could feel the damp heat from his neck, smell the childlike sweetness of his skin, like a baby at naptime. Then he stepped back abruptly. "Natalie, uh, take care."

She lifted her gaze from the table, and the elephant seemed to trip, fall and crash right on top of the table. Because shining in her gorgeous, sky-blue eyes was a world of misery and guilt and love and hopelessness, and I, who loved no one as much as I loved Natalie, felt it like a shovel to the head. "Take care, Andrew," she said briskly.

Both of us watched him walk away to rejoin his friends on the other side of the mercifully large restaurant.

"Want to go somewhere else?" Natalie suggested when Andrew was out of range.

"No, no, I'm fine. I like it here," I said heartily. "Besides, dinner should be out soon." We smiled at each other.

"Are you okay?" she asked softly.

"Oh, yeah," I lied. "Sure. I mean, I loved him and all, he really is a great guy, but…you know. He wasn't The One." I made quote marks out of my fingers.

"He wasn't?"

"Nope. I mean, he's a great guy and all, but…" I paused, pretended to think. "I don't know. There was something missing."

"Oh," she said, her eyes thoughtful.

Our dinners came. I'd ordered a steak; Nat had salmon. The potatoes were great. We ate and chatted about movies and our family, books and TV shows. When we got the check, Natalie paid and I let her. Then we stood up. My sister didn't look in Andrew's direction, just walked smoothly to the door in front of me.

But I glanced back. Saw Andrew staring at Natalie like a

junkie needing a fix, raw and hurting and naked. He didn't see me looking—he only had eyes for Nat.

I caught up to my sister. "Thanks, Nattie," I said.

"Oh, Grace, it was nothing," she answered, perhaps a bit too emotionally for the circumstances.

My heart thudded in my chest on the elevator ride down. I remembered my fourth birthday. Remembered the barrettes. The Saturday-morning cuddling. Her face as I'd left for college. I remembered that hospital waiting room, the smell of old coffee, the glare of the lights as I'd promised God anything, *anything*, if He'd save my sister. I considered what was in Natalie's eyes when she looked up at Andrew.

I imagined what kind of character it took to walk away from what might be the love of your life for the sake of another. To feel the big kablammy and not be able to do a thing about it. I wondered if I had the selflessness for an act of that magnitude. I asked myself what kind of heart I really had. What kind of sister I really was.

"I had this very strange thought," I said as we walked back toward Natalie's apartment, arm in arm.

"So many of your thoughts are strange," she said, almost hitting our usual vibe.

"Well, this one is pretty out there, but it feels right," I said, stopping on the corner of the New Haven Green. "Natalie, I think you should…" I paused. "I think you should go out with Andrew. I think he might've met the wrong sister first."

Those amazing Natalie eyes flashed again—shock, guilt, sorrow, pain…and hope. Yup. Hope. "Grace, I would never…" she began.

"I know. I really do," I murmured. "But I think you and Andrew should talk."

I met Andrew for dinner a few days later. Told him the same thing I told Natalie. The same emotions flashed over his face as had flashed across hers, with one more. Gratitude. He put up a few gentlemanly objections, then caved, as I knew he would. I suggested they meet in person, rather than talk on the phone or e-mail. They took my suggestion. Natalie called me the day after their first meeting, and in tones of gentle wonder, told me how they'd walked through New Haven, ending up shivering on a bench under the graceful trees in Wooster Square, just talking. She asked, repeatedly, if this was really okay, and I assured her it was.

And it was, except for just one problem, so far as I could see. I wasn't sure I was quite over Andrew myself.

CHAPTER NINE

ON SATURDAY MORNING, Angus shocked me into consciousness with his maniacal barking, clawing at the door as if a steak was being stuffed underneath it.

"What? Who?" I blurted, barely conscious. Glancing at the clock, I saw that it was only seven. "Angus! This house better be on fire, or you're in big trouble." Usually, my beloved pet was quite content to sleep squarely in the middle of my bed, somehow managing to take up two-thirds of it despite weighing a mere sixteen pounds.

An accidental look in the mirror showed me that my new hair tamer (which cost fifty bucks a bottle) clocked out after 1:00 a.m., which was when I went to bed the night before. So if in fact Angus *was* saving my life and our photo *did* appear on the front page of the paper, I'd better do something about that hair before rushing out into the flames. I grabbed an elastic, slapped my hair into a ponytail and felt the door. Cool. Opening it a crack, I smelled no smoke. Drat. There went my chance at meeting a hot fireman who would carry me out of the flames as if I were made of spun sugar. Still, I guessed it was a good thing that my house wasn't going up in flames.

Angus flew down the stairs like a bullet, doing his trademark Dance of the Visitor at the front door, leaping straight up so that all four paws came off the floor. Oh, yes. Today was Bull Run, and Margaret was coming along. Apparently she felt the need to rise early, but I needed coffee before I could kill any Johnny Rebs. Or was I killing Bluebellies today?

Scooping up Angus, I opened the door. "Hi, Margaret," I mumbled, squinting at the light.

Callahan O'Shea stood on my porch. "Don't hurt me," he said.

The bruise around his eye had faded considerably, still there, but yellow and brown had replaced the livid purple. His eyes were blue, I noted, and the kind that turned down at the corners, making him look a little…sad. Soulful. Sexy. He wore a faded red T-shirt and jeans, and there it was again, that annoying twinge of attraction.

"So. Here to sue me?" I asked. Angus barked—*Yarp!*—from my arms.

He smiled, and the twinge became more of a wrench.

"No. I'm here to replace your windows. Nice pajamas, by the way."

I glanced down. Crap. SpongeBob SquarePants, a Christmas present from Julian. We had a tradition of giving horrible gifts…I'd given him a Chia Head. Then his words hit home. "Excuse me? Did you say you're replacing my windows?"

"Yup," he said, poking his head in the doorway and glancing around the living room. "Your father hired me the other day. Didn't he tell you?"

"No," I answered. "When?"

"Thursday," he said. "You were out. Nice place you've got here. Did Daddy buy it for you?"

My mouth opened. "Hey!"

"So. Are you going to move aside so I can come in?"

I clutched Angus a little tighter. "No. Listen, Mr. O'Shea, I don't really think—"

"What? You don't want an ex-con working for you?"

My mouth snapped shut. "Well, actually...I..." It seemed so rude to say it out loud. "No, thank you." I forced a smile, feeling about as sincere as a presidential candidate pledging finance reform. "I'd rather hire another guy...um, someone who worked for me in the past."

"I've been hired. Your father already paid me half." He narrowed his eyes at me, and my teeth gritted.

"Well, that's inconvenient, but you'll have to give it back." Angus barked from my arms, backing me up. Good dog.

"No."

My mouth dropped open. "Well, sorry, Mr. O'Shea, but I don't want you working here." *Seeing me in my pajamas. Stirring things up. Possibly stealing my stuff.*

He cocked his head and stared at me. "How cutting, Ms. Emerson, to think that you don't like me, and also how ironic, given that if anyone has reason not to like someone else, I'd say the votes go to me."

"You get no votes, pal! I didn't ask you to—"

"But since I have better manners than you, I'll reserve judgment and say only that I don't like your propensity for violence. However, I already took your father's money, and if you want these windows before hell freezes over, I have to put in an order from a specialty place in Kansas. And to be honest, I need the work. Okay? So let's drop the feminine outrage, ignore the fact that I've seen you in your unmentionables—" his eyes traveled up and down my frame "—and get to work. I have to measure the windows. Want me to start upstairs or down?"

At this moment, Natalie's BMW pulled into the driveway, causing Angus new seizures of outrage. I clutched him to me, his little form trembling, as he tried to heave himself out of my arms, his barks bouncing off the inside of my skull.

"Can't you control the wee beastie?" Callahan O'Shea asked.

"Quiet," I muttered. "Not you, Angus, honey. Hi, Natalie!"

"Hi," she said, gliding up the front steps. She paused, giving my neighbor a questioning look. "Hello. I'm Natalie Emerson, Grace's sister."

My neighbor took her hand, an appreciative grin tugging his mouth up on one side, making me dislike him all the more. "Callahan O'Shea," he murmured. "I'm Grace's carpenter."

"He's not," I insisted. "What brings you here, Nat?"

"I thought we could have a cup of coffee," she said, smiling brightly. "I've been dying to hear about this guy you're seeing. We haven't had a chance to talk since Mom's show."

"A boyfriend?" Callahan said. "I take it he likes things rough."

Natalie's silken eyebrows popped up an inch and she grinned, her eyes studying his shiner. "Come on, Grace, how about some coffee? Callahan, is it? Would you like a cup?"

"I'd love one," he answered, smiling at my beautiful and suddenly irritating sister.

Five minutes later, I was staring sullenly at the coffeepot as my sister and Callahan O'Shea became best friends forever.

"So Grace actually hit you? With a field hockey stick? Oh, Grace!" She burst into laughter, that husky, seductive laugh that men loved.

"It was self-defense," I said, grabbing a few cups from the cupboard.

"She was drunk," Cal explained. "Well, the first time, she was drunk. The second time, with the rake, she was just flighty."

"I was *not* flighty," I objected, setting the coffeepot on the table and yanking open the fridge for the cream, which I set on the table with considerable force. "I have never been described as flighty."

"I don't know, Natalie," Callahan said, tilting his head. "Don't those pajamas say flighty to you?" His eyes traveled up and down my SpongeBobs once more.

"That's it, Irish. You're fired. Again. Still. Whatever."

"Oh, come on, Grace," Natalie said, laughing melodically. "He's got a point. I hope Wyatt won't see you in those."

"Wyatt loves SpongeBob," I retorted.

Nat poured Callahan a cup of coffee, missing the daggers shooting from my eyes. "Cal, have you met Grace's new guy?" she asked.

"You know, I haven't," he answered, cocking his eyebrow at me. I tried to ignore him. Not easy. He looked so damn... wonderful...sitting there in my cheery kitchen, Angus chewing his bootlace, drinking coffee from my limited edition Fiestaware cornflower-blue mug. The sun shone on his tousled hair, revealing very appealing streaks of gold in that rich chestnut-brown. He just about glowed with masculinity, all broad shoulders and big muscles, about to fix stuff in my house...damn it. Who wouldn't be turned on?

"So what's he like?" Natalie asked. For a second I thought she was talking about Callahan O'Shea.

"Huh? Oh, Wyatt? Well, he's very...nice."

"Nice is good. And how was your date the other night?" she continued, stirring sugar into her coffee to make herself even sweeter. Dang it. Nat had called the other night, and I could hear Andrew in the background, so I'd cut the conversation short by saying I had to meet Wyatt in Hartford. Oh, the tangled web...Callahan's soulful blue eyes were looking at me. Mockingly.

"The date was good. Pleasant. Nice. We ate. Drank. Kissed. Stuff like that."

So eloquent, Grace! Again with Callahan's eyebrow.

"Grace, come on!" my once-beloved sister said. "What's he like? I mean, he's a pediatric surgeon, so obviously he's wonderful, but give me some specifics."

"Lovely! His personality is lovely," I said, my voice a little loud. "He's very—" another glance at Cal "—respectful. Friendly. He's incredibly kind. Gives money to the homeless...and um, rescues...cats." My inner voice, disgusted at my poor lying abilities, sighed loudly.

"Sounds perfect," Natalie said approvingly. "Good sense of humor?"

"Oh, yes," I answered. "Very funny. But in a nice, nonmocking way. Not snarky, sarcastic or rude. In a gentle, loving way."

"So this is a case of opposites attract?" Callahan asked.

"I thought I just fired you," I said.

His eyes crinkled in a grin, and my knees went traitorously soft.

"I think he sounds amazing," Natalie said with a beautiful smile.

"Thanks," I said, smiling back. For a second, I was tempted to ask her about Andrew, but with the burly ex-con in the room, I decided against it.

"Are you going to the battle today, Grace?" my sister asked, taking a sip of her coffee. Honestly, everything she did looked as if it was being filmed...graceful and balanced and lovely.

"Battle?" Callahan asked.

"Don't tell him," I commanded. "And, yes, I am."

"Well, sorry to say I have to head down to New Haven," Natalie said regretfully, putting her cup aside. "It was nice to meet you, Callahan."

"The pleasure was mine," he said, standing up. Well, well, well. The ex-con had nice manners...when Natalie was around, at any rate.

I walked her to the door, gave her a hug. "Everything good with Andrew?" I asked, careful to keep my tone light.

It was like watching a beautiful sunrise, the way her face lit up. "Oh, Grace...yes."

"Excellent," I said, pushing back a lock of her cool, silky hair. "I'm glad for you, honey."

"Thanks," she murmured. "And I'm so glad for you, Grace! Wyatt sounds perfect!" She hugged me tight. "See you soon?"

"You bet." I hugged her back, my heart squeezing with love, and watched her glide out to her sleek little car and back out of my driveway. She waved, then disappeared down the street. My smile faded. Margaret knew instantly that Wyatt Dunn was fictional, and Callahan O'Shea, a virtual stranger, seemed to guess it, too. But not Natalie. Of course, she had a lot riding on me being with a great guy, didn't she? Me being attached meant...well. I knew what it meant.

With a sigh, I returned to the kitchen.

"So." Cal tipped back in his chair, hands clasped behind his head. "Your boyfriend's a cat rescuer."

I smiled. "Yes, he is. There's a problem with feral cats in his area. Very sad. He wrangles them. Herds them up into crates, gets them to foster homes. Would you like one?"

"A feral cat?"

"Mmm-hmm. They say your pet should match your personality."

He laughed, a wicked, ashy sound, and suddenly, my knees were even weaker than the time I saw Bruce Springsteen in concert. "No, thank you, Grace."

"So tell me, Mr. O'Shea," I said briskly. "How much did you embezzle, and from whom?"

His mouth got a little tight at the question. "One-point-six million dollars. From my esteemed employer."

"One point... God's nightgown!"

My checkbook, I suddenly noticed, was lying right over there, on the counter near the fridge. I should probably put that away, shouldn't I? Not that I had a million dollars there or anything. Callahan followed my nervous gaze and raised his unbruised eyebrow once more.

"So tempting," he said. "But I've turned over a new leaf. Although those are gonna be hard to resist." He nodded at a shelf containing my collection of antique iron dogs. Then he stood up, filling my kitchen. "Can I go upstairs and measure the windows, Grace?"

I opened my mouth to protest, then shut it. It wasn't worth it. How long would windows take? A couple of days?

"Um, sure. Hang on one sec, let me make sure it...um..."

"Why don't you just come with me? That way, if I'm tempted to rifle through your jewelry box, you can stop me yourself."

"I wanted to make sure the bed was made, that's all," I lied. "Right this way."

For the next three minutes, I fought feelings of lust and irritation as Callahan O'Shea measured my bedroom windows. Then he went into the guest room and did the same thing, his movements neat and efficient, zipping the measuring tape along the frames, jotting things down in his notebook. I leaned in the doorway, watching his back (ass, let's be honest) as he opened a window and looked outside.

"I might need to replace some trim when I put these in," he said, "but I won't know till I take them out. These are pretty old."

I dragged my eyes to his face. "Right. Sure. Sounds good."

He came over to me, and my breath caught. God. Callahan O'Shea was standing within an inch of me. The heat shimmered off his body, and my own body seemed to soften and sway in response. I could feel my heart squeezing and opening, squeezing and opening. His hand, still holding the tape measure, brushed the back of mine, and suddenly I had to breathe through my mouth.

"Grace?"

"Yes?" I whispered back. I could see the pulse in his neck. Wondered what it would be like to kiss that neck, to slide my fingers through his tousled hair, to—

"Can you move?" he asked.

My mouth closed with a snap. "Sure! Sure! Just…thinking."

His eyes crinkled in an all-too-knowing smile.

We went back downstairs, and a disappointingly short time later, Callahan O'Shea was done. "I'll put in the order and let you know when they come in," he said.

"Great," I said.

"Bye. Good luck at the battle."

"Thanks," I said, blushing for no apparent reason.

"Make sure you double lock the doors. I'll be home all day."

"Very funny. Now get out," I said. "I have Yankees to kill."

CHAPTER TEN

THE CANNON ROARED IN MY EARS, the smell of smoke sharp and invigorating. I watched as six Union soldiers fell. Behind the first line, the Bluebellies reloaded.

"This is so queer," Margaret muttered, handing me the powder so I could reload my cannon.

"Oh, shut up," I said fondly. "We're honoring history. And quit complaining. You'll be dead soon enough. A pox upon you, Mr. Lincoln!" I called, adding a silent apology to gentle Abe, the greatest president our nation ever saw. Surely he would forgive me, seeing as I had a miniature of the Lincoln Memorial in my bedroom and could (and often did) recite the Gettysburg Address by heart.

But Brother Against Brother took its battles very seriously. We had about two hundred volunteers, and each encounter was planned to be as historically accurate as possible. The Yankee soldiers fired, and Margaret dropped to the ground with a roll of her sea-green eyes. I took one in the shoulder, screamed and collapsed next to her. "It will take me hours to finally kick the bucket," I told my sister. "Blood poisoning from the lead. No treatment options, really. Even if I was taken to a field hospital, I'd probably die. So either way, long and painful."

"I repeat. This is so queer," Margaret said, flipping open her cell phone to check messages.

"No farbies!" I barked.

"What?"

"The phone! You can't have anything modern at a reenactment. And if this is so queer, why did you come?" I asked.

"Dad kept harassing Junie—" Margaret's long-suffering legal secretary "—until she finally begged me to say yes just to get him to stop calling and dropping by. Besides, I wanted to get out of the house."

"Well, you're here, so quit whining." I reached for her hand, imagining a Rebel soldier seeking comfort from his fallen brother. "We're outside, it's a beautiful day, we're lying around in the sweet-smelling clover." Margaret didn't answer. I glanced over. She was studying her cell phone, scowling, which wasn't an unusual expression for her, but her lips trembled in a suspicious manner. Like she was about to cry. I sat up abruptly. "Margs? Is everything okay?"

"Oh, things are peachy," she answered.

"Aren't you supposed to be dead?" my father asked, striding toward us.

"Sorry, Dad. I mean, sorry, General Jackson," I said, flopping obediently back in the grass.

"Margaret, please. Put that away. A lot of people have worked very hard to make this authentic."

Margaret rolled her eyes. "Bull Run in Connecticut. So authentic."

Dad grunted in disgust. A fellow officer rushed to his side. "What shall we do, sir?" he asked.

"Sir, we will give them the bayonet!" Dad barked. A little thrill shuddered through me at the historic words. What a war! The two officers conferred, then walked away to engage the gunmen on the hillside.

"I might need a break from Stuart," Margaret said.

I sat bolt upright once again, tripping a fellow Confederate who was relocating my cannon. "Sorry," I said to him. "Go get 'em." He and another guy hefted the cannon and wheeled it off amid sporadic gunfire and the cries of the commanding officers. "Margaret, are you serious?"

"I need some distance," she answered.

"What happened?"

She sighed. "Nothing. That's the problem. We've been married for seven years, right? And nothing's different. We do the same things day after day. Come home. Stare at each other over dinner. Lately, when he's talking about work or something on the news, I look at him and just think, 'Is this it?'"

An early butterfly landed on the brass button of my uniform, flexed its wings and fluttered off. A Confederate officer rushed by. "Are you girls dead?" he asked.

"Oh, yes, we are. Sorry." I lay back down, pulling Margaret's hand until she joined me. "Is there anything else, Margs?" I asked.

"No." Her eyes flickered away from me, belying her words. But Margaret was not one to offer something before she was ready. "It's just…I just wonder if he really loves me. If I really love him. If this is what marriage is or if we just picked the wrong person."

We lay in the grass, saying nothing more. My throat felt tight. I loved Stuart, a quiet, gentle man. I had to admit, I didn't know him terribly well. I saw him sporadically at work, usually from afar. The Manning students loved him, that was for sure. But family dinners tended to revolve around Mom and Dad bickering or Mémé's soliloquies on what was wrong with the world today, and usually Stuart didn't get a word in edgewise. But what I did know was that he was kind, smart and very considerate toward my sister. One might even say, if pressed, that he adored her a little too much, deferring to her on just about everything.

The sound of fleeing Union soldiers and the cries of triumphant Rebel soldiers filled the air.

"Can we go now?" Margaret asked.

"No. Dad's just now assembling the thirteen guns. Wait for it…wait for it…" I raised myself up on my elbows so I could see, grinning in anticipation.

"There stands Jackson, a veritable stone wall!" came the cry of Rick Jones, who was playing Colonel Bee.

"Huzzah! Huzzah!" Though supposedly dead, I couldn't help joining in the cry. Margaret shook her head, but she was grinning.

"Grace, you really need to get a life," she said, standing up.

"So what does Stuart think?" I asked, taking her proffered hand.

"He says to do whatever I need to sort things out in my head." Margaret shook her head, whether in admiration or disgust. Knowing Margaret, it was probably disgust. "So, Grace, listen. Do you think I could stay with you for a week or two? Maybe a little longer?"

"Sure," I said. "As long as you need."

"Oh, and hey, listen to this. I'm fixing you up with this guy. Lester. I met him at Mom's show last week. He's a metalsmith or some such shit."

"A metalsmith? Named Lester?" I asked. "Oh, Margaret, come on." Then I paused. Surely he couldn't be worse than my veteran friend. "Is he cute?"

"Well, I don't know. Not cute, exactly, but attractive in his own way."

"Lester the metalsmith, attractive in his own way. That does not sound promising."

"So? Beggars can't be choosy. And you said you wanted to meet someone, so you're meeting someone. Okay? Okay. I'll tell him to call."

"Fine," I muttered. "Hey, Margs, did you run down that name I gave you?"

"What name?"

"The ex-con? Callahan O'Shea, who lives next door to me? He embezzled over a million dollars."

"No, I didn't get around to it. Sorry. I'll try to this week. Embezzlement. That's not so bad, is it?"

"Well, it's not good, Margs. And it was over a million dollars."

"Still better than rape and murder," Margs said cheerfully. "Look, there's donuts. Thank God, I'm starving."

And with that, we tramped off the field where the rest of the troops already stood, drinking Starbucks and eating Krispy Kreme donuts. Granted, it wasn't historically accurate, but it sure beat mule meat and hoecake.

THAT NIGHT, I SPENT AN HOUR taming my thorny locks and donning a new outfit. I had two back-to-back dates via eCommitment…well, not dates exactly, but meetings to see if there was a reason to try a date. The first was with Jeff, who sounded very promising indeed. He owned his own business in the entertainment industry, and his picture was very pleasing. Like me, he enjoyed hiking, gardening and historical movies. Alas, his favorite was *300,* so what did that say? But I decided to overlook it for the moment. Just what his business was, I wasn't sure. Entertainment industry…hmm. Maybe he was an agent or something. Or owned a record label or a club. It sounded kind of glamorous, really.

Jeff and I were meeting for a drink in Farmington, and then I was moving onto appetizers with Leon. Leon was a science teacher, so I already knew we'd have lots to talk about…in fact, our three e-mails thus far had been about teaching, the joys and the potholes, and I was looking forward to hearing more about his personal life.

I drove to the appointed place, one of those chain places near a mall that have a lot of faux Tiffany and sports memorabilia. I recognized Jeff from his picture—he was short and kind of cute, brown hair, brown eyes, an appealing dimple in his left cheek. We gave each other that awkward lean-in hug where we weren't sure how far to go and ended up touching cheeks like society matrons. But Jeff acknowledged the awkwardness with a little smile, which made me like him. We followed the maitre d' to a little table, ordered a glass of wine and started in on the small talk, and it was then that things started to go south.

"So, Jeff, I've been wondering about your job. What exactly do you do?" I asked, sipping my wine.

"I own my own business," he said.

"Right. What kind?" I asked.

"Entertainment." He smiled furtively and straightened the salt and pepper shakers.

I paused. "Ah. And how exactly do you entertain?"

He grinned. "Like *this!*" he said, leaning back. Then, with a flourish and a sudden, sharp flick of his hands, he set the table on fire.

Later, after the firefighters had put out the flames and deemed it safe to return to the restaurant, a large portion of which was covered in the foamy fire retardant that had doused the "entertainment," Jeff turned beseechingly to me. "Doesn't anyone love magic anymore?" he asked, looking at me, as confused as a kicked puppy.

"You have the right to remain silent," a police officer duly recited.

"I didn't mean the fire to be so big," Jeff informed the cop, who didn't seem to care much.

"So you're a magician?" I asked, fiddling with the burnt end of a lock of my hair, which had been slightly singed.

"It's my dream," he said as the officer cuffed him. "Magic is my life."

"Ah," I said. "Best of luck with that."

Was it me, or did a lot of men leave in handcuffs when I was around? First Callahan O'Shea, now Jeff. I had to hand it to Callahan—he looked a lot better in restraints than poor Jeff, who resembled a crated ferret. Yes, when it came to handcuffs, Callahan O'Shea was— I stopped that train of thought. I had another date. Leon the teacher was next in line, so on I went, glad that the firefighters of Farmington were so efficient that I wasn't even late.

Leon was much more promising. Balding in that attractive Ed Harris way, wonderful sparkling blue eyes and a boyish laugh, he seemed delighted in me, which of course I found very appealing. We talked for a half hour or so, filling each other in on our teaching jobs, bemoaning helicopter parents and extolling the bright minds of children.

"So, Grace, let me ask you something," he said, pushing our potato skins aside to touch my hand, making me glad I'd splurged on a manicure/pedicure this week. His face grew serious. "What would you say is the most important thing in your life?"

"My family," I answered. "We're very close. I have two sisters, one older, one—"

"I see. What else, Grace? What would come next?"

"Um, well…my students, I guess. I really love them, and I want so much for them to be excited about history. They—"

"Uh-huh. Anything else, Grace?"

"Well," I said, a bit miffed at being cut off twice now, "sure. I mean, I volunteer with a senior citizen group, we do ballroom dancing with my friend Julian, who's a dance teacher. Sometimes I read to some of them, the ones who can't read for themselves."

"Are you religious?" Leon asked.

I paused. I was definitely one of those who'd classify herself as *spiritual* rather than *religious*. "Sort of. Yes, I mean. I go to church, oh, maybe once a month or so, and I—"

"I'm wondering what your feelings are on God."

I blinked. "God?" Leon nodded. "Um, well God is…well, He's great." I imagined God rolling His eyes at me. *Come on, Grace. I said, "Let there be light," and bada-bing! There was light! Can't you do better than "He's great," for God's sake? Get it? For* God*'s sake?* (I always imagined God had a great sense of humor. He'd have to, right?)

Leon's bright (fanatical?) blue eyes narrowed. "Yes, He is great. Are you a Christian? Have you accepted Jesus Christ as your personal savior?"

"Well…sure." Granted, I couldn't ever remember anyone in my family (Mayflower descendants, remember?) ever using the term *personal savior*… We were Congregationalists, and things tended to stay a little more philosophical. "Jesus is also so…good." And now I had Jesus, raising His head as He hung on the Cross. *Wow. Thanks, Grace. This is what I get for dying up here?*

"Jesus is my wingman," Leon said proudly. "Grace, I'd like to take you to my church so you can experience the true meaning of holiness."

Check, please! "Actually, Leon, I have a church," I said. "It's very nice. I can't say I'm interested in going anywhere else."

The fanatical blue eyes narrowed. "I don't get the impression you've truly embraced God, Grace." He frowned.

Okay. Enough was enough. "Well, Leon, let's be honest.

You've known me forty-two minutes. How the hell would you know?"

At the *H-E*-double hockey sticks word, Leon reared back. "Blasphemer!" he hissed. "I'm sorry, Grace! We do not have a future together! You're going straight to you-know-where." He stood up abruptly.

"Judge not," I reminded him. "Nice meeting you, and good luck with finding someone," I said. I was pretty sure God would be proud. Not just a quote from the Good Book, but turning the other cheek and everything.

Safely in my car, I saw with dismay that it was only eight o'clock. Only eight, and already I'd been in a fire and condemned to hell…and still no boyfriend. I sighed.

Well. I knew a good cure for loneliness, and its name was Golden Meadows. Twenty minutes later, I was sitting in Room 403.

"Her white satin chemise slid to the floor in a seductive whisper." I paused, glanced at my one-person audience, then continued. *"His eyes grew cobalt with desire, his loins burning at the sight of her creamy décolletage. 'I am yours, my lord,' she said, her lips ripe with sultry promise. Reaching for her breast, his mind raced...* Okay, that's a dangling participle if I ever heard one. His mind did not, I assure you, reach for her breast."

Another glance at Mr. Lawrence revealed the same level of attention as before—that is to say, none. Mr. Lawrence was nonverbal, a tiny, shrunken man with white hair and vacant eyes, hands that constantly plucked at his clothes and the arms of his easy chair. In all the months I'd been reading to him, I had never heard him speak. Hopefully, he was enjoying our sessions on some level and not mentally screaming for James Joyce. "Well. Back to our story. *His mind raced. Dare he take the promise of forbidden passion and sheath his rock-hard desire in the heaven of her soft and hidden treasure?"*

"I think he should go for it."

I jumped, dropping my tawdry paperback. Callahan O'Shea stood in the doorway, shrinking the size of the room. "Irish! What are you doing here?" I asked.

"What are you doing here, is a better question."

"I'm reading to Mr. Lawrence. He likes it." Hopefully Mr. Lawrence wouldn't lurch out of his two-year silence and deny that fact. "He's part of my reading program."

"Is that right? He's also my grandfather," Callahan said, crossing his arms.

My head jerked back in surprise. "This is your grandfather?" I asked.

"Yes."

"Oh. Well, I read to…to patients sometimes."

"To everyone?"

"No," I answered. "Just the patients who don't get—" My voice broke off midsentence.

"Who don't get visitors," Callahan finished.

"Right," I acknowledged.

I had started my little reading program about four years ago when Mémé first moved here. Having visitors was a huge status symbol at Golden Meadows, and one day I'd wandered into this unit—the secure unit—and found that too many folks were alone, their families too far to visit often or just unable to stand the sadness of this wing. So I started reading. Granted, *My Lord's Wanton Desire* wasn't a classic—not in literary terms, anyway—but it did seem to keep the attention of my listeners. Mrs. Kim in Room 39 had actually wept when Lord Barton popped the question to Clarissia.

Callahan pushed off from the doorway and came into the

room. "Hi, Pop," he said, kissing the old man's head. His grandfather didn't acknowledge him. My eyes stung a little as Cal looked at the frail old man, who, as always, was neatly dressed in trousers and a cardigan.

"Well, I'll leave you two alone," I said, getting up.

"Grace."

"Yes?"

"Thank you for visiting him." He hesitated, then looked up at me and smiled, and my heart swelled. "He liked biographies, back in the day."

"Okay," I said. "Personally, I think the duke and the prostitute are a little more invigorating, but if you say so." I paused. "Were you guys close?" I found myself asking.

"Yes," he answered. Callahan's expression was unreadable, his eyes on his grandfather's face as the old man plucked at his sweater. Callahan put his hand over the old man's, stilling the nervous, constant movement. "He raised us. My brother and me."

I hesitated, wanting to be polite, but curiosity got the better of me. "What happened to your parents?" I asked.

"My mother died when I was eight," he said. "I never met my father."

"I'm sorry." He nodded once in acknowledgment. "What about your brother? Does he live around here?"

Cal's face hardened. "I think he's out West. He's…estranged. There's just me." He paused, his face softening as he looked at his grandfather.

I swallowed. Suddenly, my family seemed pretty damn wonderful, despite Mom and Dad's constant bickering, Mémé's stream of criticism. The aunts and uncles, mean old Cousin Kitty…and my sisters, of course, that primal, ferocious love I felt for both my sisters. I couldn't imagine being estranged from either of them, ever.

"I'm sorry," I said again, almost in a whisper.

Cal looked up, then gave a rueful laugh. "Well. I had a normal enough childhood. Played baseball. Went camping. Fly-fishing. The usual boy stuff."

"That's good," I said. My cheeks burned. The sound of Callahan's laugh reverberated in my chest. No denying it. I found Mr. O'Shea way too attractive.

"So how often do you come here?" Callahan asked.

"Oh, usually once or twice a week. I teach Dancin' with the Oldies with my friend Julian. Every Monday, seven-thirty to nine." I smiled. Maybe he'd drop by. See how cute I looked in my swirly skirts, swishing away, delighting the residents. Maybe—

"Dance class, huh?" he said. "You don't look the type."

"And what does that mean?" I asked.

"You're not built like a dancer," he commented.

"You should probably stop talking now," I advised.

"Got a little more meat on your bones than those girls you see on TV."

"You should definitely stop talking now." I glared. He grinned.

"And aren't dancers graceful?" he continued. "Not prone to hitting people with rakes and the like?"

"Maybe there's just something about you that invites a hockey stick," I suggested tartly. "I've never hit Wyatt, after all."

"Yet," Callahan responded. "Where is the perfect man, anyway? Still haven't seen him around the neighborhood." His eyes were mocking, as if he knew damn well why. Because no cat-loving, good-looking pediatric surgeon would go for a wild-haired history teacher who enjoyed pretending to bleed to death on the weekends. My pride answered before my brain had a chance.

"Wyatt's in Boston this week, presenting a paper on a new recovery protocol in patients under ten," I said. Good Lord. Where had I pulled that from? All those Discovery Health shows were starting to pay off, apparently.

"Oh." He looked suitably impressed...or so it seemed to me. "Well. Any reason for you to hang around, then?"

I was dismissed. "No. None. So. Bye, Mr. Lawrence. I'll finish reading the book when your charming grandson isn't around."

"Good night, Grace," Callahan said, but I didn't answer, choosing instead to walk briskly (and gracefully, damn it) out of the room.

My mood was thorny as I drove home. While Callahan O'Shea was completely right to doubt the existence of Wyatt Dunn, it bugged me. Surely, were such a man to exist, he could like me. It shouldn't seem so impossible, right? Maybe, just maybe, somewhere out there was a real pediatric surgeon with dimples and a great smile. Not just magicians with tendencies toward arson and religious nut jobs and too-knowing ex-cons.

At least Angus worshipped me. God must've had single women in mind when he invented dogs. I accepted his gift of a ruined roll of paper towels and a chewed-up sneaker, praised him for not destroying anything else and got ready for bed.

I imagined telling Wyatt Dunn about my day. How he'd laugh at the bad dates—well, of course, there would be no bad dates if he were a real person—but still. He'd laugh and we'd talk and make plans for the weekend. We'd have a gentle, sweet, thoughtful relationship. We'd hardly ever fight. He'd think I was the loveliest creature to walk the earth. He'd even adore my hair. He'd send me flowers, just to let me know he was thinking of me.

And even though I knew quite well he wasn't real, I felt better. The old imaginary boyfriend was doing what he did best. I knew I was a good, smart, valuable person. If the dating pool of Connecticut failed to provide a worthy choice, well, what was the harm in a little visualization? Didn't Olympic athletes do that? Picture a perfect dive or dismount in order to achieve it? Wyatt Dunn was the same idea.

The fact that Callahan O'Shea's face kept coming to mind was purely coincidental, I was sure.

CHAPTER ELEVEN

"WHO IS JEB STUART?" Tommy Michener suggested.

"Correct!" I said, grinning. His teammates cheered, and Tommy, who was captain of his team, flushed with pride. "Pick again, Tom!"

"I'll stick with Civil War Leaders, Ms. Em," he said.

"Leaders for a thousand. This vice president of the Confederacy was sickly his whole life, never weighing more than one hundred pounds."

Hunter's team buzzed in. "Who is Jefferson Davis?" Mallory guessed.

"No, honey, sorry, he was the *president* of the Confederacy. Tommy, does your team have a guess?" The kids huddled together, conferring.

Emma Kirk, the day student with a crush on Tommy, whispered into his ear. I'd made sure they were on the same team. He asked her a question. She nodded. "Who is Little Aleck Stephens?" Emma said.

"Yes, Emma! Well done!"

Tommy high-fived Emma, who practically levitated in pleasure.

I beamed at my students. Civil War Jeopardy! was a hit. With a glance at the clock, I was shocked to see our time was almost over. "Okay, Final Jeopardy! everyone. Ready? This Pulitzer Prize–winning author, whose book details the rise and fall of the South as seen through one woman's eyes, never wrote another novel."

I hummed the theme from *Jeopardy!* with gusto, strolling back and forth between the two groups of kids. Tommy's team was kicking some serious butt; however my favorite student was showing off for Kerry, who was on the other team, and chances were he'd bet it all.

"Pens down. Okay, Hunter, your team had nine thousand points. Your wager? Oh, I see you've bet the farm. Very bold. Okay, Hunter. Your answer, please?"

He held up his team's wipe away board. I winced. "No. Sorry, Hunter. Stephen Crane is not the answer. But he did write *The Red Badge of Courage,* which is about the Battle of Chancellorsville, so nice try. Tommy? What did you bet?"

"We bet it all, Ms. Em," he said proudly, glancing over at Kerry and winking. Emma's smile dropped a notch.

"And your answer, Tom?"

Tom turned to his team. "Who is Margaret Mitchell?" they chorused.

"Correct!" I shouted.

You'd think they'd won the World Series or something—screams of victory, lots of high fives and dancing around, a few hugs. Meanwhile, Hunter Graystone's team groaned.

"Tommy's team…no homework for you!" I announced. More cheering and high-fiving. "Hunter's team, sorry, kids. Three pages on Margaret Mitchell, and if you haven't read *Gone With the Wind,* shame on you! Okay, class dismissed."

Ten minutes later, I was seated in the conference room in Lehring Hall with my fellow history department members—Dr. Eckhart, the chairman; Paul Boccanio, who was next in seniority; the unfortunately named Wayne Diggler, our newest teacher, hired last year right out of graduate school; and Ava Machiatelli, sex kitten.

"Your class sounded quite out of control today," Ava murmured in her trademark phone-sex whisper. "So much chaos! My class could hardly think."

Not that they need to for you to give them an A, I grumbled internally. "We were playing Jeopardy!" I said with a smile. "Very invigorating."

"Very noisy, too." A reproachful blink...another...and, yes, a third blink.

Dr. Eckhart shuffled to the head of the table and sat down, an activity that took considerable time and effort. Then he gave his trademark phlegmy, barking cough that caused first-years to jump in their seats until about November. A distinguished gentleman with an unfortunate aversion to daily bathing, Dr. Eckhart was from the olden days of prep schools where the kids wore uniforms and could be locked in closets for misbehaving, if not beaten with rulers. He often mourned those happy times. Aside from that, he was a brilliant man.

He now straightened and folded his arthritic hands in front of him. "This year will be my last as chairman of the history department at Manning, as you have doubtless all heard."

Tears pricked my eyes. I couldn't imagine Manning without old Dr. E. Who would huddle in a corner with me at trustee functions or the dreaded Headmaster's Dinner? Who would defend me when angry parents called about their kid's B+?

"Headmaster Stanton has invited me to advise the search committee, and of course I encourage all of you to apply for the position, as Manning has always prided itself on promotion from within." He turned to the youngest member of our staff. "Mr. Diggler, you, of course, are far too inexperienced, so please save your energy for your classes."

Wayne, who felt that his degree from Georgetown

trumped all the rest of ours put together, slumped in his seat and sulked. "Fine," he muttered. "Like I'm not headed for Exeter, anyway." Wayne often promised to leave when things didn't go his way, which was about twice a week.

"Complete your sentences, please, Mr. Diggler, until that happy day." Dr. Eckhart smiled at me, then gave another barking cough. It was no secret that I was a bit of a pet with our elderly chair, thanks to regular infusions of Disgustingly Rich Chocolate Brownies and my membership in Brother Against Brother.

"Actually, speaking of Phillips Exeter," began Paul, blushing slightly. He was a balding, brilliant man with glasses and a photographic memory for dates.

"Oh, dear," sighed Dr. Eckhart. "Are congratulations in order, Mr. Boccanio?"

Paul grinned. "I'm afraid so."

It wasn't that uncommon, prep schools poaching teachers, and Paul had a great background, especially given that he'd actually worked in the real world before becoming a teacher. Add to that his impressive education—Stanford/Yale, for heaven's sake—and it was no wonder that he'd been nabbed.

"Traitor," I murmured. I really liked Paul. He winked in response. "That leaves my two esteemed female colleagues," Dr. Eckhart wheezed. "Very well, ladies, I'll expect you to submit your applications. Prepare your presentations in paper form, none of this computer nonsense, please, detailing your qualifications and ideas for improvements, such as they may be, to Manning's history department."

"Thank you for this opportunity, sir," Ava murmured, batting her eyelashes like Scarlett O'Hara.

"Very well," Dr. Eckhart said now, straightening his stained shirt. "The search begins next week, when we shall post the opening in the appropriate venues."

"You'll be terribly missed, Dr. Eckhart," I said huskily.

"Ah. Thank you, Grace."

"Oh, yes. It won't be the same without you," Ava hastily seconded.

"Indeed." He hauled himself out of the chair on his third attempt and shuffled out the door. I swallowed thickly.

"Good luck, girls," Paul said cheerfully. "If you'd like to have a Jell-O wrestling match, winner gets the job, I'd be happy to judge."

"We'll miss you so," I said, grinning.

"It's so unfair," whined Wayne. "When I was at Georgetown, I had dinner with C. Vann Woodward!"

"And I had sex with Ken Burns," I quipped, getting a snort from Paul. "Not to mention the fact that I was an extra in *Glory*." That part was true. I'd been eleven years old, and Dad took me up to Sturbridge so we could be part of the crowd scene as the 54th Massachusetts Regiment left for the South. "It was the best moment of my childhood," I added. "Better even than when that guy from *MacGyver* opened the new mall."

"You're pathetic," Wayne mumbled.

"Grow up, little man," breathed Ava. "You don't have what it takes to run a department."

"And you do, Marilyn Monroe?" he snapped. "I'm too good for this place!"

"I'll be happy to accept your resignation when I'm chair," I said graciously. Wayne slammed his hands on the table, followed by some stomping, followed by his most welcomed departure.

"Well," Ava sighed. "Best of luck, Grace." She smiled insincerely.

"Right back at you," I said. I didn't really dislike Ava—prep schools were such tiny little worlds, so insulated from the rest of the world that coworkers became almost like family. But the idea of working under her, having her approve or disapprove my lesson plans, rankled. Watching her leave with Paul, her ass swinging vigorously under a too-tight skirt, I found that my teeth were firmly clenched.

For another minute or two, I sat alone in the conference room and allowed myself a tingling little daydream. That I got the chairmanship. Hired a fantastic new teacher to replace Paul. Revitalized the curriculum, raised the bar on grades so that an A in history from Manning meant something special. Increased the number of kids who took—and aced—the AP test. Got more money in the budget for field trips.

Well. I'd better get started on a presentation, just as Dr. Eckhart suggested. Tight sweaters and easy A's aside, Ava had a sharp mind and was much more of a political creature than I was, which would definitely help her. Now I wished I had chitchatted a bit more at last fall's faculty/trustee cocktail party, instead of hiding in the corner, sipping bad merlot and swapping obscure historical trivia with Dr. Eckhart and Paul.

I loved Manning. Loved the kids, adored working here on this beautiful campus, especially at this time of year, when the trees were coming into bloom and New England was at her finest. The leaves were just budding out, a haze of pale green, lush beds of daffodils edged the emerald lawns, the kids decorating the grass in their brightly colored clothing, laughing, flirting, napping.

I spied a lone figure walking across the quad. His head was down, and he seemed oblivious to the wonders of the day. Stuart. Margaret had e-mailed me to say that she'd be staying with me for a while, so I gathered things weren't better on that front.

Poor Stuart.

"Welcome to Meeting Mr. Right," said our teacher.

"I can't believe we've been reduced to this," I whispered to Julian, who gave me a nervous glance.

"My name is *Lou*," our teacher continued plummily, "and I've been happily *married* for sixteen *wonderful* years!" I wondered if we were supposed to applaud. Lou beamed at us. "Every single *person* wants to find The *One*. The one who makes us feel *whole*. I know that my *Felicia*—" he paused again, then, when we failed to cheer, continued. "My Felicia does that for *me*."

Julian, Kiki and I sat in a classroom at the Blainesford Community Center. (Kiki's perfect man had dumped her on Wednesday after she'd called his cell fourteen times in one hour). There were two other women, as well as Lou, a good-looking man in his forties with a wedding ring about an inch wide, just so there'd be no misunderstandings. His rhythmic way of talking made him seem like a white suburban rapper. I shot Julian a condemning stare, which he pretended to ignore.

Lou smiled at us with all the sunny optimism of a Mormon preacher. "You're all *here* for a *reason,* and there's no *shame* in admitting it. You want a *man*…um, I am correct in assuming you also want a man, sir?" he asked, breaking off from his little song to look at Julian.

Julian, clad in a frilly pink shirt, shiny black pants and eyeliner, glanced at me. "Correct," he mumbled.

"That's *fine!* There's nothing *wrong* with that! These methods work for, er…anyway. So let's go *around* and just introduce *ourselves,* shall we? We're going to get pretty *intimate* here, so we might as well be *friends*," Lou instructed merrily. "Who'd like to go first?"

"Hi, I'm Karen," said a woman. She was tall and attractive enough, dark hair, dressed in sweats, maybe around forty, forty-five. "I'm divorced, and you wouldn't believe the freaks I meet. The last guy I went out with asked if he could suck my toes. In the restaurant, okay? When I said no, he called me a frigid bitch and left. And I had to pay the bill."

"Wow," I murmured.

"And this was the best date I've had in a year, okay?"

"Not for *long,* Karen, not for *long,*" Lou announced with great confidence.

"I'm Michelle," said the next woman. "I'm forty-two and I've been on sixty-seven dates in the past four months. Sixty-seven first dates, that is. Want to know how many second dates I've been on? None. Because all those first dates were with idiots. My ex, now, he's already married again. To Bambi, a waitress from Hooters. She's twenty-three, okay? But I haven't met one decent guy, so I hear you, Karen."

Karen nodded in grim sympathy.

"Hi, I'm Kiki," said my friend. "And I'm a teacher in a local school, so is there a vow of confidentiality in this class? Like, no one's going to out me on the street, right?"

Lou laughed merrily. "There's no *shame* in taking this *class,* Kiki, but if you're more *comfortable,* I think we can all agree to keep our *enrollment* to *ourselves!* Please continue. What drove you to this *class?* Are you past *thirty?* Afraid you'll never meet Mr. *Right?*"

"No, I meet him all the time. It's just that I tend to… maybe…rush things a little?" She glanced at me, and I nodded in support. "I scare them away," she admitted.

Julian was next. "I'm Julian. Um…I'm…I've only had one boyfriend, about eight years ago. I'm just kind of…scared. It's not that I can't meet a man…I get asked out all the time." Of course he did, he looked like Johnny Depp, and already I could see the speculation in Karen's eyes… *Hmm, wonder if I could get this one to jump the fence…*

"So you're afraid to *commit,* afraid things won't work

out, so you can't *fail* if you don't *try,* correct? All right!" Lou said, not waiting for an answer. "And you, miss? What's your name?"

I took a deep breath. "Hi. I'm Grace." I paused. "I'm currently pretending to have a boyfriend. My sister's dating my ex-fiancé, and to make everyone think I was fine with that, I told my family I've been seeing this fabulous guy. How's that for pathetic? And like you, Karen, I've been on some astonishingly bad dates, and I'm getting a little nervous, because my sister and Andrew are getting serious, and I'd really like to find someone. Soon. Very soon."

There was a moment's silence.

"I've made up boyfriends, too," Karen said, nodding her head slowly. "The best man I ever dated was all in my head."

"Thank you!" I exclaimed.

"I did it, too," Michelle said. "I even bought myself an engagement ring. It was beautiful. Exactly what I wanted. For three months, I wore that thing. Told everyone I knew I was getting married. It got so I was trying on dresses on the weekends. Sick, really. Looking back, though, it was one of my happier times."

"This brings up one of my *strategies,*" Lou announced. "Men love women who are *taken,* so Grace, your little *ruse* isn't the worst idea in the *world.* It's a great way to get a man *intrigued.* A woman who is sought out by other *men* shows that she has a certain *appeal!*"

"Or a certain lack of *honesty,*" I offered.

Lou guffawed heartily. Beside me, Julian winced. "I'm sorry," he whispered. "I thought this was worth a shot."

"It's only sixty bucks," I whispered back. "Plus we can get margaritas after."

"Let's get *going* with the class. Some of these *things* are going to sound a little *silly,* maybe, a little old-*fashioned,* but the name of the class is Meeting Mr. *Right,* and my methods *work.*" He paused. "For you, Julian, I'm not so sure, but give it a try and let me know how it's going, okay?"

"Sure," Julian said glumly.

For the next hour, I bit my lip to keep from snorting and did not look at Julian, who was similarly struggling. Everything Lou said sounded silly, all right. Downright idiotic, sometimes. It was like we were stepping back in time to the 1950s or something. *Be feminine and proper.* An image of me clubbing Callahan O'Shea came to mind. So proper, so ladylike. *No swearing, smoking or drinking more than one small glass of wine, which should not be finished. Make the man feel strong. Make yourself as attractive as possible. Makeup at all times. Skirts. Be approachable. Smile. Laugh, but quietly. Flutter your eyelashes. Bake cookies often. Exude serenity and grace. Ask for a man's help and flatter his opinions.*

Gack.

"For example," Lou said, "you should go to the *hardware* store. There are lots of *men* at a *hardware* store. Pretend you don't *know* which *lightbulb* to choose. Ask for the man's *opinion.*"

"Come on!" I blurted. "Lou, please! Who would want to date a woman who can't choose her own lightbulb?"

"I *know* what you're *thinking,* Grace," Lou sang out. "This is not *me.* But let's face it. *'You'* isn't working, or *'you'* wouldn't be in this *class.* Am I right?"

"He's got us there," Karen admitted with a sigh.

"THAT WAS FAIRLY *DEMEANING,*" I said, mimicking Lou's rolling speech pattern as we sat at Blackie's a half hour later, slurping down margaritas.

"At *least* it's *over,*" Julian said.

"Okay, stop, you two. He has a point. Listen to this," Kiki said, reading one of the handouts. "'When in a restaurant or bar, square your shoulders, look around carefully and say to yourself, *I am the most desirable woman here.* This will help you exude the confidence necessary to make men notice you.'" She frowned in concentration.

"I am the most desirable woman here," Julian said with mock earnestness.

"Problem is, you are," I answered, nudging him in the ribs.

"Too bad you aren't straight," Kiki said. "Then you and I could hook up."

"If I were straight, Grace and I would be married and have six kids by now," Julian said valiantly, putting his arm around me.

"Aw," I said, tilting my head against his shoulder. "Six, though? Seems like a lot."

"I'm gonna try it," Kiki said. "It's our homework, right? So here goes nothing. By the way, *I* am the most desirable woman here, and I'm exuding confidence." She smiled and stood up, then walked over to the bar, crossing her arms and leaning on the counter so her breasts swelled like ocean waves in a storm surge.

A man noticed immediately. He turned, smiled appreciatively and said something.

It was Callahan O'Shea.

My face flushed. "Crap," I hissed. God forbid that Kiki mention the class, for one, since Callahan would know I wasn't dating anyone, and for two...well...if Kiki was turning over a new leaf with men, shouldn't she know Callahan was recently released from prison? And should he know she tended to be a little wacko when it came to men?

"Maybe I should warn her," I murmured to Julian, not

taking my eyes off the two of them. "That's my neighbor. The ex-con." I'd told Julian about Cal's past.

"Oh, I don't know. Embezzlement didn't sound so bad," Julian said, sipping his piña colada. "And God, Grace. You didn't tell me he was so hot."

"Yeah, well..." My voice trailed off. Kiki said something, Callahan replied, and Kiki threw her head back, laughing. My eye twitched. "I...I'll be right back," I said.

Walking over to the bar, I touched Kiki's arm. "Kiki, can I talk to you a sec?" I said. I turned to my neighbor. "Hi, Callahan." I was already blushing. Wondered how my hair was. Dang it. I wanted to look pretty because Callahan O'Shea was looking at me.

"Hi, Grace," he said. He smiled...just a little, but enough. The man was just unfairly attractive.

"Oh, do you two know each other?" Kiki asked.

"Yes. We live next door to each other. He just moved in."

I hesitated, not sure I was doing the right thing. But Kiki had been my friend for years. Wouldn't I want to know if a guy I was interested in had just left prison? If she knew, she could make her own decision. Right?

Callahan was watching me. Dang it. I'd bet the farm that he knew what I was thinking.

"Kiki, Julian and I have a question," I finally said.

"Sure," she said uncertainly. I dragged her off a few paces, not looking at Cal. "Um, Kiki," I whispered, "that guy just got out of prison. For embezzling over a million dollars." I bit my lip.

She winced. "Oh, damn!" she said. "Isn't this typical? Leave it to me to pick the criminal. Crap. Of course he's gorgeous, too, right?"

"And he seems...well, he's...I just figured you should know."

"No, you're right, Grace. I have a hard enough time as it is, right? Don't need to date an ex-con."

With me trailing a step or two behind, Kiki went back to the bar and took her drink from the bartender. Callahan was watching us. His smile was gone. "Cal, nice meeting you," Kiki said politely.

His eyes flicked to me in a knowing glance, but he simply inclined his head in a courtly manner. "Have a good night," he said, turning back to the baseball game on the TV above the bar. Kiki and I hightailed it back to our table.

Our artichoke dip had arrived, and Julian was already eating, gazing across the restaurant with his soulful gypsy eyes at a good-looking blond guy who was returning his gaze with equal intensity.

"Go for it," I said, nodding toward the guy. "You're the most desirable woman here."

"He looks like that football player. Tom Brady," Julian murmured.

"How do you know who Tom Brady is?" I asked.

"Every gay man in America knows who Tom Brady is," he said.

"Maybe he *is* Tom Brady," Kiki said. "You never know. Go ahead, give it a shot. Make him feel manly and smart. Use those feminine wiles."

For a second, Julian seemed to consider it, then his shoulders dropped. "Nah," he said. "Why do I need a man when I have you two beautiful girls?"

For the rest of the night, I shot little glances at Callahan O'Shea's back as he ate a hamburger and watched the baseball game. He did not look back.

CHAPTER TWELVE

ON SATURDAY MORNING, I WAS once again wrenched out of bed by Angus's hysteria and staggered down the stairs to open the door. This time, it was Margaret, a suitcase in tow, a glower on her face.

"I'm here," she said. "Got any coffee?"

"Sure, sure, let me put it on," I answered, still squinting. I'd been up late last night watching all two hundred and twenty-nine smarmily glorious minutes of *Gods and Generals,* weeping copiously as General Jackson barked out his last delirious orders to First Virginia. I think it's fair to say I had a Confederate hangover, so Margaret in all her grouchy glory, first thing in the morning...ouch. I followed her as she stomped into the kitchen.

"So what happened?" I asked as I measured out coffee grounds.

"Here's the thing, Grace," Margaret said in her master and commander voice. "Don't marry a man you love like a brother, okay?"

"Brothers, bad. Got it."

"I'm serious, smart-ass." She bent over and scooped up Angus, who was chewing on her shoe. "I said to Stuart last night, 'How come we never have sex on the kitchen table?' And you know what he said?" Margaret glared at me accusingly.

"What?" I asked, sitting down at the table with her.

She lowered her voice to imitate her husband. "'I'm not sure that's sanitary.' Can you fucking believe that? How many men would turn down kitchen-table sex? You want to know when Stuart and I do it?"

"No, I absolutely do not," I answered.

"Monday, Wednesday, Friday and Saturday," she snapped.

"Wow," I said. "That sounds pretty good to—"

"It's in his daily planner. He puts a little star in the nine o'clock slot to remind him. Intercourse with Wife. Check."

"But still, it's nice that he—"

"And that's the whole problem, Grace. Not enough passion. So I'm here."

"At the home of passion," I murmured.

"Well, I can't just stay there! Maybe he'll notice me a little more now! Maybe not! I don't really care at this point. I'm thirty-four years old, Grace. I want to have sex on the kitchen table! Is that so wrong?"

"I know I wouldn't say so," came a voice. We both turned. Callahan O'Shea stood in the kitchen doorway. Angus exploded into his usual sound and fury, struggling to get out of Margaret's arms. "I knocked," Cal said, grinning. "Hi, I'm Callahan. The good-looking neighbor."

Margaret's expression morphed from furious to rapacious, a lion staring at a three-legged baby zebra. "Hi, Callahan the good-looking neighbor," she said in a sultry voice. "I'm Margaret the horny sister."

"The horny *married* sister," I inserted. "Margaret, meet Callahan O'Shea. Cal, my sister, pretty happily married for lo these many years, currently suffering from what I believe is called the seven-year itch."

"Hey, it has been seven years, hasn't it?" Margaret

snapped out of her lustful daze. "So you're the embezzler, huh?"

"That's right." Cal inclined his head, then turned to me. "Not fit for decent company, right, Grace?"

My face went nuclear. Ah, yes. Kiki and the warning. Callahan's expression was decidedly cold.

"Grace, your windows came yesterday afternoon. If you want, I can get started today."

Closing my eyes, I tried to imagine this guy stealing my Victorian Santa collection. "Sure."

"How about if I only work when you're around?" he suggested. "That way you can keep an eye on your checkbook and family heirlooms, maybe pat me down before I go."

"Or I can do that," Margaret volunteered.

"Very funny," I said. "Install the windows. Will it take long?"

"Three days. Maybe five, depending on how the old ones come out. I might need a hand with that, if your boyfriend's around today."

Gosh. Almost forgot about that pesky boyfriend. Margaret looked at me sharply. "Mmm. He's working," I said, shooting her a silent warning.

"He doesn't seem to come around much, from what I've noticed." Cal folded his big arms and raised an eyebrow.

"Well, he's very busy," I said.

"What does he do again?" Callahan asked.

"He's a..." I really wished I'd picked something less sappy. "A pediatric surgeon," I said.

"So noble," Margaret murmured, smiling into her coffee cup.

Callahan's hair was sticking up on one side, and my fingers wondered what it would feel like to run through that silky, misbehaving, adorable mess. I told my fingers to stop daydreaming.

"So, sure, okay, you can start today, Cal," I said. "Would you like some coffee first?"

"No. Thank you," he said. So much for my peace offering. "Where do you want me to start? And do you want to make a sweep of the room first?"

"Okay, listen. I'm sorry I told my friend you just got out of the slammer. But you *are* an admitted criminal, so…"

"So?" he said.

I sighed. "So you can start in here, I guess."

"The kitchen it is." He turned and walked down the hall toward the front door.

When he was safely outside, presumably to get my first window, Margaret leaned forward. "Are you guys fighting? And why did you tell him you have a boyfriend?" she asked. "He's gorgeous. I'd do him in a New York minute."

"We're not fighting! We hardly know each other. And yes, he's gorgeous, but that's beside the point."

"Why? I thought you were looking to get laid."

"Shh! Lower your voice. I told him I was seeing someone."

"Why'd you tell him that?" Margaret took a sip of her coffee.

I sighed. "Natalie was over last weekend, asking all these questions about Wyatt…" Margaret, the least fanciful creature on earth, never did understand the comfort of my imaginary boyfriends. "Anyway. I don't think it's a bad thing for him to think there's a man who stops by occasionally. Just in case he's casing my joint."

"Wouldn't mind if he cased mine." I gave her a dirty look. "Right. Well. He's hot. Wonder if he's interested in an affair."

"Margaret!"

"Relax. Just kidding."

"Margs, speaking of dates, weren't you going to fix me up with the blacksmith? I'm getting a little desperate here."

"Right, right. Metalsmith. Lester. Weird. I'll call him."

"Great," I muttered. "I can't wait."

She took another sip of coffee. "Got anything to eat? I'm starving. Oh, and I brought some dirty laundry, hope that's all right. I just had to get out of the house. And if Stuart calls, I don't want to talk to him, okay?"

"Of course. Anything else, Majesty?"

"Can you pick up some skim milk? This half-and-half will kill me." Margaret was one of those people who ate nonfat cheese and didn't know she was missing anything.

Callahan came into the kitchen carrying a new window and leaned it against the wall.

"Are you married, good-looking neighbor?" Margs asked.

"Nope," came his answer. "Is that a proposal?"

Margaret grinned wickedly. "Maybe," she murmured.

"Margaret! Leave him alone."

"How much time did you actually serve, Al Capone?" Margs asked. "God, his ass in those jeans," she whispered to me, not taking her eyes off his backside.

"Stop it," I whispered back.

"Nineteen months," Cal answered. "And thanks." He winked at Margaret. My uterus twitched in response.

"Nineteen months on three-to-five?" Margs asked.

"Yup. You've done your homework," he said, smiling at my sister. My beautiful sister. Beautiful, red-haired, smart as a whip, razor-witted sister in a high-income bracket and a size four to boot.

"Well, Grace asked me to check you out, being that you're a threat to her security."

"Shut it, Margaret," I said, blushing.

"Any other questions?" Cal asked mildly.

"Have you had a woman since you got out?" Margaret asked, studying her fingernails.

"God's nightgown!" I yelped.

"You mean did I swing by the local whorehouse on my way into town?" Cal asked.

"Correct," Margaret affirmed, ignoring my offended squeaks.

"No. No women."

"Wow. How about in the big house? Any girlfriends?" she asked. I closed my eyes.

Callahan, however, laughed. "It wasn't that kind of prison."

"You must be so lonely," Margaret said, smiling wickedly at Cal's back.

"Are you done interrogating him?" I snapped. "He has work to do, Margaret."

"Party pooper," Margaret said. "But you're right. And I have to go into the office. I'm a lawyer, Callahan, did Grace tell you? Criminal defense. Would you like my card?"

"I'm completely reformed," he said with a grin that promised all sorts of illicit behavior.

"I know people in the parole office. Very well, in fact. I'll be watching."

"You do that," he answered.

"I'll help you get settled," I offered, hauling Margaret out of her chair and grabbing her suitcase. "You can't have an affair with him," I hissed once we were upstairs. "You will not cheat on Stuart. He's wonderful, Margaret. And he's heartbroken. I saw him at school the other day, and he looked like a kicked puppy."

"Good. At least he's noticing me now."

"Oh, for God's sake. You're so spoiled."

"I have to go to the office," she said, ignoring my last comment. "I'll see you for dinner, okay? Feel like cooking?"

"Oh." I took a deep breath. "I won't be here."

"Why? Date with Wyatt?" she asked, raising a silken eyebrow.

I reached up to smooth my difficult hair. "Um, no. Well, yes. We're going to Nat's for dinner. Double date."

"Holy Mary the Eternal Virgin, Grace," my sister muttered.

"I know, I know. Wyatt will end up in emergency surgery, bless his talented heart."

"You're an idiot. Hey, thanks for letting me crash here," Margs said at the door to the guest room, vaguely remembering that she should be grateful.

"You're welcome," I said. "Leave Callahan alone."

For the next few minutes, I found things to do upstairs, away from my neighbor. Took a shower. As the warm water streamed over me, I wondered what would happen if Callahan O'Shea walked in. Tugged his shirt over his head, unbuckled his belt, slid out of those faded jeans and stepped in here with me, enfolding me in his brawny arms, his mouth hot and demanding, his— I blinked hard, turned the water to cold and finished up.

Margaret headed into her office, calling out a cheerful goodbye to Callahan and me, seeming rather depressingly chipper about leaving her husband. I wrote up a quiz on the Reconstruction for my seniors, using my laptop and not the larger computer downstairs. Corrected essays from my sophomores on the FDR administration. Downstairs, the whine of the saw and thump of the hammer and the offhanded, tuneless whistle of Callahan O'Shea blended into a pleasant cacophony.

Angus, though he still growled occasionally, gave up trying to tunnel under my bedroom door and lay on his back in a puddle of sunlight, his crooked bottom teeth showing most adorably. I concentrated on my students' work, writing notes in the margins, comments at the end, praising them lavishly for moments of clarity, pointing out areas that could've used some work.

I went downstairs a while later. Four of the eight downstairs windows were already in. Cal glanced in my direction. "I don't think I'll have to replace those sills. If the windows upstairs are as easy as the ones downstairs, I'll be done Monday or Tuesday."

"Oh. Okay," I said. "They look great."

"Glad you like them."

He looked at me, unsmiling, unmoving. I looked back. And looked. And looked some more. His was a rugged face, and yes, handsome, but it was his eyes that got me. Callahan O'Shea had a story in those eyes.

The air seemed to thicken between us, and I could feel my face—and other parts—growing warm.

"I'd better get back to work," he said, and, turning his back on me, he did just that.

CHAPTER THIRTEEN

THE SECOND I OPENED THE DOOR, I knew that Natalie and Andrew were living together. Natalie's apartment had his smell, that baby shampoo sweetness, and it hit me in a slap of undeniable recognition. "Hello!" I said, hugging my sister, stroking her sleek hair.

"Hi! Oh, it's so good to see you!" Nat hugged me tight, then pulled back. "Where's Wyatt?"

"Hey, Grace!" Andrew called from the kitchen.

My stomach clenched. Andrew at Natalie's. So cozy.

"Hi, Andrew," I called back. "Wyatt got stuck at the hospital, so he'll be a little late." My voice was smooth and controlled. Bully for me.

"But he is coming?" Nat said, her brows puckering in concern.

"Oh, sure. He'll just be a while yet."

"I made this fabulous cream tart for dessert," Nat grinned. "Definitely wanted to make a good impression, you know?"

Natalie's apartment was in the Ninth Square section of New Haven, a rescued part of the city not far from the downtown firm where she worked. I'd been here, of course, helped her move in, gave her that iron horse statue for a housewarming gift. But things were different now. How long had Nat and Andrew been together? A month? Six weeks? Yet already his things were scattered here and there...a jacket on the coatrack, his running shoes by the door, the *New York Law Journal* by the fireplace. If he wasn't living here, he was staying over. A lot.

"Hey, there," Andrew said, coming out of the kitchen. He gave me a quick hug, and I could feel his familiar sharp angles. Angles that felt repugnant today.

"Hi," I said, stretching the old mouth in a grin. "How are you?"

"Great! How about a drink? A vodka gimlet? Appletini? White Russian?" Andrew's merry green eyes smiled behind his glasses. He'd always been proud of having bartended his way through law school.

"I'd love some wine," I said, just to deny him the exhibitionistic pleasure of making me a cocktail.

"White or red? We have a nice cabernet sauvignon open."

"White, please," I answered. My smile felt tight. "Wyatt likes cabernet, though."

At this moment, I was incredibly grateful to young Wyatt Dunn, M.D. This night would've been awful without him, even if he didn't exist in the corporeal world. I drifted over to the couch, Natalie chattering away about how she couldn't find tilapia anywhere today and had to go to Fair Haven to a little fish market down by the Quinnipiac River. I had to stifle a sigh at the picture of Natalie, a study of elegant beauty, riding her bike down to the Italian market, where, no doubt, the owner fussed over her and threw in a few biscotti, since she was so pretty. Natalie with the perfect hair and fabulous job. Natalie with the lovely apartment and Natalie with the beautiful furniture. Natalie with my ex-fiancé, telling me how she was dying to meet my imaginary beau.

I didn't relish the fact that I was lying to Natalie—and my parents, and grandmother and even Callahan O'Shea—but it was a far sight better than being Poor Grace, tossed over for her sister. Morally wrong to lie, but hey! If lying was ever justified, I'd have to say it was now.

For a brief second, another scenario flashed across the old brain cells. Callahan O'Shea sitting by my side, rolling his eyes at how Andrew was even now showing off in the kitchen, chopping parsley like a manic spider monkey. That Cal would sling his big, muscular arm around my shoulder and mutter, "I can't believe you were engaged to that scrawny jerk."

Right. That would happen, and then I'd win the Lotto and discover I was the love child of Margaret Mitchell and Clark Gable.

To distract myself, I looked around Nat's living room. My gaze stopped abruptly on the mantel. "I remember this," I said, my voice a tad tight. "Andrew, this is the clock I gave you, isn't it? Wow!"

And it was. A lovely, whiskey-colored mantel clock with a buttery face and elaborately detailed numbers, a brass key for winding it. I found it in an antiques shop in Litchfield and gave it to Andrew for his thirtieth birthday, two years ago. I planned the whole dang party, good little fiancée that I was. A picnic in the field along the Farmington. His work friends—*our* friends, back then—as well as Ava, Paul, Kiki and Dr. Eckhart, Margaret and Stuart, Julian, Mom and Dad, and Andrew's snooty parents, who looked vaguely startled at the idea of eating on a public picnic table. What a great day that had been. Of course, that was back when he still loved me. Before he met my sister.

"Oh. Yeah. I love that clock," he said awkwardly, handing me my wine.

"Good, since it cost the earth," I announced with a stab of crass pleasure. "One of a kind."

"And it's...it's gorgeous," Andrew mumbled.

I know it is, dopey. "So. You two are very cozy. Are you living here now, Andrew?" I asked, and my voice was just a trifle loud.

"Well, uh...not...I still have a few months on my lease. So, no, not really." He exchanged a quick, nervous glance with Natalie.

"Mmm-hmm. But obviously, since your things are migrating here..." I took a healthy sip of my chardonnay.

Neither of them said anything. I continued, making sure my tone was pleasant. "That's nice. Saves on rent, too. Very logical." And *fast*. But of course, they were in love. Who wouldn't be in love with Natalie, the fair flower of our family? Nat was younger. Blond, blue-eyed. Taller. Prettier. Smarter. Man, I wished Wyatt Dunn was real! Wished that Callahan O'Shea was here! Anything other than this echoing sense of rejection that just wouldn't fade away. I unclenched my jaw and took a seat next to my sister and studied her. "God, we just do not look alike, do we?" I said.

"Oh, I think we do!" she exclaimed earnestly. "Except for the hair color. Grace, do you remember when I was in high school and got that perm? And then colored my hair brown?" She laughed and reached out to touch my knee. "I was crushed when it didn't come out like yours."

And there it was. I couldn't be mad at Natalie. It was almost like I wasn't *allowed* to be mad at Natalie, ever. It wasn't fair, and it was completely true. I remembered the day she was referring to. She'd permed it, all right, permed that lovely, cool hair, then dyed it a flat, ugly brown. She was fourteen at the time, and had cried in her room as the chemical curls failed to produce the desired results. A week later, her hair was straight again, and she became the only brunette in high school with blond roots.

She'd wanted to be like me. She thought we looked

alike—me, three inches shorter, fifteen pounds heavier, the accursed hair, the unremarkable gray eyes.

"There's definitely a resemblance," Andrew said. *Piss off, buddy,* I thought. *Here I am taking a class on how to meet a husband, dredging up men on the Internet, lusting after a convict, and you have this* pearl, *you undeserving jerk.* Well. I guess the anger wasn't quite so gone after all. Not the anger caused by Andrew, that was.

He seemed to catch that thought. "I better check the risotto. I don't think it's going to thicken without some serious prayer." With that, he scurried off into the kitchen like a frightened crab.

"Grace, is everything okay?" Natalie asked softly.

I took a breath. "Oh, sure." I paused. "Well, Wyatt and I had a little fight."

"Oh, no!"

I closed my eyes. I really was becoming a masterful liar. "Yeah. Well, he's so devoted to the kids, you know?" *Yes, Grace, such a prick, your pediatric surgeon.* "I mean, he's wonderful. I'm crazy about him. But I hardly see him."

"I guess it's an occupational hazard," Natalie murmured, her eyes soft with sympathy.

"Yeah."

"But he makes up for it, I hope?" Nat asked, and I answered that yes, indeed he did. Breakfast in bed…strawberries, and the waffles were a little burnt, it was so cute, he was like a kid…the flowers he sent me (I had actually sent myself some flowers). The way he listened…loved learning about the classes I was teaching. The beautiful scarf he bought me last weekend (in fact, I did have a beautiful new scarf, except that I'd bought it for myself that day Julian and I went shopping).

"Oh, hey, did I tell you I'm up for chairmanship of the history department?" I said, seizing on a change of subject.

"Oh, Grace, that's wonderful!" my sister cried. "You would do so much for that place! It would totally come alive if you were in charge."

Then, on cue, my cell phone rang. I stood up, reached into my pocket, withdrew my phone and flipped it open. "It's Wyatt," I said, smiling at Nat.

"Okay! I'll give you a little privacy." She started to get up.

"No, stay!" I commanded, then turned to the phone. After all, she needed to hear this conversation...my end, anyway. "Hi, honey," I said.

"Hi, baby," said Julian. "I'm thinking of changing my name."

"Oh, no! Is he okay?" I asked, remembering to frown in concern, as I'd practiced in the rearview mirror on the way here.

"Something more manly, you know? Like Will or Jack. Spike. What do you think?"

"I think he's lucky you were his doctor," I answered firmly, smiling at my sister.

"Maybe that's too butch, though. Maybe Mike. Or Mack. Well, I probably won't. My mother would kill me."

"No, no, that's fine, honey! I understand. Of course she will! No, they both know what you do for a living! It's not like you're a..." I paused. "A carpenter or something. A mechanic. You're saving lives!"

"Down, girl," Julian coached.

"You're right," I said.

"What are you having for dinner?" my friend asked.

"Risotto, asparagus and tilapia. Some delicious tart my sister slaved over."

"I'll send some back with Grace!" Natalie called.

"Make sure I get that tart," Julian said. "I've earned it. Shall we chat some more? Want me to propose?"

"No, no, honey, that's fine. You have a great night," I said.

"Love you," Julian said. "Now say it back to me."

"Oh, um, same here." My face grew hot—I was not about to declare my love for an imaginary boyfriend. Even I wouldn't go that far. Then I flipped the phone closed and sighed. "Well, he can't make it. The surgery was more complicated than he thought, and he wants to stay close until the little guy's out of the woods."

"Ooh," Natalie sighed, her face morphing into something like adoration. "Oh, Grace, I'm so sorry he can't come, but God, he sounds so wonderful!"

"He is," I said. "He really is."

After dinner, Natalie walked me to my spot in the parking garage. "Well, I'm so sorry I couldn't meet Wyatt," she said. "But it was great to have you here." Her voice echoed in the vast cement chamber.

"Thanks," I said, unlocking the car. I put the Tupperware containing Julian's generous slab of tart on the backseat and turned back to my sister. "So things are really serious with you and Andrew?"

She hesitated. "Yes. I hope that's okay with you."

"Well, I didn't want you to have a fling, Nat," I replied a bit sharply. "I mean, *that* would've hurt, you know? I just... I'm glad. This is good."

"Are you sure?"

"Yes. I am."

She smiled, that serene, blissful smile of hers. "Thanks. You know, I have to thank Wyatt when I do finally meet him. To tell you the truth, I think I would've broken up with Andrew if you hadn't been seeing someone. It just felt too wrong, you know?"

"Mmm," I said. "Well. I...I should go. Bye, Nattie. Thanks for a lovely dinner."

Rain came down in sheets as I drove home, my little car's wipers valiantly battling for visibility. It was a vicious night, colder than normal, windy and wild, much like the night my tire blew out. The night I first met Wyatt Dunn. I snorted at the thought.

I imagined, for one deeply satisfying second, that I'd kept my mouth shut in the bathroom at Kitty's wedding. That I'd let the guilt work its magic and admitted, yes, it *was* wrong, a woman shouldn't date a man who was once promised to her sister. Andrew would have been out of my life forever, and I wouldn't have to see his eyes light on Natalie's face with that expression of gratitude and wonder—an expression I can tell you quite honestly I never saw before. No, when Andrew had looked at me, there was affection, humor, respect and comfort. All good things, but no kablammy. I had loved him. He hadn't loved me back the same way.

Despite Margaret's sleeping presence in the guest room when I came home, and though Angus did his best to tell me that I was the most wonderful creature on God's green earth, the house felt empty. If only I did have that nice doctor boyfriend to call. If only he was on his way home to me now. I'd hand him a glass of wine and rub his shoulders, and he'd smile up gratefully. Maybe we'd cuddle on the couch there, then head up to bed. Angus wouldn't so much as nip Wyatt Dunn, because Angus, in this fantasy anyway, was an excellent judge of character and just adored Wyatt.

I brushed my teeth and washed my face and grimaced over my hair, then found myself wondering if the attic needed, well, a little visit. Yes. Sure it did. It was quite wet out, after all, though the hard rain had stopped around Hartford and it was just kind of foggy and damp now. Surely Callahan O'Shea wouldn't be out on his roof. This was simple homeownership...perhaps a window was open up there. It might rain again later. You never knew.

Callahan O'Shea *was* out there. *Good for you, Cal,* I thought. Not the type to let a little New England weather stop him from doing his thing.

He must've missed the outdoors in prison. Granted, he'd been in a Club Fed, apparently, but when I pictured him, he was in an orange jumpsuit or black-and-white stripes, in a cell with bars and a metal cot. (There just weren't enough movies featuring Club Feds, and so the one in my imagination was identical to the prison in *The Shawshank Redemption*.)

For one second, I imagined what it would be like to be down there with Callahan O'Shea, his arm around me, my head on his shoulder, and the image was so powerful that I could feel the thud of his heartbeat under my hand, his fingers playing in my hair. Occasionally, one of us would murmur something to the other, but mostly, we'd just be still.

"Don't waste your time," I whispered sagely to myself. "Even without the prison record, he's not your type." *Besides,* my irritating little voice told me, *he doesn't even like you.* Add to that the roiling discomfort I felt around the large, muscular man next door...no. I wanted comfort, security, stability. Not bristling tension and sex appeal. No matter how good it looked from here.

CHAPTER FOURTEEN

"GRACE?"

Angus growled fiercely then bounded off to attack a moth. I looked up from the pansies I was potting on the back patio. It was Sunday morning, and Callahan O'Shea was back, standing in the kitchen at the sliding glass door. He'd gotten right to work this morning; Margaret was off for a run (she ran marathons, so there was no telling when she'd be back) so apparently Cal had no reason to hang around and flirt.

"I need to move the bookcase in front of the window. Do you want to move your little...things?"

"Sure," I said, getting up and brushing off my hands.

My "things" were mostly DVDs and collectibles. Wordlessly, I placed the items on the couch...a tobacco tin from the 1880s, a tiny cannon, a porcelain figure of Scarlett O'Hara in her green velvet curtain dress and a framed Confederate dollar.

"I guess you like the Civil War," he commented as he glanced at the movie cases. *Glory, Cold Mountain, The Red Badge of Courage, Shenandoah, North and South, The Outlaw Josey Wales, Gods and Generals, Gettysburg,* and the Ken Burns documentary, special edition DVD, a Christmas gift from Natalie.

"I'm a history teacher," I said.

"Right. That explains it," he said, looking more closely

at the movies. "*Gone With the Wind*'s never been opened. You have more than one copy?"

"Oh, that. My mom gave this to me, but I always thought I should see it on the big screen first, you know? Give the movie its due."

"So you've never seen it?"

"No. I've read the book fourteen times, though. Have you?"

"I've seen the movie." He smiled a little.

"On the big screen?"

"Nope. On TV."

"That doesn't count," I said.

"I see." He smiled a little, and my stomach tightened. We moved the bookcase. He picked up his saw and waited for me to move out of the way. I didn't.

"So, Cal…why did you embezzle a million dollars?" I asked.

"One point six million," he said, plugging the saw in. "Why does anyone steal anything?"

"I don't know," I answered. "Why did you?"

He looked at me with those dark blue eyes, weighing his answer. I waited, too. There was something in his face that told a story, and I wanted to hear it. He was sizing me up, wondering what to tell me, how to say it. I waited.

"Hi, honey, I'm home!" The front door banged open. Margaret stood there, sweaty and flushed and gorgeous. "Bad news, campers. Mom's on her way. I saw her car at Lala's Bakery. Hurry. I almost set a world record getting here before she did."

My sister and I bolted for the cellar. "Callahan, give us some help!" Margs ordered.

"What's wrong?" Cal asked, following us. At the foot of the cellar stairs, he stumbled to a halt. "Oh, my God." He looked slowly around.

My cellar was the sculpture repository. Mom, alas, was generous with her art, and so my cellar was littered with glass girl parts.

"I love it here," Callahan said distantly.

"Hush, you. Grab some sculptures and get upstairs. No time for chitchat," Margaret ordered. "Our mom will have a fit if she knows Grace hides her stuff. I speak from experience." Grabbing *The Home of Life* (a uterus) and *Nest #12* (ovary), my sister ran lightly back upstairs.

"Do you rent this place out?" Callahan asked.

"Stop," I said, unable to suppress a grin. "Just bring that upstairs and put it on a shelf or something. Make it look like it belongs." I shoved *Breast in Blue* into his hands. It was heavy—I should've warned him, and for a second, he bobbled the breast, and I grabbed for it, and so did he, and the end result was that we both were sort of holding it, our hands overlapping as we both supported the sculpture. I looked up into his eyes, and he smiled.

Kablammy.

My knees practically buckled. He smelled like wood and soap and coffee, and his hands were big and warm, and God, the way those blue eyes slanted down, the heat from his body beckoning me to lean in over *Breast in Blue* and just…you know…just… Really, who cared if he was an ex-con? Stealing, shmealing. Though I was distantly aware that I should probably change my expression from *unadulterated lust* to something more along the lines of *cheerful neighbor*, I was paralyzed.

A car horn sounded. Upstairs, Angus burst into a tinny thunderstorm of barking, hurling his body against the front door, from the thumping sound of it.

"Hurry up down there!" Margaret barked. "You know what she's like!"

The spell was broken. Cal took the sculpture, grabbed another one and went upstairs. I did the same, still blushing.

I shoved *Hidden Treasure* onto the bookcase and lay *Portal in Green* on the coffee table, where it splayed most obscenely.

"Hello, there!" Mom called from the porch. "Angus, down. Down. Quiet, honey. No. Stop. Quiet, dear. No barking."

I picked up my dog and opened the door, my heart still thumping. "Hi, Mom! What brings you here?"

"I have pastries!" she chirped. "Hello, Angus! Who's a sweet baby? Hi, Margaret, honey. Stuart said we'd find you here. And oh, hello. Who are you?"

I glanced back. Cal stood in the kitchen doorway. "Mom, this is my neighbor, Callahan O'Shea. Callahan, my mother, the renowned sculptor, Nancy Emerson."

"A pleasure. I'm a big fan of your work." Cal shook my mother's hand, and Mom turned a questioning gaze on me.

"Dad hired him to put in some new windows," I explained.

"I see," said Mom suspiciously.

"I need to run next door and then head to the hardware store, Grace. Anything you need?" Cal said, turning to me.

I need to be kissed. "Um, nope. Not that I can think of," I said, blushing yet again.

"See you later, then. Nice meeting you, Mrs. Emerson." The three of us watched as he went out the front door.

Mom snapped out of it first. "Well. Margaret, we need to talk. Come on, girls. Let's sit in the kitchen. Oh, Grace, this shouldn't go here! It's not funny. This is serious artwork, honey."

Callahan O'Shea had placed *Breast in Blue* in my fruit bowl amid the oranges and pears. I grinned. Margaret snorted with laughter and opened the pastry bag. "Oh, goody. Poppy seed rolls. Want one, Grace?"

"Sit, girls. Margaret. What's this about you leaving Stuart, for heaven's sake?"

I sighed. Mom wasn't here to see me. I was her trouble-free daughter. Growing up, Margaret had been (and proudly still was) the drama queen, full of adolescent rebellion, collegiate certainty, academic excellence and a gift for confrontation. Natalie, of course, was the golden one from the moment of her birth and since her brush with death, her every feat had been viewed as miraculous.

So far, the only exceptional thing that had happened to me was my breakup with Andrew. Sure, my parents loved me, though they viewed becoming a teacher as a bit of an easy route. ("Those who can, do," Dad had said when I announced I'd forgo law school and get a master's in American History with the hope of becoming a teacher. "And those who can't, teach.") My summers off were treated as an affront to those who "really worked." The fact that I slaved endlessly during the school year—tutoring and correcting and designing lesson plans, staying well past school hours to meet with students in my office, coaching the debate team, going to school events, chaperoning dances and field trips, boning up on new developments in teaching and handling the sensitive parents, all of whom expected their children to excel in every way—was viewed as irrelevant when compared with all of my delicious vacation time.

Mom sat back in her chair and eyed her eldest child. "So? Spit it out, Margaret!"

"I haven't left him completely," Margaret said, taking a huge bite of pastry. "I'm just...lurking here."

"Well, it's ridiculous," Mom huffed. "Your father and I

certainly have our problems. You don't see me running off to Aunt Mavis's house, do you?"

"That's because Aunt Mavis is such a pain in the ass," Margaret countered. "Grace is barely even half of the pain that Mavis is, right, Gracie?"

"Oh, thanks, Margs. And let me say what a privilege it was to see your dirty clothes scattered all over my guest room this morning. Shall I do your laundry for you, Majesty?"

"Well, since you don't have a real job, sure," she said.

"Real job? It's better than getting a bunch of drug dealers—"

"Girls, enough. Are you really leaving Stuart?" Mom asked.

Margaret closed her eyes. "I don't know," she said.

"Well, I think that's ridiculous. You married him, Margaret. You don't just leave. You stay and work things out till you're happy again."

"Like you and Dad?" Margaret suggested. "Kill me now, then. Grace, would you do the honors?"

"Your father and I are perfectly..." Her voice trailed off, and she studied her coffee cup as if a light was abruptly dawning.

"Maybe you should move in with Grace, too," Margaret suggested, raising an eyebrow.

"Okay, very funny. No. You can't, Mom." I shot Margs a threatening look. "Seriously, Mom," I said slowly. "You and Dad love each other, right? You just like to bicker."

"Oh, Grace," she sighed. "What's love got to do with it?"

"Thank you, Tina Turner," Margaret quipped.

"I'm hoping love has a lot to do with it," I protested.

Mom sighed. "Who knows what love is?" She waved her hand dismissively.

"Love is a battlefield," Margaret murmured.

"All you need is love," I countered.

"Love stinks," she returned.

"Shut up, Margs," I said. "Mom? You were saying?"

She sighed. "You get so used to someone...I don't know. Some days, I want to kill your father with a dull knife. He's a boring old tax attorney, for heaven's sake. His idea of fun is to lay down and play dead at one of those stupid Civil War battles."

"Hey. I love those stupid battles," I interjected, but she ignored me.

"But I don't just walk away, either, Margaret. We did, after all, vow to love and cherish each other, even if it kills us."

"Gosh. That's beautiful," Margaret said.

"But my word, he gets on my nerves, making fun of my art! What does *he* do? Runs around in dress-up clothes, firing guns. *I* create. *I* celebrate the female form. *I* am capable of expressing myself by more than grunts and sarcasm. *I*—"

"More coffee, Mom?" Margs asked.

"No. I have to go." Still, she remained in her chair.

"Mom," I asked cautiously, "why *do* you, uh, celebrate the female form, as you put it? How did that get started?" Margaret gave me a dark look, but I was a little curious. I was in graduate school when Mom discovered herself, as it were.

She smiled. "The truth is, it was an accident. I was trying to make one of those little glass balls that hang in the window or on a Christmas tree, you know? And I was having trouble tying off the end, and your father came in and said it looked like a nipple. So I told him it was, and he turned absolutely purple and I thought, why not? If your father had that kind of a reaction to it, what would someone else think? So I took it down to Chimera, and they loved it."

"Mmm," I murmured. "What's not to love?"

"I mean it, Grace. The *Hartford Courant* called me a postmodern feminist with the aesthetic appeal of Mapplethorpe and O'Keeffe on acid."

"All from a screwed up Christmas ornament," Margaret interjected.

"The first one was accidental, Margaret. The rest are a celebration of the physiological miracle that is Woman," Mom pronounced. "I love what I do, even if you girls are too Puritanical to properly appreciate my art. I have a new career and people admire me. And if it tortures your father, that's just gravy."

"Yes," Margs said. "Why not torture Dad? He's only given you everything."

"Well, Margaret, dear, I'd counter that by saying he's the one who got everything, and you of all people should appreciate my position. I became wallpaper, girls. He was more than happy to come home, be served a martini and a dinner I slaved over for hours in a house that was immaculate with children who were smart, well-behaved and gorgeous, then pop into bed for some rowdy sex."

Margaret and I recoiled in identical horror.

Mom turned a hard eye on Margaret. "He was completely spoiled, and I was invisible. So if I'm torturing him, Margaret, darling firstborn of my loins, you of all people might say, 'Well done, Mother.' Because at least he's noticing me now, and I didn't even have to go running to my sister's house."

"Youch," Margaret said. "I'm bleeding, Grace." Oddly, she was smiling.

"Please stop fighting, you two," I said. "Mom, we're very proud of you. You're, um, a visionary. Really."

"Thank you, dear," Mom said, standing up. "Well, I have

to run now. I'm giving a talk at the library on my art and inspiration."

"Adults only, I'm guessing," Margaret murmured, taking Angus from my lap to make kissing faces at him.

Mom sighed and looked at the ceiling. "Grace, you have cobwebs up there. And don't shlunch, honey. Walk me to the car, all right?"

I obeyed, leaving Margaret, who was hand-feeding Angus bits of her roll.

"Grace," my mother said, "who was that man who was here?"

"Callahan?" I asked. She nodded. "My neighbor. Like I told you."

"Well. Don't go screwing up a good thing by falling for a manual laborer, dear."

"God, Mom!" I yelped. "You don't even know him! He's very nice."

"I'm just pointing out that you have a lovely thing going with that nice doctor, don't you?"

"I'm not going to date Callahan, Mother," I said tersely. "He's just some guy Dad hired."

Ah, shit. There he was, getting into his truck. He heard, of course. Judging from his expression, he heard the "just some guy Dad hired," not the "very nice" bit.

"Well, fine," Mom said in a quieter voice. "It's just that ever since Andrew and you broke up, you've been wandering around like a ghost, honey. And it's nice to see your young man has put some roses back in your cheeks."

"I thought you were a feminist," I said.

"I am," she said.

"Well, you could've fooled me! Maybe it's just that enough time passed and I actually got over him on my own. Maybe it's springtime. Maybe I'm just having a really good time at work these days. Did you hear that I'm up for the chairmanship of the department? Maybe I'm just doing fine on my own and it has nothing to do with Wyatt Dunn."

"Mmm. Well. Whatever," Mom said. "I have to go, dear. Bye! Don't shlunch."

"She'll be the death of me," I announced as I went back inside. "If I don't kill her first, that is."

Margaret burst into tears.

"God's nightgown!" I said. "I didn't mean it! Margs, what's wrong?"

"My idiot husband!" she sobbed, slashing her hand across her face to wipe away the tears.

"Okay, okay, honey. Settle down." I handed her a napkin to blow her nose and patted her shoulder as Angus happily licked away her tears. "What's really going on, Margs?"

She took a shaky breath. "He wants us to have a baby."

My mouth dropped open. "Oh," I said.

Margaret never wanted kids. Actually, she said that the memory of Natalie hooked up to a respirator was enough to crush any maternal instincts she might've had. She always seemed to like kids well enough—gamely holding our cousins' babies at family gatherings, talking to older kids in a pleasingly adult way. But she also was the first to say she was too selfish to ever be a mother.

"So is this up for discussion?" I asked. "How do you feel?"

"Pretty fucking awful, Grace," she snapped. "I'm hiding at your house, flirting with your hunky neighbor, not speaking to my husband, and *Mom* is giving me lectures on marriage! Isn't it obvious how I feel?"

"No," I said firmly. "You're also bawling into my dog's fur. So spill, honey. I won't tell anyone."

She shot me a watery, grateful look. "I feel kind of…betrayed," she admitted. "Like he's saying I'm not enough. And you know, he's...he can be really irritating, you know?" Her breath started hitching out of her again. "He's not the most exciting person in the world, is he?"

I murmured that, no, of course he wasn't.

"And so I feel like he just hit me upside the head."

"So what do you think, Margs? Do you think you might want a baby?" I asked.

"No! I don't know! Maybe! Oh, shit. I'm gonna take a shower." She stood up, handed me my doggy, who snagged the last bit of poppy seed roll from my plate and burped. And thus ended the sisterly heart-to-heart.

CHAPTER FIFTEEN

ON WEDNESDAY EVENING, I was getting ready for my date with Lester the metalsmith. He'd called at last, sounded normal enough, but let's be honest. With a name like Lester, being a member of an artisan's cooperative and having his looks summarized as *attractive in his own way*...well. My hopes were flying pretty low.

Nonetheless, I figured it wouldn't be the worst thing in the world for me to get out of the house. I could practice my feminine wiles on him, try a few of the techniques Lou had urged during our Meeting Mr. Right class. Yes, I was that desperate.

Margaret was working—since our chat over the weekend, she'd kept mum on the subject of her husband. Angus watched as I resignedly followed Lou's advice...a skirt short enough to show that, yes, I had fabulous legs. A little lipstick, a little holy water on the hair, and I was ready to go. I kissed Angus repeatedly, asked him not to feel jealous, lonely or depressed, told him he could watch HBO and order pizza, realized that I was far, far down the path to "Weird Dog Lady" and headed out.

Lester and I were meeting at Blackie's, and I figured I'd walk. It was a beautiful night, just a little cool, and in the west, there was the thinnest line of red as the sunset held on a little longer. I looked for a moment at my own house. I'd left the Tiffany lamp on for Angus, and my hanging porch light was on. The buds of the peonies were tight with promise...in another week or so, they'd burst into fragrant, lush blossoms that scented the whole house. The slate walk was edged with lavender, ferns and heather, and hostas huddled in a thick green mass at the base of my mailbox.

It was a perfect house, sweet enough to be featured on the cover of a magazine, cozy, welcoming, unique. Only one thing was missing—the husband. The kids. The whole adorable family I'd always envisioned...the one that was getting harder and harder to imagine.

You might wonder why I didn't sell the house after Andrew broke it off with me. It was, after all, supposed to be *our* house. But I loved it, and it had so much potential. The thought of not hearing the Farmington River shushing gently in the distance, of letting someone else plant bulbs and hang ferns on the front porch...I just couldn't do it. And yes, maybe I was holding on to the last piece I had of Andrew and me. We'd planned to be so happy here....

So rather than becoming our house, it became mine. That house was my grief therapy, and as I polished it and made it a sanctuary of comfort and beauty and surprising little delights, you can bet that I imagined my revenge on Andrew. That I'd meet someone else, someone better, smarter, taller, funnier, richer, nicer...someone who freakin' adored me, thank you so much. And Andrew would see. It was his stupid loss. And he could just be lonely and miserable for the rest of his stupid life.

Obviously, it didn't turn out that way, or I wouldn't be standing here on the sidewalk, a fake boyfriend on one hand, a metalsmith on the other, an ex-con who made my girl parts sit up and bark in the background.

"Get going," I told myself. Margaret might be a bit off

love these days, but she wouldn't fix me up with a bad person. Lester the metalsmith. It was kind of hard to get excited about him. Lester. Les. Nope. Nothing.

Blackie's was packed, and immediately, I regretted arranging the date this way. What was I supposed to do, just start tapping men on the shoulder and asking if they were Lester the metalsmith? *Is there a metalsmith in the building? Please, if you're a metalsmith, report to the bar immediately.*

"What can I get you?" the bartender asked as I pushed my way forward.

"A gin and tonic, please?" I asked.

"Coming up," he said.

Well, here I was, once again trying to convey The Look, the confidence, the appeal, the *I'm just an amused observer of life* look that didn't say *Quite eager to find boyfriend so I won't have to be alone when sister marries ex-fiancé, which seems like it'll be happening soon, damn it. Good dancer a plus*.

"Excuse me, are you Grace?" came a voice at my shoulder. "I'm Lester."

I turned. My eyes widened. Heart rate stopped entirely, then kicked in at about one hundred and eighty beats per minute.

"You are Grace, right?" the man asked.

"Thank you," I murmured. As in "Thank you, *God!*" Then I closed my mouth and smiled. "Hi. I mean, yes. I'm Grace. Hello. I'm fine, thanks."

So I was a babbling idiot. So would you be, if you'd seen this guy. Dear God in heaven, oh, Margaret, thank you, because before me stood a man the likes that every woman on the face of the earth would want to devour with whipped cream and chocolate sauce. Black hair. Black gypsy eyes. Killer dimples. Shirt open to reveal swarthy skin and completely lickable neck. Like Julian, sort of, but more dangerous, less adorable. Swarthier. Taller. Heterosexual. Praise be.

The bartender handed me my drink, and I passed him a twenty in a daze. "Keep the change," I murmured.

"I got us a table," Lester said. "Over there, in the back. Shall we?"

He led the way, which meant I got to look at his ass as we twisted our way through the crowd. Vowing to send Margaret some flowers, do her laundry and bake her brownies, I mentally thanked her for fixing me up with Lester the metalsmith, who was so much more than "attractive in his own way."

"I was really psyched when Margaret called," Lester said, sitting down. He already had a beer, and he took a sip from it now. "She's so cool."

"Oh," I said, still in full idiot mode. "That's…yes. She is. I love my sister."

He grinned, and a little whimper came from the back of my throat.

"So you work at a school?" he said.

I gave myself a mental shake. "Yes, I do," I answered. "I'm a history teacher at Manning Academy."

I managed to complete several sentences on what I did and where, but I couldn't relax. This man was just unbelievably good-looking. His hair was thick and kind of long, waving gracefully around his face. He had incredible hands, strong and dark with long fingers and a healing cut I yearned to kiss better.

"So, Lester, what kind of metalsmithing do you do?" I asked, swallowing.

"Well, actually, I brought you one of my pieces. A little gift to say thanks for meeting me." He reached into a battered leather bag next to him and fumbled for something.

A gift. Oh! I melted like…well, like a hunk of molten metal, of course. He *made* me something.

Lester straightened up and put the object on the table.

It was beautiful. Made from iron, an abstract person rose up from the base, the metal twisting gracefully in a fluid arc, arms raised to heaven, iron hair flowing as if greeting a gust of wind on a summer day. "Oh, my gosh," I breathed. "It's beautiful."

"Thanks," he said. "That's one of a series I'm doing now, and they're selling really well. But yours is special, Grace." He paused, looked at me with those dark, dark eyes. "I think you're great, Grace. I'm hoping that we'll really connect. This is sort of a good faith gift."

"Wow," I said. "Yes." As in Yes, *I* will *marry you and bear us four healthy children.*

He grinned again, and I fumbled for my drink and drained it.

"Excuse me one second," Lester said. "I have to make one quick call, and I'll be right back. I'm so sorry."

"Oh, no, not at all," I managed. I could use the time to get myself under control, since I was practically teetering on the brink of orgasm. Who could blame me? Mr. Beautiful Gypsy Man *liked* me. Wanted a *relationship* with me. Could it really be this easy? Imagine bringing him home to meet the gang! Imagine having him as my date the next time Natalie and Andrew invited me over. Imagine Callahan O'Shea seeing me with Beautiful Gypsy Man! Wouldn't that be the coolest! Good God!

I snatched my cell phone from my bag and punched in my home number.

"Margaret," I muttered urgently when she picked up. "I love him! Thank you! He's amazing! He's not attractive in his own way! He's unbelievably gorgeous!"

"I just turned on *Gods and Generals,*" Margaret said. "Do you really watch this crap?"

"He's amazing, Margs!"

"Okay. Glad to be of service. He seemed pretty hot to meet you. Actually, he asked me out first, but I flashed the wedding ring. I regret that now," she said, sounding mildly surprised.

"Oh, here he comes. Thanks again, Margs. Gotta go." I pushed End and smiled as Lester returned and sat down. My whole body pulsated with desire.

For the next half hour or so, we managed to talk. Actually, I was the one having a hard time of it and so tried instead to show that I was a good listener, despite the fact that I was barely paying attention, thanks to the lust that roiled inside me. Dimly, I heard Lester tell me about his family, how he became a metalsmith, where he showed in New York and San Francisco. He'd been in a long-term relationship (with a woman, which put any lingering fears to bed), but things hadn't worked out. Now he was looking to settle down. He loved to cook and couldn't wait to make me dinner. He wanted children. He was perfect.

Then his cell phone rang. "Oh, shoot, I'm sorry, Grace," he said with an apologetic smile, glancing at the screen of the phone. "I've been waiting for this call."

"No, no, go ahead," I said, sipping my G&T. *Do whatever you want, baby. I'm yours.*

Lester flipped open his phone. "What do you want, bitch?" he demanded, his face contorting with fury.

I choked and sputtered, lurching up straight in my seat. Around us, patrons grew still. Lester ignored us all.

"Well, guess where I am?" he barked, turning slightly away from me. "I'm at a *bar* with a *woman!* So there, you disgusting whore! And I'm going to take her back to our house and I'm going to have *sex* with her!" His voice grew louder and louder, cracking with intensity. "That's right! On the *couch,* in our *bed,* on the kitchen *floor,* on the goddamn *kitchen table!* How do you like that, you cheating, miserable skank?" Then he flipped his phone shut, looked at me and smiled. "So where were we?" he asked pleasantly.

"Uh…" I said, glancing around in frozen horror. "Was that your ex?" I asked.

"She means nothing to me anymore," Lester said. "Hey, feel like going back to my place? I can cook us some dinner."

All my internal organs seemed to retract in horror. Suddenly, I wanted no part of Lester's kitchen, thanks very much. "Gee…um, Lester. Do you think I'd be out of line if I suggested you, uh, weren't really over her yet?" I tried to smile.

Lester's face crumpled. "Oh, crap," he sobbed, "I still love her! I love her and it's killing me!" He lowered his head to the table and banged his forehead repeatedly, sobbing, snuffling, tears spurting out of his eyes.

I caught the eye of our waitress and pointed to my drink. "I'll have another," I called.

An hour and a half later, I finally walked Lester to his car, having heard all about Stefania, the coldhearted Russian woman who'd left him for another woman…how he'd gone to her house and bellowed her name over and over and over until the police were summoned and dragged him away… how he'd called her one hundred and seven times in a single night…how he'd defaced Russia from an antique map in the public library and had to serve a hundred hours of community service. I nodded and murmured, sipping my much-needed alcohol (I was walking home, what was the harm?). *Artists,* I thought as I listened to his tirade. I'd been dumped, too, yet you didn't see me crapping on anyone's lawn. Maybe Kiki would like him….

"So, hey. Good luck, Les," I said, rubbing my hands on my upper arms. The night had grown cooler, and mist hung around the streetlamps.

"I hate love," he declared to the heavens. "Just crush me now, why don't you? Kill me, universe!"

"Chin up," I said. "And...well. Thanks for the drinks."

I watched as he drove out of the parking lot—no way in hell I was getting in the car with him, no matter how benign his offer of a ride had been. Sighing, I looked at my watch. Ten o'clock on a Wednesday night. Another man down.

Drat. I'd forgotten my statue inside, and whether its maker was insane or not, I liked it. In fact, it might well have more value in the near future. *Metalsmith institutionalized. Prices soar.* I made a mental note to strangle Margaret as soon as I got home. She was a lawyer, after all. Maybe next time she fixed me up, she could run a quick background check.

I went back inside, retrieved my little statue, wove my way once again through the sea of bodies crammed into Blackie's and pushed the door to leave. It was stuck. I pushed harder and it opened abruptly, thudding against someone who was trying to come at the same moment.

"Ouch," he said.

I closed my eyes. "Watch where you're going," I muttered by way of greeting.

"I should've known it was you," Callahan O'Shea said. "Hitting the sauce, Grace?"

"I was on a date, thanks very much. And you're in no position to point fingers. An Irishman in a bar. How novel."

"I see we're drunk again. Hope you're not driving." His gaze wandered past me toward the bar. I turned to look. An attractive blond woman gave him a little wiggle of her fingers and smiled.

"I'm not drunk! And I'm not driving, so don't worry.

Enjoy your date. Tell her to order a double." With that, I walked past him into the chilly night.

Callahan O'Shea may have been an arrogant, irritating man, but I had to admit, he was right about my ability to hold my liquor. Granted, I had planned on having some food, but when the waitress did come by, Lester had been at the height of his tirade against love, and ordering buffalo wings seemed insensitive. Well. I wasn't exactly drunk, just a bit buzzed. Add to that the thick scent of lilacs, and it was actually a rather nice sensation.

The mist was heavier now, and I could only imagine what my hair was doing, but I could practically feel it spreading, growing, expanding like a feral creature. I sucked in more lilac-scented air and tripped—the price of closing one's eyes on Peterston's erratic sidewalks—but recovered nicely.

"I can't believe your boyfriend let you walk home alone in this condition, Grace. Such a cad."

I scowled. "You again. What are you doing here?"

"Walking you home. I see we won an Emmy," Callahan said, tilting his head to get a better look at my statue.

"This is a very lovely gift. From Wyatt. Who bought it for me. And you don't have to walk me home."

"Someone should. Seriously, where's that boyfriend of yours?"

"He has surgery in the morning and he had to go. So he left."

"Mmm-hmm," Callahan said. "Why didn't he at least drive you home? Did he have feral cats to round up?"

"I wanted to walk. I insisted. Besides, what about your date? Did you just leave her all alone in the bar like that? *Tsk, tsk.*"

"She's not my date."

"Yet I saw her wave to you in definite recognition and anticipation."

"Yet she's not my date," he said.

"Yet I find that hard to believe," I said. "So who is she, then?"

"My parole officer." Callahan grinned. "Now tell Uncle Cal the truth, Grace. Did we have a little spat with our boyfriend tonight?"

"No, we didn't spat. Spit—whatever. And that is God's honest truth." Perhaps now was a good time to change the subject. "Are you really Irish?"

"What do you think, genius?"

I think you're a jerk. Oops. May have said that aloud.

"Maybe you should stick with a nice Coke the next time you go out, hmm?" he suggested. "How many drinks did you have?"

"I had two gin and tonics—actually, one and a half—and I don't drink very often, so yes, maybe I'm feeling the effects. That's all." We came to a trestle bridge that crossed the railroad tracks.

"So you can't hold your liquor. How much do you weigh, anyhow?"

"Cal, it's a cardinal sin to ask a woman about her weight, so back off, bub."

He laughed, that ashy, deliciously naughty sound. "I love it when you call me 'bub.' And I'll call you 'lush,' how's that?"

I sighed loudly. "Listen, Callahan O'Shea of the leprechauns, thank you for escorting me this far. It's only a few blocks to home. Why don't you head back to your woman?"

"Because this isn't the greatest neighborhood and I don't want you walking home alone."

Aw. It *was* one of the scruffier parts of town...in fact, when a drug deal went down, it usually happened right here under the bridge. I sneaked a look at Cal's face. Aside from his being far too good-looking, I had to admit, he was being really...well, considerate.

"Thank you," I said. "You sure your date doesn't mind?"

"Why would she mind? I'm doing a public service."

Going down the metal steps of the little bridge, I slipped a little. Callahan reached out and grabbed me before any harm was done, and for a second, I just clung to his arms. Warm, solid, reassuring arms. Wouldn't mind staying here all night. He smelled good, too, dang it, like soap and wood.

He reached up and gently pulled something from my hair...a leaf. Looked at it for a second before dropping it. Resumed his hold on me, his hand warm on my upper arm.

"So. Your date," I blurted. "Um. She seems nice. Looks nice, I mean." My heart was flopping around like a dying fish in my chest.

Cal let go of my arms. "She's nice. Not my date, though. As I told you already."

"Oh." Relief flooded my knees, making them tingle painfully. No. I didn't want Callahan O'Shea to be dating anyone. And what did that say? We started walking once more, side by side, the mist cocooning us from the occasional headbeams that passed, muffling the sound of the cars. I swallowed. "So, Cal, are you...um...seeing anyone?"

He shot me a veiled glance. "No, Grace, I'm not."

"Not the marrying type, I guess? Don't want to settle down just yet?"

"I'd love to settle down," he said. "A wife, a couple of kids, a lawn to mow."

"Really?" I asked. Yelped, actually. Callahan struck me as the type who walked into the room while *Bad to the Bone* was playing. Mowing the lawn while the kiddies frolicked? Hmm. Hmm.

"Really." He shoved his hands in his pockets. "Isn't that what you and Dr. Wonderful want?"

"Oh. Uh, sure. I guess. I don't know." This was not a conversation I wanted to have while slightly inebriated. "It would be hard to be with a guy who's married to his work," I finished lamely.

"Right," Cal said.

"So you know, things aren't as wonderful as they seem," I added, surprising myself.

"I see." Cal turned to look at me. He smiled, just a little, and I looked down suddenly. I didn't know anything about this guy. Only that he was undeniably attractive. That he wanted to settle down. That he'd served time for criminal acts.

"Hey, Cal, are you sorry you embezzled that money?" I asked abruptly.

He tilted his head and considered me. "It's complicated."

"Why don't you just spit it out, Irish? What did you do?"

He laughed. "Maybe I'll tell you someday. We're almost home, anyway."

We're almost home. As if we had a place together. As if he might come in, and Angus wouldn't bite him. As if I might make us a snack—or he might—and we'd pop in a movie. Or not. Or we'd just go upstairs, heck. Take off a few articles of clothing. Get a little exercise.

"Here you go," Callahan said, walking up the path with me. The iron porch railing was slick and cold, and Callahan's hand on my back felt even warmer by comparison. Whoa. Wait a sec. His *hand* on my *back*. He was *touching* me, and man, it felt good, like a small sun was resting there, radiating heat into the far regions of my body.

I turned to him, about to say something—what, I had no idea. The sight of his smile, his downturning, lovely eyes, wiped all thought from my mind.

My knees went soft and tingly, and my heart swelled against my ribs in a warm surge. For a second, I could *feel* what it would be like to kiss Callahan O'Shea, and the strength of that image caused a buzz in the pit of my stomach. My lips opened slightly, my eyes fluttered closed. He was like a magnet, pulling me in.

"Good night, my little lush," he said.

My eyes snapped open. "Great! Good night, bub. Thanks for walking me home."

And with one more grin that I felt down to my bone marrow, he turned and left, back to the woman who was not his date, leaving me not at all sure if I was greatly relieved or hugely disappointed.

CHAPTER SIXTEEN

"Hey, Dad," I said one evening after school. Dropping by the family domicile was a habit of mine—sometimes you just can't learn from experience, right? The truth was, taken individually, my parents were great people. My father was methodical and reliable, as dads should be, I thought, and his love of the Civil War gave us a special bond. And my mother was a vibrant, intelligent woman. Growing up, she'd been a devoted mom, the kind who sewed our Halloween costumes and baked cookies from scratch. Granted, my parents had always seemed to do things separately; I had very few memories of them going out just the two of them. They had friends and socialized normally enough, but as far as a deep and abiding love or passion…let's just say that if it was there, they hid it well.

It worried me. What if that was the kind of marriage I ended up with, stifled and irritated with my spouse all day, wishing I'd chosen another life? Look at Margaret. Look at Mémé and her three husbands, none of whom she ever recalled fondly.

Dad was sitting at the kitchen table, his daily six ounces of red wine (for health reasons only) next to him. I let go of Angus's leash so my puppy could go see his second favorite person on earth.

"Hello, Pudding," he said, glancing up from the *Wall*

Street Journal. Then he caught sight of my dog. "Angus! How are you, buddy?" Angus leaped in the air, barking with love. "Who's a good boy, huh? Are you a good dog?"

"He's really not," I admitted. "He bit my neighbor. The carpenter."

"Oh, how are the windows coming along?" Dad asked, picking up Angus to better worship.

"They're done, actually." And I had to admit, I was disappointed. No more Callahan O'Shea in my house. "He did a great job. Thanks again, Daddy."

He smiled. "You're welcome. Hey, I heard you're Jackson at Chancellorsville."

"I get a horse and everything," I said, smiling modestly. Brother Against Brother's members included a stable-owner who would loan out horses here and there, so long as we passed a riding class. Alas, I was only allowed to ride Snowlight, a fat and elderly white pony with a fluffy mane and a narcoleptic tendency to lie down when hearing loud noises, which made my rallying the troops a bit less dramatic than planned. However, as Colonel Jackson, I was to be shot at this battle, so Snowlight's narcolepsy would come in handy.

"You were great at Bull Run, by the way," I said. He nodded in acknowledgment, turning the page of his paper. "Where's Mom?"

"She's in the garage," Dad answered.

"The studio!" Mom's voice could be heard clearly from the *studio*—she hated when we referred to it as garage, feeling that we were demeaning her self-expression.

"She's in the *studio!* Making her porno statues!" Dad bellowed back, slapping the paper down on the table. "God help me, Grace, if I'd known your mother would have a meltdown when you kids left for college—"

"You know, Dad, you could try to be a little more supportive of Mom's—"

"It's not porn!" My mother stood in the doorway, her face flushed from the heat of her glassblowing fire. Angus raced into the garage to bark at her artwork.

"Hi, Mom," I said. "How are the, uh, sculptures coming along?"

"Hello, honey," Mom replied, kissing my cheek. "I'm trying to use a lighter glass. The last uterus I sold weighed nineteen pounds, but these light ones keep breaking. Angus, no! Stay away from that ovary, honey!"

"Angus! Cookie!" I said. My dog raced back into the kitchen, and Mom closed the door behind her, then went to the special doggy cookie jar they kept on hand for my dog (no grandchildren, you understand).

"Here you go, you sweet thing!" Mom cooed. Angus sat, then raised his front paws in the air, nearly causing Mom to faint with joy. "So sweet! Yes, you are! You're a sweet baby! You're my little Angus-Pooh!" Finally, she straightened up to look at her biological child. "So what brings you here, Grace?"

"Oh, I was just wondering if you guys had talked to Margaret lately," I said. Angus, miffed that the attention was no longer upon him, trotted off to destroy something. Since her little tear jag in my kitchen, I'd barely spoken to my sister, who'd been drowning herself even more than usual in work.

Mom gave Dad a sour look. "Jim, our daughter is visiting. Think you could drop your paper and pay attention to her?"

Dad just rolled his eyes and continued reading.

"Jim!"

"Mom, it's okay. Dad's just relaxing. He's listening, right, Dad?"

My father nodded, giving my mother a resigned stare.

"Well, about Margaret and Stuart, who knows?" Mom said. "They'll find their way. Marriage is complicated, honey. You'll find out someday." Mom flicked Dad's paper, earning a glare. "Right, Jim? Complicated."

"With you it is," my father grumbled.

"Speaking of marriage, honey, Natalie wanted to make sure everyone was free for brunch on Sunday, did she tell you?"

"Marriage? What?" My voice cracked.

"What?" Mom asked.

"You said, 'speaking of marriage.' Are they engaged?"

Dad lowered his paper and peered at me over his bifocals. "Would you be all right with that, Pudding?"

"Um, yeah! Of course! Sure! Did she say? She didn't tell me anything."

Mom patted my shoulder. "No, no, she didn't say anything. But, Grace, sweetie…" She paused. "It seems like it might be coming."

"Oh, I know! Sure! I hope it does come to marriage. They're great together."

"And now you have Wyatt, so it doesn't sting as much, right?" Mom said.

For a second, I almost blurted out the truth about Wyatt Dunn, saintly doctor. *I actually just made that guy up so Nat wouldn't feel so guilty, Mom, Dad. And oh, by the way, I may have a thing for the ex-con next door.* But what would they say to that? I could imagine their faces, the consternation, the worry, the fear that I'd chugged around the bend. The certainty that I wasn't over Andrew, that I'd been crushed beyond repair, that a crush on Cal indicated my wobbly emotional state. "Right," I said slowly. "I have Wyatt. And also papers that need grading."

"And I have to finish my *art*," Mom said, once again poking Dad's paper. "So make your own damn dinner."

"Fine! I'd love to! Your cooking has really gone down the drain, you know. Ever since you became an *artist*."

"Grow up, Jim." Mom turned to me. "Honey, wait. We want to meet Wyatt." She reached for the calendar that hung next to the fridge. "Let's make a date right now."

"Oh, Mom, you know how it is. He's so busy. And plus he's working in Boston a few days a week, um, consulting. Up at Children's. Oops, gotta go. See you soon. I'll get back to you on a date."

As I drove around town on my errands, Angus on my lap, helping me steer, it seemed like everyone's story—their how-they-met story—echoed in my head. My own parents had gotten together when Dad was a lifeguard and Mom had been swimming at Lake Waramaug, pretending to drown for her friends. She was sixteen at the time, just goofing around, and had Dad been a less literal person, he probably could've seen that. As it was, he hauled her out of the lake and, learning that her lungs were water-free, chastised her so fiercely that she burst into tears. And just like that, he fell in love.

Margaret and Stuart met during a fire drill at Harvard. It was a frigid January night, and Margs was clad only in her pajamas. Stuart wrapped her in his coat and let her sit on his lap so her feet wouldn't have to touch the snow. He carried her back into the dorm (and right into her bed, as the story went).

I wanted a story. I didn't want to say, "Oh, Daddy and I met on a Web site because we were both so damned desperate we couldn't think of anything else." Or, "I tricked Daddy into loving me by pretending I couldn't pick out my own lightbulb and wearing makeup at all times."

Andrew and I had had a story. A pretty great story. How many people could say they'd met their husbands while lying dead at Gettysburg, after all? It was damn cute. And of course, I reminded myself harshly, gently pushing Angus's head out of the way so I could see, Natalie and Andrew had a great story, too. *I was engaged to her sister, but one look at Natalie, and I knew I had the wrong Emerson girl! Hahaha!*

"Stop it," I told myself, my voice grating. "You'll find someone. You will. He doesn't have to be perfect. Just good enough. And, yes, Natalie and Andrew are probably going to get married. We know this. We are not surprised. We'll take the news very well."

But I couldn't shake the funk that lowered as I did my errands...grocery store, dry cleaner, wine shop for some good and cheap chardonnay. Everywhere I went, I imagined the story. At the package store: *He recommended some wine, we got to talking...I saved the bottle, see, it's over there, on the shelf.* Unfortunately, the man behind the counter at the package store was sixty years old, wedding ring in place, as well as a couple of hundred extra pounds. At the market: *We ran into each other at the Ben & Jerry's case, argued over which was better, Vanilla Heath Bar or Coffee Heath Bar, and we still can't agree.* But, no, the only person in front of Ben & Jerry's was a girl of about twelve, stocking up on Cinnamon Bun from the look of things. At the cleaners: *He was picking up a suit, I needed my Confederate officer's uniform...* Alas, the only one in the cleaner's was the sweet and tiny woman who owned the place. "Watch you don't get shot!" she said, handing me my dress grays.

"Getting shot is the whole point," I said. My smile felt forced.

When I got home, I stashed my groceries, took a box of tampons away from Angus and gave him a chew stick instead, poured a healthy glass of wine and went up to the attic with my uniform. Did I usually stow my uniform in the attic? Well, no, not until winter, usually, but it seemed like a good idea tonight. And I left the light off, because I knew the way by heart.

He was there. Callahan O'Shea was back on the roof, hands clasped behind his head, looking up at the sky.

We met when I clocked him with my field hockey stick. I thought he was robbing the house next door. Turned out he wasn't, simply a guy on his first night out of prison. What for, you ask? Oh, he stole over a million dollars.

Sighing, I tore myself away from the view and went back downstairs. Pictured Wyatt Dunn coming home, hugging me, resting his cheek against my hair. Angus wouldn't bite him or even bark. We'd sit down in my seldom-used dining room, and I'd pour him a glass of wine, and he'd ask to hear about my students, and I'd cheer him up by telling him about how I divided the class into Confederates and Union citizens and made them debate why their side was right, how the entire Southern side spoke in drawls and got the giggles when Emma Kirk said, "Fiddle-dee-dee."

So intense was my little daydream that when a knock came on the door, I almost expected it to be Wyatt, that I somehow conjured him. Angus went into his yapping frenzy, so I picked him up and peeked. It was Callahan O'Shea, down from the roof. My face went lava-hot.

"Hi," I said, clutching my dog, who growled fiercely.

"Hi," Callahan said, leaning in the doorway.

"Everything okay?" It was dark, after all.

"Yup." He just looked at me from those denim-blue eyes, and I noticed for the first time that his irises were flecked with gold. His shirt was a soft green, and the smell of freshly cut wood drifted toward me.

"What can I do for you?" I asked, my voice husky.

"Grace."

"Yes?" I breathed.

"I want you to stop spying on me," he said.

Dang it! I sucked in a guilty breath. "Spying? I'm not... I...I don't..."

"From the attic. Do you have a problem with me being up on my roof?"

"No! I just was..." *Hrrrr. Hrrrr. Yarp!* Angus was struggling to get out of my arms, giving me a great excuse to stall. "Hang on a second. Or just come in. I have to put Angus in the cellar."

I stashed Angus, took a few deep breaths, then turned to face my neighbor, who stood just inside the doorway, a sarcastic eyebrow raised. If eyebrows could be sarcastic, that is.

"Cal, I was just putting some things away up there. I saw you and yes, I wondered what you were doing out there, okay? I'm sorry."

"Grace, we both know that you've been spying. Just knock it off."

"Well, someone has quite an ego, doesn't he?" I said. "I was putting away my general's uniform. Go upstairs and check if you want." Angus barked from the cellar, backing me up.

Callahan took a step closer and looked down at me—literally and figuratively, I imagined. His eyes wandered to my hair, then...oh, God...to my mouth. "Here's what I want to know," he said. "Why does that boyfriend of yours leave you alone so damn much?" His voice was soft.

My whole body responded with a giant, hot, pulsating throb. "Oh...well..." My voice was breathy. "I'm not sure that's gonna work out. We're, um...reevaluating."

Tell him you're free, Grace. Just say you and Wyatt broke up.

I didn't. Honestly, it was just too scary. My entire body was quivering with Callahan's nearness, and fear. Fear that he was playing me, all too aware that I was a heartbeat away from wrestling him to the floor and ripping off his clothes.

That stirring image was almost immediately replaced with another, much less desirable picture—Cal pushing me back and saying, quite firmly, *No thanks,* that sardonic expression on his too-appealing face.

"So." My voice was brisk and teacherly. "Anything else, Mr. O'Shea?"

"No." But he looked at me, really looked, and it was awfully hard to maintain eye contact, let me tell you. Surely I was blushing, since my face was burning hot.

"No more spying," he finally said, his voice gentle. "Got it?"

"Yes," I whispered. "Sorry."

And then he turned and left, leaving me standing in the middle of my living room, shaky and feeling like my stays were a little too tight.

Okay, okay, I admitted that I was desperately attracted to Callahan O'Shea. And that was not a good thing. First of all, I wasn't sure he liked me very much. Secondly...well. It wasn't just the ex-con thing. Sure, if he'd beaten someone with a pipe or something, obviously he'd be out of the running. Embezzlement, yes, it was also a crime. But not that bad, right? If he was sorry...plus, he'd served his debt to society and all that crap....

No. It wasn't his past, though obviously, I put a lot of weight on the past. It was the fact that my whole life, I knew what I wanted. Andrew had been The One, and look how that turned out. What I wanted now, God help me, was another Andrew, just without the whole sister-loving complication.

Callahan O'Shea was ridiculously appealing, but I'd never

relax around him. He was not the type to look at me adoringly. He...he...ah, crap, he was just too *much*. Too big, too good-looking, too appealing, too *stirring*. I felt too many things around him. It was disturbing, really. He made me irritable and lustful and sharp when I wanted to be sweet and loving and soft. I wanted to be...well, like Natalie. And I wanted a man who looked at me the way Andrew looked at Natalie. Not like Callahan, who looked like he knew my every dirty little secret.

CHAPTER SEVENTEEN

I WAS WORKING LATE AT MANNING one evening, putting together my presentation for the board of trustees, when Stuart paid me a visit.

"Hey, Stuart!" I exclaimed, getting up to kiss his cheek.

"How are you, Grace?" he asked politely.

"I'm okay," I said. "Have a seat. Want some coffee or anything?"

"No, thank you. Just a few minutes of your time."

Stuart looked awful. His eyes were shadowed and tired, and there seemed to be gray in his beard that wasn't there a few weeks ago. Although we worked at the same school, Stuart's office was in Caybridge Hall, a newer building on the southern side of the campus, far from Lehring, where the history department nestled appropriately in the oldest building at Manning. I rarely encountered Stuart at work.

I sat back behind my desk and took a deep breath. "You want to talk about Margaret?" I asked softly.

He looked down. "Grace..." He shook his head. "Has she told you why we're...apart?"

"Um..." I paused, not sure how much I should reveal. "She's said a few things."

"I brought up the idea of us having a baby," Stuart said quietly. "And she basically exploded. Suddenly, it seems, we're having all sorts of troubles that I was completely unaware of. I'm quite boring, apparently. I don't talk about work enough. She feels like she's living with a stranger. Or a brother. Or a ninety-year-old man. We don't have enough fun, we don't just grab a toothbrush and rush off to the Bahamas—and here she works seventy hours a week, Grace! If I suggested we fly off somewhere, she'd kill me!"

He certainly had a point. Margaret was mercurial, putting it kindly.

He sighed wearily. "All I wanted was to talk—just talk—about the idea of having a baby. We decided we wouldn't have kids when we were twenty-five, Grace. That was a long time ago. I figured we could revisit the idea. And now she said she's filing for divorce."

"A divorce?" I squeaked. "Oh, crap. I didn't know that, Stuart." I was quiet for a minute, then said, "But you know Margaret, buddy. She's all thunder and lightning. I doubt she really wants…" My voice trailed off. I had no idea what Margaret really wanted. On the one hand, I couldn't imagine her divorcing Stuart just like that. On the other, she'd always been impulsive. And completely unable to admit when she was wrong.

"What should I do?" he asked, and his voice broke just a little.

"Oh, Stuart." I got out of my seat and went to him, patted his shoulder awkwardly. "Listen," I murmured, "one thing she said to me was that…" *you only have sex on scheduled days*… I grimaced. "Um, maybe things were a little… routine? With you guys? So maybe a little surprise now and again—" *on the kitchen table* "—wouldn't be a bad thing. Just sort of to show that you really…noticed her."

"I do notice her," he protested, wiping his eyes with one hand the way men do. "I love her, Grace. I've always loved her. I don't understand why that's not enough."

Mercifully, my sister wasn't home when I got there. As Stuart pointed out, she worked a very long day. Bemused, I threw together some dinner, then went upstairs to change for Dancin' with the Oldies.

Callahan was busy these days at his own house, and I hadn't seen him since he busted me for spying. I looked out the window at the new shingles on the roof, the curving and lovely little deck in the back. For the past two days, he'd been doing something inside, so I hadn't been able to ogle him. Pity.

"Come on, Angus, buddy. Let's go," I said. I got my things and left the house, Angus trotting and leaping with delight at my side. He knew what Mommy's swirly-twirly skirt meant. I got in the car, put it in Reverse and backed out onto the street as I had done a thousand times before.

Unlike those thousand other times, however, I heard a horrifying metallic crunch.

Callahan's pickup truck was parked on the street, very close to my driveway. Well, okay, maybe not that close, but having gotten used to a clear runway ever since I'd lived here, I guess I took the turn kind of…yes. Okay. It was my fault.

I got out of the car to inspect the damage. Crap. I guessed that Callahan would be less than amused when I told him I'd just crushed his rear left taillight. Lucky for me, my own car was made of sturdy German stock, and there was only a little scrape where I'd hit the truck.

Glancing at my watch, I sighed, then dutifully trotted down the path to fess up.

I knocked briskly. No answer. "Callahan?" I called. "I just hit your truck!" Nothing. Fine, he was out. I didn't have a pen, either, dang it, and if I went inside, I'd be late for dancing. I was cutting it close as it was.

He'd have to wait. I ran back down the path, shooed

Angus out of the driver's seat and headed off for Golden Meadows.

As I drove, Angus sitting on my lap, his adorable front paws resting on the steering wheel, I found myself wishing I was the single-mother type. I could just pop into a sperm bank and bingo. No man necessary. Life would be so much simpler.

I drove past the lake. The sun was setting, and a pair of Canada geese cruised in for a landing, their graceful black necks outstretched. The minute they touched water, each swam to the other, checking that the other was safe. Beautiful. That was the kind of tenderness I wanted. Super. I was now envying geese.

Pulling into the visitors' lot at Golden Meadows, I bucked up a bit. This place was good for the spirit. "Hi, Shirley," I said to the receptionist as I went in.

"Hello, Grace." She smiled. "And who have we here? Why, it's Angus! Hello, honey! Hello! Do you want a cookie?" I watched in amusement as Shirley convulsed in delight at the sight of my dog, who was extremely popular here. Angus, knowing he had a captive audience, raised his right paw and tilted his little head as Shirley swooned with joy.

"You sure you don't mind watching him?" I asked as Angus delicately (we were in public, after all) ate the proffered cookie.

"Mind? Of course not! I love him! Yes, I do! I love you, Angus!"

Smiling, I walked down the hall. "Hey, everyone!" I called as I went into the activity room where we held Dancin' with the Oldies each week.

"Hello, Grace!" they chorused. I hugged and kissed and patted, and my heart was eased a good bit.

Julian was there, too, and the sight of my old buddy made me just about burst into tears. "I miss you, ugly," I said to him. Dancin' with the Oldies hadn't met last week, due to a conflict with a free blood pressure screening.

"I miss you, too," he said, pulling a face. "This dating thing isn't working for me, Grace. I say forget it."

"What happened?" I asked.

"A whole lot of nothing," he answered. "It's just...I'm not meant to be with anyone, I think. Romantically, anyway. It's not the worst thing to be alone, is it?"

"No," I lied. "Not at all! Come over for *Project Runway* tomorrow, okay?"

"Thank you. I've been so lonely." He gave me a sad smile.

"Me, too, buddy." I squeezed his hand in relief.

"Okay, good people!" Julian called, patting my head and pushing Play. "Tony Bennett wants you to *Sing, You Sinners!* Gracie, let's jitterbug!"

Three dances later, flushed and panting, I took a seat next to my grandmother. "Hello, Mémé," I said, giving her withered cheek a kiss.

"You look like a tramp," she hissed.

"Thank you, Mémé! You also look so pretty today!" I said loudly.

My grandmother was odd...her utmost pleasure in life was to put other people down, but I knew she was also proud of the fact that I came here, that everyone loved me. She might not have a kind word to say, but she liked having me around nonetheless. Somewhere in her sour old soul, I believed, was Nice Mémé, a woman who just had to have a little affection for her three granddaughters. So far, though, Mean Mémé had gagged and bound Nice Mémé, but you never knew.

"So what's new, Mémé?" I asked, sitting next to her.

"What do you care?" she answered.

"I care. A little. I'd care more if you were nice to me once in a while."

"What's the point? You're just after my money," she said, waving her liver-spotted hand dismissively.

"I thought two hundred years of hard living would've used up your money by now," I answered.

"Well, I have plenty. I buried three husbands, missy, and what's the point of marriage if you're not making money?"

"That's so romantic, Mémé. Really. I have tears in my eyes."

"Oh, grow up, Grace. A woman your age doesn't have time to waste. And you should show me more respect. I might cut you out of my will."

"Tell you what, Mémé," I said, patting her bony little shoulder, "you take my portion and you spend it. Go on a cruise. Buy yourself some diamonds. Hire a gigolo."

She harrumphed, but didn't look my way. Instead, she was watching the dancers. I might've been wrong, but it seemed that her pinkie was keeping time to "Papa Loves Mambo." My heart swelled with unwilling sympathy. "Want to dance, Mémé?" I asked softly. She could, after all, walk pretty well. The wheelchair was more for effect—she was better able to ram people if her center of gravity was lower.

"Dance?" she snorted. "With whom, dimwit?"

"Well, I'd—"

"Where's that man you're always talking about? Scared him off, did you? I'm not surprised. Or did he fall in love with your sister?"

I flinched. "Jesus, Mémé," I said, my throat thickening with tears.

"Oh, get over it. It was a joke." She glanced at me with disdain.

Still stunned, I moved away, accepting a rather stiff waltz from Mr. Demming. Mémé was my only living grandparent. I never met my biological grandfather—he was the first of the husbands that Mémé buried, but I loved him in theory, since my father had an arsenal of wonderful stories about him. Mémé's other two husbands had been lovely men; Grandpa Jake, who died when I was twelve, and Poppa Frank, who died when I was in graduate school. My mom's parents had died within months of each other when I was in high school. They, too, were quintessentially wonderful people. But because the fates were cruel, the only surviving grandparent I had was as mean as camel spit.

When Dancin' with the Oldies was done, Julian kissed my cheek and said farewell. Mémé watched and waited, vulture-like, so I could follow her, slavelike, to her apartment. I knew from experience that if I told her she'd hurt my feelings, she'd just make it worse, tell me I had no sense of humor and then call my dad to complain about me. Resigned, I took the handles of her wheelchair and pushed her gently down the hall.

"Edith," Mémé said loudly, stopping a fearful looking woman in her tracks. "This is my granddaughter, Grace. She's visiting me. Grace, Edith is new here." A Grinchy smile spread over her face. "Did *you* get any visitors this week, Edith?"

"Well, actually, my son and his—"

"Grace comes every week, don't you, Grace?"

"I do. I help with the ballroom dancing class," I said. "You'd be more than welcome to come."

"Oh, I love dancing!" Edith cried. "Really? I can just stop in?"

"Seven-thirty to nine," I answered with a smile. "I'll look for you next week."

Mémé, irritated that she wasn't having better luck making

Edith feel inferior, began her hacking cough-on-demand to get the attention back to herself.

"So nice to meet you," I said to Edith, taking my cue to continue pushing the wheelchair. We continued through the foyer.

"Stop," Mémé commanded. I obeyed. "You there! What do you want?"

A man was coming down one of the hallways that led off the main foyer. It was Callahan O'Shea.

"If you're thinking this would be a good place to rob, let me set you straight, young man. We have security cameras, you know! Alarms! The police will be here in seconds."

"You two must be related," Callahan said drily.

I smiled. "My grandmother. Eleanor Winfield, meet my neighbor Callahan O'Shea."

"Oh, the Irish." She sneered. "Don't loan him any money, Grace. He'll drink it away. And for God's sake, don't let him in your house. They steal."

"I've heard that," I answered, grinning. Cal smiled back and there it was, that soft, hot feeling in my stomach.

"We had an Irish maid when I was a child," Mémé continued, looking sourly at Callahan. "Eileen, her name was. Or Irene. Possibly Colleen. Do you know her?"

"My mother," he said instantly. I choked on a laugh.

"She stole seven spoons from us before my father caught on. Seven."

"We loved those spoons," he said. "God, the fun we had with your spoons. Eating, hitting each other on the head, throwing them at the pigs in the kitchen. Happy times."

"It's not funny, young man," Mémé sniffed.

I thought it was funny. In fact, I was wiping my eyes, I was laughing so hard. "Visiting your grandfather, Callahan?" I managed to ask.

"That's right," he answered.

"How's he doing? Think he wants me to come back and finish with the duke and Clarissia?"

Cal grinned. "I'm sure he does."

I smiled back. "For a second, I thought you were here about your truck."

His smile dropped. "What about my truck?"

I felt my face warming. "It's hardly noticeable."

"What, Grace?" His voice was hard.

"Just a little dent," I answered, cringing a little. "Maybe a broken taillight." He scowled. "Actually, it's definitely...hey. I have insurance."

"You need insurance," he muttered.

"Grace! Take me back to my apartment," Mémé ordered.

"Easy, Pharaoh," I said. "I'm talking to my neighbor."

"So talk to him in the morning." She glared up at Callahan. He glared back, and I found myself grinning again. I liked a man who wasn't scared of Mémé, and there weren't many around.

"How'd you get here, Cal? I'm assuming you didn't drive."

"I rode my bike," he answered.

"Would you like a ride? It's dark out," I said.

He looked at me for a second. Then the corner of his mouth pulled up in a smile, and my lady parts buzzed once more. "Sure. Thank you, Grace."

"You shouldn't give him a ride, Grace!" Mémé snapped. "He's likely to strangle you and dump your body in the lake."

"Is this true?" I asked Callahan.

"I was thinking about it," he admitted.

"Well. Your guilty secret is out."

He smiled. "Allow me." He took the handles of Mémé's chair and started off. "Which way, ladies?"

"Is that Irishman pushing me?" Mémé demanded, craning her neck around to see.

"Oh, come on now, Mémé," I said, patting her shoulder. "He's a big, brawny, good-looking guy. You just sit back and enjoy the ride."

"You sound like a tramp," she muttered. But she did, bidding us a sharp good-night at her apartment door. She stared pointedly at Callahan until he took the hint and walked a few paces down the hall so as not to see the heaps of gold lying about in her dragon lair and thus be tempted to rob her blind.

"Good night, Mémé," I said dutifully.

"Don't trust that man," she whispered. "I don't like the way he looks at you."

I glanced down the hall, tempted to ask just how he looked at me. "Okay, Mémé."

"What a sweet old lady," Callahan said as I rejoined him.

"She's pretty horrible," I admitted.

"Do you visit her a lot?" he asked.

"Oh, yes, I'm afraid."

"Why?"

"Duty," I answered.

"You do a lot for your family, don't you?" he asked. "Do they do anything for you?"

My head jerked back. "Yes. They're great. We're all really close." For some reason, his comment stung. "You don't know my family. You shouldn't have said that."

"Mmm," he said, cocking his eyebrow. "Saint Grace the Martyr."

"I'm not a martyr!" I exclaimed.

"Your sister moved in with you and bosses you around, your grandmother treats you like dirt, but you don't stick up for yourself, you lie to your mother about liking her sculptures...yes, that sounds pretty martyrish to me."

"You have no idea what you're talking about," I snapped. "To the best of my knowledge, you have two relatives, one of whom isn't speaking to you and one who can't. So what do you know about family?"

"Well, looky here. She has teeth after all." He sounded perversely pleased.

"You know, you are certainly not obliged to take me up on my offer of a ride, Callahan O'Shea. Feel free to ride your bike and get hit by a car for all I care."

"And with you on the road, there's a good chance of that happening, isn't there?"

"I repeat. Shut up or go home alone."

"All right, all right. Settle down," he said. I walked faster, irritated, my dancing shoes tapping loudly on the tile floor.

We walked back to the front desk to fetch my wee beastie from Shirley. "Was he a good boy?" I asked her.

"Oh, he was an angel!" she cooed. "Weren't you?"

"What sedative did you use?" Callahan asked.

"You're the only one he doesn't like," I lied as Angus bared his crooked little teeth at Callahan O'Shea and growled his kitten-purr growl. "He's an excellent judge of character."

It was raining outside, a sweet-smelling rain that would have my peonies (and hair) three inches taller by morning. I waited, still miffed, as Cal unchained his bike from a lamppost and wheeled it to my car. I popped open the trunk and waited, but Cal just stood there, getting rained on, looking at me.

"Well?" I asked. "Put it in."

"You don't have to give me a ride if you don't want to, Grace. I made you mad. I can ride my bike home."

"I'm not mad. Don't be dumb. Put your bike in the car. Angus and I are getting wet."

"Yes, ma'am."

I watched as he picked it up and maneuvered it in. It wouldn't fit all the way, so I made a mental note to drive slowly so as not to damage two forms of Callahan's transportation in one night, then got in the car with my dog. A quick look in the rearview mirror assured me that, yes, my hair was in fact possessed by evil spirits. I sighed.

"You're cute when you're mad," Callahan said as he got in.

"I'm not mad," I answered.

"It's all right with me if you are," he answered, buckling his seat belt.

"I'm not!" I practically shouted.

"Have it your way," he said. His arm brushed mine, and a hot jolt of electricity shot through my entire body. I stared straight ahead, waiting for it to fade.

Cal glanced at me. "Does that dog always sit on your lap when you're driving?"

"How's he going to learn if he doesn't practice?" Callahan smiled, and I felt my anger (yes, yes, so I was still a little bit mad) fade away. The lust remained. I backed (carefully) out of my parking space. Callahan O'Shea smelled good. Warm, somehow. Warm and rainy, the ever-present smell of wood mingling in an incredible combination. I wondered if he'd mind if I buried my face in his neck for a while. Probably shouldn't do that while I was driving.

"So how's your grandfather doing these days?" I asked.

"He's the same," Cal answered, looking out his window.

"Does he recognize you, do you think?" I asked, belatedly realizing that that was none of my business.

Callahan didn't answer for a second. "I don't think so."

A hundred questions burned to be asked. *Does he know you were in prison? What did you do before prison? Why doesn't your brother speak to you? Why'd you do it, Cal?*

"So, Cal," I began, taking a left on Elm Street, Angus helping me steer, "how's your house coming along?"

"It's pretty nice," he said. "You should come over and take a look."

I glanced at him. "Sure." I hesitated, then decided to go for it. "Callahan, I was wondering. What did you do in your pre-prison life?"

He looked at me. "I was an accountant," he said.

"Really?" I'd have guessed something outdoor-related—cowboy, for example. Not a desk job. "Don't want to do that again, then? Kind of boring, is it?"

"I lost my license when I broke the law, Grace."

Oh, crap, right. "So why *did* you break the law?" I asked.

Cal merely looked at me. "Why do you want to know so badly?"

"Because!" I answered. "It's not every day you live next door to a convicted felon."

"Maybe I don't want to be thought of as a convicted felon, Grace. Maybe I want to be thought of as the person I am now. Make up for lost time and leave the past behind and all that crap."

"Ah, how sweet. Well, I am a history teacher, Mr. O'Shea. The past matters very much to me."

"I'm sure it does." His voice was cool.

"The best indicator of the future is past behavior," I intoned.

"Who said that? Abe Lincoln?"

"Dr. Phil, actually." I smiled. He didn't smile back.

"So what are you saying, Grace? You expect me to embezzle from you?"

"No! Just…well, you obviously felt the need to break the law, so what does that say? It says something, but since you won't open your mouth and speak, I don't know what it is."

"What does your past say about you?" he asked.

My past was Andrew. What did it say? That I wasn't a good judge of character? That when compared with Natalie, I didn't measure up? That I wasn't quite good enough? That Andrew was a jerk?

"There's the lake," I commented. "If you're planning on dumping my body there, you'd better get to it."

His mouth pulled up in one corner, but he didn't answer.

We pulled onto our street. "About your truck," I said. "I'm really sorry. I'll call my insurance agent tomorrow."

"I take it you have him on speed dial," Callahan said.

"Very funny."

He laughed, an ashy, low laugh that hit me right in the pit of my stomach. "Thanks for the ride, Grace," he said.

"If you ever want to confess your sins, I'm available."

"Now you've gone from a martyr to a priest. Good night, Grace."

CHAPTER EIGHTEEN

"IT'S...UH, BEAUTIFUL," I said, blinking down at the ring. Oh, heck, it was. The diamond was about a carat, maybe a little more, a nice chunky thing, pear-shaped, pretty setting. I loved it. I *owned* it, in fact. Well, no, that's not quite true. I *owned* its twin, which sat in my jewelry box at home, waiting for me to pawn it. For heaven's sake. Couldn't Andrew be a little more original? I mean, come on! He'd picked sisters to become his fiancées...at least he could've picked out different rings, for crying out loud.

"Thanks," Nat said, blissfully unaware that we now had matching engagement rings from the same man. We were sitting in the backyard of our parents' house, just Nat and me. The rest of the gang was inside—Andrew, Mémé, Margaret, Mom and Dad.

"You're sure this is okay with you?" Natalie asked, slipping her hand into mine.

"The only thing that's not okay is you constantly asking if I'm okay," I said a bit sharply. "Really, Natalie. Please stop." Then, guilty at my irritation, I squeezed her hand. "I'm glad you're happy."

"You've been just amazing, Grace. Getting Andrew and me together...that was above and beyond the call."

You're telling me. I gave a snort, then glanced at my little sister. The sun was shining on her hair, her dark gold eyelashes brushing her cheeks as she gazed at her ring.

"So have you set a date?" I asked.

"Well, I wanted to ask your opinion on that," she said, looking at me. "Andrew and I kind of felt it should be soon. Get it out of the way, you know? Then we could just be married. Nothing huge. Just the family and a few friends and some dinner afterward. What do you think?"

"Sounds pretty," I said.

"Grace," she began hesitantly, "I was wondering if you'd be my maid of honor. I know the circumstances are pretty weird, but I had to ask you. And if you don't want to, of course I understand. But ever since I was little, I always imagined it would be you. Margaret as a bridesmaid, of course, but you as my number one, you know?"

It was impossible to say no. "Sure," I murmured. "I'd be honored." My heart was beating in slow, rolling thumps, making me feel a little ill.

"Thank you," Nat whispered, hugging me. For a minute, it was like we were little again, her face warm and smooth against my neck, me petting her silky blond hair, breathing in the sweet smell of her shampoo.

"I can't believe you're getting married," I whispered, a couple tears slipping out of my eyes. "I still want to give you piggyback rides and braid your hair."

"I love you, Grace," she murmured.

"I love you, too, Nattie Bumppo," I said around the rock in my throat. My little sister, whom I had helped bathe and diaper, whom I'd read to and cuddled, was leaving me in one of the most profound ways a sister could. For twenty-five years, I had been Natalie's favorite person, and she'd been mine, and now that was changing. When I was with Andrew, let's face it, he hadn't deposed Natalie from the throne in my heart. Sure, I loved him…but Natalie was *part* of me. Part of my soul and heart, the way only sisters could be.

Dozens of memories flashed through my head. Me at age ten, when I'd had my tonsillectomy, waking up from a restless, narcotic-induced sleep to find that Natalie had drawn eighteen pictures of horses for me, laying them on my bedroom floor, propping them on my chair and desk so everywhere I looked, I'd see horses. The time I beat up Kevin Nichols when he put gum in her hair. Me leaving for William & Mary, and Natalie's face contorting with the effort of smiling so I wouldn't see that she was, in fact, sobbing.

I loved her, and had always loved her, so much that it hurt. I could not—would not—let Andrew come between us.

She squeezed me hard, then sat up. "I can't believe I still haven't met Wyatt," she said.

"I know," I seconded. "He's dying to meet you, too." Wyatt was, alas, at a medical convention in San Francisco. I'd briefly flirted with the idea of telling my family Wyatt and I had broken up, then I decided I needed him a little longer. This morning, I'd Googled *medical conventions* and *surgeons* and found one in the City by the Bay. Extremely convenient.

"Things are good with you two?" Nat asked.

"Oh, I guess. He works too much. If there's one fly in the ointment, it's that." My evil plan was to plant these seeds so I could ease everyone into the idea of a breakup. "He's always at the hospital, and now he's up in Boston… He's so devoted to his work. I guess it's the classic complaint of the doctor's wife."

Oops. Hadn't actually meant to say that last sentence. Natalie's face glowed even more beautifully, if possible.

"Do you think you guys might get married?"

Oh, crap. "Um, well…I don't know. The work thing is something we have to figure out. And of course, I've been burned before."

And again. Didn't mean to say that last bit. Natalie flinched.

"I mean, I've picked the wrong guy before, so I want to be careful and all. Make sure he's the right one."

"But you think he is?"

I tipped my head, pretending to consider the question. After all, Wyatt and I were going to have to break up. Rather soon, in fact, since obviously I couldn't keep this up forever. "He's…" I smiled at Natalie in what I imagined was modest adoration. "He's pretty wonderful, Nat. I just wish we had more time together."

The back door banged open, and Margaret appeared before us. "Grace, your dog just broke a vulva. And Mom wants you to come in and eat, anyway." She fisted her hands on her hips. "And did it ever occur to you two that I might be jealous of your little club? Christ Almighty and His five sacred wounds, girls! Can't I be included once in a while?"

"She swears like some ex-nun turned sailor," Natalie murmured.

"Yeah. You have to wonder how she spends her free time," I seconded.

"Quit your whining," Nat called to our big sis. "You two are living together, so don't talk to me about clubs, okay?"

Margaret tromped over to us. "Move over, favorite," she grumbled, shoving my shoulder so she could sit down. "Is everything okay out here? I've been spying through the windows."

"Everything's great. I'm Nattie's maid of honor," I said. It felt okay. Yes. It would be fine.

"God's sandals, Natalie! You want Andrew's former fiancée to be your fucking maid of honor?"

"Yes," Nat answered calmly. "But only if she wants to be."

"And I do," I said, sticking my tongue out at Margaret.

"So? What am I, Nat? Can I maybe sweep up for you? Maybe I could do dishes at the reception and peek out at you once in a while, if you don't think I'll be blinded with your golden beauty, your majesty."

"God, listen to her," Nat giggled. "Would you be my bridesmaid, Margaret dear?"

"Oh, gosh, thanks, yes. I can't wait." Margaret shot me a look. "Maid of honor, huh? Freaky."

"Margs, you've met Wyatt, right?" Natalie asked.

Margaret stuck her tongue in her cheek. "Sure," she answered. I closed my eyes.

"What do you think?" Nat sat up straighter, grinning. She always did love girl talk.

"Well, aside from that sixth toe on his left foot, he's pretty cute," Margs said.

"Very funny," I answered. "It's barely a nub, Natalie."

Natalie was laughing. "What else, Margs?"

"Well, the way he sucks on Grace's ear is pretty disgusting. Especially in church. Yick."

"Come on, I'm serious," Natalie wheezed, wiping her eyes.

"That wandering eye freaks me out."

When our mother came out to find what was keeping her girls, she found us helpless with laughter on the bench under the maple tree.

My good humor remained as Angus and I walked home along the Farmington. A path meandered through the state forest that bordered the river, and though the gnats were out, they were harmless enough if I ignored them. Angus trotted ahead on his long leash, stopping frequently to pee, sniff and pee some more, making sure that all the other dogs who came down this path would know that Angus McFangus had been there before them.

Natalie and Andrew had set a date after poring over Mom's calendar. June fourth, the day after Manning's graduation. Four weeks from now. Four weeks to break up with my imaginary boyfriend, four weeks to possibly find a date for yet another wedding. I imagined being stag at this one. Bleecch. Yet the thought of turning myself inside out to find someone was equally distasteful.

Angus barked and trembled. Up ahead, someone was fly-fishing in the river, hip boots on, the long line of his pole arcing out in a golden, serpentine flash. The sun shone on his messy hair, and I smiled, somehow not surprised to see my neighbor.

"Catching anything, or are you just trying to look pretty?" I called.

"Howdy, neighbor," he called back. "Haven't caught a thing."

"You poor slob." I picked my way over the rocks to get closer. "Don't blind me with your hook, okay?"

"Why? Seems like I owe you a few cuts and bruises," he said, sloshing over toward me. Angus began yarping. "Quiet, you," Cal said sternly, which set Angus off into hysterics. *Yarpyarpyarpyarp! Yarpyarpyarpyarp!*

"You have such a way with animals," I said. "Do small children burst into tears at the sight of you?"

He laughed. "What are you doing out here, Grace?"

"Oh, just headed for home," I answered.

"Want to sit for a while? I have cookies," he said temptingly.

"Are they homemade?" I asked.

"If by *homemade,* you mean *bought at the bakery,* then yes," he answered. "They're good. Not compared to your brownies, though. Those things were out of this world. Worth all the pain I had to go through to get them."

"Aw. Well, that was such a nice compliment, maybe I'll bake you some more." I sat on a rock that jutted over the river, holding Angus on my lap, where he growled at the man in front of us.

"Why don't you let Angus off the leash?" Cal suggested.

"Oh, no," I said. "He'd go right for the water and get swept away." I hugged my little pal a little closer. "We don't want you to drown, do we, sweet coconut baby? Hmm? No. We don't."

"Some of us do," Callahan said. The cookies were from Lala's—sad, really, that I could recognize baked goods from twenty yards—crumbly and delicious peanut butter cookies with crystals of sugar sparkling in the crisscross marks.

Cal offered a cookie to Angus who snapped it up, catching part of Cal's finger. Cal jerked his hand back, sighed, looked at the wounded extremity and held out his finger for my inspection. Two tiny drops of blood showed.

"You poor thing," I said. "Shall I call 911?"

"Why don't you call a lawyer?" he said, raising an eyebrow. "Possibly Margaret. Your dog is becoming a menace. Between the two of you, I can't believe I'm still alive."

"Tragic, really. Well, you'll be moving soon, right?"

"Yup. I'm sure you'll miss me."

Dang it. I would miss him. The sun shone on his hair, illuminating all the shades of brown and caramel and gold. It wasn't fair that this guy could look like an ad for *Outdoor Living,* oozing sex appeal in wader boots and a flannel shirt. The sleeves were rolled up to reveal his tanned forearms. His lashes were golden and straight and really just pointlessly attractive, and my girl parts were begging me to do something.

I cleared my throat. "So, Cal, how's your love life? I happened to see you again with that blonde from the bar."

"Spying again, Grace? I thought we had an understanding."

I sighed in exasperation. "She was right on the front porch. I was weeding." I paused. "You kissed her."

"On the cheek," he said.

"Mmm-hmm. Which some women find very romantic." He said nothing. "So? What about the lawn you want to mow?"

"That's kind of a crude way to refer to sex, isn't it, Grace?"

I blinked, then laughed. "I meant what you said that time. You wanted a wife, some kids, a lawn to mow."

"And I do." He cast the line out again, not looking at me.

"So how's the search going?" I asked.

"Not bad," he answered after a beat or two. Angus growled.

Not bad. What did that mean? "Well." I stood up and brushed off my jeans. "Thanks for the cookie, mister. Good luck with your fishing. For the wife *and* the trout."

"Have a nice day, Grace."

"You, too."

As I walked the rest of the way home, I tried to talk myself out of lusting after Callahan O'Shea. Reminded myself that he wasn't husband material, not for me. We weren't compatible. Because…um…well, because…

Let's face it. Callahan O'Shea was very fun to look at, that was true. Maybe he liked me. He *flirted* with me…a little. Sometimes. He flirted more with Margaret, to be honest. I'd seen them talking the other day, laughing like old friends over the back fence. Regrettably, I'd been on the phone at the time, so I hadn't been able to eavesdrop.

One thing was certain however. I did not feel safe around him. Not that he would rob me, no, of course not. But if

Andrew had broken my heart, imagine what Callahan O'Shea could do to it. Crush it until there was nothing left but rubble. Let's be honest. For someone like me—the little schoolteacher who danced with old people, loved Civil War movies and playing pretend—to be with someone like him, this vital, vaguely dangerous man who radiated and bristled with sex appeal...it had to be a bad idea. A disaster waiting to happen.

I just wished I could stop thinking about it.

CHAPTER NINETEEN

IT WAS QUITE A RELIEF to have Julian back as a regular feature in my life. And not only did I have him, but also the handsome and debonair Tim Gunn, since *Project Runway* was on. Margaret had deigned to come downstairs, I'd made popcorn and brownies, and it was the happiest I'd felt in a good while.

This week had been tough at school. The kids were dying to do anything but learn, and the seniors' year had basically ended once they'd heard from the colleges. I understood, had shown *Glory* instead of making them work, but still. I couldn't do nothing, either, which was what Ava was doing...letting the seniors text their friends and gossip, despite the fact that classes wouldn't end for weeks.

Speaking of Ava, her presentation to the board had been (from her own account, anyway) dazzling. The fact that she was sleeping with the chairman (according to Kiki, seconded by Paul and hinted at by Ava herself) certainly wasn't hurting her cause. My presentation was soon, and I'd been going over it feverishly, wondering if I should pull back on the changes I wanted to make, stick with the status quo a bit more.

On the dating front, eCommitment had offered up a mortician whose passion was taxidermy (understandable, I guess, but that didn't mean I had to date him) and an unemployed man who lived in his parents' basement and collected Pokémon cards. Come on! I was tired of looking. Granted, I hadn't been at it very long, but I wanted a break. I'd break up with Wyatt and just tell my family he was a workaholic, the end. Then I could relax and just enjoy life. I thought it was a great plan.

"Which one is that again?" Margaret asked, stuffing more popcorn into her mouth. She was supposedly working on a brief and did indeed have a yellow legal pad next to her, but it was forgotten as she succumbed to the siren call of my favorite show.

"That's the one who made his mother a gown when he was six," Julian answered, stroking Angus's back. "The prodigy. He's cute, too. I think he might be gay."

"Really," Margaret said. "Hmm. A guy who designs women's clothing. Gay. Who knew?"

"Now, now. No need for stereotypes," Julian chided.

"Said the gay male dance instructor," Margaret added, grinning.

"Replied the angry, driven, heterosexual female defense attorney," Julian countered.

"Retorted the man who spends thirty minutes on his hair each day, owns three cats and knits them sweaters," Margaret said.

"Sniped the beautiful, bitter workaholic who walked out on her mild-mannered husband, essentially castrating him," returned Julian. They grinned fondly at each other.

"You win," Margaret said. "The angry hetero concedes to the dancing fairy." Julian batted his impressive eyelashes at her.

"Children. Stop your bickering or there's no ice cream for you," I said, spreading my middle-child peacekeeping karma among them. "Oh, look, Tim's giving them the challenge." We fell silent, hanging on Tim Gunn's every word. Of course, that was when the phone rang.

"Don't get it," hissed Julian, turning up the TV from the remote.

I disobeyed after glancing at the caller ID. "Hey, Nat."

"Hi, Gissy! How's it going?"

"I'm great," I said, trying to listen to the show. Ooh. Dresses out of materials found at the dump. This would be a good one.

"What are you doing?" Natalie asked.

"Oh, um, we're just watching *Project Runway*," I answered.

"He's there? Wyatt's there?" Natalie squealed.

"No, Julian's here. Wyatt's in, um, Boston."

Julian's head snapped around, and he scootched closer to me so he could listen. *Project Runway* went into commercial.

"Well, listen, I wanted to ask you a favor. Andrew and I are going to come up on Friday for a family dinner. You know, the Carsons and you guys, and I wanted to make sure you could make it. With Wyatt."

I winced.

"I think he can finally get away, don't you, Grace? I mean, there are other doctors in Boston, right?" She chuckled.

"Uh, dinner? With the Carsons?" Margaret recoiled at the name, Julian looked stricken. They remembered the Carsons. I simulated shooting myself in the temple.

"Um...Friday?" I gestured to Margaret and Julian for help. "Gee, we, um...we sort of have plans."

"Grace, come on!" Natalie said. "This is getting ridiculous."

You have no idea, I thought.

Margaret jumped up and pried the phone out of my hand. "Nat, it's Margs." Margaret listened for a second. "Well, shit, Nat, did you ever think that maybe Grace is afraid Wyatt will fall for you, too?"

"Stop! That's not nice. Give me the phone, Margaret." I wrestled the receiver out of my older sister's hand and spoke soothingly to my younger sister. "I'm back, Nattie."

"Grace, that's not true, is it?" she whispered.

"Of course not! No!" I glared at Margaret, then lowered my voice. "I can tell you this, because I know you'll understand." Margaret sighed loudly. "Nat," I continued, "you know how Wyatt and I don't get to spend too much time together. And I told him I was losing patience. So he made these special plans…"

Nat was quiet for a minute. "Well, I guess you need a little time alone together."

"Exactly. You understand. But tell the Carsons I said hello, and of course I'll be seeing them soon at the wedding and all that."

"Okay. Love you, Grace."

"Love you, too, honey." I clicked End and turned to my other sister and friend. "Wyatt and I are going to have a big fight," I announced.

"Poor bastard. If only he wasn't so committed to healing children," Margaret said.

"I'm sure he'll be heartbroken," Julian said kindly.

I went into the kitchen for a drink of ice water, Angus pattering after me, hoping for a cookie. I obliged, knelt down and made my little dog sit up for his treat, then gave it to him and patted his head.

I was tired of Wyatt, tired of Margaret, too, tired of my parents' bickering, tired of mean old Mémé, tired of Natalie and Andrew. For a second, I remembered Callahan O'Shea asking me if my family did anything for me. Well. I was tired of thinking about him, too, because that just got me all hot and bothered and tingly in places long neglected, and then I didn't sleep well, which made me feel more tired than ever.

When Natalie's wedding was over, I was going to take a nice long vacation. Maybe go to Tennessee, see some of the battle sites down there. Maybe go to England. Or Paris, where I could possibly meet a real-life Jean-Philippe.

Angus rested his sweet head on my foot. "I love you, McFangus," I said. "You're Mommy's best boy."

Straightening up, I couldn't help but check out Callahan O'Shea's house for signs of life. A soft light glowed in an upstairs window. Maybe a bedroom window. Maybe he was having sex with a potential wife. If I went upstairs, to the attic, for example, I might be able to see...or if I just bought some really good binoculars...or if I climbed up the lilac tree and went hand-over-hand along the drainpipe, then, yes, I'd have a perfect view of what was in that room. God's nightgown, I was pathetic.

"Grace." Margaret stood in the kitchen doorway. "Hey, you okay?"

"Oh, sure," I said.

"Listen, I'm sending you and Julian out for dinner, okay? As a thank-you for letting me be such a pain in the ass and stay here." Her voice was uncharacteristically kind.

"That's nice of you."

"I'll have Junie make reservations, okay? Somewhere really swanky. Order lots to drink, get two desserts, the works." She came over to me and put her arm around my shoulder, and from the porcupine sister, it was a horribly tender gesture. "And you can have all the more fun thinking of how you're missing the Carsons."

ON FRIDAY NIGHT, Julian and I were shown to a lovely table at Soleil, a beautiful restaurant overlooking the Connecticut

River in Glastonbury. It was the kind of place I'd never eat in—very modern and expensive. We passed not only a glassed-in wine storage room on our way to our table, but a special, clear glass freezer full of designer vodka. On one end, the kitchen was exposed so we could see the chefs working madly away, sliding plates under the lights, chattering away in French. Our waiter, whose name was Cambry, handed us menu after menu—wine list, today's specials, martini list, regular menu, staff picks, each bound in leather and printed in an elegant font. "Enjoy your meal," he said, gazing at Julian. My friend ignored him, as was his custom.

"Look at this place, Grace," Julian said as we pored over the martini list. "Just the sort of place Wyatt would take you."

"You think? It's a little too high pressure for me."

"But he wants to impress you. He adores you."

"That's not enough, Wyatt," I said with mock seriousness. "I understand how devoted you are to your work, but I want more. You're a lovely man. Good luck. I'll always care for you, but goodbye."

Julian placed both of his hands over his heart "Oh, Grace, I'm so sorry. I'll always love you and regret that my work came between us, but I cannot abandon those poor children to some ham-handed caveman when I alone possess the necessary..." Julian's head whipped around as a waiter passed. "Oh, that looks good. What is that, salmon? I think I might order that." Julian looked back at me. "Where was I?"

"It doesn't matter. It's over. My family will be crushed." My buddy laughed. "Julian," I said more quietly, "you know how you said we weren't going to keep looking for a man?"

"Yeah?" he said, frowning.

"Well, I still want a man."

He sat back in his seat and sighed. "I know. Me, too. It's just so hard."

I sat back. "I have a crush on my neighbor. The ex-con."

"Who wouldn't?" Julian muttered.

"He's just a little…"

"Much?" my friend suggested.

"Exactly," I agreed. "I think he might like me, but as for doing anything about it, I'm just too…"

"Chickenshit?"

"Yes," I admitted. Julian nodded in sympathy. "But what about you, Julian? You must have to fight men off with a stick. The waiter keeps looking at you. He's cute. You could talk to him, at least."

"Well, maybe I will."

I gazed out the window at the river. The sun was sinking into a spectacular pile of buttery clouds, and the sky was pale peach and rose. It was lovely, and I felt myself relaxing.

"Okay, give it a try, Grace," Julian said, once we'd ordered dinner (he'd ignored the cute waiter) and were sipping our cool and unusual martinis. "Remember Lou from Meeting Mr. Right? We already know rule number one."

"I'm the most beautiful woman here," I said obediently.

"Yes, Grace, but you have to feel it. Sit up straight. Stop shlunching."

"Yes, Mother," I said, taking another sip.

"Rule number two. Look around the room and smile, because you know that every man here would be lucky to have you, and you can have any man you want."

I did as told. My eyes stopped on an elderly man, well into his eighties. Sure, *he'd* be lucky to have me. As proven with Dave of the Leg Bag, I had a certain *je ne sais quoi* when it came to older men. But would the bartender, who looked hauntingly like a young Clark Gable *sans* moustache, feel that way?

"'Believe in yourself,'" Julian intoned. "No, Grace, you're doing it wrong. Look. What's the problem?"

I rolled my eyes. "The problem is that it's stupid, Julian. Put me next to I don't know, Natalie, for example, or Margaret, for another, and I'm *not* the most beautiful woman in the room. Ask Andrew if he was lucky to have me, and he'd probably say hell yes! Because if it weren't for me, he'd never have met his darling bride-to-be."

"Ooh! Are we having our period? Sit and watch, darling," Julian said, ignoring my diatribe. I watched sulkily as my buddy sat back in his seat and gazed around the room. Bing, bang, boom. Three women at three different tables stopped midsentence and blushed.

"Sure, you're great with *women*," I said. "But you don't want to date *women*. Think I didn't see you just about crawl under the table when our waiter was fawning all over you? Try it on the guys, Julian."

He narrowed his lovely eyes at me. "Fine." His own face grew a little pink, but I had to give him credit for trying.

And sure enough, his eyes met our waiter's, who snatched a plate from the kitchen counter and practically vaulted over a table to get to us. "Here you are," he breathed. "Oysters Rockefeller. Enjoy."

"Thank you," Julian said, looking up at him. The waiter's lips parted. Julian didn't look away.

Well, well. Would my friend actually break his self-imposed chastity and find Mr. Right after all? Smiling, I took a bite of the oysters—yummy—and decided to check my messages while the two good-looking men gazed soulfully at each other. Gracious! Julian was actually initiating conversation! Would wonders never cease.

I'd turned off my phone in last period today when giving my freshmen a test and hadn't turned it back on. I wasn't a cell phone lover, to be honest. Many was the day that I forgot to turn it on at all. But wait. This was odd. I had six messages.

I'd never had six messages before. Was something wrong? Had Mémé died? An unexpected wave of sadness hit me at the idea. Hitting the code for my voice mail, I glanced out the window and waited as Julian and Cambry the waiter flirted.

"You have six new messages. Message one." My older sister's voice came on. "Grace, it's Margaret. Listen, kid, don't go to Soleil tonight, okay? I'm really sorry, but I think Junie told Mom where you were going when Mom called my office this afternoon. I guess Mom's all hell-bent for leather to meet Wyatt, and she made a reservation for tonight. With the Carsons. So don't go there. I'll pick up the tab somewhere else, just charge it. Call me when you get this."

The message was left at 3:45.

Oh...my...God.

Message two. "Grace, Margs again. Mom just called me. The dinner is definitely at Soleil, so head somewhere else, okay? Call me." That one was at 4:15.

Messages three through five were the same, I dimly noted, though Margaret's language deteriorated as they went on. Horror rose like an icy tide. Message six was as follows. "Grace, where the hell are you? We're leaving for the stupid restaurant right now. The Carsons, Andrew, Nat, Mom and Dad and Mémé. Call me! Our reservation is at seven."

I looked at my watch. It was six-fifty-three.

Julian and Cambry were laughing now as Cambry wrote his phone number on a piece of paper. "Julian?" I said, my voice barely a whisper.

"One sec, Grace," said Julian. "Cambry and I—" Then he saw my expression. "What is it?"

"My family is on their way. Here," I said.

His eyes popped. "Oh, shit."

Cambry looked at us, confused. "Is there a problem?" he asked.

"We need to leave right away," I said. "Immediately. Family emergency. Here." I fumbled in my pocketbook for the gift certificate Margaret's secretary had printed off the Internet. Dread raced through my veins. I couldn't be found here. I couldn't! I'd just tell the family we'd gone somewhere else. That was it. No problem.

Just as we stood up to go, I heard the horrible sound of my mother's nervous society laugh. *Ahahaha! Ahahaha! Oooh...ahahaha.* I looked at Julian. "Run," I whispered.

"We need another exit," Julian said to Cambry.

"Through the kitchen," he answered instantly. The two of them were off, me right on their heels, when the strap of my pocketbook snagged on the chair of a nearby diner. He looked up.

"Oopsy," he said. "You're caught, honey." *In more ways than one, mister.* I flashed him a panicked smile and tugged. The strap didn't come free.

Years of dance training made Julian lithe and fast as a snake. He zigged and zagged through the tables toward the busy, open kitchen, failing to notice I wasn't with him.

"Here you go," said the diner, sliding the strap off the back of his chair. And just as I turned to gallop after my friend, I heard my mother's voice.

"Grace! There you are!"

My entire family walked in. Margaret, wide-eyed. Andrew and Nat, holding hands. Dad pushing Mémé's wheelchair, followed by Mom. And the Carsons, Letitia and Ted.

My mind was perfectly blank. "Hi, guys!" I heard myself saying in that out-of-body way. "What are you doing here!"

Nat gave me a hug. "Mom insisted that we crash. Just to say hello, not to spoil your special night." She pulled back to look at me. "I'm really sorry. I told her no a million times, but you know how she is."

Margaret caught my eye and shrugged. Well, hell, she tried. I could feel my heart thumping in sick, rolling beats, and hysterical laughter wriggled like a trout in my stomach.

"Grace, darling! You've been so secretive!" Mom burbled, her eyes darting to my table, where two martinis and an order of oysters Rockefeller sat abandoned. "I told Letitia here about your wonderful doctor boyfriend, and she said she couldn't wait to meet him, and then I had to tell her that *we* haven't met him, and then I thought, well, I'll just kill two birds with one stone. You remember the Carsons, don't you, dear?"

Of course I remembered them. I got to within three weeks of being their daughter-in-law, for heaven's sake. Someday, a long, long time from now, I might forgive my mother. On second thought, no. In my experience, Mr. and Mrs. Carson were aloof, undemonstrative people, completely devoid of humor. They never expressed anything but the coolest politeness toward me.

"Hi, Mrs. Carson, Mr. Carson. Good to see you again." The Carsons smiled insincerely at me. I returned their smile with equal affection.

"What are you eating? Are those oysters? I don't eat shellfish," Mémé boomed. "Disgusting, slimy, riddled with bacteria. I have irritable bowel syndrome as it is."

"Grace, honey, I'm sorry if we're horning in," Dad murmured, giving me a kiss on the cheek. "Your mother went a little berserk when she heard you weren't coming. Don't you look pretty! So where is he? As long as we're here."

Andrew caught my eye. He knew me pretty well, after all. He tilted his head to one side and smiled curiously.

"He's...uh...he's in the bathroom," I said.

Margaret closed her eyes.

"Right. Um, not feeling that well, actually. I'd better go check on him. Tell him you're here."

My face burned as I walked (and walked, and walked, God, it seemed to be taking forever) through the restaurant. In the foyer, Cambry gestured down the hall toward the restrooms. Sure enough, there was Julian, lurking just inside the men's room, peering out through the cracked door. "What should we do?" he whispered. "I told Cambry what was going on. He can help us."

"I just told them Wyatt's not feeling well. And you're playing the part of Wyatt." I glanced back toward the dining room. "Jesus, Mary and Joseph on rye bread, here comes my dad! Get in a stall. Hurry up!"

The door closed, and I heard the sound of a stall door slamming as Dad lumbered down the hall. "Honey? How's he doing?"

"Oh, well, not so good, Dad. Um, he must've eaten something that didn't agree with him."

"Poor guy. Helluva way to meet your sweetheart's family." Dad leaned amiably against the wall. "Want me to check on him?"

"No! No, no." I pushed the men's room door open a crack. "Hon? You doing okay?"

"Uhhnnhuh," Julian said weakly.

"I'm here if you need me," I said, letting the door close again. "Dad, I really wish you guys hadn't come. This is—" *a ridiculous farce* "—our special night."

He had the decency to look ashamed. "Well, your mother...you know how she is. She felt the whole family should be there to show the Carsons...well, that you're okay with everything."

"Right. And I am," I said, cursing myself. I should've just

gone to the stupid dinner, said that Wyatt had plans or emergency surgery or something. Instead, here I was, lying to my father. My dear old dad who loved me and played Civil War with me and paid for my new windows.

"Dad?" I said hesitantly. "About Wyatt..."

Dad patted my shoulder. "Don't worry, Pudding. It's embarrassing, sure, but no one will hold a little diarrhea against him."

"Well, the thing is, Dad—"

"We're just glad you're seeing someone, honey. I don't mind admitting that I was worried about you. Breaking up with Andrew, well, that was one thing. Everyone's heart gets broken once or twice. And I knew it wasn't your idea, honey."

My mouth dropped open. "You did?" I'd taken such pains to tell everyone that it was mutual, that we just weren't sure we were right for each other...

"Sure, Pudding. You loved him, clear as day. Letting your sister date him..." Dad sighed. "Well, at least you found someone else. The whole way here, Natalie was chattering on and on about how wonderful your young man was. I think she still feels pretty guilty."

Well. There went my feeble desire to confess. A man came down the hall and paused, looking at us.

"My daughter's boyfriend is sick," Dad explained. "The runs." I closed my eyes.

"Oh," the man said. "Um...thanks. I guess I can wait." He turned and headed back to the dining room.

Dad pushed the door open a little. "Wyatt, son? This is Grace's dad, Jim Emerson."

"Hello, sir," Julian mumbled in a lower than normal voice.

"Anything I can get for you?"

"No, thanks." Julian threw in a groan for authenticity. Dad winced and let the door close.

"Why don't we go back, too, Dad?" I suggested. I cracked the door again. "Honey? I'll be back in a sec."

"Okay," Julian said hoarsely, then coughed. Frankly, I thought he was overdoing it a bit, but hey. I owed the guy my firstborn. Dad took my hand as we went back to the dining room, and I gave him a grateful squeeze as we approached my family, who was now seated around a large table. The Carsons frowned at the menu, Mémé inspected the silverware, Mom looked like she could levitate with the amount of nervous energy buzzing through her. Andrew, Nat and Margaret all looked up at me.

"How's he doing?" Natalie asked.

"Not that great," I said. "A bad oyster or something."

"I told you. Oysters are filthy bits of rubbery phlegm," Mémé announced, causing a nearby diner to gag noticeably.

"You're looking well, Grace," Mrs. Carson said, tearing her eyes from the menu. She tilted her head as if impressed that I hadn't slashed my throat when her son dumped me.

"Thanks, Mrs. Carson," I said. For about a month, I'd called her Letty. We had lunch together once to talk about the wedding.

"I have some Imodium in here somewhere," Mom said, fumbling through her purse.

"No, no, that's okay. It's more of…well. We're going to head home. I'm so sorry. Wyatt would just love to meet everyone, but you understand." I stifled a sigh. Not only was I dating an imaginary man, he had diarrhea, as well. So classy. Definitely the kind to make Andrew jealous.

Wait a second. To the best of my knowledge, Wyatt Dunn was not invented to make anyone jealous. I glanced at Andrew. He was looking at me, still holding Natalie's hand,

and in his eyes was a hint of something. Affection? His mouth tugged up on one side, and I looked away.

"I'll walk you to the car," Natalie said.

"Stay here," Margs all but barked. "He doesn't want to meet you under these circumstances, dummy." Natalie sank back down, looking wounded.

I kissed my mother's cheek, waved to Mémé and finally left the dining room. Cambry the waiter was waiting outside the bathroom door. "You can leave the back way," he murmured, pushing open the bathroom door. "Julian? Coast is clear."

"I'm so sorry," I said to my friend. "And thank you," I added, pressing a twenty on Cambry. "You were really nice."

"You're welcome. It was kind of fun," Cambry said. He led us to another exit, farther away from the main dining room, shook hands with Julian, holding on a little too long.

"Well, I know I had a good time," Julian announced as we pulled out of the parking lot. "And, Grace, guess what? I have a date! So every cloud has a silver lining."

I glanced at my buddy. "You were great in there," I said.

"Faking diarrhea is a specialty of mine," he said, and with that, we laughed so hard I had to pull over.

CHAPTER TWENTY

"Why would you teach the American Revolution at the same time as the Vietnam War?" asked Headmaster Stanton, frowning.

Ten of us—the Headmaster, Dr. Eckhart, seven trustees and me—sat around the vast walnut conference table in Bigby Hall, the main administrative building of Manning, the one that was featured on the cover of all our promotional brochures. I was making my presentation to the Board of Trustees, and I felt ill. I'd been up till 2:00 a.m. perfecting my talk, practicing over and over till I thought I had it right. This morning, I'd gotten up at six, dressed in one of my Wyatt outfits, taking care to combine conservatism with creativity, tamed my hair, ate a good breakfast despite the churning stomach and now was wondering if I should've bothered.

It wasn't going well. I'd finished my talk, and the seven members of the board, including Theo Eisenbraun, Ava's reputed lover, stared at me with varying degrees of confusion. Dr. Eckhart appeared to be dozing, I noted with rising panic.

"That's an excellent question," I said in my best teacher voice. "The American Revolution and the Vietnam War have a lot in common. Most history departments teach chronologically, which, to be honest, I think can get a little stale. But in the Revolution, we have a situation of an invading foreign army up against a small band of poorly armed citizens who won the war through cunning, use of the terrain and just a simple refusal to give up. The same can be said for Vietnam."

"But they happened in different centuries," said Adelaide Compton.

"I'm aware of that," I said, a bit too sharply. "I feel that teaching by theme and not simply by timeline is the way to go. In some cases, anyway."

"You want to teach a class called 'The Abuse of Power'?" asked Randall Withington, who'd been a U.S. senator for our fair state some time ago. His already-florid face seemed a bit more mottled than usual.

"I think it's a very important aspect of history, yes," I said, cringing internally. Senator Withington had been ousted on charges of corruption and, er, abuse of power.

"Well, this is all very interesting," said Hunter Graystone III, who was Hunter IV's father and a Manning alumnus. He indicated my fifty-four-page document—curriculum for all four years, required courses, electives, credits, budget, field trips, staffing suggestions, teaching strategies, the role of parents, meshing the history curriculum with other subjects. I'd color-coded it, included pictures, graphs, charts, had it printed up and bound at Kinko's. Mr. Graystone had yet to open it. Damn it. I'd given Hunter a B on his midterm (quite fair, let me tell you), and Mr. Graystone had reminded me of this very fact when I introduced myself a half hour ago. "Why don't you just sum things up for us, Ms. Emerson?"

Dr. Eckhart looked up—not asleep, thank goodness—and gave me a little nod of encouragement.

"Sure," I said, trying to smile. "Well, here it is in a nutshell." Taking a deep breath, I decided to give it all I had, my blank-faced audience aside. "I want Manning students to understand the impact of history on where we are today. I want the past to come alive for them, so they can appreciate the sacrifices that have gotten us to this point." I looked around at each board member in turn, willing them to *feel* my love for the subject. "I want our students to learn from the past in a way much more profound than memorizing dates. I want them to feel how the whole world shifted because of the act of a single person, whether it was Henry VIII creating a new religion or Dr. King calling for equality on the steps of the Lincoln Memorial."

"And who is Dr. King?" Adelaide asked, frowning.

My mouth dropped open. "Martin Luther King, Jr.? The civil rights activist?"

"Of course. Right. Go on."

Taking a steadying breath, I continued. "So many kids today see themselves as isolated from even the recent past, disconnected from their country's policies, living in a world where there are too many distractions from true knowledge. Text messaging, video games, online chatting…they all detract from living in this world and understanding it. These kids have to see where we've been and how we got here. They have to! Because it's our past that determines our future—as individuals, as a nation, as a *world*. They have to understand the past, because these kids *are* the future."

My heart pounded, my face was hot, my hands shook. I took a shaking breath and folded my sweaty hands together. I was finished.

No one said anything. Not a word. Nothing, and not in a good way. Nope, it was fair to say there was the proverbial sound of crickets.

"So…you believe the children are our future," Theo said, suppressing a grin.

I closed my eyes briefly. "Yes," I said. "They are. Hopefully, they'll have the ability to think when the fates call on them to act. So." I stood up and gathered my papers. "Thank you all so much for your time."

"That was...very interesting," Adelaide said. "Er...good luck."

I was assured that I'd be notified if I got through the next round. They were, of course, looking outside Manning, yadda yadda ding dong, blah blah blah. As for making it to the next round, my chances were dubious. Dubious at best.

Apparently, word of my impassioned speech got out, because when I ran into Ava later that day in the Lehring staff room, she smiled coyly. "Hello, Grace," she said. Blink...blink...here it comes...and, yes, blink. "How was your presentation to the board?"

"It was great," I lied. "Very positive."

"Good for you," she murmured, washing out her coffee cup, singing as she did. "'I believe the children are our future...teach them well and let them lead the way—'"

I gritted my teeth. "How did yours go, Ava? Did the push-up bra sway the board in your favor, do you think?"

"Oh, Grace, I feel sorry for you," she said, pouring herself some more coffee. "It's not my cleavage they loved, hon. It's my way with people. Anyway. Best of luck."

At that moment, Kiki stuck her head in the door. "Grace, got a minute? Oh, hi, Ava, how are you?"

"I'm fantastic, thanks," Ava half whispered. Blink. Blink. And blink again.

"You okay?" Kiki asked when I came into the hall and closed the door behind me.

"I'm crappy, actually," I said.

"What happened?"

"My presentation didn't go very well," I admitted. All that work reduced to a Whitney Houston song. To my irritable disgust, my throat tightened with tears.

"I'm sorry, kid." She patted my arm. "Listen, do you want to go to Julian's Singles' Dance Night this Friday? Take your mind off your troubles? I still haven't met someone. God knows why. I've been trying those methods from Lou like they were sent from Mount Sinai, you know?"

"Kiki, that class was dumb, don't you think? Do you really want to trick a guy into dating you by pretending you're someone you're not?"

"Is there another way?" she asked. I sighed. "Okay, okay, I know. But come to the dance with me. Please? Just to distract yourself?"

"Yick," I answered. "I don't think so."

She lowered her voice. "Maybe you'll find someone to take to your sister's wedding," she suggested, evil, black-hearted woman that she was.

I grimaced.

"It's worth a shot," she cajoled.

"Satan, get thee behind me," I muttered. "Maybe. I'm not promising, but maybe."

"Okay, great!" She glanced at her watch. "Dang it, I have to run. Mr. Lucky needs his insulin, and if I'm late, he craps all over the place and then has seizures. Talk to you later!" And she was off, running down the hall to the medical disaster that was her cat.

"Hello, Grace."

I turned around. "Hi, Stuart! How are you? How's everything?"

He sighed. "I was hoping you'd tell me."

I bit down on a wave of impatience. "Stuart, um…listen. You need to do something. I'm not your intermediary, okay?

I want very much for you guys to work this out, but you need to take action. Don't you think so?"

"I just don't know what action to take," he protested, taking off his glasses to rub his eyes.

"Well, you've been married to her for seven years, Stuart! Come on! Think of something!"

The door to the teacher's lounge opened. "Is there a problem here?" Ava's chest said. Well, her mouth said it, but with the amount of boob she was showing today, who could pay attention?

"No, no problem, Ava," I said shortly. "Private conversation."

"How are you, Stu?" she purred. "I heard your wife left you. I'm so sorry. Some women just don't appreciate a truly decent man." She shook her head sadly, blinked, blinked, blinked, then sashayed down the hall, her ass swaying.

Stuart stared after her.

"Stuart!" I barked. "Go see your wife. Please."

"Right," he muttered, tearing his eyes off Ava's butt. "Will do, Grace."

LATE THAT EVENING, I sighed, triple circling *would of* in red pen and writing *would HAVE* in the margin of Kerry Blake's paper. I was correcting papers on my bed, as Margaret was using the computer to play Scrabble downstairs in my tiny office. Would of. Come on!

Kerry was a smart enough girl, but even at the age of seventeen, she knew she'd never have to really work for a living. Her mother was a Harvard grad and managing partner at a Boston consulting firm. Her father owned a software company with divisions in four countries, which he often visited in his private jet. Kerry would get into an Ivy League school, regardless of her grades and test scores. And, barring some miracle, if she did decide to work instead of take the Paris Hilton route, she'd probably get some high-paying job with a great office, take three-hour lunches and jet around to meetings, where she'd do a negligible amount of work, taking credit for the grunts who worked under her. If Kerry didn't know a past participle from a preposition, no one would care.

Except me. I wanted her to use her brain instead of coast on her situation, but Kerry didn't really care what I thought. That was clear. The board of trustees might well share her ennui.

"Grace!" Margaret's voice boomed through the house, making Angus jump. I swear, my older sister was becoming more and more like Mémé every day. "I'm making whole grain pasta with broccoli for dinner. Want some?"

I grimaced. "No, thanks. I'll throw something together later on." Something with cheese. Or chocolate. Possibly both.

"Roger that. Oh, shit. Stuart's here."

Thank *God.* I leaped to the window, Angus bouncing merrily behind me. Sure enough, my brother-in-law was coming up the path. It was almost dark, but his standard white oxford glowed in the dimming light. I moved out into the hallway to eavesdrop better, shutting the door behind me so Angus wouldn't blow my cover. Margaret stomped to answer the soft knock. I could see the back of her head, but no more.

"What do you want?" she asked ruthlessly. I detected a note of pleasure under her tone…Stuart was finally *doing* something, and Margaret appreciated that kind of thing.

"Margaret, I think you should come home." Stuart's voice was quiet, and I had to strain to hear. He didn't say anything else.

"That's it?" Margaret barked, echoing my own thought. "That's all you've got?"

"What more would you like me to say, Margaret?" he asked wearily. "I miss you. I love you. Come home."

My eyes were suddenly wet.

"Why? So we can stare at each other every night, bored out of our minds?"

"I never felt that way, Margaret. I was very happy," Stuart said. "If you don't want to have a baby, that's fine, but all these other complaints...I don't know what you want me to do. I'm no different from how I've always been."

"Which may be the problem," Margaret said sharply.

Stuart sighed. "If there's something specific you want me to do, I'll do it, but you have to tell me. This isn't fair."

"If I tell you, then it doesn't count," Margaret retorted. "It's like planned spontaneity, Stuart. An oxymoron."

"You want me to be unexpected and surprising," Stuart said, his voice suddenly hard. "Would you like it if I ran naked down Main Street? How about if I started shooting heroin? Shall I have an affair with the cleaning woman? Would that be surprising enough?"

"You're being deliberately obtuse, Stuart. Until you figure it out, I have nothing to say. Goodbye." Margaret closed the door and leaned against it, then, a second later, peeked out the transom window. "Goddamn it," she muttered. I heard the sound of a car motor starting. Apparently, Stuart was gone.

Margaret caught sight of me, crouched at the top of the stairs. "So?" she asked.

"Margaret," I began cautiously, "he loves you and he wants to make you happy. Doesn't that count, honey?"

"Grace, it's not that simple!" she said. "He'd love it if every night of our life was the same as the night before.

Dinner. Polite conversation about literature and current events. Sex on the prescribed days. The occasional dinner out, where he takes half an hour to order a bottle of wine. I'm so bored I could scream!"

"Well, here's what I think, roomie," I said, my own voice growing hard. "He's a decent, hardworking, intelligent man and he adores you. I think you're acting like a spoiled brat."

"Grace," she said tightly, "since you've never been married, your opinion really doesn't count a whole heck of a lot right now. So mind your own business, okay?"

"Oh, absolutely, Margs. Hey, by the way, how much longer do you think you'll be staying?" Sure, it was bitchy, but it felt good.

"Why?" Margaret said. "Am I cutting in on your time with Wyatt?" With that, she stomped back into the kitchen.

Ten minutes later, feeling that I really should have control of my own house and shouldn't have to hide in my bedroom, I went downstairs. Margaret was standing at the stove, stirring her pasta, tears dripping off her chin. "I'm sorry," she said in a small voice.

"Sure," I sighed, my anger evaporating. Margaret never cried. Never.

"I do love him, Grace. I think I do, anyway, but sometimes I just felt like I was suffocating, Grace. Like if I started screaming, he wouldn't even notice. I don't want a divorce, but I can't be married to a piece of cardboard, either. It's like we work in theory, but when we're actually together, I'm dying. I don't know what to do. If just once he could move outside the stupid box, you know? And the idea of a baby…" She started to sob. "It feels like Stuart wanting a baby means I'm not enough anymore. And he was the one who was supposed to adore me."

"Which he does, Margs!"

She didn't listen. "Besides, I'm such a bitch, Grace, who would want me for a mother?"

"You're not a bitch. Not all the time," I assured her. "Angus loves you. That's a good sign, isn't it?"

"Do you want me to move out? Stay at a hotel or something?"

"No, of course not. You know damn well you can stay with me as long as you want," I said. "Come on. Give us a hug."

She wrapped her arms around me and squeezed fiercely. "Sorry about the Wyatt crack," she muttered.

"Yeah, yeah," I said, squeezing her back. Angus, jealous that there was love and it wasn't directed at him, began leaping and whining.

Margaret stepped back, breaking our hug, grabbed a tissue and wiped her eyes. "Want some dinner?" she offered. "I made enough for us both."

I looked at what she called dinner. "I try to avoid eating rope," I said, getting a little grin in response. "I'm actually not hungry. Think I'll just sit outside for a bit." I poured myself a glass of wine, patted her shoulder to assure her I wasn't mad, and went out with my dog into the sweet-scented night.

Sitting in an Adirondack chair, I looked around my yard. Angus was sniffing the back fence, patrolling the perimeter like the good guard dog he was. All the flowers I planted last year were coming up beautifully. The peonies along the back fence were heavy with blooms, the sugary smell of their blossoms heady in the night. Bee balm waved over near pine trees that shielded me from 32 Maple, and on Callahan's side, the irises rose in graceful lines, white and indigo, vanilla and grape scented. The lilacs along the eastern side of the house had faded, but their scent was indescribably lovely, calming and invigorating at the same time. The only sound was of the Farmington River, full and fast at this time of year, gushing over the rocks. A train whistle sounded somewhere, its melancholy note underscoring the loneliness that shrouded my heart.

Why couldn't people be happy alone? Love took your heart hostage. I'd sell my soul for Margaret and Natalie, my parents, Julian, even sweet little Angus, my faithful friend. As proven by my recent actions, I'd do anything to find someone who'd love me with the same wholeheartedness I wanted to love him. Those distant days with Andrew seemed like they'd happened to someone else. And even if I did find someone, what guarantee was there that it would last? Look at my parents, so pissed off with each other all the time. Margaret and Stuart...seven years crumbling away. Kiki, Julian and me, all floundering.

I seemed to be crying a little bit. I wiped my eyes on my sleeve and took a healthy slug of wine. Stupid love. Margaret was right. Love sucked.

"Grace?"

My head jerked up. Callahan O'Shea was out on his roof, looking down at me like a blue-collar *deus ex machina*.

"Hi," I said.

"Everything okay?" he asked.

"Oh...sure," I said. Feeble, even for me.

"Want to come up?"

My answer surprised me. "Okay."

I left Angus examining a clump of ferns, went through the little gate that separated my backyard from the front, and headed for Callahan's back deck. The fresh boards, sharp and clean-smelling, glowed dimly in the night, and the metal rungs of the ladder were cool under my hand. Up I went, peeking over the roof to where my neighbor stood.

"Hi," he said, taking my hand to help me.

"Hi," I said back. His hand was warm and sure, and I was glad, never being a huge fan of ladders. That hand made me feel safe. Just one hand, that was all it took. It was with great reluctance that I let it go.

A dark-colored blanket was spread on the rough shingles. "Welcome to the roof," Callahan said. "Have a seat."

"Thanks." Self-consciously, I sat down. Cal sat next to me. "So what do you do out here?" I asked, my voice sounding a bit loud in the quiet, cool air.

"I just like to look at the sky," he answered. But he wasn't looking at the sky. He was looking at me. "I didn't get to do that a lot in prison."

"The sky's pretty," I said. *Clever, Grace. Very witty.* I could feel the warmth of his shoulder next to mine. "So."

"So." He was smiling a little, and my stomach did a slow, giddy roll. Then he stretched out so that he was lying on the blanket, clasping his hands behind his head. After a second's hesitation, I did the same thing.

It *was* pretty. The stars were winking, the sky velvety and rich. The river's lush song was pierced by a night bird of some kind, trilling softly every few minutes. And there was Callahan O'Shea, the solid warmth of him just inches from me.

"Were you crying before?" His voice was gentle.

"A little," I admitted.

"Everything all right?"

I paused. "Well, Margaret and Stuart are having a tough time of it these days. And my other sister, Nat—remember her?" He nodded. "She's getting married in a few weeks. I guess I was just feeling sentimental."

"You and that family of yours," he commented mildly. "They sure have a choke hold on you."

"They sure do," I agreed glumly.

The far-off bird trilled again. Angus barked once in reply. "Were you ever married?" Callahan asked.

"Nope," I said, staring at the hypnotic stars. "I was engaged a couple of years ago, though." God. A couple of years ago. It sounded like such a long time.

"Why'd you call it off?"

I shifted to look at him. Nice, that he assumed it had been my decision. Nice, but untrue. "I didn't, actually. He did. He fell for someone else." Funny...saying it like that didn't sound all that bad. *He fell for someone else.* It happened.

Callahan O'Shea turned his head. "Sounds like he was an idiot," he said softly.

Oh. *Oh.* There it was again, that warm, rolling squeeze of my insides. I swallowed. "He wasn't that bad," I said, looking back at the sky. "What about you, Callahan? Ever get close to the altar?"

"I was seeing someone before prison. I guess it was serious." His voice was level, unperturbed.

"Why'd you guys break up?" I asked.

"Well, we were struggling a bit as it was," he answered. "But me being arrested was the final nail in my coffin."

"Do you miss her?" I couldn't help asking.

"A little," he said. "Sometimes. It's like our happy times were in another life, though. I can barely remember them."

His statement so echoed my own earlier thoughts about Andrew that my mouth opened in amazement. He must've noticed my shocked expression, because he smiled. "What?" he asked.

"Nothing. I just...I know how that feels." We were quiet for another minute, then I asked him another question, one I'd wondered about more than once. "Hey, Cal, I read that you pled guilty. Didn't you want to go to trial?"

He kept his eyes on the sky and didn't answer for a second. "There was a lot of evidence against me," he finally said.

As I had once before, I got the impression that Callahan wasn't telling me all there was to tell. But it was *his* crime, *his* past, and the night and being here were just too comfortable to press on. I was out on the roof with Callahan O'Shea, and it was enough. It was, in fact, lovely.

"Grace?" God, I loved the way he said my name, his voice deep and soft and with just a hint of roughness in it, like distant thunder on a hot summer night.

I turned my head to look at him, but he was just staring at the stars. "Yes?"

He still didn't turn my way. "Are you finished with the cat wrangler?"

My heart jolted, my breath froze. For a flash of a second, I imagined telling Callahan the truth about Wyatt Dunn. Imagined him turning to look at me, his expression incredulous, then disgusted, rolling his eyes and muttering something less than flattering about my emotional state. I sure as hell didn't want that. Callahan O'Shea was asking if I was done with Wyatt because he…yes, there was no denying it…he was interested. In me.

I bit my lip. "Um…Wyatt's…he was better on paper than in real life," I said, swallowing hard. Not exactly a lie. "So yeah. So we called it quits."

"Good." Then he did turn to look at me. His face was serious, his eyes unreadable in the dim light from the stars. My heart slowed, and suddenly the smell of lilacs was dizzying. Cal's lashes were so long, his eyes so lovely. And it was scary, too, looking at him like that, so close and available, so warm and solid.

Very slowly, he reached out to touch my cheek with the

back of his fingers. Just a little caress, but I sucked in a sharp breath at the contact. He was going to kiss me. Oh, God. My heart clattered so hard it practically bruised my ribs. Cal smiled.

Then Margaret's voice split the quiet air. "Grace? Grace, where are you? Nat's on the phone!"

"Coming!" I called, abruptly lurching to my feet. At the realization that his mistress was on the roof, Angus exploded into yarps, breaking the quiet into shards of noise. "Sorry, Cal. I—I have to go."

"Coward," he said, but he was smiling.

I took another step closer to the ladder, then stopped. "Maybe I could come back up here again sometime," I said.

"Maybe you could," he agreed, sitting up in one quick, graceful move. "I hope you do."

"Gotta run," I breathed, then scuttled down the ladder as fast as I could. Cal's low, ashy laugh followed me as I trotted into my own yard where Angus finally quieted. My heart thundered as if I'd run a mile.

"What were you doing out there?" Margaret hissed as I burst onto the patio. "Were you up there with Callahan?"

"Hi, Margaret," Cal called from his roof.

"What were you guys doing up there?" she called back.

"Monkey sex," he answered. "Wanna give it a try?"

"Don't tempt me, Bird Man of Alcatraz," she said, shoving the phone into my hand.

"Hello?" I panted.

"Hi, Grace. I'm sorry. Was I interrupting?" Nat's voice was small.

"Oh, no. I was just..." I cleared my throat. "Just talking to Callahan next door. What's up?"

"Well, I was wondering if you were free this Saturday," she said. "Do you have anything at school? Or any battles?"

I went through the slider into the kitchen and glanced at my calendar. "Nope. All clear."

"Think you'd like to go dress shopping with me?"

My head jerked back slightly. "Sure!" I said heartily. "What time?"

"Um, maybe around three?" Nat sounded so hesitant that I could tell something was wrong.

"Three would be great," I answered.

"You sure?"

"Yes! Of course, Bumppo. Why do you sound so weird?"

"Margaret said maybe I should cut you a break and go without you."

Good old Margs. My older sister was right—it would be awfully nice to skip out on this particular wedding event, but I had to go. "I want to come, Nat," I said. Part of me did, at any rate. "I'll see you at three."

"Why do you baby her so much?" Margaret demanded the minute I hung up. Angus raced in, almost tripping her, but she ignored him. "Tell her to open her eyes and think of someone else for a change. She's not lying in a hospital bed anymore, Grace."

"I know that, Margaret dear. But for crying out loud, it's her wedding dress. And I'm over Andrew. I don't care if she's marrying him, she's our little sister and we should both be there."

Margaret dropped into a kitchen chair and picked up Angus, who licked her chin with great affection. "Princess Natalie. God forbid she think of someone else for a change."

"She's not like that! God, Margs, why do you give her such a hard time?"

Margaret shrugged. "Maybe I think she needs a little hard time once in a while. She's lived a charmed life, Grace. Adored, beautiful, smart. She gets everything."

"Unlike your poor, orphaned, troll-like self?" I asked.

"Yes, I'm all soft edges and peachy glow." She sighed. "You know what I'm talking about, Grace. Admit it. Nat has glided through life on a fluffy white cloud with a fucking rainbow over her head while bluebirds sang all around her. Me, I've stomped through life, and you...you've..." Her voice broke off.

"I've what?" I asked, bristling.

She didn't answer for a second. "You've hit a few walls."

"Andrew, you mean?"

"Well, sure. But remember when we first moved to Connecticut, and you were kind of lost?" Sure I remembered. Back when I was dating Jack of Le Cirque. Margaret continued. "And that year you lived with Mom and Dad after college, when you waitressed for a year?"

"I was taking time off to figure out what I wanted to do," I bit out. "Plus, waitressing is a life skill I'll always have."

"Sure. Nothing wrong with that. It's just that Nat's never had to wonder, never been lost, never doubted herself, never imagined that life would be anything less than perfect for her. Until she met Andrew and finally found something she couldn't have, which you ended up giving her. So if I think she's a little self-centered, that's why."

"I think you're jealous of her," I said, smarting.

"Of course I'm jealous of her, dummy," Margaret said fondly. Honestly, I would never figure Margaret out. "Hey," she added, "what were you doing up on that roof with Hottie the Hunk Next Door?"

I took a deep breath. "We were just looking at the sky. Talking."

Margaret squinted at me. "Are you interested in him, Grace?"

I could feel myself blushing. "Sort of. Yes. Definitely. I am."

"Mmm-hmm." Margs gave me her pirate smile.

"So?"

"So nothing. He's a huge improvement on Andrew the Pale. God, imagine screwing Callahan O'Shea. Just his name practically gives me an orgasm." She laughed, and I smiled reluctantly. Margaret stood up and patted my shoulder. "Just make sure you're not doing it to show Andrew that there's a man who wants what's in your pants, okay?"

"Wow. That's so romantic, I think I might cry."

She grinned again like the pirate she should've been. "Well, I'm beat. I have to write a brief and then I'm hitting the hay. 'Night, Gracie." She handed me my wee doggie, who rested his head on my shoulder and sighed with devotion. "And, Grace, one more thing as long as I'm doing the big sister shtick." She sighed. "Look. I know you're trying to move on and all that crap, and I don't blame you. But no matter how great Cal looks without a shirt, he's always going to have a prison record, and these things have a habit of following a person around."

"I know," I admitted. Ava and I had both made it to the second round of interviews for the chairmanship, much to my surprise. I still wasn't entirely hopeful, but Margs was right. Callahan O'Shea's past would matter at Manning. Maybe it shouldn't, but it would.

"Just be sure you know what you want, kiddo," Margs said. "That's all I'm saying. I think Cal's pretty damn fun, and you could probably use some fun. But keep in mind that you're a teacher at a prep school, and this just might matter to the good people at Manning. Not to mention Mom and Dad."

I didn't answer. As usual, Margaret was right.

CHAPTER TWENTY-ONE

"I'VE BEEN COMMISSIONED to do a sculpture of a baby in utero for Yale New Haven's Children Hospital," Mom announced the next night at dinner. We were at the family domicile—me, Margaret, Mémé, Mom and Dad—eating dinner.

"That sounds nice, Mom," I said, taking a bite of her excellent pot roast.

"It's coming along beautifully, if I do say so myself," she agreed.

"Which you do say, every half hour," Dad muttered.

"I almost died in childbirth," Mémé announced. "They had to put me under. When I came to three days later, they told me I had a beautiful son."

"My kind of labor and delivery," Margaret murmured, knocking back her wine.

"The problem with the sculpture is that the baby's head keeps breaking off—"

"Less than reassuring for the expectant mothers, I'm guessing," Margaret interjected.

"—and I can't find a way to keep it on," Mom finished, glaring at Margs.

"How about duct tape?" Dad suggested. I bit down a laugh.

"Jim, must you constantly belittle my work? Hmm? Grace,

stop shlunching, honey. You're so pretty, why do you shlunch?"

"You can always tell breeding by good posture," Mémé said, fishing the onion out of her martini and popping it into her mouth. "A lady never hunches. Grace, what is wrong with your hair today? You look like you just stepped out of the electric chair."

"Oh, do you like it, Mémé? It cost a fortune, but, yes, electrocution was just the look I was going for. Thanks!"

"Mother," Dad said, "what would you like to do for your birthday this year?"

Mémé raised a sparse eyebrow. "Oh, you remembered, did you? I thought you forgot. No one has said a word about it."

"Of course I remembered," Dad said wearily.

"Has he ever forgotten, Eleanor?" Mom asked sharply in a rare show of solidarity with Dad.

"Oh, he forgot once," Mémé said sourly.

"When I was six," Dad sighed.

"When he was six. I thought he'd at least make me a card, but, no. Nothing."

"Well, I thought we'd take you out to dinner on Friday," Dad said. "You, Nancy and me, the girls and their boys. What do you think? Does that sound nice?"

"Where would we go?"

"Somewhere fabulously expensive where you could complain all night long," Margaret said. "Your idea of heaven, right, Mémé?"

"Actually," I said on impulse, "I can't come. Wyatt's presenting a paper in New York, and I said I'd go down to the city with him. So sorry, Mémé. I hope you have a lovely night."

Granted, yes, I'd been planning to tell the family that Wyatt and I had parted ways—Natalie's wedding would demand attendance, and obviously Wyatt couldn't show, being imaginary and all. But the idea of spending a Friday night listening to Mémé detail her nasal polyps and having Mom and Dad indulge in their endless bickering, sitting in the glow of Andrew and Natalie while Margaret sniped at everyone...nope. Callahan O'Shea was right. I did a lot for my family. More than enough. Wyatt Dunn could give me one last excuse before, alas, we were forced to break up for good.

"But it's my birthday." Mémé frowned. "Cancel your plans."

"No," I said with a smile.

"In my day, people showed respect to their elders," she began.

"See, I was thinking the Inuit have it right," Margaret said. "The ice floe? What do you say, Mémé?"

I laughed, receiving a glare from my grandmother. "Hey, listen, I have to go. Papers to grade and all that. Love you guys. See you at home, Margs."

"Cheers, Grace," she said, toasting me with a knowing grin. "Hey, does Wyatt have a brother?"

I smiled, patted her shoulder and left.

When I pulled into my driveway ten minutes later, I looked over at Callahan's house. Maybe he was home. Maybe he'd want company. Maybe he'd almost kiss me again. Maybe there'd be no "almost" about it.

"Here goes nothing," I said, getting out of the car. Angus's sweet little head popped up in the window, and he began his yarping song of welcome. "One second, sweetie boy!" I called, then walked over to 36 Maple. Right up the path. Knocked on the door. Firmly. Waited.

There was no answer. I knocked again, my spirits slipping a notch. Glancing down the street, I noticed belatedly that Cal's truck wasn't there. With a sigh, I turned around and went home.

The truck wasn't there the next day, or the next. Not that I was spying, of course…just glancing out my window every ten minutes or so in great irritation, acknowledging the fact that…yikes…I missed him. Missed the joking, the knowing looks, the brawny arms. The tingling wave of desire that one look from Callahan O'Shea could incite. And God, when he touched my face that night on the roof, I'd felt like the most beautiful creature on earth.

So where was he, dang it? Why did it bug me so much that he'd gone off for a few days? Maybe he was back in an orange jumpsuit, stabbing trash on the side of the freeway, having broken parole somehow. Maybe he was a CIA mole and had been called up to serve, like Clive Owen's assassin character in *The Bourne Identity*. "Must go kill someone, dear…I'll be late for dinner!" Seemed to fit Callahan more than being an accountant, that's for sure.

Maybe—maybe he had a girlfriend. I didn't think so, but I just didn't know, did I?

On Friday night, tired of torturing myself about Callahan, I decided that going to Julian's singles' night with Kiki was a better way to spend my time than wondering where the hell Callahan O'Shea had gone. I was supposed to be in New York with Wyatt, and Margaret was growling in the kitchen, surrounded by piles of paper and an open bottle of wine, complaining about having to go to dinner with our family.

And so it was that at nine o'clock, instead of watching Mémé wrestle food past her hiatal hernia and listening to my parents snipe, I was instead dancing to Gloria Estefan at Jitterbug's singles' night. Dancing with Julian, dancing with Kiki, dancing with Cambry the waiter and having a blast.

There were no men here for me…Kiki had claimed the only reasonably attractive straight guy, and they seemed to be hitting it off. Apparently, Cambry had brought a lot of his friends, so aside from a scattering of middle-aged women (Julian's usual crowd for this event), the night had taken on a decidedly gay-man feel.

I didn't mind a bit. This only meant that the men danced well, dressed beautifully and flirted outrageously in one of the unfairnesses of life—gay men were generally better boyfriends than straight guys, except on the sex front, where things tended to fall apart. Still, I'd bet a gay boyfriend would at least tell me if he was going out of town for a few days. Not that Callahan was my boyfriend, of course.

I let the music push those thoughts away and found that after a while, I was twirling, laughing, showing off my dancing skills, being told I was *fabulous* again and again by Cambry's pals.

As the music pulsed in my ears and I salsa-stepped with one good-looking guy after another, I felt a warm wave of happiness. It was nice to be away from my family, nice not to be looking for love, nice to be just out having fun. Good old Wyatt Dunn. This last date was definitely our best.

When Julian went to the back to change the music, I followed him. "This is great!" I exclaimed. "Look at all the people here! You should make this a regular thing. Gay Singles' Night."

"I know," he said, grinning as he shuffled through his song list. "What should we do next? It's ten o'clock already. Man! The night has flown by. Maybe some slower stuff, what do you think?"

"Sounds good to me. I'm beat. This is quite a bit livelier than Dancin' with the Oldies. My feet are killing me." Julian grinned. He looked as ridiculously handsome as ever, but happier, too. The shadow that made him so tragically appealing seemed to have lifted. "How are things with Cambry?" I asked.

Julian blushed. "Fairly wonderful," he admitted shyly. "We've had two dates. I think we might kiss soon."

I patted my friend's arm. "I'm glad, honey," I told him. "You're not feeling...neglected?"

"No! I'm happy for you. It's been a long time coming."

"I know. And, Grace, you'll—" He looked up suddenly, his expression changed to one of horror. "Oh, no, Grace. Your mother's here."

"What?" I said, instantly imagining the worst. Mémé had died. Dad had a heart attack. Mom was tracking me down to break the news. *Please, not Nat or Margs,* I prayed.

"She's dancing," Julian said, craning his neck. "With one of Cambry's friends. Tom, I think."

"Dancing? Is my father here?" I stood behind Julian, peeping over his shoulder.

"I don't see him. Maybe she just...felt like dancing," he said. "Oh, she's coming our way. Hide, Grace! You're supposed to be in New York!"

I slipped into Julian's office before my mother could see me. Mature? No. But why ruin a happy night when good old hiding would do the trick? I pressed my ear against the door so I could hear.

"Hello, Nancy!" Julian's voice, purposefully loud, came to me easily. "How nice to see you!"

"Hello, Julian dear," Mom said. "Oh, isn't this fun! Now, I know I'm not single, but I just felt like dancing! Is that all right?"

"Of course!" Julian said heartily. "You'll leave a few broken hearts behind, but of course! Stay a while! Have fun! Shall we dance?"

"Actually, sweetheart, could I use your phone for one second?"

"My phone? In my office?" Julian practically yelled.

"Yes, dear. Is that all right?"

"Um, well, sure! Of course you can use the phone in my office!"

With that, I leaped away from the door, jerked open the closet door and popped in, closing the door behind me. Just in the nick of time.

"Thanks, Julian dear. Now you go! Shoo! Don't let me keep you from your guests."

"Sure, Nancy. Um, take your time." I heard the door close, smelled the leather from Julian's jacket. Heard the beeping of the phone as my mother called someone. Waited with thudding heart.

"The coast is clear," she murmured, then replaced the receiver.

The coast is clear? Clear for what? For whom? I was tempted to crack the closet door, but didn't want to give myself away. After all, not only was I *not* in New York City with my doctor boyfriend, but I was hiding in a closet, spying on my mother. The coast was clear. That did not sound good.

Crap. I knew things weren't great with my parents, but then again, that was the norm. Did Mom have someone on the side? Was she cheating on Dad? My poor father! Did he know?

Indecision kept me standing where I was, my throat tight, heart galloping. I realized I was gripping the sleeve of Julian's coat. *Calm down, Grace,* I urged myself. Maybe *the coast is clear* didn't sound quite as clandestine as I thought. Maybe Mom was talking about something else...

But, no. The office door opened again, then closed.

"I saw you dancing out there," came a man's gruff voice. "You're that sculptor, aren't you? Every man was watching you. Wanting you."

Okay, well, *that* statement wasn't true. I frowned. Every

man out there, save about two, was gay. If they were watching my mother, it was for fashion tips.

"Lock the door." Mom's voice was low.

My eyes widened in the dark closet. God's nightgown! I clenched the sleeve more tightly, my fingernails digging into the soft leather.

"You're so beautiful." The voice was hoarse...but familiar.

"Shut up and kiss me, big boy," Mom ordered. There was silence.

Cold with dread, I cracked the door the smallest fraction and took a peek. And just about peed my pants.

My parents were making out in Julian's office.

"What's your name?" my father asked, breaking off from the kiss and looking at Mom with smoky eyes.

"Does it matter?" Mom said. "Kiss me again. Make me feel like a woman should."

My astonishment turned to horror as dear old Dad grabbed my mother and kissed her sloppily...oh, God, there was tongue. I jerked back, shuddering, and closed the door as quietly as I could...not that it mattered, they were moaning rather loudly...and stuffed the jacket sleeve into my mouth to keep from screaming, a massive case of the heebie-jeebies rolling through me from head to toe. My parents. My parents were *role-playing*. And I was stuck in a closet.

"Oh, yes. More. Yes," my mother groaned.

"I want you. Since the moment I walked into this seedy little joint, I wanted you."

I jammed my fingers in my ears hard. *Dear God,* I prayed. *Please strike me deaf right now. Please? Pretty please?* I could, of course, just open the closet door and bust them. But then I'd have to explain what I was doing in there in the first place. Why I was hiding. Why I hadn't revealed myself sooner. And then I'd have to hear my parents explain what they were up to.

"Oh, yes, right there!" my mother crooned. My fingers weren't working, so I tried the heels of my hands. Alas, I could still hear a few words. "Lower...higher..."

"Ouch! My sciatica! Not so fast, Nancy!"

"Just stop talking and do it, handsome."

Oh, please, God. I'll become a nun. Really. Don't you need nuns? Make them stop. At the sound of another groan, I tried to go to my happy place...a meadow full of wildflowers, guns firing, cannons booming, Confederate and Yankee soldiers dropping like flies...but no.

"Oh, baby," my mother crooned.

I could not stay in here and listen to my parents doing the wild thing, but just as I was about to burst forth and stop them in the name of decency, my mother (or God) intervened.

"Not here, big boy. Let's get a room."

Thank you, Lord! Oh, and about that nun thing...how about a nice fat donation to Heifer International instead?

I waited a few more minutes, taking cleansing breaths, then risked another look. They were gone.

The door burst open and I flinched, but it was just Julian.

"Everything okay?" Julian exclaimed. "Did she find you? She didn't say a word, just scooted out the door." Julian took a better look at me. "Grace, you're white as a ghost! What happened?"

I made a strangled noise. "Um...you might want to burn that desk."

Then, eager to leave this office and never return, I sidled past him, waved to Kiki, who was still dancing with the straight guy, and headed for home. As I drove, shuddering, feeling that Satan had cigarette-burned a hole into my soul, there was part of me that was...*shudder*...quite happy that my parents...*gack*...could still get it on. That there was more than irritation and obligation driving their marriage, no matter how yucky it was for their child. I rolled down the window and took a few gulps of the clean spring air. Perhaps a strong dose of hypnotherapy could erase this night from my mind forever.

But yes. It was good to know that my parents still, er, loved each other.

Shudder. I pulled into my driveway.

Callahan's house was still dark.

CHAPTER TWENTY-TWO

THE NEXT DAY, I found myself once again sitting in the bosom of my family—Margs, Natalie and the sexpot formerly known as my mother were dress shopping at Birdie's Bridal.

Well, Mom and Natalie were dress shopping. Margaret and I were drinking strawberry margaritas from a thermos Margs had thoughtfully brought along as we sat in the dressing room, waiting for Natalie to emerge in another dress. Actually, dressing room was a misnomer. Dressing hall, really, because Birdie's had couches, an easy chair, coffee table and a huge, curtained area for the bride to try on dresses before coming out to dazzle her entourage.

"You've earned this," Margaret muttered, taking a slug herself straight from the thermos.

"I really have," I agreed. Mom and Nat were behind the curtain, Mom fussing away. "A little tuck in here, move your arm, honey, there…"

Mom seemed so normal today. I wondered if she was thinking about almost *shtupping* Dad at Jitterbug's last night. Blecch. Or perhaps she was remembering the day she and I went wedding dress shopping. Margaret had had a deposition, Nat was still at Stanford, so it was just Mom and me, and we'd had a lovely time. Granted, I bought the first dress I tried on…not really the princess bride–type, to be honest, and one white dress looked about as good as another. (I'd kind of been hoping for a hoop skirt, sort of like the one Ms. Mitchell described Scarlett wearing in Chapter Two of *Gone With the Wind,* but Mom's look of incredulity had squashed that one.) I barely remembered what my actual wedding dress really looked like, aside from being white and simple. I'd have to sell it on eBay. Wedding dress: Never been worn.

"Ooh, that one's pretty, too!" I chirped as Nat emerged from behind the curtain. She looked like a bride should... flushed, beaming, eyes sparkling, sweetly modest.

"The first one was better," Margaret said. "I don't like those froufrou things along the neckline."

"Froufrou's out," I seconded, taking another slug of my drink.

"I don't know," Natalie murmured, staring at herself. "I kind of like froufrou."

"It's nice froufrou," I amended hastily.

"You look beautiful," Mom announced staunchly. "You could wear a garbage bag and you'd look beautiful."

"Yes, Princess Natalie," Margaret said, rolling her eyes. "You could wear toad skins and you'd be beautiful."

"Sack cloth and ashes, I was thinking," I added, earning a gratifying snort from my older sister.

Nat grinned, but her eyes were distant. "I don't care what I wear. I just want to be married," she murmured.

"Blecch," said Margaret. I grinned.

"Of course you do," Mom said, patting her shoulder. "I felt the same way. So did Margaret."

"Did I?" Margaret mused.

Mom, belatedly aware that perhaps there were other feelings to be considered, glanced at me with a nervous smile. I smiled back. Once, yes, I'd felt that way about marriage. Once, being married to Andrew was all that I'd wanted, too. Nights of movies and Scrabble games, weekends spent antiquing or on the battlefield, leisurely sex on a bed strewn with sections of the *New York Times*. A couple of kids down the road. Long summers spent vacationing on Cape Cod or driving across country. Yadda yadda ding dong, blah blah blah.

And sitting here, admiring my sister, I could finally see that, even back then before Andrew's revelation, all those imaginings had felt a little...thin. I'd pictured that future with a determination that should've clued me in. It was all too good to be true.

"How was your overnight in the city, Grace?" Natalie asked, snapping out of her daze.

I glanced at Margaret, who'd been clued in before. "Well, I'm sorry to say that Wyatt and I are—" I paused for regretful effect "—taking a break."

"What?" Natalie and Mom chorused.

I sighed. "You know, he's such a great guy, but really, his work is just too demanding. I mean, you guys never even got to meet him, right? What does that say about the kind of husband he'd be?"

"Crappy," Margaret announced. "Plus, I never thought he was all that."

"Quiet, Margaret," Mom said, coming to sit at my side to administer a few maternal pats.

"Oh, Grace," Natalie said, biting her lip. "He sounded so wonderful. I—I thought you were madly in love. You were talking about getting married a little while ago!"

Margaret choked on her drink. "Well," I said, "I just don't want a husband who can't really, um, be devoted to the kids and me. You know. Running off all the time to the hospital was getting a little old."

"But he was saving children's lives, Grace!" Natalie protested.

"Mmm," I said, taking a sip of margarita. "True. Which

makes him a great doctor, but not necessarily a great husband."

"Maybe you're right, honey. Marriage is hard enough," Mom said. I forced myself not to picture last night, but of course, it was seared onto my eyelids, Mom and Dad... bleccch!

"How are you taking it, Grace?" Margaret asked, as she'd been instructed in the car ride here.

"You know, I'm actually fine with it," I answered blithely.

"You're not heartbroken?" Natalie asked, kneeling in front of me, a vision in her white dress.

"No. Not even a little. It's for the best. And I think we'll stay friends," I said, getting an elbow in the ribs from Margaret. "Or not. He might be transferring to Chicago. So we'll see. Mom, how's your art coming along?" A subject guaranteed to take the focus off my love life.

"It's getting a little dull," Mom said. "I'm thinking of going male. I'm tired of all those labias and ovaries. Maybe it's time for a good old-fashioned penis."

"Why not flowers, Mom? Or bunnies or butterflies? Does it have to be genitalia?" Margs asked.

"How are we doing in here?" Birdie of Birdie's Bridal bustled in holding another dress. "Oh, Natalie, honey, you look dazzling! Like an ad in a magazine! Like a movie star! A princess!"

"Don't forget Greek goddess," Margaret added.

"Aphrodite, rising from the waves," Birdie agreed.

"That would be Venus," I said.

"Oh, Faith, here's your dress," Birdie said, handing me a rose-colored, floor length dress.

"It's Grace. My name is Grace."

"Try it on, try it on!" Nat said, clapping her hands. "That color will be gorgeous on you, Grace!"

"Yes, maid of honor. Your turn to be super special," Margaret growled.

"Oh, get over it," I said, rising from the couch. "Try on your dress, Margaret, and behave."

"Yours is right here," Natalie said, swatting Margaret on the head. Birdie handed Margs a dress a few shades paler than mine, and Margaret and I went into separate dressing rooms to try our garments on.

Behind the curtain I went. I hung the dress on a hook, slid out of my jeans and T-shirt, glad for the new bra and panties set that kept me from feeling like a total slob. I slipped the dress over my head, freed my hair from the zipper and managed to rescue my left breast from where it got stuck in the bodice. There. A tug here, a push there, and I was zipped.

"Come on, let's see!" Natalie called impatiently.

"Ta-da!" I said gamely, coming out to join my sisters.

"Oh! Gorgeous! That is really your color!" Nat cried, clapping her hands. She'd put on another wedding dress, a shimmering white silk creation with a demure neckline, a snug bodice that glistened with beads and huge, puffy skirt. Margaret, fast and efficient at everything she did, was already waiting, looking sulky and gorgeous in her pale pink.

"Come on, Grace," Mom said. "Stand with your sisters and let's see how you look."

I obeyed. Stood on the little dais next to cool, blond, elegant Natalie Rose. On Nat's other side was Margaret, her reddish gold hair sleekly cut into a stylish bob, sharply attractive, thin as a greyhound, cheekbones to die for. My sisters were, simply put, beautiful. Stunning, even.

And then there was me. I noticed that my dark hair hadn't taken kindly to the weather today and was doing its wild-animal thing again. A few dark circles lurked under my eyes. (Who could sleep after Mom and Dad's foreplay?) In the past few months, I'd managed to gain weight in my upper arms, courtesy of all that quality time with Ben & Jerry's. Based on the one picture we had of her, I looked like my great-grandmother on my mother's side, who'd immigrated from Kiev.

"I look like Great-Grandma Zladova," I commented.

Mom's head jerked back. "I always wondered where you got that hair," she murmured in wonder.

"You do not," Natalie said staunchly.

"Wasn't she a washerwoman?" Margaret asked.

I rolled my eyes. "Great. Nat is Cinderella, Margaret is Nicole Kidman, and I'm Grandma Zladova, laundress to the czars."

Ten minutes later, Birdie was completing the sale, Mom was fussing over headpieces, Margaret was checking her BlackBerry, and I needed a little air. "I'll meet you outside, Nat," I said.

"Grace?" Natalie put her hand on my arm. "I'm sorry about Wyatt."

"Oh," I said. "Well, thanks."

"You'll find someone," she murmured. "The right one will come along. It'll be your turn soon."

The words felt like a slap. No, more than the words was… damn it, my eyes were stinging…the pity. In all the time since Andrew and I broke up, Natalie had felt sympathy, and guilt, and a whole lot of other feelings, no doubt, but she'd never *pitied* me. No. My younger sister had always, *always* looked up to me, even when my chips were down. Never before had she given me the kind of look I was getting now. I was Poor Grace once more.

"Maybe I'll never meet someone," I said tartly. "But hey. You and Andrew could use me as a nanny, right?"

She blanched. "Grace…I didn't mean it like that."

"Sure," I said quickly. "I know. But you know, Nat, me

being single isn't the worst thing in the world. It's not like I lost a limb."

"Oh, no! Of course not. I know." She smiled uncertainly.

I took a deep breath. "I...I'll be outside," I said.

"Okay," she chirped. "Meet you at the car," she said, then went back to our mother and her wedding dress.

When I got home from dress shopping, I was limp from the effort of all that damn fun. Dinner and drinks had followed the dress shopping, full of good cheer and talk of the wedding. We were joined by a few other female relatives—Mom's sisters and, alas, Cousin Kitty, Queen of the Newlyweds, who gushed and beamed about how wonderful it was to be married. For the third time, that was...numbers one and two hadn't been so great, but that was in the past, of course, and now Kitty was an expert on Happily Ever After.

In just a few weeks, Andrew and Natalie would be husband and wife. I couldn't wait. Seriously, I just wanted to be done with it. Then, finally, it'd seem like a new chapter of my life could start.

Angus clawed at the kitchen door to be let out. It was raining now, thunder rumbling distantly in the east. Angus wasn't one of those dogs who feared storms—he had the heart of a lion, my little guy—but he didn't like being rained on. "Come back soon," I said.

The minute I opened the door, I saw the dark shape against the fence at the end of my property. Lightning flashed. A skunk...damn it! I lunged after my dog. "No, Angus! Come here, boy!"

But it was too late. My dog, a blur of white ferocity, streaked across the backyard. Another flash of lightning showed me that the animal was a raccoon. It looked up in alarm, then was gone, under the fence in a hole that Angus had probably dug. A raccoon could do serious damage to my little dog, who wasn't smart enough to know better. "Angus! Come! Come, boy!" It was no use. Angus rarely obeyed when in pursuit of another animal, and just like that, he, too, was gone, under the fence, after the raccoon.

"Damn it!" I cursed. Turning around, I ran back into the house, grabbed a flashlight then ran back outside, into Callahan's yard to avoid having to climb over the back fence in my own yard.

"Grace? Everything okay?" The back porch light came on. He was back.

"Angus is chasing a raccoon," I blurted, running past the deck without stopping, tearing down Cal's yard to the woods, my breath coming in gasps already. Visions of my adorable little dog with his eye torn out, with slash marks down his back, blood staining his white fur… Raccoons were fierce, and this one could very well tear up my little dog. It had looked much bigger than Angus.

"Angus!" I called, my voice high with fear. "Cookie, Angus! Cookie!"

My flashlight illuminated the raindrops and dripping branches of the state forest. As I crashed forward, twigs snapping in my face, a new fear lanced my stomach. The river. The Farmington River was a hundred yards away, full and dark from the spring rains and snow melt. It was more than strong enough to sweep away a small and not-very-bright dog.

Another light flashed next to mine. Callahan, wearing a slicker and Yankees cap, had caught up.

"Which way did he go?" he asked.

"Oh, Callahan, thank you," I panted. "I don't know. He went under the fence. He tunnels. I usually fill them in, but this time…I…I…" Sobs ratcheted out of me.

"Hey, come on. We'll find him. Don't worry, Grace." Callahan slipped his arm around my shoulder, gave me a quick squeeze, then aimed his light overhead into the canopy branches.

"I don't think he can climb, Cal," I said wetly, rain and tears mixing on my face as I looked up.

Cal smiled. "The raccoon can, though. Maybe Angus treed him. If we find the raccoon, maybe we'll find your little dog."

Smart idea, but after five minutes of shining our flashlights into the branches, we had found neither the raccoon nor my dog. There was no sign of him, not that I was a tracker or anything. We were closer to the river now. That which had once sounded sweet and comforting now sounded menacing and cruel...the uncaring river rushing past, carrying anything along with it.

"So where have you been the past few days?" I asked Callahan, shining my light under a fallen branch. No Angus.

"Becky needed me to do a quick job down in Stamford," he answered.

"Who's Becky?"

"The blonde from the bar. She's an old friend from high school. Works in real estate. That's how I found this house."

"You could've let me know you were going out of town," I said, glancing at him. "I was worried."

He smiled. "Next time I will."

I called Angus again, whistled, clapped my hands. Nothing.

Then I heard a distant, sharp bark, followed by a yelp, that sickening surprised cry of pain. "Angus! Angus, buddy, where are you?" I called, tripping forward toward the direction of the cry. It came from upriver. In the river? I couldn't tell.

It was hard to hear over the noise of the rain and flowing water. Images of Angus when I first bought him, a tiny ball of shivering, coconutty fluff...his bright eyes staring at me each morning, willing me to wake up...his funny little Super Dog pose...the way he slept on his back with his paws in the air, his crooked little bottom teeth showing. I was crying harder now. "Angus!" I kept calling, my voice harsh and scared.

We came to the edge of the river. Usually I thought it so beautiful, the rushing, silken water, the stones beneath, the flashes of white where the current collided with a rock or branch. Tonight, it was sinister and dark as a black snake. I guided my beam over the water, dreading the sight of a little white body being swept along.

"Oh, shit," I sobbed.

"He probably wouldn't go in," Cal said soothingly, taking my hand. "He's dumb, but he's got some instincts, right? He wouldn't drown himself."

"You don't know Angus," I wept. "He's stubborn. When he wants something he just doesn't stop."

"Well, if he's chasing the raccoon, the raccoon would have enough sense, then," Cal said. "Come on. Let's keep looking."

We walked along the river, through the woods, farther and farther away from home, calling my dog's name, promising treats. There were no more yelps, just the sound of the rain hissing through the leaves. I didn't have socks on, and my feet were freezing inside my plastic gardening clogs, which were covered in mud. This was all my fault. He dug all the time. I knew this. Usually, I checked the fence line on weekends for just this reason. Today, I hadn't. Today, I'd been dress shopping with stupid Natalie.

I didn't want to picture life without my dog. Angus who

slept on my bed after Andrew left me. Angus who needed me, waited for me, whose little head popped up in the living-room window each and every time I came home, overjoyed at the miracle of my very being. I'd lost him. I should've filled in that stupid hole, and I didn't, and now he was gone.

I sucked in a ragged breath, tears, hot and endless, cutting down my rain-soaked face.

"There he is," Cal said, shining his light.

He was right. About thirty yards west of the river, Angus stood next to a small house that, like mine, backed up to the state forest. He was sniffing a tipped over garbage can and looked up at the sound of my voice. His tail wagged, he barked once, then went back to investigating the trash.

"Angus!" I cried, lurching up the slight hill that separated me from my dog. "Good puppy! Good boy! You worried Mommy! Yes, you did!" He wagged his tail in agreement, barked again, and then I had him. Gathering my dog in my arms, I kissed his soggy little head over and over, tears dropping into his fur as he wriggled and nipped me in delight.

"There you go, then," Cal said, coming up behind me. He was smiling. I tried to smile back, but my mouth was doing that wobbling contortion thing, so I didn't quite pull it off.

"Thank you," I managed. Callahan reached out to pet Angus, who suddenly realized that his nemesis was there, turned his little head and snapped.

"Ingrate," Cal said, giving my dog a mock scowl. He bent down and scooped the trash back into the garbage can, then set it aright.

"You've been really great," I said shakily, clutching my dog against my chest.

"Don't sound so surprised," Cal returned.

We walked down the driveway of the house to the street.

I recognized the neighborhood—it was about half a mile from Maple Street, a bit posher than where Cal and I lived. The rain gentled, and Angus snuggled up on my shoulder, doing his baby impression, cheek against my neck, front paws on my shoulder. I stretched my jacket around his little body and thanked the powers that be for the safety of my dopey little dog, whom I loved more than was probably advisable.

The powers that be, and Callahan O'Shea. He came with me on this cool, rainy night and didn't leave till we found my dog. Said nothing irritating like, "Oh, he'll come back." Nope. Callahan had stuck with me, reassured me, comforted me. Picked up trash for me. I wanted to say something, though I wasn't sure what, but when I glanced at my strong, solid neighbor, my face burned hot enough to power a small city.

We turned onto Maple Street, and the lights of my house glowed. I glanced down. Cal and I were covered in mud from our feet to our knees, and soaked to the skin. Angus resembled a mop more than a dog, his fur soaked and matted.

Cal noticed my glance. "Why don't you come over to my house?" he suggested. "We can get washed up there. Your house is kind of a museum, isn't it?"

"Well, not really a museum," I said. "It's just tidy."

"Tidy. Sure. Well, want to come over? It won't matter if we get my kitchen dirty. I'm still working on it."

"Sure. Thanks," I said. I had been wondering about the house, what it was like inside, what Callahan had been doing. "How's that been going, anyway? You flipping the house and all?"

"It's going fine. Come in. I'll give you a tour," he offered, reading my mind.

Cal let me in the back door.

"I'll get a couple towels," he said, taking off his work boots and disappearing into another room. Angus, still on my shoulder, gave a little snore, making me smile. I slipped off my filthy gardening clogs, pushed my hair out of my face with one hand and took a look around.

Cal's kitchen was nearly done. A trestle table with three mismatched chairs overlooked a new bay window. The kitchen cabinets were maple with glass panes, and the counters were made from gray soapstone. Spaces gapped where the appliances would go, though there was a two-burner stove and a dorm-size fridge. I should definitely invite him over for dinner, I thought. Seeing as he was so nice to me. Seeing as he'd held my hand. Seeing as I had the hots for him and couldn't seem to remember the reasons that I'd once thought Callahan O'Shea made a bad choice.

Cal came back into the room. "Here," he said, taking my sleeping pooch from me and wrapping him in a big towel. He rubbed the dog's fur, causing Angus to blink sleepily at the strange man holding him. "No biting," Cal warned. Angus wagged his tail. Cal smiled.

Then he kissed my dog on the head.

That was it. Without even quite realizing that I'd moved, I found that my arms were somehow around Callahan's neck, that I'd knocked off his Yankees cap, that my fingers were in his wet hair, that I was squishing Angus and that I was kissing Callahan O'Shea. Finally.

"It's about time," he muttered against my mouth. Then he was kissing me back.

CHAPTER TWENTY-THREE

His mouth was hot and soft and hard at the same time, and he was so solid and warm, and he was licking my chin while he kissed me…or no, wait. That was Angus, and Callahan laughed, a low, scraping laugh. "Okay, okay, hang on," Cal murmured, pulling back. One of his hands held Angus, the other cupped the back of my head. Oh, crap, my hair. The man could lose a finger in there. But he gently disentangled himself, then set my damp little dog on the floor and straightened up, looking at me in the eyes. Angus yarped once, and then he must've run off somewhere, because I heard his toenails clicking away. But I wasn't looking at anything except the man in front of me. His lovely, utterly kissable mouth, the slight scrape of razor stubble, those downward slanting, dark blue eyes.

Now those were eyes I could look into for a long, long time, I thought. The heat of him shimmered out to me, beckoning, and my lips parted.

"Want to stay over?" he asked, breathing hard.

"Sure!" I squeaked.

And then we were kissing again. His mouth was hot and fierce on mine, my hands clenched his hair. His arms went around me, crushing me against him, and God, he felt good, so big and safe and a little scary at the same time, so masculine and hard. And his mouth, oh, Lord, the man knew how to kiss, he kissed me like I was the water at the end of a long stretch of burning sand. I felt the wall against my back, felt his weight pressing against me, and then his hands were under my wet shirt, burning the damp skin of my waist, my ribs. I tugged his shirt out of his jeans and slid my hands across the hot skin of his back, my knees practically buckling as his mouth moved to my neck. Then his hand moved a little higher and my knees did buckle, but he held me against the wall and kept kissing me, my neck, my mouth. All that time in prison must have made Callahan O'Shea a little desperate, and the fact that he was with *me*, kissing *me*...it was overwhelming. A man like this. With me.

"You sure about this?" he asked, pulling back, his eyes dark and his cheeks flushed. I nodded, and just like that, he kissed me again and lifted me, his hands cupping my ass, and carried me into another room. One with a bed, thank God. Then Angus yarped and jumped against us, and Callahan laughed. Without putting me down, he gently shoved my dog out with his foot and closed the door with his shoulder.

So it was just the two of us. Outside the room, Angus whined and scratched wildly. Cal didn't seem to notice, just set me down, slid his hands up my face and stepped closer, erasing the space between us.

"He's going to ruin that door," I whispered as Cal nuzzled my neck.

"I don't care," he muttered. Then Callahan O'Shea pulled my shirt over my head and I stopped worrying about my dog.

Whatever urgency he'd felt before seemed to melt, and suddenly things moved in slow motion. His hands were so hot on my skin, and he bent to kiss my shoulder, sliding the strap of my camisole down, his five o'clock shadow scraping the tender skin there, his mouth hot and silky smooth. His own skin was like velvet, his hard muscles sliding underneath with hypnotic power.

Without me quite realizing that we'd moved, I found that we'd made it to the bed, because he was pulling me down with him, smiling that wicked, slow smile that caught me in the stomach. Then his hand moved to the waistband of my jeans, playing there before cleverly undoing the button. He kissed me again, hot and slow and lazy, and then he rolled over so I was on top of him, his big muscular arms around me, and I kissed that smiling mouth, slid my tongue against his. God, he tasted so good, I just couldn't believe he'd been living next door to me for all these long, lonely weeks when there was this kind of kissing waiting for me. I heard him groan deep in his throat as he wove his fingers into my wet hair, and I pulled back to see his face.

"About time," he whispered again, and after that, there was no more talking.

AN HOUR LATER, MY LIMBS were filled with that almost-forgotten, heavy sweetness. I lay on my side, my head on Callahan's shoulder, his arm around me. I sneaked a peek at his face. His eyes were closed, those long, straight lashes brushing the tops of his cheeks. He was smiling. Possibly asleep, but smiling.

"What are you looking at?" he murmured, not opening his eyes. Not sleeping, but apparently omniscient.

"You're pretty gorgeous, Irish," I said.

"Would it break your heart to hear that I'm actually Scottish?"

"Not if it means I can see you in a kilt." I grinned. "Plus, then you're related to Angus."

"Great," he said, still smiling. My heart expanded almost painfully. Callahan O'Shea. I was in bed, naked, with Callahan O'Shea. Pretty damn nice.

"Scottish, hmm?" I asked, tracing a line on his shoulder.

"Mmm-hmm. Well, Pop's Scottish. My father was Irish, I guess. Hence the mick name." He opened his eyes like a lazy dragon and grinned. "Any other questions at the moment?"

"Um, well…where's the bathroom, Cal?" I asked. Not exactly the most romantic thing, but nature was calling.

"Second door on the left," he said. "Don't be long."

I grabbed the afghan that had been neatly folded at the bottom of the bed and ventured into the hall, wrapping myself in the blanket as I went. There was Angus, asleep on his back in front of the fireplace in the living room, which was illuminated only by the kitchen lights spilling in. My dog was snoring. Good boy.

In the bathroom, I flicked on the light and blinked, then winced as I saw my reflection. Jeez Louise! A streak of mud lined my jaw, my forehead bore a red stripe from the twig that had caught me in the face, and my hair…my hair…it looked more like wool than hair. Rolling my eyes, I finger-combed it a bit, wet it down on the left side, took care of business and washed my hands. Noticed that my feet were rather dirty. Washed those, one at a time, in the sink.

"What are you doing in there?" Cal called. "Stop rifling through my medicine cabinet and get back to bed, woman!"

The mirror showed my grin. My cheeks glowed. I rewrapped the afghan around my shoulders—modesty, you know?—and walked back down the hall to Callahan's room. At the sight of me, he lurched abruptly into a sitting position.

"It's the rain," I said, running a hand over my hair. "It goes a little crazy in the rain."

But he simply looked at me. "You're so beautiful, Grace," he said, and that pretty much sealed the deal.

I was rather crazy about Callahan O'Shea.

THE NEXT MORNING, I opened one eye. The clock on the night table read 6:37 a.m. Callahan was asleep next to me.

It took a minute for that to sink in, and as it did, I felt a glow in my chest. Callahan O'Shea was sleeping next to me. After shagging me. Three times. Ahem! And quite fabulously, I might add. So much so that the second time, I'd awakened Angus, who then tried to tunnel under the bedroom door to ascertain why his mistress was making all that noise.

Not only that, it was…fun. Hot and steamy, yes, that I'd expected from a guy like Callahan O'Shea. But maybe I hadn't expected that he'd make me laugh. Or to tell me how soft my skin was, his voice in a tone of near wonder. When I woke up somewhere around 3:00 a.m., he'd been looking at me, smiling like I was Christmas morning.

"Hey, Cal?" I whispered. He didn't move. "Callahan?" I kissed his shoulder. He smelled *so* good. God, three times last night, you'd think I'd have had enough. "Hey, gorgeous. I have to go." I thought about adding *honey,* but that felt a little… sweet. Bub, maybe. Not honey. Not yet. "Wake up, bub."

Nope. Nothing. I'd worn him out, poor lad.

I realized I was grinning. Ear to ear. Maybe humming a bit. Felt a little Cole Porter coming on. With one more kiss and one more look at the beautiful Callahan O'Shea, I slipped out of the warm bed and tiptoed out of the room, gathering my mud-stained clothes as I went. Angus bounced up in the living room the minute he saw me. "Shh," I whispered. "Uncle Cal's still sleeping."

Taking a quick look around the living room, I could see

that Callahan had been hard at work. The floors still held the faint bite of polyurethane, and the walls were painted a pale gray. Planks of some sort were piled in the corner, and beveled wooden trim framed two of the four living room windows.

It was a lovely home, or it would be when he was finished. The fireplace tiles were painted blue, and though the stairs leading to the second floor had no railing, they were wide and welcoming. It was the kind of home that had been carefully built, with surprising little windows with deep sills, crown molding and a pattern inset in the oak floors. The kind of house that just wasn't made anymore.

Angus whined. "Okay, boy," I whispered. In the kitchen, I found a pen and piece of paper by the phone. "Dear Mr. O'Shea," I wrote.

Thank you ever so much for your kind assistance in helping me find my beloved Angus last night. I trust you slept well. I have the unfortunate duty of fighting off the Yankee hordes this morning at Chancellorsville (also known as Haddam Meadows on Route 154 just off of Route 9, should you be interested in watching us drive back the Northern aggressors). Should I survive unscathed, I very much hope that our paths will cross again in the near future. Very best wishes, Grace Emerson (Miss).

Dumb or cute? I decided it was cute and tucked it by the phone. Then I took one more peek at the gorgeous sleeping man, picked up Angus and let myself out. My dog needed a bath, and so did I.

CHAPTER TWENTY-FOUR

"THIS WAY, FIRST VIRGINIA!" I called, safely aboard Snowlight. Granted, the fat little white pony was not exactly a warrior steed, but he was better than nothing.

Margaret trotted up to my side. "I really need to stop doing this," she said, pulling at the corner of her wool uniform. "I'm dying here."

"Actually, you're supposed to die over there, by the river," I corrected.

"I can't believe this is your social life," she said.

"Yet here you are, tagging along." I turned toward my troops. "'Who could not conquer, with troops such as these?'" I quoted loudly. My soldiers cheered.

"So you went to bed early last night," Margs commented. "Lights out, Angus quiet, and it was only 9:30 p.m. when Mom dropped me off."

"Yup. Early to bed, early to rise," I said, my face prickling with telltale heat. Margs had found me this morning in the kitchen, hair wrapped in a towel, red bathrobe firmly cinched, very proper. She'd driven down to the battlefield herself, since she had a deposition in Middletown at two, so I hadn't had the chance to tell her of recent developments with Hottie the Hunk Next Door.

"Hey, I met a guy in court and thought you might want his number," Margaret said, aiming her rifle at a Union soldier.

"Oh, wait, don't fire," I said. "Snowlight will fall asleep if you do. He has narcolepsy." I patted the pony's neck fondly.

"Gentle Jesus of the three iron nails, Grace," Margs muttered. She pointed her gun at the soldier and said, without much conviction, "Bang." The soldier, well aware of my steed's shortcomings, fell with obliging dramatics, clawed the ground for a few seconds, then lay tragically still. "So, should I have him call you?"

"Well, actually, I don't think I'll be needing anyone's number," I said.

"Why?" Margs asked. "Did you find someone?"

I looked at her and smiled. "Callahan O'Shea."

"Holy shit," she yelped, her face incredulous. At that moment, Grady Jones, a pharmacist by day, fired a cannon from fifty yards away, and Margaret dropped dutifully to the ground. "You slept with him!" she exclaimed. "With Callahan, didn't you?"

"A little quieter, please, Margaret, you're supposed to be dead, okay?" I dismounted from Snowlight and gave him a carrot from my pocket, stalling so I could talk to my sister. "And, yes, I did. Last night."

"Oh, shit."

"What?" I asked. "What about 'Grace, you deserve some fun'?"

Margaret adjusted her rifle so she wasn't lying on it. "Grace, here's the thing. You do deserve fun. You definitely do. And Callahan is probably a tremendous amount of fun."

"He is. So what's the problem?"

"Well, fun's not really what you're looking for, is it?"

"Yes! It...well, what do you mean?"

"You. You're looking for happily ever after. Not a fling."

"Quiet down! You're supposed to be dead!" snapped a passing Union soldier.

"This is a private conversation," Margaret snapped back.

"This is a battle," he hissed.

"No, honey, this is called *pretending*. I hate to break it to you, but we're not really in the Civil War. If you'd like to feel a bit more authentic, I'd be happy to stick this bayonet up your ass."

"Margaret! Stop. He's right. Sorry," I said to the Union soldier. Luckily, I didn't know him. He shook his head and continued, only to be shot a few yards later.

I looked back down at my sister, who had draped her arm across her face to shield her eyes from the sun. "About Callahan, Margs. He happens to be looking for the whole shmere, too. Marriage, a couple of kids, a lawn to mow. He said so."

Margaret nodded. "Well. Good for him." She was quiet for a minute. Shots rang in the distance, a few cries. In another minute, I'd have to remount Snowlight, join a reconnaissance party and catch a little friendly fire in the arm, resulting in a gruesome amputation and my eventual death, but I lingered a little longer, the sun beating on my head, the sharp, sweet scent of grass rising all around us.

"One more thing, Gracie." Margaret paused. "Did Callahan ever tell you exactly what happened with his embezzlement?"

"No," I admitted. "I've asked once or twice, but he hasn't told me."

"Ask again," she advised.

"Do you know?" I asked.

"I know a little. I did some digging."

"And?" I demanded.

"He ever mention a brother to you?" Margaret asked, sitting up and squinting at me.

"Yes. They're estranged."

Margaret nodded. "I bet they are. It seems the brother was the president of the company Cal embezzled from."

God's nightgown! I guess my stupefaction showed, because Margaret reached out to pat my shin. "Ask, Grace. I bet he'll come clean now, since you're bumping uglies and all."

"Such a way with words. No wonder juries love you," I murmured automatically.

"General Jackson! Your opinion is required over here!" called my father, and so I remounted and left my sister to nap in the grass.

For the rest of the battle, my mind fretted over Margaret's little bombshell, and though I went through the motions, being Stonewall Jackson was a bit wasted on me this day. When I finally took the bullet, taking care to slide off Snowlight as he fainted from fear at the barrage of blanks, I was relieved. I uttered the General's poetic last words... "'Let us cross over the river and rest in the shade of the trees,'" and our battle was over. Granted, it actually took Stonewall Jackson eight days to die, but even Brother Against Brother wasn't willing to spend a week reliving the deathwatch.

BY THE TIME I CAME HOME, it was almost five o'clock. It felt like I'd been away from home for days, not hours. Of course, last night, I'd been at Callahan's. The very thought weakened the old knees, and a pleasant tightness squeezed my chest. But now, mingling with that was knowledge that it was time for Cal to tell me about his past.

First, though, I had a dog to worship, a dog who was leaping repeatedly at my side, barking to remind me just who my true love was supposed to be. I apologized profusely to Angus for my absence (despite the fact that my mother had come by and fed him hamburger meat, taken him for a walk, brushed him and given him a new and very jaunty red bandana). Grand-maternal devotion apparently not enough,

Angus had chewed up a slipper to punish me for my absence. He was a bad doggy, but I didn't have the heart to say so, him being so dang adorable and all.

A hard knock came at the front door. "Coming!" I said.

Callahan O'Shea stood on my front porch, hands on his hips, looking mad as hell.

"Hi," I said, blushing in spite of his expression. His neck was beautiful, tanned to the color of caramel, just waiting to be tasted.

"Where the hell have you been?" he barked.

"I—I was at a battle," I said. "I left you a note."

"I didn't get a note," he said.

"I left it by the phone," I replied, raising my eyebrows. He scowled, quite steamed, apparently. It was rather adorable.

"Well, what did it say?" he demanded.

"It said…well, you'll read it when you get home," I said.

"Was this a one-night stand, Grace?" His voice was irritable and hard.

I rolled my eyes. "Come in, Cal," I said, tugging his hand. "I wanted to talk to you anyway, but, no, this wasn't a one-night stand. God's nightgown! What kind of girl do you think I am, huh? First things first, though. I'm starving. You want to order a pizza?"

"No. I want to know why I woke up alone."

He sounded so mad and sullen and adorable that I couldn't suppress a smile. "I tried to wake you, bub. You were out cold." He narrowed his eyes. "Look, if you want me to go over and show you the note, I'll be happy to."

"No. It's fine." He didn't smile.

"Fine, huh?"

"Well, no, Grace, it's not fine. I stomped around all day, not knowing where you were. I practically scared your mother to death when I came over, and she wouldn't unlock the door to talk to me, and, yes, I'm in a pretty crappy mood."

"Because you didn't find the note, Grumpy. Which was very cute, if I do say so, and gave no indication of a one-night stand. Now how about that pizza, or should I chew off my own arm? I'm starving."

"I'll cook," he grunted, still glaring.

"I thought you were mad at me," I reminded him.

"I didn't say it would be good." Then he wrapped his arms around me, lifting me so my toes were off the ground, and kissed the stuffing out of me.

"Dinner can wait," I breathed.

Oh, it wasn't the smartest thing to do, given that we had Things To Discuss, but come on! Those soft blue eyes, that tousled hair... Did I mention he carried me? All the way up the stairs, over his shoulder, caveman style? And he wasn't even out of breath at the top? Come on! And God, the way he kissed me, urgent, hungry kisses that melted my bones and heated my core to the point that I didn't even notice Angus chewing on Cal's leg until he started laughing against my mouth, then grabbed Angus and put him out in the hall, where my little dog barked twice before trotting off to destroy something else.

Looking at Callahan there, leaning against my bedroom door, his shirt unbuttoned, his eyes heavy-lidded and hot... well, I almost didn't need the sex, if I could just stare at him, that little smile finally playing at the corner of his mouth... Actually, what was I saying? I *did* need the sex. No point in wasting a man who looked at me like that.

Margaret was sitting on the chaise lounge on the patio when we came downstairs a good while later. Angus lay sprawled on her lap, groaning occasionally as she stroked his fur.

"I heard zoo noises," Margs called, turning her head as we entered the kitchen. "Figured it was safer to stay outside."

"Want a glass of wine, Margaret?" I asked.

"Sure," she said listlessly.

Callahan did the honors, opening the fridge as if he lived there and getting out a bottle of chardonnay. "This okay?" he asked.

"That's great," I said, handing him the corkscrew. "Thanks, bub. And not just for uncorking the wine."

He grinned. "You're very welcome. To all my skills. Want me to cook something?"

"Yes, I do," I said. "Margs, you want to eat with us?"

"No, thanks. The pheromones alone in there would choke me."

I opened the screen door and sat next to my sister, sliding my bare feet against the brick of the patio. "Everything all right, Margaret?" I asked.

"Stuart's on a date," she announced. "With your coworker, Eva or Ava or some other sex-kitten, porn-star name."

My mouth dropped open. "Oh, Margs. Are you sure it's a date?"

"Well, he's having dinner with her, and he took great pains to remind me who she was." Her voice deepened to impersonate Stuart's formal voice. "'You remember, Margaret. Rather attractive, teaches history with Grace...' Asshole." Margaret's mouth gave a telltale wobble.

"You know, she might just be trying to butter him up for his support on her being chairman of our department," I suggested. "She must know he's friends with the headmaster."

"He wouldn't go against you, Grace," she replied.

"I'm harboring his wife. He might," I said. She didn't say anything else. I glanced at Callahan through the screen door. He was chopping something at the counter, and he looked so *right* there that it made me a little dizzy. Then I immediately felt a pang of guilt for feeling so happy when Margaret was suffering.

"Margaret," I said slowly, turning back to my sister, who was staring at her knees, "maybe it's time for you to go back to Stuart. Get some counseling and all that. Things aren't getting any better with you staying here."

"Right," she said. "Except it would look like I'm crawling back because I'm jealous, which is true, now that I think of it, and I don't want to give him the satisfaction of thinking that if he's going to cheat on me, I'll come to heel like some trick dog." Angus barked in solidarity. "If he wants me back, he should bloody well do something!" She paused. "Other than screwing another woman," she added.

"What can I do?" I asked.

"Nothing. Listen, I'm going down cellar, okay? To watch one of your geeky movies or something, is that all right?"

"Sure," I said. "Um, I might stay over at Cal's tonight."

"Okay. See you later." She got up, gave my shoulder a squeeze and went into the kitchen. "Listen, Shawshank, you need to talk to my sister about your sordid past. Okay? Have fun." She took her glass of wine and disappeared down cellar.

I sat alone on the patio, listening to the birds begin their evening chorus. The peace of the season, the smell of freshly cut grass, the gentling sky made me so happy. From the kitchen came the sounds of Callahan cooking, the hiss of something in the frying pan, the cheerful clatter of plates. I felt such a surge of…well, it was too early to say *love,* but you know. Contentment. Pure, underrated contentment. Angus licked my ankle as if he understood.

Cal opened the door and brought out our plates, setting one in my lap. An omelet and whole wheat toast. Perfect. He sat down in the chair vacated by Margaret and took a bite of toast. "So. My sordid past," he said.

"Maybe I should know what you did that landed you in prison."

"Right," he answered tightly. "You should know. You eat, I'll talk."

"I just think I should hear it from you, Cal. Margaret knows—"

"Grace, I was planning to tell you today, okay? That's why I was ticked when you weren't around. So eat."

Obediently, I took a bite of the omelet, which was hot and fluffy and utterly delicious. Giving him what I hoped was an encouraging smile, I waited.

Cal put his plate down and turned his chair so it faced me better. He sat leaning slightly forward, his big hands clasped loosely in front of him, and stared at me for a minute, which made chewing a bit awkward. Then he sighed and looked down.

"I didn't exactly embezzle the money. But I knew about it, I didn't report the person who did embezzle it, and I helped it stay hidden."

"Well, then, who took it?" I asked.

"My brother."

I nearly choked. "Oh," I whispered.

For the next half hour, Callahan told me a pretty fascinating story. How he and his brother, Pete, owned a large construction company. About Hurricane Katrina and an endless supply of reconstruction the government was paying for. About the frenetic nature of the business, the orders that went missing, the insurance claims, the criminal underbelly of New Orleans. And then, one night, how he found a Cayman Islands account under his own name with $1.6 million in it.

"Holy crap, Cal," I breathed.

He didn't answer, just nodded.

"What did you do?"

"Well, it was four in the morning, and I was fairly stunned, seeing my own name there on the computer screen. I was afraid to look away, too, thinking my brother—because it couldn't have been anyone but him—that he might move the money. Or spend it. God, I don't know. So I opened another account and transferred the whole amount."

"Aren't those accounts password protected and all that?" I asked. (I did read John Grisham, after all.)

"Yeah. He used our mother's name. He never was really smart when it came to PIN numbers and that kind of thing. Always used his birthday or our mom's name. Anyway, I figured I'd confront him, and we'd find a way to get the money back to where it belonged. We were working in the Ninth Ward, rebuilding neighborhoods, and I figured we'd just slip the money back in."

"Why didn't you call the Feds or the police?" I asked.

"Because it was my brother."

"But he was cheating all those people! And he was using you to do it! God, the Ninth Ward was hardest hit of anyone—"

"I know." Cal sighed and scrubbed his hand through his hair. "I know, Grace. But..." His voice trailed off. "But he was also the brother who let me sleep in his room for a year after our mom died. The one who showed me how to hit a baseball and taught me to drive. He always said we'd go into business together. I wanted to give him a chance to make things right." Cal looked at me, his face looking older, and sad. "He was my big brother. I didn't want him to go to jail."

Yes. I also knew about putting family before common sense, didn't I? "So what happened?" I asked more quietly. "What did he say?" I set my empty plate aside.

"Well, what could he say? He was sorry, he got caught up in it all, everyone else was doing it... But he agreed that we'd just funnel the money back into the projects and make things right." He paused, remembering. "Unfortunately for us, the Feds had been watching the company. When I moved the money, I gave them a trail, and they pounced." He looked down and shook his head.

"Did your brother go to jail, too?" I asked softly.

Cal didn't look up. "No, Grace. He testified against me."

I closed my eyes. "Oh, Cal."

"Yeah."

"Did you...what did you do?"

Another weary sigh. "My brother had taken steps, you know? My name was all over this, and it was his word against mine. And I was the accountant. Pete said even if he'd wanted to, he wouldn't have known how to do it, I was the college boy and all that. The prosecutors found him a lot more convincing, I guess. My lawyer said the world wasn't going to go easy on someone who stole from Katrina victims, so when they offered a plea, I took it."

Angus jumped onto my lap, and I petted him, thinking. "Why didn't you ever tell me this before, Cal? I would've believed you."

"Would you?" he asked. "Doesn't every convict say he's innocent? That he was set up?"

He had a point. I didn't answer. "I have no way of proving that I didn't do exactly what my brother said I did," he added quietly.

My heart ached in a sudden, sharp tug as I tried to imagine what it would feel like to be turned in by Margaret or Natalie. To be betrayed by one of them. I couldn't. Yes, of course Nat had fallen for Andrew, but that wasn't her fault. I never thought so, anyway, and I knew my sister. But to have your own brother send you to jail for his crime…man. No wonder Cal had an edge when it came to discussing his past.

"So you were going to tell me all this? Even without Margs digging around in your records?"

"Yes."

"Why now? Why not all the other times I asked?"

"Because we started something last night. I thought we did, anyway." His voice was hard. "So that's the story. Now you know."

We sat in silence for a few more minutes. Angus, weary of being ignored, yarped once and wagged his tail, inviting me to adore him. I petted his fur idly and adjusted his bandana, idly noting that he'd eaten Cal's omelet while we were talking.

"Cal?" I finally said.

"Yeah." His voice was flat, his shoulders tight.

"Would you like to have dinner with my family sometime?"

He didn't move for a second, then practically sprang across the distance between us. His smile lit up the gloom. "Yes."

He wrapped his big arms around me and kissed me hard, and Angus nipped him. Then we cleared the dishes and went to his place.

CHAPTER TWENTY-FIVE

THE NEXT DAY was Memorial Day, so I didn't have to crawl out of Cal's bed at the crack of dawn. Instead, we walked down to Lala's for pastries and meandered back along the Farmington.

"Do you have plans this afternoon?" Callahan asked, taking a long pull from his coffee.

"What if I did?" I asked, tugging Angus's leash so he wouldn't eat or roll on the poor dead mouse at the edge of the path.

"You'd have to cancel them." He grinned, slipping his arm around my waist.

"Oh, really?"

"Mmm-hmm." He wiped a little frosting off my chin, then kissed me.

"Okay, then. I'm yours," I murmured.

"I like the sound of that," he said, kissing me again, long and slow and sweet, so that my knees wobbled when he let me go. "I'll pick you up around two, but I have to run now. The appliances are being installed today."

"You're almost done with the house, aren't you?" I asked, a sudden pang hitting my heart.

"Yup," he answered.

"What happens after that?"

"I have another house to work on, couple towns north. But

if you want, I can come back and lie on the roof of this house so you can spy on me. If the new owners don't mind."

"I never spied. It was more of a gazing thing."

He grinned, then glanced at his watch. "Okay, Grace. Gotta run." He kissed me once more, then went up the path to his house. "Two o'clock, don't forget."

I let out some line on Angus's retractable leash so my puppy could sniff a fern and took a pull of my own coffee. Then I headed back home to correct papers.

As I sifted through my kids' essays, I had an uneasy thought. I needed to tell the Manning search committee about Callahan. He was, after all, in my life now, and I should be upfront about that. However it happened, Cal had served time in a federal prison, had covered up a crime, even though his intentions had been honorable. That wasn't something I should try to hide. That was also something that would probably tank whatever chance I had at becoming chairman of the history department. Nonprofit institutions tended to frown on embezzling and felons and prison records, especially where impressionable children were concerned.

My shoulders drooped at the thought. Well. I had to do it just the same.

At two o'clock sharp, Cal came up the walk. "You ready, woman?" he called through the screen door as Angus leaped and snarled from the other side.

"I have four papers left to grade. Can you wait half an hour?"

"No. Do it in the car, okay?"

I blinked. "Yes, Master." He grinned. "Where are we going?"

"You'll find out when we get there. When do you think this dog will like me?"

"Possibly never," I said, picking up my dog and kissing his head. "Goodbye, Angus, my darling boy. Be good. Mommy loves you."

"Ouch. That's really...wow. Sad," Cal said. I punched him in the shoulder. "No hitting, Grace!" he laughed. "You need to get those violent urges looked at. God. I never got beat up in prison, but I move in next to you, and look at me. Hit by sticks, bitten by your dog, my poor truck dented..."

"Such a baby. I'd think prison would've toughened you up a bit. Made you a man and all that."

"It wasn't that kind of prison." He smiled and opened his truck door for me. "We did have tennis lessons. No shivving, though. Sorry to disappoint you, honey."

Honey. I sort of flowed into the truck. Honey. Callahan O'Shea called me honey.

Ten minutes later, we were on the Interstate, heading west. I took out a paper and started to read.

"Do you like being a teacher?" Callahan asked.

"I do," I answered immediately. "The kids are fantastic at this age. Of course, I want to kill them half the time, but the other half, I just love them. And they are sort of the point of teaching."

"Most people don't love teenagers, do they?" He smiled, then checked the rearview mirror as we merged.

"Well, it's not the easiest age, no. Little kids, who doesn't love them, right? But teenagers—they're just starting to show signs of who they could be. That's really great to watch. And of course, I love what I teach."

"The Civil War, right?" Callahan asked.

"I teach all areas of American history, actually, but yes, the Civil War is my specialty."

"Why do you love it? Kind of a horrible war, wasn't it?"

"Absolutely," I answered. "But there was never a war

where people cared more about their cause. It's one thing to fight a foreign country, a culture that you don't know, cities that you've never visited, maybe. But the Civil War...imagine what would drive you to raise troops against your own country, the way Lincoln did. The South was fighting for rights as individual states, but the North was fighting for the future of the nation. It was heartbreaking because it was so personal. It was *us*. I mean, when you compare Lincoln with someone like—"

I heard my voice rising, becoming that of a television preacher on Sunday morning. "Sorry," I said, blushing.

Callahan reached over and squeezed my hand, grinning. "I like hearing about it," he said. "And I like you, Grace."

"So it's more than the fact that I was the first woman you saw out of prison," I said.

"Well, we can't discount that," he said somberly. "Imprinting, they call it, right, Teacher?"

I swatted his arm. "Very funny. Now leave me alone. I have papers to grade."

"Yes, ma'am," he said.

And grade them I did. Cal drove smoothly, not interrupting, commenting only when I read a snippet out loud. He asked me to check his MapQuest directions once or twice, which I did, quite amiably. It was surprisingly comfortable.

About an hour later, Callahan pulled off the highway. A sign announced that we'd arrived in Easting, New York, population 7512. We drove down a street lined with a pizzeria, hair salon, package store and a restaurant called Vito's. "So, Mr. O'Shea, why have you brought me to Easting, New York?" I asked.

"You'll see it in about a block if these directions are right," he said, pulling into a parking space on the street. Then he hopped out and opened my door. I made a mental note to thank Mr. Lawrence the next time I read to him.

Callahan O'Shea had beautiful manners. He took my hand and grinned.

"You look very confident," I said.

"I am," he answered, kissing my hand. All the qualms I'd felt about his past and my chances at the chairman job vanished, replaced with a tight band of happiness squeezing my chest. I couldn't remember the last time I'd felt so light. Maybe, in fact, I'd never felt this good.

Then I saw where Cal was taking me, lurched to a halt and burst into tears.

"Surprise," he said, sliding his arms around me in a hug.

"Oh, Cal," I snuffled into his shoulder.

A small movie theater stood just down the block, brick entrance, wide windows, the smell of popcorn already seducing the senses. But it was the marquee that got me. Framed in lightbulbs, black letters against a white background were the following words: *Special Anniversary Showing! See It As It Was Meant To Be Seen!* And below that, in huge letters...*Gone With the Wind.*

"Oh, Cal," I said again, my throat so tight I squeaked.

The teenager behind the counter stared wonderingly at me as I wept, while Cal bought us tickets, popcorn and root beer. The place was mobbed—I wasn't the only one, apparently, who yearned to see the greatest love story of all time on the big screen.

"How did you find this?" I asked, wiping my eyes once we were seated.

"I Googled it a few weeks ago," he answered. "You said you'd never seen it before, and it made me wonder if it ever got shown anymore. I was just going to tell you, but then you finally jumped me, so I figured I'd make it a date."

A few weeks ago. He'd been thinking about me weeks ago. Wow.

"Thank you, Callahan O'Shea," I said, leaning in to kiss him. His mouth was soft and hot, and his hand slid behind my neck, and he tasted like popcorn and butter. Warm ripples danced through my stomach until the white-haired lady sitting behind us accidentally (or purposefully) kicked our seats. Then the lights dimmed, and I found that my heart was racing. Cal grinned, gave my hand a squeeze.

For the next few hours, I fell in love with Scarlett and Rhett all over again, my emotions as tender and raw as when I was fourteen and first read the book. I winced when Scarlett declared her love to Ashley, beamed when Rhett bid for her at the dance, cringed when Melly had her baby, bit a nail as Atlanta burned. By the last line, when Katie Scarlett O'Hara Hamilton Kennedy Butler raised her head, once again determined to get what she wanted, unbowed, unbroken, I was out and out sobbing.

"I guess I should've brought some Valium," Callahan murmured as the credits rolled, handing me a napkin, since I'd run out of tissues when Rhett joined the Confederate troops outside of Atlanta.

"Thank you," I squeaked. The white-haired lady behind us patted my shoulder as she left.

"You're welcome," Cal said with that grin that I was coming to love.

"Did you like it?" I managed to ask.

He turned to me, his face gentle. "I loved it, Grace," he said.

IT WAS ALMOST NINE WHEN WE got back to Peterston. "You hungry?" Callahan asked as we passed Blackie's.

"I'm starving," I said.

"Great." He pulled into the parking lot, got out and took my hand. Holding hands had to be one of the most wonderful things God ever invented, I thought as we went into the restaurant. A small but undeniable claim on someone, holding hands. And holding hands with Callahan O'Shea was thrilling and comforting at the same time, his big hand smooth and callused and warm.

We found a booth, and Cal sat next to me, rather than across. He slid his arm around my shoulder and pulled me close, and I breathed in the clean, soapy smell of him. Damn. I was in deep.

"Want some wings?" he asked, scanning the menu.

"You are definitely getting shagged tonight," I said. "First *Gone With the Wind,* now buffalo wings. I can't resist you."

"Then my dastardly plan is working." He turned and kissed me, that hungry, hot, soft kiss that was like caramel sauce, and I thought to myself that for the rest of my life, I would remember this as the most perfect, most romantic date I or any other woman had ever had. When I opened my eyes, Callahan O'Shea was grinning. He pinched my chin and turned back to the menu.

I looked around the restaurant, smiling, feeling that the world was a beautiful place. A good-looking guy caught my eye and raised his beer glass. He looked familiar. Oh, yes. Eric, the window washer from Manning who loved his wife. And wasn't she cute. They were holding hands. Another happy couple. Aw! I waved back.

"Hello there, Grace," came a soft voice. I looked up and tried to suppress a grimace.

"Hi, Ava," I said. "How are you?" My voice was chilly. She had, after all, gone on a date with Stuart.

"Very well, thank you," she purred, looking at Callahan. Blink...blink...and blink again. "I'm Ava Machiatelli."

"Callahan O'Shea," my boyfriend said, shaking her hand.

"I heard you had dinner with Stuart the other night," I said.

"Mmm." she smiled. "Poor lad. He needed a little…company." My teeth clenched. Damn Stuart for being just another typical man, and damn Ava for being the kind of woman who had no morals when it came to sex.

Ava turned and waved toward the bar. "Kiki! Over here!" She turned back to Cal and me. "Apparently, Kiki broke up with someone over the weekend and is feeling rather devastated," she said. "I'm administering margaritas."

Kiki joined us, looking indeed quite tragic (and a little tipsy). "Hey, Grace. I called you about ten times today. Remember that guy from Jitterbug's? Well, he dumped me!" Her voice broke. She turned her gaze to Callahan. "Hi—" Her voice broke off abruptly. "My God, it's the ex-con!" she exclaimed, heartbreak forgotten.

"Nice to see you again," Cal said, raising an eyebrow at her.

"Ex-con?" Ava said.

There was an uncomfortable pause. I didn't say anything…visions of trustees danced in my head. Shit.

"Embezzling, right?" Kiki said, shooting me a decidedly cool look. Ah, yes. I'd warned her off Callahan for just that reason. Damn it.

"That's right," Cal said.

Ava's eyes lit up. "Embezzling. Fascinating."

"Well," I said. "Nice seeing you guys. Have fun."

"Oh, we will," Ava said with a huge smile. "So nice to meet you, Callahan." And with that, they returned to their table.

"Everything okay?" Cal asked.

"They work at Manning," I said, watching as Ava and Kiki sat at a table not too far away.

"Right."

"So now everyone will know I'm dating an ex-con," I said.

"I guess so." His eyes were expectant.

"Well," I said briskly, squeezing his hand. "I guess I *am* dating an ex-con. So there you go." Ava's and Kiki's heads were together. My stomach hurt. "So. Buffalo wings it is."

Unfortunately, I wasn't hungry anymore.

CHAPTER TWENTY-SIX

I WENT TO SCHOOL EARLY the next morning, straight to the headmaster's office.

I wasn't fast enough.

"Grace. I was expecting you," Dr. Stanton said as I sat in front of his desk like a repentant student. "I had a rather disturbing phone call from Theo Eisenbraun this morning."

"Right," I said, sweat breaking out on my forehead. "Um…well, I wanted to tell you myself, but I guess the news is out. But yes, I just started dating someone, and he, uh, served time for embezzlement."

Dr. Stanton sighed. "Oh, Grace."

"Dr. Stanton, I'd hope that my credentials stand on their own," I said. "I love Manning, I love the kids, and I really don't think my personal life should have anything to do with how I'm viewed as a teacher. Or, um, as a potential department chairman."

"Of course," he murmured. "And you're quite right. We value you tremendously, Grace."

Right. We both knew I was screwed. If I'd had any chance of getting the chairmanship, it was gone now. "The search committee is meeting this week, Grace. We'll let you know."

"Thanks," I said, then went on to Lehring Hall, to my casket-size office and sat in the old leather chair Julian and I had found at a yard sale. Damn it. Glum, I gnawed on a fingernail, staring out the window at the beautiful campus. The cherry blossoms waved thick and foamy, as if the tree branches had been sprayed with pink whipped cream. Graceful dogwood blossoms seemed to float on the air, and the grass glowed emerald. It was Manning's most beautiful time. Classes ended next Wednesday, with graduation two days after that. The day before Natalie and Andrew's wedding, actually.

Being chairman might've been a stretch for me—I was only thirty-one, after all, and I didn't have a doctorate in history. Add to that the fact that I just wasn't a political creature with minimal administrative experience, aside from heading up the curriculum committee. Maybe I'd never had a chance at all.

Still, I had made it to the final round. It might've just been a courtesy to a Manning faculty member. But if being with Callahan O'Shea had tanked my chances...well. He was worth it. I hoped. No. I knew. If being passed over for chairman was the price I had to pay, so be it. Thus resolved, I left my poor fingernail alone, sat up straight and booted up my computer.

"Hello, Grace." Ava blinked sleepily from the doorway, a knowing smile on her glossy lips. "How are you this morning?"

"I'm perfect in every way, Ava, and you?" I slapped a chipper smile on my face and waited.

"I heard you met with Dr. Stanton this morning." She grinned. Nothing was secret at a prep school. "Dating an ex-con, Grace? Not much of a role model for the young minds of Manning, is it?"

"Well, if we're examining morals, I'd say it beats dating a married coworker, Ava. One wonders."

"One does," she murmured. "The search committee meets Thursday, you know."

"I heard they already made their decision," came a rusty voice. "Good morning, ladies."

"Good morning, Dr. Eckhart," I said.

"Hello, there," whispered Ava.

"A word, please, Ms. Emerson?" he croaked.

"Ta-ta," Ava said, then swung off down the hall, her lush bottom straining the seams of her skirt.

"Have you heard?" I asked as Dr. Eckhart came into my office.

"Yes, I've heard, Grace. I'm here to reassure you." He broke off into a coughing fit, sounding, as he usually did, as if he were trying to expel a small child from his lungs. When he caught his breath, he smiled with watery eyes. "Grace, many of our own board members have had a brush with the law, especially concerning matters of creative financing. Try not to worry."

I gave the old man a halfhearted smile. "Thanks. Have they really reached a decision?"

"From what I've heard, they're finalizing the package this afternoon, but yes, I was told they agreed on someone last week. I recommended you, my dear."

My throat tightened. "Thank you, sir. That means more to me than I can say."

The chimes rang for first period. Dr. E. shuffled off to Medieval History with his sophomores, and I went down the hall to my seniors. Two more Civil War classes with them, then they'd be out in the world. Many of them, I'd never see again.

I pushed open the door and went in, my arrival unnoticed by my students. Hunter IV lounged in front of Kerry Blake, who was wearing a cropped, low-cut shirt that wouldn't have looked out of place on a prostitute, but which probably cost a week of my salary. Four students were checking their

BlackBerry, despite the rules against having them in class. Molly, Mallory, Madison and Meggie were trying to out-impress each other with their summer plans—one was going to Paris to intern at Chanel, another would be mountain climbing in Nepal, one had plans to white-water raft on the Colorado, and one would be, in her words, committing slow suicide by spending the summer with her family. Emma sat staring at Tommy Michener, who was dozing with his head on the desk.

Maybe I wasn't as good a teacher as I thought. For all my best intentions, had I really taught these kids what I wanted them to learn? Would they ever understand how important it was to know our past? And add to that the fact that I'd just killed my chances of becoming chairman, and I felt something inside me snap.

"Good morning, princes and princesses!" I barked, earning a gratifying jump from many of them. "This weekend, my lovely children, is the reenactment of the Battle of Gettysburg." Groans. Eye rolling. "You are required to attend. Failure to do so will result in an F in class participation, which, as I'm sure you remember, is worth one third of your grade, and even though you've all gotten into college, I do believe you're supposed to maintain a healthy grade point average. Am I right? I am. Meet me in front of the building Saturday morning, 9:00 a.m."

Their mouths hung open with horror, and for a second, they were unable to find their voices. And then came the chorus. "It's not fair! I have lacrosse/soccer/tickets! My parents will—"

I let them protest for a minute, then smiled and said simply, "Nonnegotiable."

WHEN I GOT HOME that afternoon, Angus was looking cuter than ever, so I figured a waltz was in order. Scooping my little dog up into my arms, I swooped around the living room, one-two-three, one-two-three, humming *Take It to the Limit* by the Eagles, one of Angus's favorites. "'So put me on a highway, and show me a sign,'" I sang. Angus began to croon along. As I said, it was one of his favorites.

I wasn't sure why I felt so happy, given that my chances of being history chair were smaller than ever. "I guess there's more to life than work, right, McFangus?" I asked the Wonder Pup. He wriggled in delight.

It was true. In just a little while, Natalie and Andrew would be married, putting the final nail in the coffin of Andrew and me. Summer was fast approaching, the time of reading and relaxing and battling down South.

And Callahan O'Shea was my boyfriend. A warm tide of happiness rose from my ankles on up. Callahan O'Shea was looking for a wife, kids and a lawn to mow. I figured I might just be able to help him out on that quest.

"Can I cut in?"

Speak of the devil, there he was on my porch, sinful grin in place. Angus stiffened and yarped in my arms.

"Come on in," I said, setting down my faithful beastie, who leaped onto Cal's ankle with great enthusiasm. *Hrrr. Hrrr.* Cal ignored him, took my hand and put his hand on my waist.

"I don't really know what I'm doing," he admitted, his eyes crinkling most appealingly as he tried to execute a box step, stepping on my foot.

"I'll teach you," I said. The back of his neck was warm under my hand, and the lovely smell of wood and man and sweat made my heart beat a little faster. The tide of happiness became a flood.

"I always kind of liked the eighth-grade shuffle myself," he said, pulling me into a hug. Our feet barely moved...well, except when Cal tried to shake Angus off. My hands drifted down Cal's back...I figured I'd cop a feel, why not...when I touched paper.

"Oh, right," Callahan said, stepping back. "This is yours. The mailman put it in my box by mistake." He pulled an envelope from the back pocket of his jeans and handed it to me.

The envelope was thick and creamy, my name done in stylish calligraphy, the ink a dark green. "This must be my sister's wedding invitation," I said, opening it. Sure enough, it was. Stylish and classic, just like Natalie. I smiled a little at the pretty design, the traditional words. *Together with their parents, Natalie Rose Emerson and Andrew Chase Carson warmly request the honor of your attendance...* I looked up at Callahan. "Want to be my wedding date?" I asked.

He smiled. "Sure," he said.

Sure. Just like that. Such a contrast from the superhuman effort I'd put into finding a date for Kitty's wedding. I paused. "Um, I don't think I told you this, Cal, but remember I said I'd been engaged once?" Cal nodded. "Well, it was to Andrew. The guy who's marrying my sister."

Cal's eyebrows bounced up in surprise. "Really?"

"Yup," I said. "But once he and Natalie met, it seemed pretty clear that she was the one for him. Not me."

He didn't say anything for a minute, just looked at me, frowning slightly. "Are you okay with them being together?" he asked finally. Angus shook the cuff of his jeans.

"Oh, sure," I answered. I paused. "It was really tough at first, but I'm fine now."

Cal studied me for another minute. Then he bent, picked up Angus, who replied with a growl before gnawing on Cal's thumb. "I'd say she's more than fine, wouldn't you, Angus?"

he asked. Then he leaned in and kissed my neck, and it dawned on me in a sweetly painful rush that I was crazy in love with Callahan O'Shea.

CHAPTER TWENTY-SEVEN

BUT BEING CRAZY ABOUT HIM didn't mean things were perfect.

"I think we should just wait a little bit," I said to Cal a few days later as we drove to West Hartford.

"I think it's a bad idea," he said, not looking at me. We were on our way to that most distressing of family gatherings—Mom's art show. Well, actually, most of my family gatherings were distressing, but Mom's shows were special. However, it was the only night before Nat's wedding that my family could get together. The official Meet the Family horror show.

"Callahan, trust me. It's my family. They're going to... well, you know. Flip a little. No one wants to hear that their baby girl is dating a guy with a record."

"Well, I do have a record, and I think we should just get it out in the open."

"Okay, listen. First of all, you've never been to one of my mother's shows. They're weird. My dad will be tense as it is, Mom will be fluttering all over the place... Secondly, my grandmother is deaf as a stone, so I'd have to yell, and it's a public place and all that. It's just not the time, Cal."

I'd told my parents and Natalie that I was dating the boy next door. I hadn't told them anything else.

My parents were concerned, thinking I had dumped a

perfectly good workaholic doctor for a carpenter. That was bad enough...wait till they found out about his nineteen months behind bars. Not that there were bars at his prison, but such a distinction was going to be lost on the Emerson family, whose line could be traced back to the Mayflower.

"I'm actually surprised you haven't told them yet," Cal said.

I glanced over at him. His jaw was tight. "Listen, bub. Don't worry. I'm not trying to hide anything. I just want them to know you and like you a little bit first. If I walk in and say, 'Hi, this is my boyfriend who was recently released from prison,' they'll have kittens. If they see what a great guy you are first, it won't be so bad."

"When will you tell them?"

"Soon," I bit out. "Cal. Please. I have a lot on my mind. School's ending, I still haven't heard about the chairmanship, one sister's getting married, the other's ready to jump out of her skin... Can we just let my folks meet you without dumping your prison record on them? Please? Let me have one major crisis at a time? I promise I'll tell them soon. Just not tonight."

"It feels dishonest," he said.

"It's not! It's just...parceling out information, okay? We don't have to go around introducing you as Callahan O'Shea, ex-con. Do we?"

He didn't answer for a minute. "Fine, Grace. Have it your way. But it doesn't feel right."

I took his hand. "Thanks." After a minute, he squeezed back.

"You're dating the help? You threw over that nice doctor for the help?" Mémé's expression was that of a woman who'd just bitten into a lizard. Actually, of a lizard biting into a lizard. She wheeled a little closer, hitting a pedestal and causing *Into the Light* (supposedly a birth canal, but actually more resembling the Holland Tunnel) to wobble precariously. I steadied it, then looked down at my disapproving grandmother.

"Mémé, please stop calling Callahan the help, okay? You're not in Victorian England anymore," I started. "And as I said—" here I took a breath, weary with the lie "—Wyatt, though a very nice man, just wasn't a good fit. Okay? Okay. Let's move on."

Margaret, lurking nearby, raised an eyebrow. I yearned for more wine and ignored her *and* Mémé, who was once again labeling the Irish as beggars and thieves.

Chimera Art Gallery was littered with body parts. Apparently, Mom wasn't the only one who was doing anatomy these days, and she was quite irritable that another artist was also featured (joints…ball-and-socket, gliding and cartilaginous, not nearly as popular as Mom's more, ah, intimate items, most of which looked like they belonged in a sex shop). I dragged my eyes off *Yearning in Green* (use your imagination) and sidled over to Callahan, who was talking to my father.

"So! You're a carpenter!" Dad boomed in the hearty voice he used on blue-collar workers, a little loud and with an occasional grammatical lapse to show that he, too, was just an average joe.

"Dad, you hired Cal to replace my windows, remember? So you already know he's a carpenter."

"Restoration specialist?" Dad suggested hopefully.

"Not really, no," Callahan answered evenly, resisting Dad's efforts to glam him up. "I wouldn't say a specialist in anything, though. Just basic carpentry."

"He does beautiful work," I added. Cal gave me a veiled look.

"What I wouldn't give to trade in my law books for a hammer!" Dad trumpeted. I snorted—in my memory, at least, it had always been Mom who did the needed household repairs; Dad couldn't even hang a picture. "You always a carpenter?" my father continued, dropping a verb to demonstrate his camaraderie with the working man.

"No, sir. I used to be an accountant." Cal looked at me again. I gave him a little smile and slipped my hand in his.

My mom, apparently having overheard, pounced on us. "So you had a *revelation,* Callahan?" she asked, caressing a nearby sculpture in a most pornographic way. "The same happened with me. There I was, a mother, a housewife, but inside, an artist was struggling for recognition. In the end, I just had to embrace my new identity."

"Dance hall hussy?" I muttered to Margaret. I'd told Margs about our parents' attempted tryst—why should I suffer alone?—and she snorted. Mom shot me a questioning look but dragged Cal over to *Want,* describing the wonders of self-expression. Callahan tossed me a wink. Good. He was relaxing.

"Hey, guys! We made it!" My younger sister's mellifluous voice floated over the hum of the crowd.

Natalie and Andrew were holding hands. "Hi, Grace!" my younger sister said, leaping over to hug me.

"What about me?" Margaret growled.

"I was getting there!" Nat said, grinning. "Hello, Margaret, I love you just as much as I love Grace, okay?"

"As you should," Margs grumbled. "Hi, Andrew."

"Hi, ladies. How's everyone?"

"Everyone's suffering, Andrew, so join the crowd," I said with a smile. "Nice of you guys to come."

"We wanted to meet Callahan officially," Natalie said. "You and Wyatt were together for what, two months? And I never got to even shake his hand." Nat looked over at Cal. "God, Grace, he is really gorgeous. Look at those *arms*. He could pick up a horse."

"Hello, I'm standing right here," Andrew said to my sister. I smiled at my wineglass, a warm glow in the pit of my stomach. *That's right, Andrew,* I thought. *That big, strong, gorgeous man is your replacement.* I wondered what Cal would think of my ex. Cal glanced over at me, smiled, and the glow became a lovely ache. I smiled back, and Cal returned his attention to my mom.

"Crikey, look at her," Nat said to Margaret. "She's in love."

I blushed. Andrew caught my eye, a questioning eyebrow raised.

"I'm afraid you're right, Nat," Margs replied. "Grace, you're in deep, poor slob. And hey, speaking of poor slobs, Andrew, make yourself useful and get us more wine."

"Yes, sir," Andrew answered obediently.

"By the way," I said, "Mom wants you to pick out a wedding present. A sculpture." I lifted an eyebrow.

"Oh, sweetie, let's pick fast," Natalie said. "The smallest one, whatever it is. My God, look at that. *Portals of Heaven.* Wow. That is large." They meandered off.

Dad approached Margs and me. "Gracie-Pudding," he said, "can I have a word?"

Margaret heaved a sigh. "Rejected again. People wonder why I'm so mean. Fine. I'll just go browse the labias." Dad flinched at the word and waited till she was out of hearing range.

"Yes, Dad?" I said, picking up a shoulder joint to admire. Oops. It came apart in my hands.

"Well, Pudding, I just have to ask myself if maybe you broke things off prematurely with the doctor," Dad said, watching me fumble the joint parts. "Sure, he has to work a lot, but think of what he's working on! Saving children's lives! Isn't that the kind of man you want? A carpenter... he...well, not to be snobby or anything, honey..."

"You're sounding pretty snobby, Dad," I said, trying to fit the humerus (or was it the ulna? I got a B- in biology) back into the socket. "Of course, you think being a teacher is akin to being a field hand, so..."

"I think nothing of the sort," Dad said. "But still. You'd probably make more picking cotton."

Callahan, having been released from my mother's death grip, came over to me.

"Here y'are!" Dad barked heartily, slapping Callahan on the back hard enough to make his wine slosh. "So, big guy, tell me about yourself!"

"What would you like to know, sir?" Cal asked, taking my hand.

"Grace says you used to be an accountant," Dad said with an approving smile.

"Yes," Cal answered.

"And I take it you went to college for this?"

"Yes, sir. I went to Tulane."

I gave Dad a look that was meant to convey *See? He's really nice* and also *Lay off the questions, Dad.* He ignored it. "So, Callahan, why'd you leave—"

Mom interrupted. "Do you have family in the area, Callahan?" she asked, smiling brightly.

"My grandfather lives at Golden Meadows," Cal answered, turning to her.

"Who is he? Do I know him?" Mémé barked, wheeling closer and almost toppling a breast from a nearby pedestal.

"His name is Malcolm Lawrence," Cal answered. "Hello, Mrs. Winfield. Nice to see you again."

"Never heard of him," Mémé snapped.

"He's in the dementia unit," Callahan said. I squeezed his hand. "My mother died when I was little, and my grandfather raised my brother and me."

Mom's eyebrows raised. "A brother? And where does he live?"

Cal hesitated. "He...he lives in Arizona. Married, no kids. So not much family to speak of."

"You poor thing!" Mom said. "Family is such a blessing."

"Is it?" I asked. She clucked at me fondly.

"You. Irishman." Mémé poked Cal's leg with a bony finger. "Are you after my granddaughter's money?"

I sighed. Loudly. "You're thinking of Margaret, Mémé. I don't really have a lot, Cal."

"Ah, well. I guess. I'll have to date Margs, then," he said. "And speaking of sister swapping," he added, lowering his voice so only I could hear.

"Hi, I'm Andrew Carson." The Pale One approached, my glowing, beautiful sister in tow. Andrew pushed up his glasses and stuck out a hand. "Nice to meet you."

"Callahan O'Shea," Cal returned, shaking Andrew's hand firmly. Andrew winced, and I bit down on a smile. *That's right, Andrew! He could beat you to a pulp.* Not that I was a proponent of violence, of course. It was just true.

"It's great to see you again, Callahan," Natalie said.

"Hello, Nat," Cal returned with a smile, the one that could charm the paint off walls. Natalie blushed, then mouthed *Gorgeous!* I grinned back in complete agreement.

"So you're a...plumber, is it?" Andrew said, his eyes flicking up and down Cal's solid frame, a silly little grin on his face, as if he were thinking, *Oh, yes, I've heard of blue-collar workers! So you're one of those!*

"He's a carpenter," Natalie and I said at the same time.

"It's so great to work with your hands," Dad boomed. "I'll probably do more of that once I retire. Make my own furniture. Maybe build a smokehouse."

"A smokehouse?" I asked. Cal smothered a smile.

"Please, Dad. Don't you remember the radial saw?" Natalie said, grinning at Callahan. "My father almost amputated his thumb the one time he tried to make anything. Andrew's the same way."

"That was a rogue blade," Dad muttered.

"It's true," Andrew said amenably, slipping an arm around Natalie. "Grace, remember when I tried to fix that cabinet when we first moved in together? Practically killed myself. Never tried that again. Luckily, I can afford to pay someone to do it for me."

Natalie shot him a surprised glance, but he ignored it, smiling insincerely at Cal. Who didn't smile back. Well, well. Andrew was jealous. How pleasing. And how classy of Cal, not to rise to his bait. Still, I could feel him tensing next to me.

"Such a shame to waste your education, though, son," Dad continued. Oh, God. He was doing his "Earn a Decent Wage" speech, one that I'd heard many times. And by decent wage, Dad didn't mean the simple ability to pay your own bills and maybe sock a little away. He meant six figures. He was a Republican, after all.

"Education is never wasted, Dad," I said hastily before Cal could answer.

"Are you from around here, Calvin?" Andrew asked, tilting his head in owlish fashion.

"It's Callahan," my guy corrected. "I'm originally from Connecticut, yes. I grew up in Windsor."

"Where'd you live before you moved back?" Andrew asked.

Callahan glanced at me. "The South," he said, his voice a little tight. I tried to convey my gratitude by squeezing his hand. He didn't squeeze back.

"I love the South!" my mother exclaimed. "So sultry, so passionate, so *Cat on a Hot Tin Roof!*"

"Control yourself, Nancy," Mémé announced, rattling her ice cubes.

"Don't tell me what do to, old woman," Mom muttered back, knowing full well that Mémé was too deaf to hear.

"So why'd ya leave accounting?" Dad asked. Cripes, he was like a dog with a bone.

"Maybe we can stop interrogating Cal for now, hmm?" I suggested sharply. Cal had grown very still next to me.

Dad shot me a wounded look. "Pudding, I'm just trying to figure out why someone would trade in a nice secure job so he could do manual labor all day."

"It's an honest question," Andrew seconded.

Ah. Honest. The key word. I closed my eyes. *Here it comes,* I thought. I was right.

Callahan let go of my hand. "I was convicted for embezzling over a million dollars," he stated evenly. "I lost my accounting license and served nineteen months at a federal prison in Virginia. I got out two months ago." He looked at my father, then my mother, then Andrew. "Any other questions?"

"You're a convict?" Mémé said, craning her bony neck to look at Cal. "I knew it."

BY THE TIME THE GALLERY SHOW was over, I had managed to tell my family about Cal's situation. Granted, I did a piss-poor job, given that I was completely unprepared. I'd been planning to figure out something a bit more convincing than *It's not as bad as it sounds...* Plus, Margs had abandoned me, saying there was an emergency at work and she wouldn't be home till midnight at the earliest.

"Happy?" I asked Callahan, getting into the car and buckling myself in with considerable vigor.

"Grace, it's best to be honest right up front," he said, his face a bit stony.

"Well, you got your way."

"Listen," he said, not starting the car. "I'm sorry if it was uncomfortable for you. But your family should know."

"And I *was* going to tell them! Just not tonight."

He looked at me for a long minute. "It felt like lying."

"It wasn't lying! It was introducing the idea bit by bit. Going slow. Considering the feelings of others, that's all."

We sat in the idle car, staring ahead. My throat was tight, my hands felt hot. One thing was clear. I was going to be spending a lot of time on the phone for the next day or so.

"Grace," Callahan said quietly, "are you sure you want to be with me?"

I sputtered. "Cal, I shot myself in the foot for you this week. I told the headmaster of my school that I was dating you! I'm taking you to my sister's wedding! I just don't think you need to walk around with a scarlet letter tattooed on your forehead, that's all!"

"Did you want me to lie to your dad?" he asked.

"No! I just…I wanted to finesse this, that's all. I know my family, Cal. I just wanted to ease them into the idea of your past. Instead, you went in with guns blazing."

"Well, I don't have a lot of time to waste."

"Why? Do you have a brain tumor? Are there bloodhounds tracking you at this very moment? Is an alien spaceship coming to abduct you?"

"Not that I'm aware of, no," he answered drily.

"So. I'm a little…mad. That's all. I just… Listen, let's go

home. I have to make some calls. And I should stay at my place tonight," I said.

"Grace," he began.

"Cal, I probably have twenty messages on my machine already. I have to correct the final essays for my sophomores and post all my classes' grades by next Friday. I still haven't heard about the chairmanship thing. I'm stressing. I just need a little alone time. Okay?"

"Okay." He started the car, and we drove home in silence. When we pulled in my driveway, I jumped out of the car.

"Good night," he said, getting out.

"Good night," I answered, starting up the walk. Then I turned around, went back and kissed him. Once. Another time. A third. "I'm just a little tense," I reminded him in a gentler voice, finally pulling back.

"Okay. Very cute, too," he said.

"Save it, bub," I answered, squeezing his hand.

"I just couldn't out and out lie, honey," he added, looking at the ground.

Hard to be mad at a guy for that. "I understand," I said. Angus yarped from inside. "But I really do have to work now."

"Right." He kissed my cheek and walked over to his place. With a sigh, I went inside.

CHAPTER TWENTY-EIGHT

A FEW HOURS LATER WHEN my parents had been called (if not soothed) and my schoolwork was done, I found myself once again staring over at Cal's house from my darkened living room.

When I told Dr. Stanton about Callahan this week, I'd done it with the idea that Callahan would be part of my future. It was funny. A couple of months ago, when I pictured the man I'd end up with, I was still picturing Andrew. Oh, not his face...it wasn't that obvious. But so many of his qualities. His soft voice, gentle sense of humor, his intelligence, even his flaws, like how inept he was at changing tires or unclogging a sink. Now, though...I smiled. Callahan O'Shea could change a tire. He could probably hot-wire an entire car.

I stroked Angus's head, earning a little doggy moan in response and a love bite to my thumb. When I was alone with Callahan, I was crazy about him. When his past came into my narrow little world of teaching and family...things were a little harder. But as Cal had pointed out, at least it was done now. Everyone knew. No more parceling out of information. There was something to be said for that.

A soft knock came on my front door, and I glanced at the clock. Eight minutes past nine. Angus had fallen too deeply asleep to go into his usual rage, luckily, so I tiptoed to the door, turning on a light as I went, figuring it was Callahan.

It wasn't.

Andrew stood on my porch. "Hey, Grace," he said in his quiet voice. "Do you have a minute?"

"Sure," I answered slowly. "Come on in."

The last time Andrew had seen the home we were going to live in together, it had been only half-Sheetrocked, wires and insulation exposed, the kitchen just a gaping hole. The floors had been rough and broken in places, the stairs stained and dark with age.

"Wow," he said, turning in a slow circle. Angus popped up from the couch. Before he could maul Andrew, however, I picked him up.

"Want a tour?" I asked, clearing my throat.

"Sure," he answered, ignoring Angus's purring snarls. "Grace, it's beautiful."

"Thanks," I said, bemused. "Well, here's the dining room, obviously, and the kitchen. That's my office, remember, it was a closet before?"

"Oh, my God, that's right," he said. "And wow, you knocked down the bedroom wall, didn't you?"

"Mmm-hmm," I murmured. "Yup. I figured...well, I just wanted a bigger kitchen."

The original plan was that there'd be a downstairs bedroom, you see. We were planning to have at least two kids, possibly three, so we planned on both upstairs bedrooms being theirs. Then, later, when our clever children went off to college and Andrew and I got older, we wouldn't have to worry about schlepping up and down the stairs. Now what was once going to be a bedroom—our bedroom—was my office.

My Fritz the Cat clock ticked loudly on the wall, tail swishing in brittle motion. *Tick...tick...tick...*

"Can I see upstairs, too?" Andrew asked.

"Of course," I said, holding Angus a little tighter. I followed Andrew up the narrow stairs, noticing how he was still so scrawny and slight. Had I once found that endearing? "So this is my bedroom," I said tersely, pointing, "and there's the guest room, where Margaret's staying, that's the door to the attic—I haven't done anything up there yet. And at the end of the hall is the bathroom."

Andrew walked down the hall, peeking in the various doorways, then stuck his head in the loo. "Our tub," he said fondly.

"My tub," I corrected instantly. My voice was hard.

He gave a mock grimace. "Oops. Sorry. You're right. Well, it looks beautiful."

We'd found the old porcelain claw-foot tub in Vermont one weekend when we'd gone antiquing and bed-and-breakfasting and lovemaking. It had been in someone's yard, an old Yankee farmer who once had his pigs use it as a water trough. He sold it to us for fifty bucks, and the three of us had practically killed ourselves getting it into the back of Andrew's Subaru. I found a place that reglazed tubs, and when it came back to us, it was shiny and white and pure. Andrew had suggested that, while it wasn't yet hooked up to the plumbing, maybe we could get naked and climb in just the same. Which we had done. A week later, he dumped me. I couldn't believe I'd kept the thing.

"It's amazing. What a great job you've done," he said, smiling proudly at me.

"Thanks," I said, heading downstairs. Andrew followed. "Would you like a glass of water? Coffee? Wine? Beer?" I rolled my eyes at myself. *Why not just bake the man a cake, Grace? Maybe grill up a few shrimp and a filet mignon?*

"I'll take a glass of wine," he said. "Thanks, Grace."

He followed me into the kitchen, murmuring appreciatively as he noticed little details—the crown molding, the cuckoo clock in the hall, the cluster of heavy architectural stars I'd bolted to the wall behind the kitchen table.

"So why the visit, Andrew?" I asked, carrying two glasses of wine into the living room. He sat on the Victorian sofa that had cost so much to reupholster. I took the wing chair, handed Angus a misshapen hunk of rawhide to discourage him from eating Andrew's shoes and looked at my sister's fiancé.

He took a deep breath and smiled. "Well, this is a little awkward, Grace, but I felt I should...well, ask you something."

My heart dropped into my stomach, sitting there like a peach pit. "Okay."

He looked at the floor. "Well, I...this is uncomfortable for me." He broke off, looked up and made one of his goofy faces.

I smiled uncertainly.

"I guess I'll just blurt this out," he said. "Gracie, what are you doing with that guy?"

The peach pit seemed to turn, scraping my insides unpleasantly, and my smile dropped from my face as if it was made from granite. Andrew waited, a kindly, concerned expression on his face. "What do you mean?" I asked, my voice quiet and shaky.

Andrew scratched his cheek. "Grace," he said very softly, leaning forward, "forgive me for asking this, but does this have something to do with Natalie and me?"

"Excuse me?" I asked, my voice squeaking. I reached for my dog and lifted him to sit protectively on my lap. Angus dropped the rawhide and growled obediently at Andrew. Good dog.

Andrew took a quick breath. "Look, I'll just come right

out with this, Grace. That guy doesn't seem, well, right for you. An ex-con, Gracie? Is that really what you want? I...well, I never met the other guy, Wyatt, was it? The doctor? But from what Natalie said, he sounded great."

I closed my eyes. *Natalie never met him, you dope. I never met him.* But God knew Natalie had a lot dependent on me dating Wyatt Dunn, so perhaps her imagination had gotten the better of her. As mine had with me.

"Grace," Andrew continued, "this guy... I have to ask myself if you're doing this out of...well..."

"Desperation?" I suggested with a bite.

He winced slightly but didn't correct me. "You've been... well, generous, Grace," he said. "I'm sure the whole situation with Natalie and me has been...uncomfortable. It has been for me, anyway, so I can only imagine how it's been for you."

"How kind of you to consider my feelings," I murmured. The peach pit scraped deeper.

"But—what's his name again? The embezzler?"

"Callahan O'Shea."

"Well, Grace, to me it just seems like he's not for you."

I smiled tightly. "Well, you know, Andrew, he does have this one really wonderful quality. He's not in love with my sister. Which, you know, I find quite refreshing."

Andrew flushed, acknowledging that with a half nod. "Point taken, Gracie. But even with—"

"And I feel compelled to mention," I said, my voice taking on my *silence in the classroom* tone, causing Angus to whine sympathetically, "that my love life is no longer any of your business."

"I still care about you, that's all," he protested softly, and in that moment, I wanted to kick him in the nuts.

"Don't trouble yourself, Andrew," I said, trying to keep

my voice from breaking with rage. "I'm fine. Callahan is a good man."

"Are you sure, Grace? Because there's something I don't trust about him."

I set Angus down and looked steadily at Andrew. "How interesting that you should say that, Andrew. After all, look what happened with you and me. I thought you loved me. I thought we were pretty damn perfect together. And I was wrong. So it's funny. You don't trust Callahan, and I don't quite trust you, Andrew, and I have no idea what you're doing here right now, questioning my taste in men."

He started to say something, but I cut him off. "Here's what I know about Callahan. He uncovered a crime and he tried to make it right. At the same time, he was trying to protect his brother. He risked everything for the person he loved best, and he got screwed in the process."

"Well, that's a nice spin, Grace, but—"

"It's not spin, Andrew. Have *you* ever risked anything? You…" My voice grew choked with anger, my heart thudding, face burning. "You asked me to marry you, knowing I was head over heels for you and knowing damn well you didn't feel the same way. But you figured it was time to settle down, and there I was, ready, willing and able. Then you met my sister, fell in love, never said boo about it. Instead you waited until three weeks before our wedding to call things off. Three weeks! Jesus, Andrew! Think you might have spoken up a little sooner?"

"I never—"

"I'm not finished." My voice was hard enough to cause his mouth to snap shut. "Even with Natalie, you just sat back and did nothing. Yet she's the love of your life, isn't she? But if it weren't for me, you would never have even spoken to her again."

His face reddened even more. "I said I'm grateful for how you got Nat and me together."

"I didn't do it for you, Andrew. I did it for her. You, though...you didn't fight for her, you didn't try to talk to her...you just sat there like a fern or something, doing nothing."

His shoulders slumped. "What was I supposed to do?" he said, his voice small. "I wasn't about to date my ex-fiancée's sister. I didn't want to put you in a bad spot."

"And yet here you are, a week away from marrying her."

He sighed, slumping back against the sofa, and ran a hand through his pale blond hair. "Grace, you're right. I never would've even spoken to Natalie without your blessing. The last thing I wanted to do was hurt you more. I thought it was the right thing to do. Wasn't it?" He looked so genuinely confused that I wanted to shake him.

Then I saw the tears in his eyes. The sight took the fight out of me, and I drooped back against my chair. "I don't know, Andrew. It was a complicated situation."

"Ex*act*ly," he said, and *God,* I was sick of him! For the past three years, I'd been obsessed with Andrew, happily and miserably, and enough was enough.

"Listen," I said wearily. "I guess I appreciate your concern over Cal, but...well, you just don't get a say, Andrew. I'm none of your business anymore."

He smiled, a little sadly. "Well, you'll be my sister-in-law soon. You are my business, a little."

"Save it, pal." But I said the words with a smile. For Nat's sake.

He set his wineglass on the coffee table and stood. "I should go," he said, looking around again. "The house is beautiful, Grace. You did a wonderful job."

"I know," I said opening the door.

He went out on the porch, and I followed, closing the screen door so Angus wouldn't get out. Andrew turned back to face me. "You'll always be special to me, you know," he said, not looking in my eyes.

I paused. "Well. Thank you."

He put his skinny arms around me and gave me a stiff hug. After a second, I patted his shoulder. Then, quite out of the blue, Andrew turned his head and kissed me.

It wasn't a romantic kiss…not quite. Too puckery. But neither was it a brother-in-law peck on the cheek. In typical Andrew fashion, he hadn't been able to decide. Idiot.

I jerked back. "Andrew, are you out of your mind?"

"What?" he said, his quirky eyebrows raised.

"Well, call me crazy, but I don't think you should ever do that again, okay? Ever."

"Shit. Sorry," he said, grimacing. "I just—I'm sorry. Force of habit. I don't know. I just…forget it. I'm really sorry."

I just wanted him gone. "Bye, Andrew."

"Good night, Grace." Then he turned and walked down the steps to his car. He opened the door, got in, started the car and waved, then backed down the driveway.

"Good riddance," I muttered. I turned to go into the house, then started in fright.

Callahan O'Shea was standing at the border of our yards, looking at me with an expression that made me surprised I hadn't burst into flames.

CHAPTER TWENTY-NINE

"CALLAHAN!" I STAMMERED. "Hey! You surprised me."

"What the hell was that?" he growled.

I waved my hand dismissively. "That was nothing." *He just doesn't think you're good enough for me, that's all.* "Want to come in?"

"Grace," he bit out. "It didn't look like *nothing*. It looked like your sister's fiancé just kissed you. The guy you were going to *marry!*"

"So I've got a lot of 'splainin' to do?" I said. He narrowed his eyes. Aw! He was jealous! Funny how pleasing that can be, isn't it? Unfortunately, Callahan didn't seem to share my amusement. "Well, don't just stand there brooding, Mr. O'Shea. Come in. You can grill me all you want."

With a muttered curse, he came up the steps and into the house, not even glancing down as Angus launched himself through the air to attack. Instead, he took in the wineglasses on the coffee table. The scowl deepened.

"It's not what you think," I said.

"And what do I think?" Callahan asked tightly.

"You think..." I squashed a smile. "You think Andrew's hitting on me."

"That seemed obvious."

"Wrong. Sit down, Cal. Want some wine?"

"No. Thank you." He sat in the spot recently vacated by

Andrew. "So? Why was he here? And does he always kiss you on the mouth?"

I nestled into my chair and took a sip of my wine, considering my honey. Yep. Definitely jealous. Perhaps now wasn't the time to say I found it incredibly sexy. "Andrew hasn't kissed me for a long, long time. Why he did tonight, who knows? He said it was force of habit."

"That's the stupidest thing I ever heard."

Angus growled, his teeth firmly sunk into Cal's work boot.

"You're jealous, aren't you?" I couldn't help asking.

"Yes! I am, actually! You loved that scrawny little idiot, and he came over tonight and kissed you. How am I supposed to feel?"

"Well, for one, you should feel happy, because as you said, Andrew's a scrawny little idiot. And you're the opposite."

Callahan started to say something, then stopped. "Thanks." The corner of his mouth pulled up.

"You're welcome," I smiled.

"Do you still have feelings for him, Grace?" he asked carefully. "Tell me right now if you do."

"I don't. As you said, scrawny little idiot."

Callahan considered me for a moment, then reached down to dislodge Angus's teeth from his shoes. "Go see your mommy," he said. Angus obeyed, leaping onto my lap and curling in a tight circle. Callahan sat back and looked at me, his face considerably more at ease than when he first came in. "Does it worry you? Andrew kissing someone who's not Natalie?"

I thought on that. "No. The first time those two saw each other, they fell in love, just like that. Kablammy, like they were hit by lightning."

"Or a field hockey stick," Cal added.

Oh. *Oh.* My heart swelled. "Anyway," I said, blushing. "Andrew came over because he was..." I paused. "Concerned."

"Because you're dating someone with a record?"

"Correct." I stroked Angus's sweet, bony head, earning a little groan in response.

"So the man who left you for your sister has a problem with my morals."

"Bingo." I smiled across at my sweetie. "And I told him I thought you were pretty wonderful and quite honorable, and I may have mentioned how great you look without your clothes on." Callahan smiled. "Plus, I told him one of the things I liked best was the fact that you hadn't fallen for Natalie *or* Margaret, so I thought you might be a keeper."

"Grace," Cal said seriously, leaning forward, "I can't imagine falling for Natalie or Margaret. Not after meeting you."

My throat tightened abruptly. No one...*no one*...had ever compared me with my sisters and found me superior. "Thanks," I whispered.

"You're welcome," he murmured, gazing into my eyes. "You want me to find Andrew and beat him up?"

"Nah," I said. "It'd be like shooting fish in a barrel."

He laughed, then reached down to retie the work boot Angus had mauled. "You planning to tell Natalie that her fiancé's going around kissing people?"

I thought about that for a second, playing with my puppy's fur. "No. I honestly don't think it meant anything. I mean, really, Angus has given me a more passionate kiss than that one." *Not to mention you, bub,* I added silently. "I think it was just a reflex."

"What if it wasn't?" Cal asked.

My head jerked back. "It was. I'm sure. He loves Natalie! They're crazy about each other. You saw that."

Cal hesitated, then gave a nod. "I guess."

He guessed? Everyone could see that Natalie and Andrew were meant to be. It was obvious. Wasn't it?

Angus snapped awake from his brief nap and leaped off my lap, trotting into the kitchen to see if God had miraculously refilled his bowl.

Callahan leaned back against the couch, looking like a contender for Sexiest Man Alive. In all the time I'd spend with Andrew, I could honestly say I'd never felt like this...the thrilling rush of Cal's presence mingling with the comfort that came from the certainty that he...well...he liked me. He chose me. He *wanted* me. He even put up with Angus.

"So how's your family taking the news that Princess Grace is dating an ex-con?" he asked, grinning a little.

I decided not to tell him about Dad's eleven-point argument on why Cal was a bad idea or the fact that Mom had already talked to a private investigator. "They'll get used to it."

"I guess they thought your cat-wrangling pediatrician was a better choice, huh?"

Those words were Arctic water on my heart. Oh, yeah. Wyatt Dunn, M.D. "Um...well." I nibbled on a thumbnail. "Callahan. About that."

"What?" Cal said, grinning. "Don't tell me he dropped by for some kissing, too."

My stomach twisted. "No, no. Um, Cal. As long as we're talking. I need to tell you something. Something you might not like." I realized I was chewing my thumb again and put my hands in my lap. Taking a deep breath, I looked into Callahan's eyes.

The smile slipped off his face, leaving it blank and inscrutable. "Go ahead," he said silkily.

"Well...this is actually kind of funny," I said, attempting a chuckle. My heart raced in a manic patter. "Here's the thing. I...I never actually dated Wyatt Dunn. The doctor. The pediatric surgeon."

Cal didn't move. Didn't even blink.

"Yeah," I continued, swallowing twice, my mouth dry as Arizona in July. "Um...I...I made him up."

The only sound was Fritz the Cat, ticking away, and the jingle of Angus's tags as he snuffled around the kitchen. *Tick...tick...tick.*

"You made him up."

"Well, yeah!" A panicky laugh burst out of my tight throat. "Of course! I mean, come on! You suspected, right? A good-looking, single, straight pediatric surgeon? I could never get a guy like that!"

Oh, boy, did that ever come out wrong.

"But you could get a guy like me." Callahan's voice was dangerously calm.

Shit. "I...well, I didn't mean it that way. I meant that there's no such animal. He's...you know. Too good to be true."

"You made him up," Cal repeated.

"Mmm-hmm," I squeaked, clenching my toes in discomfort.

"Tell me, Grace, why would you do something like that?" The calm in his voice was downright ominous.

I didn't answer for a minute. The day I made up Wyatt Dunn seemed a long, long time ago. "Well, see, we were at a wedding." As quickly as I could, I told him about the comments, the bouquet toss, Nat in the bathroom. The words fell out of my mouth like hailstones. "I guess I didn't want Natalie thinking I wasn't over Andrew," I said. "And to be honest—" Cal lifted a sardonic eyebrow but remained silent

"—I was tired of everyone looking at me like I was...well, the dog no one wants at the pound."

"So you lied." His voice was very quiet. He sat still as a bronze statue, and my heart raced a little faster, making me feel ill. "To your entire family."

"Well, you know, it made everyone feel better. And Margaret knew," I mumbled, looking to the floor. "And my friend Julian. And Kiki, actually."

"I seem to remember you on at least one date with this man," Cal said. "And flowers...didn't he send you flowers?"

My face was so hot it hurt. I glanced at Callahan's face. "I, um, sent them to myself. And...I pretended to be on a date or two." I winced, then cleared my throat. "Cal, look. It was dumb, I know that. I just wanted everyone to think I was okay."

"You lied, Grace," he said, his voice no longer so quiet. Getting a bit loud, in fact, and one could even say rather angry. "I can't believe this! You lied to me! You've been lying for months! I asked you if you were done with that guy, and you said you weren't seeing him anymore!"

"And I wasn't, right?" My nervous laugh came out like a dry heave. "Yes, right. I lied. I did. It was a mistake, probably."

"Probably?" he barked.

"Okay, it was definitely a mistake! I admit it, it was stupid and immature and I shouldn't have done it, but my back was against the wall, Cal!"

"I've got to hand it to you, Grace." His voice was flat and calm. "You're a great liar. I did suspect, you're right. But you convinced me. Well done."

Youch. I took a quick breath. "Cal, listen. It was juvenile. I know that. But cut me some slack here."

"You lied to me, Grace. You lied to just about everyone

you know!" He jammed a hand through his hair and turned away from me. My temper started to bubble. It wasn't *that* bad. No one was hurt. In fact, it's fair to say that my lie spared people from worrying over poor tragic Grace who was dumped. I know it had made *me* feel better.

"Callahan, look," I said more calmly. "I did a stupid thing, I admit it. And I hate to be the one to tell you this, Callahan, but people are flawed. Sometimes they do dopey things, especially around people they love. Surely you've heard of such occasions."

This earned me another glare, but he remained silent. No slack, no understanding, no sympathy. And so, alas, I continued talking, my voice rising.

"I mean, come on, Cal. You're not perfect, either. Remember? You yourself did a stupid thing to protect someone you loved. I have to say, it's a little ironic, getting a morality lecture from you, of all people!"

"And just what does that mean?" he asked, his mouth tight.

"It means you're the ex-con who covered up a crime for his brother and just got out of clink two months ago!"

Oops. Probably shouldn't have said that. His face went from tight to completely furious. And calm. It was a horrible combination.

"Grace," he said quietly, standing up. "I can't believe I was so wrong about you."

It was like a punch in the heart. I jolted out of my chair, standing in front of him, my eyes flooding with tears. "Wait a second, Callahan. Please." I took a deep breath. "I'd think that you of all people would understand. We were both doing the wrong thing for the right reason."

"You're not over Andrew," he stated.

"I most certainly *am* over Andrew," I said, my voice shaking. I *was*. And it killed me that he didn't believe that.

"You lied so people would think you were, and you kept lying, and you're still lying, and you don't even see that there's something wrong with this picture, do you?" Cal stared at the floor like he couldn't bear to look at me. When he spoke next, his voice was quieter. "You're lying to your family, Grace, and you lied to me." He dragged his eyes up to mine. "I'm leaving now. And just in case it's not clear, we're done."

He didn't slam the door. Worse, he closed it quietly behind him.

CHAPTER THIRTY

"THIS IS, LIKE, SO LAME." Kerry's expression combined disgust, incredulity and martyrdom the way only a teenager's could.

"I thought we got to ride horses," Mallory whined. "You said we were in the cavalry. That guy has a horse. Why can't I have a horse?"

"Picture us dismounted," I said tightly. Suffice it to say, my mood over the past forty-eight hours had been poor at best.

My righteous indignation had faded about ten minutes after Callahan had closed the door with such finality, leaving hot shards of shock flashing across an echoing emptiness. Callahan O'Shea, who thought I was beautiful and funny, who smelled of wood and sun, didn't want anything more to do with me.

Last night, despite Julian and Margaret's best efforts to distract me with a *Project Runway Season 1* DVD marathon and mango martinis, I'd sat in a daze of self-disgust, not eating, not drinking, tears leaking out of my eyes as Tim Gunn urged on the troops in the background. Well into the wee hours of this very morning, hard little sobs hiccupped out of me like pebbles until I finally fell asleep around 6:00 a.m. Then, realizing I'd ordered my Civil War class to attend the Gettysburg reenactment, I jolted out of bed, drank three cups of coffee and now stood before them, a sickly caffeine buzz in my head, an ache in my chest.

"Children, the Battle of Gettysburg lasted for three days," I said, dressed in my Yankee blues. "When it was over, fifty-one *thousand* men would be dead. The Confederates' line of wounded stretched fourteen miles. Ten thousand injured. One in three men killed. The bloodiest battle in American history. The beginning of the end for the South."

I looked into the eleven dubious faces before me. "Look, kids," I said wearily. "I know you think this is lame. I know we're in Connecticut, not Pennsylvania. I know that having a couple hundred oddball history geeks like me running around, firing blanks, isn't the real thing."

"So why'd you make us come?" Hunter asked, earning an admiring "Like, exactly!" from Kerry.

I paused. "I want you to try…just try, just for the next couple hours, to put yourselves as best you can in the minds of those soldiers. Imagine believing in something so passionately that you'd risk your life for it. For an idea. For a way of life. For the future of your country, a future you knew you might never see. You're here, you lucky, nice, well-fed rich kids, because you stand on the shoulders of this country's history. I just want you to feel that, just a little bit."

Kaelen and Peyton rolled their eyes in unison. Hunter discreetly checked his cell phone. Kerry Blake examined her manicure.

But Tommy Michener stared at me, his mouth slightly open, and Emma Kirk's eyes were solemn and wide.

"Let's go, kids," I said. "Remember, you're part of First Cavalry now. General Buford is over there. Do what he says, and just…well. Whatever."

With a few groans and giggles, the kids straggled after me. I got them in line with the other Brother Against Brother members. General Buford (better known as Glen Farkas, an accountant from Litchfield), rode his horse up and down the line.

The kids sobered at the sight of the snorting bay mare, the sword flapping at the general's side. Glen was really good at this.

"When does it start?" Tommy whispered.

"As soon as General Heth attacks," I whispered back.

"My heart's kind of pounding," Tommy said, grinning at me. I patted his arm, smiling back.

And here they came. The Rebel yells pierced the air, and over the hill streamed dozens of Confederates.

"Onward, men!" called General Buford, wheeling his horse. And with a mighty yell, First Cavalry followed, Tommy Michener at the front of the pack, his empty musket held high, yelling at the top of his lungs.

Five hours later, I was driving the Manning minibus back to school, grinning like an idiot.

"That was so cool, Ms. Em!"

"Did you see me nail that guy with my bayonet?"

"I was actually, like, scared!"

"I thought that horse was gonna trample me!"

"Tommy and I took over that cannon! Did you see that?"

"And when those other dudes came up behind us, when we were, like, losing it?"

Kerry Blake kept up her ennui, but the rest of them were chattering like wild monkeys. And I was soaring. Finally. Finally, the subject we'd been studying all semester had had a tiny impact on their polished, protected worlds.

Once at Manning, they piled out of the car. "I'll e-mail you a copy of that picture, Ms. Em," called Mallory. Even though modern inventions were frowned upon at reenactments, we'd bent the rules and taken a picture in front of a cannon. My kids and me. I'd have it blown up, frame it and put it in my office, and if I was head of the department, I'd...

Well. Chances were, I wasn't going to be head of the department. The announcement still hadn't been made, but telling Dr. Stanton about Callahan O'Shea had pretty much killed my chances. I wondered if I should tell him I wasn't seeing my ex-con anymore. But no. If I wasn't going to get the promotion because of some guy I was or wasn't seeing, I guess I didn't really want it.

Maybe Callahan had cooled off, I thought as I drove home. Maybe he'd see my point. Maybe he'd been missing me, too. Maybe my lie didn't seem so bad, now that some time had passed. Maybe—

As I turned onto my street, I saw a real estate sign up in front of Cal's house. My heart stuttered. Yes, I'd known Cal was planning to sell the house. I just hadn't thought it would be so soon.

The front door opened, and a woman emerged...the blonde from the bar. His real estate friend. Callahan followed right behind.

Margaret's car was not in the driveway, which meant no backup for me. She had a big case pending, so chances were she was at her office. I was on my own. I opened the car door and got out.

"Hey, Cal," I called. My voice was fairly steady.

He looked up. "Hi," he said, closing his front door behind him. He and the woman came down the walk where I'd once smacked Callahan O'Shea with a rake.

"Hi, I'm Becky Mango, as in the fruit," she chirped, sticking out her hand.

"Hi," I said. "Grace Emerson, as in Ralph Waldo." Well, didn't I sound nice and snooty. "I live next door," I added, glancing at Callahan. He was looking at the new landscaping, which had gone in this past week. Not at me.

"Beautiful house!" Becky exclaimed, gazing at my place. "If you ever want to sell it, give me a call!" She stuck her hand in her bag and pulled out a card. *Becky Mango, Mango Properties Ltd. Licensed Realtor.* The logo matched the one on the For Sale sign.

"Thanks. I will," I said, then turned to the brooding male next to her. "Cal, do you have a minute?"

He looked at me, those blue eyes that had once smiled so wickedly now so guarded. "Sure," he said.

"Callahan, I'll see you next week?" Becky asked. "I think I might have a property you'd be interested in down in Glastonbury. Real fixer-upper, going on the market next month."

"Okay. I'll call you." We both watched as she got in her car and drove off.

"So you're…you're done here?" I asked, though the answer was rather obvious.

"Yup." He slung his bag into the bed of his pickup truck.

"Where to now?" My eyes stung, and I blinked hard.

"I'm working on a place up in Granby," he said. "I'll be in the area until my grandfather…as long as he's around." He took his keys out of his pocket, not looking at me. "But I don't think he's long for the world."

My throat tightened. Cal's last relative, except for the estranged brother. "I'm sorry, Cal," I whispered.

"Thank you. Thank you for visiting him, too." His dark blue eyes flickered to mine, then dropped to the driveway once more.

"Callahan," I said, putting my hand on his warm, solid arm. "Can we just…can we talk?"

"What about, Grace?"

I swallowed. "About our fight. About…you know. You and me."

He leaned against the truck and folded his arms. Body language not promising, folks. "Grace, I think you're…I think you have things you need to work out." He started to say something else, then stopped, shaking his head. "Look," he continued. "You've been lying to me since the day we met. I have a problem with that. I don't know if you're over Andrew, frankly, and I don't want to be your rebound fling. I was looking for...well, you know what I was looking for." He looked at me steadily, his expression was neutral.

A wife, a couple of kids, a lawn to mow on weekends. "Cal, I..." I stopped and bit my thumbnail. "Okay. You have a thing about honesty, so I'll be honest now. You're partly right. I made up the boyfriend because I wasn't completely over Andrew. And I didn't want anyone to know because it made me feel so...small. So stupid, carrying a torch for the guy who dumped me for my sister. Even pretending that I had a great boyfriend was better than people knowing that. Having people think some wonderful guy out there adored me...it was a nice change."

He gave a half nod, but didn't say anything.

"When Andrew fell for Natalie..." I paused, then went on. "I loved him, he didn't love me quite so much, then he took one look at Nat, who's basically perfect in every way and my baby sister, too, and he fell in love with her. That's hard to get over."

"I'm sure it is," he said, not unkindly.

"But what I'm trying to say is that I *am* over Andrew, Callahan. I know I should've told you the truth about Wyatt, but—" My voice cracked. I cleared my throat and forced myself to continue. "I didn't want you to see me as someone who got traded in."

He sighed. Looked at the ground and shook his head a little. "I was thinking about that time I walked you home from Blackie's," he said. "You were on a date, weren't you?" I nodded. "I bet you were pretty...desperate."

"Yup," I admitted in a whisper.

"So I was just about your last shot, wasn't I, Grace? Your sister's wedding was coming fast, and you hadn't found anyone. The ex-con next door was the best you could do."

I flinched. "No, Cal. That's not how it was."

"Maybe," he said. He didn't say anything more for a minute, and when he did, his voice was gentle. "Look, if you are over Andrew, I'm glad for you, Grace. But I'm sorry."

Well, dang it. I was going to cry. Tears burned my eyes, and my throat hurt like I was being strangled. He noticed. "To be really blunt here," he said very quietly, "I don't want to be with someone who lies to make herself look better. Someone who can't tell the truth."

"I did tell the truth! I told you everything," I squeaked.

"What about your family, Grace? You planning on coming clean with your folks? With Andrew and your sister?"

I cringed at the thought. Like Scarlett O'Hara, I'd been planning on thinking about that tomorrow. Or the next day. Possibly never. It's fair to say that I was hoping the Wyatt Dunn fantasy would just fade into the past.

Callahan glanced at his watch. "I have to go."

"Cal," I said, my voice breaking, "I really would like you to forgive me and give me another chance."

He looked at me a long moment. "Take care of yourself, Grace. I hope you work things out."

"Okay," I whispered, looking down so he wouldn't see my face crumple. "You take care, too."

Then he got in his truck and drove away.

BACK IN THE HOUSE, I sat at my kitchen table, tears dripping off my chin, where Angus cheerfully licked them off. Great. Just great. I blew it. How I ever thought my Wyatt-Dunn idea was a good one was completely beyond me. I should never have... If only I'd... Next time I'd just...

Next time. Right. It occurred to me in a dizzyingly painful

flash that guys like Callahan O'Shea didn't grow on trees. That God had thrown a man down right next door, and I'd spent weeks in judgment. That just like my best friend Scarlett O'Hara, I hadn't seen what was right in front of my face. That any guy who'd drive an hour and a half so I could see *Gone With the Wind* was worth ten—a hundred—of the type of guy who'd string me along until twenty days before our wedding. *It's about time,* Callahan had said the first time I'd kissed him. He'd been waiting for me.

The thought caused a hard sob to ratchet out of me. Angus whined, nuzzling his little face against my neck. "I'm okay," I told him unconvincingly. "I'll be fine."

I blew my nose, wiped my eyes and stared at my kitchen. It was so pretty here. Actually, now that I looked at it, it was rather…well, perfect. Everything had been chosen with an eye toward getting over Andrew—colors that would soothe my heartache, furniture that Andrew would never like. The whole house was a shrine to Getting Over Andrew.

And yet it wasn't Andrew I kept seeing here. Nope. I saw Callahan sitting in my kitchen, teasing me about my pajamas…Callahan holding my mother's sculptures in his big hands…Cal shaking Angus off his foot, or sinking onto his knees because I hit him with the field hockey stick or cooking me an omelet and telling me everything about his past.

Before long, someone was going to buy the house next door. A family, maybe, or an older couple, or a single woman. Or even a single man.

I knew one thing. I didn't want to see it. Almost without realizing it, I fished out the business card in my pocket and grabbed the phone. When Becky Mango answered, I simply said, "Hi, this is Grace Emerson and we just met. I'd like to sell my house."

CHAPTER THIRTY-ONE

MANNING'S GRADUATION was the same day as Natalie's rehearsal dinner. Classes had ended a week after Gettysburg, and I gave everyone except Kerry Blake an A+ for their participation. Kerry got a C, bringing her final mark to a dreaded B- and resulting in seven phone calls to the school from her enraged parents. As his final act as chairman of the history department, Dr. Eckhart upheld my grade. I would really miss that man.

The hall echoed as I made my way down to my classroom, which I'd spent yesterday cleaning. For the summer program in August, I'd be teaching a class on the American Revolution, but for the next two months, I wouldn't be here. The familiar end of term lump came to my throat

Looking around the room, I smiled at the sight of the picture, which Mallory had not only given me, but matted and framed, bless her heart. My seniors, my First Cavalry. I would never see most of those kids again. Maybe a few e-mails from some of my favorites for the next six months or so, but most of them would leave Manning and not return for years, if ever. But I planned on making a battle reenactment a permanent requirement for my class.

My gaze wandered to the huge copy of the Gettysburg Address, another of the Declaration of Independence, which I read aloud on the first day of school, in every class, every year. And in my continual effort to get the kids to feel a connection to our country's history, I'd shamelessly covered the walls with movie posters. *Glory. Saving Private Ryan. Mississippi Burning. The Patriot, Full Metal Jacket, Flags of Our Fathers.* And on the back of the door, *Gone With the Wind,* tawdry enough that I felt it should be hidden from direct view. Scarlett's bosom was scandalously exposed, and Rhett's eyes bored into hers. Now that I'd seen the movie, I loved that poster more than ever.

The lump in my throat grew. Luckily, I was interrupted by a gentle knock on the door. "Come in," I called. It was Dr. Eckhart.

"Good morning, Grace," he said, leaning on his cane.

"Hello, Dr. Eckhart." I smiled. "How are you?"

"A bit sentimental today, Grace, a bit sentimental. My last Manning graduation."

"It won't be the same without you, sir," I said.

"No," he agreed.

"I hope we can still meet for dinner," I said sincerely.

"Of course, my dear," he said. "And I'm sorry you didn't make chairman."

"Well. Sounds like they picked a winner."

The new department chair was someone named Louise Steiner. She came to Manning from a prep school in Los Angeles, had significantly more administrative experience under her belt than either Ava or I and held a doctorate in European history and a master's in American. In short, she'd kicked our butts.

Ava had been furious enough to break up with Theo Eisenbraun, Kiki told me. Ava was actively interviewing at other prep schools, but I didn't really think she'd leave. Too much work, and Ava never was much of a worker.

"Will you be going to Pennsylvania this year?" Dr. Eckhart asked. "Or any other battle sites?"

"No," I answered. "I'm moving this summer, so no travel for me." I hugged the old man gently. "Thank you for everything, Dr. Eckhart. I'll really miss you."

"Well," he harrumphed, patting my shoulder. "No need to get emotional."

"Hello? Oh, damn, I'm sorry. I didn't mean to interrupt." Both Dr. Eckhart and I looked up. An attractive woman in her fifties with short gray hair and a classy linen suit stood in my doorway. "Hi, I'm Louise. Hello, Dr. Eckhart, nice to see you again. Grace, isn't it?"

"Hi," I said, going over to shake the hand of my new boss. "Welcome to Manning. We were just talking about you."

"I wanted to meet you, Grace, and talk about a few things. Dr. Eckhart showed me a copy of your presentation, and I loved the curriculum changes you came up with."

"Thank you," I said, shooting a look at Dr. E., who was examining his yellowed fingernails.

"Maybe we can have lunch next week, talk about things," Louise suggested.

I smiled at Dr. Eckhart, then looked back at Louise. "I'd love to," I said sincerely.

When the caps had been thrown and the children celebrated the accomplishment of not having flunked out, when the graduation brunch was over, I made my way back to the parking lot. I had about two hours to shower, change and head on over to Soleil, the site of my faked date with Wyatt Dunn and where Natalie's rehearsal dinner would take place.

"Another school year gone," said a familiar voice.

I turned. "Hi, Stuart." He looked...older. Grayer. Sadder.

"I hope you have a nice summer," he said politely, looking at a particularly beautiful pink dogwood.

"Thanks," I murmured.

"How's...how's Margaret?" His gaze flickered to mine.

I sighed. "She's tense, jealous and difficult. Miss her?"

"Yes."

I looked at his sorrowful face for a beat or two. "Stuart," I asked quietly, "did you have an affair with Ava?"

"With that piranha?" he asked, looking shocked. "Goodness, no. We had dinner. Once. All I talked about was Margaret."

What the heck. I decided to throw him a bone. "We'll be at Soleil in Glastonbury, Stu. Tonight. Reservations are for seven-thirty. Be spontaneous."

"Soleil."

"Yup." I looked at him steadily.

He inclined his head in a courtly nod. "Have a lovely day, Grace." With that, Stuart walked away, the sun shining on his graying hair. *Good luck, pal,* I thought.

"Ms. Em! Wait up!" I turned to see Tommy Michener and a man, presumably his father, judging by the resemblance between them, coming toward me. "Ms. Emerson, this is my dad. Dad, this is Ms. Em, the one who took us to that battle!"

The father smiled. "Hello. Jack Michener. Tom here talks about you all the time. Says your class was his favorite."

Tommy's dad was tall and thin, with glasses and salt-and-pepper black hair. Like his son, he had a nice face, cheerful and expressive, sort of an Irish setter enthusiasm about the both of them. His grip was warm and dry when he shook my hand.

"Grace Emerson. Nice to meet you, too. You have a great kid here," I said. "And I don't say that just because he adores history, either."

"He's the best," Mr. Michener said, slinging his arm around Tommy's shoulders. "Your mom would be so proud," he added to his son, a little spasm of pain crossing his face. Ah, yes. Tommy's mom had died the year before he came to Manning.

"Thanks, Dad. Oh, hey, there's Emma. I'll be right back," Tommy said, then bolted off.

"Emma, huh?" Mr. Michener said, smiling.

"She's a great girl," I informed him. "Been nursing a crush on your son all year."

"Young love," Jack Michener said, grinning. "Thank God I'm not a teenager anymore." I smiled. "Did Tom tell you he's majoring in history at NYU?"

"Yes, he did. I was so pleased," I answered. "As I said, he's a fantastic kid. Really bright and interested. I wish I had more students like him."

Tommy's dad nodded in enthusiastic agreement. I glanced at my car. Jack Michener made no move to leave, and being that he was the father of my favorite senior, I decided I could chat a little longer. "So what do you do for a living, Mr. Michener?"

"Oh, hey, call me Jack." He smiled again, Tommy's open, wide grin. "I'm a doctor."

"Really?" I said politely. "What kind?"

"I work in pediatrics," he said.

I paused. "Pediatrics. Let me guess. Surgery?"

"That's right. Did Tom tell you that?"

"You're a pediatric surgeon?" I asked.

"Yes. Why? Did you think it was something else?"

I snorted. "No, well…no. I'm sorry. Just thinking of something else." I took a deep breath. "Um…so. How rewarding your work must be." The irony sloshed around my ankles in thick waves.

"Oh, it's great." He grinned again. "I tend to log in too many hours at the hospital—hard to leave sometimes—but I love it."

I bit down on a giggle. "That's wonderful."

He stuffed his hands in his pockets and tipped his head. "Grace, would you like to join Tom and me for dinner? It's just the two of us here today…"

"Um, thanks," I said, "but I can't. My sister's getting married tomorrow, and tonight's the rehearsal."

His smile dropped a few notches. "Oh. Well, maybe some other time?" He paused, blushing. "Maybe even without Tommy? We live in New York. It's not that far."

A date. The pediatric surgeon was asking me out on a date. A burst of hysterical laughter surged up my throat, but I clamped down on it just in time. "Um…wow, that's really nice of you." I took a quick breath. "The truth is, I'm…"

"Married?" he said with a no-hard-feelings shrug.

"No, no. I just broke up with someone, and I'm not over him yet."

"Well. I understand."

We were quiet for a second, both of us mildly embarrassed. "Oh, here comes Tommy," I said, relieved.

"Excellent. It was great meeting you, Grace. Thanks again for all you did for my son."

Tommy enveloped me in a hug. "Bye, Ms. Em," he said. "You're the best teacher here. I've had a crush on you since my first day of class."

I hugged him back chastely, my eyes wet. "I'll really miss you, buddy," I said honestly. "Write to me, okay?"

"You bet! Have a great summer!"

And with that, my favorite student and his pediatric surgeon dad left, leaving me more bemused than ever.

CHAPTER THIRTY-TWO

"Ahahaha. Ahahaha. Oooh. Ahahaha." Mom's society laugh rang out loud and false over the table.

"Hoohoohoohoo!" Andrew's mother, not to be out-faked, chortled right back. From the other side of the table, Margaret kicked me meaningfully, making me wince in pain.

"Aren't you glad you're not marrying into that family?" she hissed.

"So glad," I whispered back.

"Margaret, are you drunk?" Mémé asked her loudly. "I had a cousin who couldn't hold her liquor, either. Disgraceful. In my day, a lady never overindulged."

"Aren't you glad those days are gone now, Mémé?" Margaret quipped. "Would you like another Rusty Nail, by the way?"

"Thank you, dear," Mémé said, mollified. Margaret signaled the waiter, then made a mocking toast to me.

"Oh, yes, a toast!" Natalie cried. "Honey, make a toast!"

Andrew stood up, his parents gazing at him with servantile adoration. "This is such a happy day for us," he said. Awkwardly. His eyes paused on me, then moved on. "Nattie and I are so happy. And we're so happy that you're all here to share our happiness."

"I know I'm happy," I muttered to Margs, rolling my eyes.

"Hardly a great orator, is he?" she said, loud enough for

our mother to hear. Mom covered with another round of "Ahahaha. Ahahaha. Oooh. Ahahaha."

The waiter appeared with our appetizers. Looking up, I saw it was Cambry. "Hey!" I exclaimed. "How are you?"

"I'm fine," he said, grinning.

"I hear we're all having dinner next week chez Julian."

"If he doesn't bolt," Cambry answered, setting down the oysters Rockefeller in front of me.

Julian was in a relationship. Granted, the mere word caused him stomach cramps and a cold sweat, but he was dating, and even he couldn't find much fault with Cambry, who was waiting tables while he finished law school.

"You hang in there," I said. "You're good for him. He hardly ever wants to come over and watch *Dancing with the Stars* these days. I should probably hate you."

"Do you?" he asked, raising a concerned eyebrow.

"No, of course not. But you have to share. He's been my best friend since high school."

"Duly noted," he said.

"Grace, I thought the oysters here caused food poisoning," Mémé bellowed, causing a nearby diner to spit abruptly into his napkin.

"No, no!" I said loudly. "No. They're great. So fresh!" I smiled encouragingly to the napkin spitter and took a bite as he watched nervously.

"Well, didn't they just about kill your doctor?" Mémé asked, turning to the Carsons, who were smiling politely. "He was in the toilet for twenty minutes," she informed them, as if they hadn't been there. "The trots, you know. My second husband had stomach problems. We couldn't leave the house some days! And the smell!"

"It was so bad, the cat fainted," Margaret intoned.

"It was so bad, the cat fainted!" Mémé announced.

"Okay, Mother," Dad said, his face burning. "Perhaps that's enough."

"Ahahaha. Ahahaha. Oooh. Ahahaha," laughed Mom, her eyes murderous upon her mother-in-law, who was knocking back another cocktail. Personally, I'd never been fonder of Mémé, for some reason. Cambry was struggling unsuccessfully to hide his laughter, and in a rush of warm sincerity, I said a quick little prayer that he and Julian would make it. Even if it meant I had no one to cushion my loneliness, poor lonely spinster that I was. Perhaps Angus needed a wife. Maybe I could have his little snipping reversed and I could become a dog breeder for people who loved to have things destroyed by adorable barking balls of fur. Or not.

I looked down the table at Natalie. She wore a pale blue dress, and her smooth, honey-colored hair was swept up and held with the kind of clip my own hair ate like a Venus flytrap. She looked so happy. Her hand brushed Andrew's over a roll, and she blushed at the contact. Aw. Then she caught my eye, and I smiled at her, my beautiful sister. She smiled back.

"Grace, where's Callahan?" she asked abruptly, her head snapping around to look for him. "Is he coming separately?"

Drat. The truth was, I'd been kind of hoping not to have to discuss it. I hadn't mentioned my breakup to anyone but Margaret. For two reasons. One, I'd been holding on to the hope that Cal might, well, forgive me, realizing that I was the one for him and he couldn't live without me. And two, I didn't want to rain on Nattie's parade. She'd be worried about me, cluck and pat my back and puzzle over how someone could not want to date her big sister. Someone other than Andrew, that was.

Lucky for me, I'd just taken a bite of my oysters, so I

grinned and pointed and chewed. And chewed. Chewed a bit more, stalling as the oyster was ground into flavored saliva.

"Who's Callahan?" asked Mrs. Carson, turning her beady eyes on me.

"Grace is dating someone wonderful," Mom announced loudly.

"A convict," Mémé said, then belched. "An Irish convict with big hands. Right, Grace?"

Mr. Carson choked, Mrs. Carson's slitty eyes grew wider with malicious glee. "Well," I began.

"He used to be an accountant," my father said heartily. "Went to Tulane."

Margaret sighed.

"He's a handyman, right, Grace?" Mémé bellowed. "Or a gardener. Or a lumberjack. I can't remember."

"Or a coal miner. Or a shepherd," Margaret added, making me snort.

"He's wonderful," Mom said firmly, ignoring both her eldest child and Callahan's criminal past. "So, er, handsome."

"Oh, he is!" Natalie said, turning her shining eyes to the Carsons. "He and Grace are so good together. You can tell they're just crazy about each other."

"He dumped me," I announced calmly, wiping my mouth. Across the table, Margaret choked on some wine. As she sputtered into her napkin, she gave me a thumbs-up.

"The gardener dumped you? What? What did she say?" Mémé asked. "Why are you mumbling, Grace?"

"Callahan dumped me, Mémé," I said loudly. "My ethics aren't up to snuff."

"The prisoner said that?" Mémé barked.

"Pish!" my mother said. No one else said a word. Natalie looked like I'd clubbed her over the head.

"Thanks, Mom," I said. "Sorry to say, I think he's right."

"Oh, Pudding, no. You're wonderful," Dad said. "What does he know, after all? He's an idiot. An ex-con and an idiot."

"An ex-con?" Mr. Carson wheezed.

"No, he's not, Dad. He's not an idiot, that is. He *is* an ex-con, Mr. Carson," I clarified.

"Well," Mom said, her eyes darting between the Carsons and me, "do you think you might get back with your pediatric surgeon? He was such a nice young man."

Wow. Amazing how a lie could be so powerful. I looked at Margaret. She looked back, lifted an eyebrow. I turned back to my mother.

"There was no pediatric surgeon, Mom," I said, enunciating so Mémé could hear. "I made him up."

You know, it was almost fun, dropping a bomb like that. Almost. Margaret sat back and smiled broadly. "You go, Grace," she said, and for the first time in a long time, she looked genuinely happy.

I sat up a little straighter, though my heart was thudding so hard I thought I might throw up. My voice shook…but it carried, too. "I pretended to date someone so Natalie and Andrew wouldn't feel so guilty. And so everyone would stop treating me like I was some sort of abandoned dog covered in sores."

"Oh, Grace," Nat whispered.

"What? Grace, you can't be serious!" Dad exclaimed.

"I am, Dad. I'm sorry," I said, swallowing hard. Here it was at last…my confession. I started talking again, and my voice grew faster and faster. "Andrew broke up with me because he fell in love with Natalie, and it hurt. A lot. But I was getting over it. I was, and if they wanted to be together, I didn't want to be the reason they stayed apart. So I made up Wyatt Dunn, this impossibly perfect guy, and everyone felt much better, and I just ran with it because to tell you the truth, it felt great, even just pretending I had a boyfriend who was so wonderful. But then I fell for Callahan, and obviously I had to break up with Wyatt, and then, that night that Andrew came over and kissed me on the porch, Cal was really unhappy about that, and we talked and then I ended up telling him about Wyatt Dunn. And he dumped me. Because I lied."

My breath came in shaky little gasps, and my back was damp with sweat. Margaret reached across the table and put her hand over mind. "Good girl," she murmured.

Natalie didn't move. The Carsons' heads swiveled to gape at their son, who looked like he'd just been shot in the stomach, eyes wide with horror, face white. The rest of the restaurant was so quiet, you could almost hear the crickets cheeping.

"Wait a minute, wait a sec," my father said, his face slack with confusion. "Then who was I talking to in the bathroom that night?"

"Shut it, Jim," my mother hissed.

"That was Julian, pretending to be Wyatt," I said. "Any other questions? Comments? No? Okay, then, I'm going out for some air."

On shaking legs, I walked across the restaurant, past the now-silent diners, my face on fire. As I entered the foyer, Cambry leaped over to open the front door. "You are one magnificent creature," he said in an admiring voice as I walked out.

"Thanks," I whispered.

He had the grace to leave me alone. I was shaking like a leaf, my heart thudding. Who said that confession was good for the soul? I wanted to throw up. Going over to a small bench that sat in the restaurant's front garden, I sat down heavily. Pressed my cold fingers against my burning cheeks and closed my eyes, just trying to breathe normally. In and out. In and out. Not hyperventilating or passing out would be enough for now.

"Grace?" Natalie's voice was timid. I hadn't heard her footsteps.

"Hey, Nattie," I said wearily without looking up.

"Can I sit with you?" she asked.

"Sure. Of course." Natalie sat next to me. When she slipped her hand into mine, I looked down at our entwined hands. Her engagement ring caught the light. "My ring looked just like this," I murmured.

"I know. Who buys the same ring for sisters?"

"He probably didn't remember the one he gave to me. He can't even pick out matching socks."

"Pathetic," she murmured.

"Men," I muttered.

"So dumb."

I agreed…in Andrew's case, anyway. "Did he tell you about that kiss?" I whispered.

I hadn't meant to ruin anything for Natalie. Should've thought about that before I opened my mouth.

She was quiet for a moment. "Yes, he told me." A mockingbird twittered above us, a long stream of notes.

"What did he say?" I asked, more out of curiosity than anything.

"He said it was a lapse in judgment. That being in the house with you, having seen you with another guy…it made him feel a little jealous."

I sneaked a glance at my sister. "What did you think about that?"

"Well, I thought he was an asshole, Grace," she said, making my mouth drop open in shock. "It was our first fight. I told him he'd screwed up our lives enough already, and kissing you was unacceptable. Then I slammed a few doors and stomped around for a while."

Natalie's face was red. "How refreshing," I murmured.

She snorted. "And I was...jealous. Not that I had a right to be, given what I did to you."

I squeezed her hand. "You can't help the big kablammy," I said.

Natalie shot me a questioning glance.

"You know," I said. "The thunderbolt. Just one look, that's all it took, all that garbage." I paused. "But you made up, obviously. You guys are okay, right?"

She gave a little nod. "I think so," she whispered, looking straight ahead and squeezing my hand a little tighter. Her eyes were full of tears. "Grace, I'm so sorry that of all the people in the world, I had to fall for him. That I hurt you." She drew a shaking breath. "I never said it, but I'll say it now. I'm so, so sorry."

"Well, you know, it really sucked," I admitted. It was a relief to say the words.

"Are you mad at me?" Two tears slipped down her cheeks.

"No," I assured her. Then I reconsidered. "Well...not anymore. I tried not to be. I was more mad at Andrew, to be honest, but yeah, part of me was just screaming. It wasn't fair."

"Grace, you know you're my favorite person in the world. The last person I'd ever willingly hurt. I never meant to. I never wanted to. I hated that I fell for Andrew. I hated it." She was crying harder now.

I slipped my arm around her, pulling her so that our heads touched as we sat, side by side, not looking at each other. I didn't like to have my sister crying, but maybe she just needed to. And maybe I needed to see it. "Well," I admitted softly, "it hurt. Quite a bit. I didn't want you to know it. But I'm over that now. I really am."

"Making up Wyatt..." Her voice trailed off. "I think that might be the nicest thing anyone's ever done for me. And man, I jumped all over that." She gave a grim laugh. "I kind of suspected he wasn't real, you know. You had me up until the bit about the feral cats." She grinned.

I rolled my eyes. "I know."

Nat sighed. "I guess I didn't want to know the truth." We were quiet for a moment. "You know, Grace," she said softly, "you don't have to watch out for me anymore. You don't have to protect me from every sad emotion."

"Well," I said, my own eyes filling. "I kind of do. That's my job. I'm your big sister."

"Forget the job," she suggested, reaching out to tuck a wayward strand of frizz behind my ear. "Forget that you're the big sister. Let's just be plain old sisters. Equals, okay?"

I looked into the blue, clear sky. Ever since I was four, I'd been watching out for Natalie, admiring her, protecting her. It might be nice, just…just liking her. Instead of adoration, friendship. Equals, like she said.

"Like Margaret," I mused.

"Oh, God, don't be like Margaret!" she blurted with mock earnestness, and we both burst into laughter. Then Nat opened her purse and handed me a tissue—of course, she was armed with a cunning little tissue pack with roses on the cover—and we sat for another minute, listening to the mockingbird, holding hands.

"Grace?" she said eventually.

"Yeah?"

"I really liked Callahan."

Hearing that was like pressing on a bruise to see if it still hurt. It did. "Me, too," I whispered. She squeezed my hand and had the sense not to say anything else. After a moment, I cleared my throat and glanced around at the restaurant. "Want to get back?"

"Nah," she said. "Let everyone wonder. Maybe we could fake a cat fight, just for fun."

I laughed. My Nattie of old. "I missed you," I admitted.

"I missed you, too. It's been so hard, wondering if you're really as okay as you seemed, but afraid to ask. And I've been jealous, you know. You and Margs, living together."

"Oh, well, then, you can take her. You and Andrew," I said. "For as long as you want."

"He wouldn't survive the week." She grinned.

"Nattie," I said slowly, "about us being equals…" She nodded encouragingly. "I want you to do me a favor, Nat."

"Anything," she said.

I turned a little to better face her. "Nat, I don't want to be maid of honor tomorrow. Let it be Margaret. I'll be your bridesmaid, go down the aisle and all that, but not maid of honor. It's too weird, okay? A little pimp-ish, you know?"

"Okay," she said instantly. "But make sure Margaret doesn't roll her eyes and make faces."

"I'm sorry, I can't guarantee anything," I said with a laugh. "But I'll try."

Then I stood up and pulled my little sister to her feet. "Let's go back, okay? I'm starving."

We held hands all the way back to our table. Mom hopped up like an anxious sparrow when she saw us. "Girls! Is everything all right?"

"Yes, Mom. We're fine."

Mrs. Carson rolled her eyes and gave a ladylike snort, and suddenly, our mother wheeled on her. "I'll thank you to wipe that look off your face, Letitia!" she said, her voice carrying easily through the restaurant. "If you have something to say, speak up!"

"I'm…I don't…"

"Then stop treating my girls like they're not good enough for your precious son. And Andrew, let me say this. We only tolerate you because Natalie asked us to. If you screw up any of my girls' lives again, I will rip out your liver and eat it. Understand me?"

"I...I definitely do understand, Mrs. Emerson," Andrew said meekly, forgetting that he was supposed to call Mom by her first name.

Mom sat back down, and Dad turned to her. "I love you," he said, his voice awed.

"Of course you do," she said briskly. "Is everyone ready to order?"

"I can't eat beets," Mémé announced. "They repeat on me."

WE ALMOST GOT THROUGH the dinner without further incident. In fact, I was trying to resist the urge to lick my bowl clean of crème brûlée when there was a commotion at the front of the restaurant.

"I'm here to see my wife," came a raised voice. "Now."

Stuart.

He came into the dining room, dressed in his usual oxford and argyle sweater vest, tan trousers and tasseled loafers, looking like the gentle, sweet man he was. But his face was set, and his eyes, God bless him, were stormy.

"Margaret, this has gone on long enough," he announced, ignoring the rest of us.

"Hmm," Margaret said, narrowing her eyes.

"If you don't want to have a baby, that's fine. And if you want sex on the kitchen table, you'll get it." He glared down at his wife. "But you're coming home, and you're coming home now, and I will be happy to discuss this further once you're naked and in my bed." He paused. "Or on the table." His face flushed. "And the next time you leave me, you'd better mean it, woman, because I'm not going to be treated like a doormat. Understand?"

Margaret rose, put her napkin by her plate and turned to me. "Don't wait up," she said. Then she took Stuart's hand and let him lead her through the restaurant, grinning from ear to ear.

CHAPTER THIRTY-THREE

THE MINUTE I CAUGHT SIGHT of Andrew, I saw it.

Trouble.

The organ played Mendelssohn's *Wedding March,* the fifty or so guests, most related to either the bride or groom, stood and turned to look at us, the freaky Emerson sisters. There was Stuart, looking smugly blissful, the expression of a man who saw a lot of action last night. I grinned at him. He nodded and touched his forehead with two fingers in a little salute. There were Cousin Kitty and Aunt Mavis, who both smiled with great false sympathy as I passed. Resisting the urge to give them the finger (we were in church, after all, and Mayflower descendants and all that crap), I looked ahead and, for the first time that day, saw the groom.

He ran a hand through his hair. Pushed up his glasses. Coughed into his fist. Didn't look at me. Bit his lip.

Uh-oh. This did not look like a man whose dreams were all about to come true. This was more than the discomfort of standing in front of dozens of people. This was bad.

I gave Andrew a questioning look, but he wouldn't meet my eyes. His gaze bounced around the church, flitting from guest to guest like a housefly bouncing against a window, relentlessly seeking escape.

I hiked my skirt up a bit and stepped onto the altar, then made room for Margs. "We have a problem," I whispered.

"What are you talking about? Look at her face," she whispered back.

I looked at Natalie, beautiful, glowing, her sky-blue eyes shining. Dad looked tall and proud and dignified, nodding here and there as he walked his baby girl down the aisle to the grand music. "Take a look at Andrew," I whispered.

Margaret obeyed. "Nerves," she muttered.

But I knew Andrew better than that.

Nattie got to the altar. Dad kissed her cheek, shook Andrew's hand, and then sat down with Mom, who patted his arm fondly. Andrew and Natalie turned to the minister. Nat was beaming. Andrew…not so much.

"Dearly beloved," Reverend Miggs began.

"Wait. I'm sorry," Andrew interrupted, his voice weak and shaking.

"Holy Mary, Queen of Heaven," Margaret breathed. "Don't you dare, Andrew."

"Honey?" Nat's voice was soft with concern. "You okay?" My stomach clenched, my breath stopped. Oh, God…

Andrew wiped his forehead with his hand. "Nattie…I'm sorry."

There was a stirring in the congregation. Reverend Miggs put a hand on Andrew's arm. "Now, son," he began.

"What's wrong?" Natalie whispered. Margaret and I moved as one to flank her, instinctively wanting to protect her from what was about to come.

"It's Grace," he whispered. "I'm sorry, but I still have feelings for Grace. I can't marry you, Nat."

A collective gasp came from the assembled guests.

"Are you fucking kidding me?" Margaret barked, but I barely heard her. A white roaring noise was in my ears. I watched as the blood drained from Natalie's face. Her knees buckled. Margaret and the minister grabbed her.

Then I dropped my bouquet, shoved past Margaret, and punched Andrew as hard as I could. Right in the face.

The next few minutes were somewhat unclear. I know that Andrew's best man tried to pull him to safety (my punch had knocked him down) as I repeatedly kicked my once-fiancé and very nearly brother-in-law in the shins with my pointy little shoes. His nose was bleeding, and I thought it was a great look for him. I remember my mother joining me to beat him about the head with her purse. She may have tried to rip out his liver and eat it, but I didn't remember the details. Vaguely, I heard Mrs. Carson screaming. Felt Dad wrap his arms around my waist as he bodily dragged me off Andrew, who was half lying on the altar steps, trying to crawl away from my kicks and Mom's ineffective but highly satisfying blows.

In the end, the groom's guests scuttled out the back, leaving the Carsons, the best man and Andrew, a handkerchief pressed to his face, huddled on one side. Natalie sat stunned in the first pew on the bride's side, surrounded by Margaret, me, Mom and Dad as Mémé herded people out of the church like some geriatric border collie in a wheelchair.

"Left at the altar," Natalie murmured blankly.

I knelt in front of her. "Honey, what can we do?"

Her gaze found mine, and for a minute, we just looked at each other. I reached out and took her hand. "I'll be okay," she whispered. "It's okay."

"He's not worth your spit, Nattie," Margaret said, stroking Natalie's silky hair.

"Not worth the tissue you used to blow your nose," Mom seconded. "Bastard. Idiot. Penis-head."

Nat looked up at Mom, then burst out laughing, a hysterical edge to her voice. "Penis-head. That's a good one, Mom."

Mr. Carson came over warily. "Um, very sorry about all this," he said. "Change of heart, obviously."

"We got that," Margaret snapped.

"We're sorry," he repeated, looking at Natalie, then at me. "Very sorry, girls."

"Thanks, Mr. Carson," I said. He nodded once, then went back to his wife and son. A moment later, the Carsons were gone, out the side door. I hoped vigorously that we'd never see them again.

"What do you want to do right now, honey?" Dad asked.

Nat blinked. "Well," she said after a minute, "I think we should go to the club and eat all that good food." Her eyes filled once more. "Yes. Let's all do that, okay?"

"You sure?" I asked. "You don't have to be brave, Bumppo."

She squeezed my hand. "I learned from the best."

AND SO IT WAS that the Emerson side of the guest list went to the country club, ate shrimp and filet mignon and drank champagne.

"I'm better off without him," Nat murmured as she drank what had to be her fifth glass of champers. "I know that. It's just gonna take a while for that to sink in."

"Personally, I hated him from the day Grace brought him home," Margs said. "Smug little weenie. Estate law, please. Such a sissy."

"How many men are stupid enough to dump two Emerson girls?" Dad asked. "Too bad we're not mobbed up. We could have his body dumped in the Farmington River."

"I don't think the Mafia accepts white Anglo-Saxon Protestants, Dad," Margaret said, patting Nat's shoulder and pouring her more champagne. "But it's a sweet thought."

Nattie would be okay, I could tell. She was right. Andrew didn't deserve her, and he never had. Her heart would heal. Mine did, after all.

I wandered over to sit with Mémé for a bit. She was

watching Cousin Kitty, who was as sensitive as a rhino, dancing with her new husband to "Endless Love." "So what do you think of all this, Mémé?" I asked.

"Bound to happen. People should be more like me. Marriage is a business arrangement. Marry for money, Grace. You won't be sorry."

"Thanks for the advice," I said, patting her bony shoulder. "But really, Mémé, were you ever in love?"

Her rheumy eyes were faraway. "Not especially," she said. "There was a boy, once…well. He wasn't an appropriate match for me. Not from the same class, you see."

"Who was he?" I asked.

She gave me a sharp look. "Aren't we nosy today? Have you gained weight, Grace? You look a little hefty in the hips. In my day, a woman wore a girdle."

So much for our heart-to-heart. I sighed, asked Mémé if she wanted another drink and wandered off to the bar. Margaret was already there.

"So?" I asked. "How was the kitchen table?"

"It actually wasn't that comfortable," she said, grinning. "You know, it was muggy last night, the humidity made me stick like Velcro, so when he actually—"

"Okay, that's enough," I broke in. She laughed and ordered a glass of seltzer water.

"Seltzer, hmm?" I asked.

She rolled her eyes. "Well, when I was living at your house, I kind of decided that maybe a baby…well, maybe it wouldn't be awful. Someday. Maybe. We'll see. Last night he said he wanted a little girl just like me—"

"Is he insane?" I asked.

She turned to look at me, and I saw her eyes were wet. "I just thought that was the sweetest thing, Grace. It really got to me."

"Yes, but then you'd have to raise it. The Mini-Margs," I said. "That man must really love you."

"Oh, shut up, you," she said, laughing in spite of herself. "The baby idea seems kind of...well. Kind of okay."

"Oh, Margs." I smiled. "I think you'd be a great mom. On many levels, anyway."

"So you'll babysit, right? Whenever I have spit-up in my hair and a screaming baby in my arms and I'm ready to stick my head in the oven?"

"Absolutely." I gave her a quick hug, which she tolerated, even returned.

"You doing okay, Grace?" she asked. "This whole Andrew thing has come full circle, hasn't it?"

"You know, if I never hear that name again, I'll be glad," I said. "I'm fine. I just feel so bad for Nat."

But she'd be okay. Even now, she was laughing at something my father said. Both my parents were glued to her side, Mom practically force-feeding her hors d'oeuvres. Andrew wasn't worthy of her.

Or of me, for that matter. Andrew never deserved me. I could see that now. A man who accepts love as if it's his due is, in a word, a jerk.

Callahan O'Shea...he was another matter altogether.

"So what are your plans for the summer?" Margs asked. "Any offers on the house yet?"

"Two, actually," I answered, taking a sip of my gin and tonic.

"I have to say, I'm surprised," Margs commented. "I thought you loved that house."

"I do. I did. I just... It's time for a fresh start. Change isn't the worst thing in the world, is it?"

"I guess not," she said. "Come on, let's go sit with Nattie."

"Here they are!" Dad boomed as we approached. "Now

the three prettiest girls in the world are all together. Make that four," he quickly amended, putting his arm around Mom, who rolled her eyes.

"Dad, did Grace tell you she's selling her house?" Margaret asked.

"What? No! Honey! Why didn't you tell me?"

"Because it's not a group decision, Dad."

"But we just put new windows in there!"

"Which the Realtor said would help it sell," I said calmly.

"Where are you going, then?" Mom asked. "You wouldn't go far, would you, honey?"

"Nope. Not far." I sat next to Nat, who was doing that mile-long stare I had mastered myself a year and a half ago. "You okay, kiddo?" I asked.

"Yeah. I'm fine. Well, not fine. But you know." I nodded.

"Hey, did you ever hear about the history department job?" Margs asked.

"Oh, yes," I answered. "They hired someone from outside. But she seems great."

"Maybe she'll give you a raise," Dad speculated. "It'd be nice if you earned more than a Siberian farmer."

"I was thinking of picking up work as a high-class hooker," I said. "Do you know any politicians who are looking?"

Natalie laughed, and the sound made us all smile.

A while later, after dinner had been served, I headed into the ladies' room. From the stalls came the voice of my smug cousin Kitty.

"...so apparently, she just was pretending to date someone so we wouldn't feel sorry for her," Kitty was saying. "The doctor was completely made up! And then there was something about a convict she'd been writing to in prison..." The toilet flushed, and Kitty emerged. From the next stall came Aunt Mavis. Upon sighting me, they both froze.

"Hello, ladies," I said graciously, smoothing my hair in the mirror. "Are you enjoying yourselves? So much to gossip about, so little time!"

Kitty's face turned as red as a baboon's butt. Aunt Mavis, made of stronger stuff, simply rolled her eyes.

"Do you have any questions about my love life? Any gaps in your information? Anything you need from me?" I smiled, folded my arms across my chest and stared them down.

Kitty and Mavis exchanged a look. "No, Grace," they said in unison.

"Okay," I answered. "And just for the record, he was on death row. Sorry to say, the governor turned down his stay of execution, so I'm on the prowl again." I winked, smiled at their identical looks of horror, and pushed my way into a stall.

When I rejoined my family, Nat was getting ready to go. "You can stay with me, Bumppo," I said.

"No, thanks, Grace. I'll stay with Mom and Dad for a few days. But you're sweet to offer."

"Want me to drive you?" I asked.

"No, Margs is taking me. We have to make a stop first. Besides, you've done enough today. Beating up Andrew... thanks for that."

"My pleasure," I said with complete sincerity. I kissed my sister, then hugged her a long, long time. "Call me in the morning."

"I will. Thanks," she whispered.

Walking to my car, I fished the car keys out of my bag. What seemed like aeons ago, I had promised my little old lady friends at Golden Meadows that I'd stop by tonight. They wanted to see my fancy dress and hear how the wedding went. Well, Dad had taken Mémé home before dinner. Chances were, the residents of Golden Meadows knew quite well how the wedding went.

But I figured I'd go just the same. Tonight was the Saturday Night Social. I could probably scare up someone to dance with, and though he wouldn't be under eighty years old, I felt like dancing, oddly enough.

I drove across town and pulled into Golden Meadows's parking lot. There was no sign of Callahan's battered pickup truck. I hadn't seen him since the day he left Maple Street, though I had stopped in to see his grandfather. As Cal had mentioned, the old man wasn't doing well. We'd never even finished the book.

On impulse, I decided to stop in and see Mr. Lawrence. Who knew? Maybe Callahan would be there. Betsy, the nurse on duty, buzzed me in with a wave. "You just missed the grandson," she said, cupping her hand over the receiver.

Drat. Well, Callahan wasn't my reason for coming, not really. I walked down the hall amid the familiar, sad sounds of this particular ward—faint moans, querulous voices and too much quiet.

Mr. Lawrence's door was open. He was asleep in his hospital bed, small and shrunken against the pale blue sheets. An IV, new from the last time I'd come by, snaked from a clear plastic tube into his arm, and tears pricked my eyes. I'd been coming to Golden Meadows long enough to know that in cases like this, an IV usually meant the patient had stopped eating and drinking.

"Hi, Mr. Lawrence, it's Grace," I whispered, sitting down next to him. "The one who reads to you, remember? *My Lord's Wanton Desire?* The duke and the prostitute?"

Of course, he didn't answer. To the best of my recollection, I'd never heard the voice of Cal's grandfather. I wondered what he'd sounded like when he was a younger man, teaching Cal and his brother to fly-fish, helping them with their homework, telling them to finish their vegetables and drink their milk.

"Listen, Mr. Lawrence," I said, putting my hand on his thin and vulnerable arm. "I just wanted to tell you something. I was dating your grandson for a little while. Callahan. And basically, I screwed things up and he broke up with me." I rolled my eyes at myself, not having planned on a deathbed confession. "Anyway, I just wanted to tell you what a good man he is."

A lump came to my throat, and my voice dropped back to a whisper. "He's smart and funny and thoughtful, and he's always working, you know? You should see the house he just fixed up. He did such a beautiful job." I paused. "And he loves you so much. He comes here all the time. And he's...well, he's a good-looking guy, right? Chip off the old block, I'm guessing."

The sound of Mr. Lawrence's breathing was barely audible. I picked up his gnarled, cool hand and held it for a second. "I just wanted to say that you did a great job raising him. I think you'd be really proud. That's all."

Then I leaned over and kissed Mr. Lawrence's forehead. "Oh, one more thing. The duke marries Clarissia. He finds her in the tower and rescues her, and they live...you know. Happily ever after."

"What are you doing, Grace?"

I jumped like someone had just pressed a brand against my flesh. "Mémé! God, you scared me!" I whispered.

"I've been looking for you. Dolores Barinski said you were supposed to come to the social, and it started an hour ago."

"Right," I said with a last glance back at Mr. Lawrence. "Well, let's go, then."

So I wheeled my grandmother down the hall, away from

the last link I had to Callahan O'Shea, knowing that I would probably not see Mr. Lawrence again. A few tears slipped down my cheeks. I sniffed.

"Oh, cheer up," Mémé snapped omnisciently from her throne. "At least you have me. That man isn't even related to you. I don't know why you even care."

I stopped the wheelchair and went around to face my grandmother, ready to tell her what a sour old pain in the butt she was, how vain and rude, how selfish and insensitive. But looking down on her thinning hair and wrinkled face, her spotted hands adorned with too-big rings, I said something else.

"I love you, Mémé."

She looked up, startled. "What's wrong with you today?"

"Nothing. I just wanted to tell you."

She took a breath, frowning, her face creasing into folds. "Well. Are we going or not?"

I smiled, resumed pushing and headed to the social. It was in full swing, and I danced with all my regulars and a few people I didn't recognize. I even took Mémé out for a spin in the wheelchair, but she hissed at me that I was making a fool of myself and wondered loudly if I'd had too much to drink at the club, so I took her back. Eventually. After two songs, that is.

My dress was admired, my hands were patted and held, even my hair was deemed pretty. I was, in other words, happy. Nat was heartbroken, and my own heart wasn't doing too well, either. I'd ruined something lovely and rare with Callahan O'Shea and made an idiot of myself in front of my family by faking a boyfriend. But that was okay. Well, the idiot part was okay. Callahan, though…I'd miss him for a long time.

CHAPTER THIRTY-FOUR

WHEN I GOT HOME from Golden Meadows, it was nearly ten. Angus presented me with two rolls of shredded toilet paper, then trotted into the kitchen to show me where he'd vomited up a few wads. "At least you did it on the tile," I said, bending down to pet his sweet head. "Thank you for barfing in the kitchen." He barked once, then stretched out in Super Dog pose to watch me clean.

"I hope you'll like our new place," I said, donning the all-too-familiar rubber gloves I used when cleaning Angus's, er, accidents. "I'll pick us out a winner, don't you worry." Angus wagged his tail.

Becky Mango had called yesterday. "I know this might be weird," she said, "but I was wondering if you might be interested in the house next door to you. The one Callahan fixed up? It's just charming."

I'd hesitated. I loved that house, heaven knew. But I'd already lived in a house that was all about one failed relationship. Buying Cal's, though it cost roughly the same as mine, would've been too Miss Havisham for me. No. My next house would be about my future, not about my past. "Right, Angus?" I said now. He barked helpfully, then burped and flipped onto his back, craftily suggesting that I take a break from cleaning up his vomit to scratch his tummy. "Later, McFangus," I murmured.

I blotted up his little mess, taking care not to let my hem get soiled. It was a pretty dress, but I was planning on taking it to the Salvation Army. I never wanted to see it again. That, and my wedding dress. Maybe Nat would want me to bring hers, too.

Tomorrow, I'd start packing. Even though I hadn't found a house yet, I'd be moving soon. I could go through all my old tag sale finds, maybe have a sale of my own. Fresh start and all that.

As I Windexed the last traces of barf off of the floor and stuffed the paper towels into the trash, Angus leaped to his feet and flew out of the room in an explosion of barking. *Yarp! Yarpyarpyarp!*

"What's wrong, honey?" I asked, coming into the living room

Yarpyarpyarp!

I peeked around the curtains through the window and my heart surged into my throat so hard I nearly choked.

Callahan O'Shea was standing on the front porch.

He looked at me, raised an eyebrow and waited.

My legs barely held me as I opened the front door. With a snarl, Angus launched himself on Cal's work boot. Cal ignored him.

"Hi," he said.

"Hi," I whispered.

His gaze went to my hands, which were still protected by the rubber gloves. "What are you doing?"

"Um...cleaning up dog puke."

"Pretty."

I just stood there. Callahan O'Shea. Here. On my porch, where we'd first met.

"Mind calling off your dog?" he asked as Angus, his

mouth clamped onto a good part of Cal's pant leg, swung his little head back and forth, growling his kittenish growl.

"Um...sure. Of course," I said. "Angus! Down cellar, boy! Come on!" My knees were shaking, but I managed to pick up Angus and shove him through the cellar door, down with the girl part sculptures. He whined, then accepted his fate and grew quiet.

I turned back to Callahan. "So. What brings you to the neighborhood?" My throat was so tight my voice squeaked.

"Your sisters paid me a visit," he said quietly.

"They did?" I asked, my mouth dropping open.

"Mmm-hmm."

"Today?"

"About an hour ago. They told me about Andrew."

"Right." I closed my mouth. "Big mess."

"You beat him up, I hear."

"Yes, I did," I murmured. "One of my finer moments." A thought occurred to me. "How did they know where to find you?" Callahan had certainly not left a forwarding address with me.

"Margaret called her pals at the parole office."

I bit down on a smile. Good old Margs.

"Natalie told me I was an idiot," Callahan murmured, his voice low enough to cause a vibration in my stomach.

"Oh," I squeaked, leaning back against the wall for support. "Sorry. You're not an idiot."

"She told me how you came clean with everyone." Cal took a step closer to me, and my heart thudded so hard I felt like I might imitate Angus and throw up myself. "Said I was an idiot if I was going to just walk away from a woman like you."

Callahan took my limp hand and removed the rubber glove, smiling a little as he did. He repeated the action on the other hand, I found myself staring at our hands, because it was hard to look in Cal's eyes.

"The thing is, Grace," he said gently, holding my sweaty hands in his own much more appealingly dry ones, "I didn't really need to hear it. I'd already figured that out."

"Oh," I breathed.

"But I have to admit, I thought it was nice that your sisters were finally doing something for you, instead of the other way around." He tipped up my chin, forcing me to look into his pretty eyes. "Grace," he whispered, "I *was* an idiot. I should know better than anyone that people get stupid around the folks they love. And that everyone deserves a second chance."

I sucked in a shaky breath, my eyes filling with tears.

"Here's the thing, Grace," Cal said, a smile playing at the corner of his mouth. "Ever since that first day when you smacked me in the head with your field hockey stick—"

"You just can't let that go, can you?" I muttered.

He grinned fully now. "—and even when you hit me with the rake and dented my truck, and when you were spying on me from your attic and your dog was mauling me, Grace, I always knew you were the one for me."

"Oh," I whispered, my mouth wobbling like crazy. Not my best look, to be sure, but I couldn't help it.

"Give us another chance, Grace. What do you say?" His smile told me he was fairly sure of the answer.

Instead of answering, I just wrapped my arms around him and kissed him for all I was worth. Because when you meet The One, you just know.

EPILOGUE

Two years later

"WE ARE NOT NAMING OUR SON Abraham Lincoln O'Shea. Think of something else." My husband pretended to scowl at me, but his look was somewhat marred by Angus licking his chin. We were lying in bed on a Sunday morning, the sun streaming in through the windows, the smell of coffee mingling with the sweet scent drifting from the small vase of roses on the night table.

"You already rejected Stonewall," I reminded him, rubbing my enormous stomach. "Stonewall O'Shea. There certainly wouldn't be any other little boys in kindergarten with that name."

"Grace. Your due date was four days ago. Come on. Be serious. This is our child. And if he has to have a Civil War name, it's got to be Yankee. Okay? We're both from New England, after all. Angus, get your tongue out of my ear. Yuck."

I giggled. When we first moved in together, Callahan took Angus to an eight-week-long obedience course. Children need structure, Cal had told me, and ever since, the dog had been insanely devoted to him.

I tried again. "How about Ulysses S. O'Shea?"

"I'd settle for Grant. Grant O'Shea. That's a compromise, Grace."

"Grant O'Shea. Nope. Sorry. How about Jeb?"

"That's it, missy." He pounced, tickled, and a second later we were making out like a couple of teenagers.

"I love you," he whispered, his hand on my tummy.

"I love you, too," I whispered back.

Yep, we got married. I got the boy next door. And for that matter, the house next door, as well. Cal said it didn't seem right that it belong to anyone but us, and we bought it together, two weeks after Natalie's nonwedding.

Living next door to my old place didn't bother me a bit. I was grateful to that house, where my sore and sad heart had slowly mended. It was where I first met my husband, after all.

Speaking of Natalie, she was doing fine. She was single still, working a lot, and seemed happy. She dated a little here and there, but nothing serious yet. Stuart and Margaret had become parents about a year ago—James, a colicky baby who cried the first four months of his life before transforming into a dimpled, chubby little Buddha of smiles and drool, and Margaret loved him beyond reason.

"God, you smell good," Cal muttered from the region of my neck, which he was nuzzling most pleasantly. "Want to fool around?"

I looked at him, his long, straight lashes and perpetually tousled hair, those soft, dark blue eyes...*I hope our son looks just like him,* I thought, and my heart ached with such love that I couldn't answer. Then there was a different ache, and soggy feeling to go with it.

"Honey?" Callahan asked. "You okay?"

"You know what? I think my water just broke."

Thirty minutes later, Cal was trying to get me out the front door as Angus barked maniacally in the cellar, enraged at the unceremonious way Callahan had dumped him there, but Cal was in no mood for niceties, racing around like the house was on fire. I knew from Margaret's long and gruesome labor, which she enjoyed discussing in great detail, that the baby would probably take the better part of a day to come. The obstetrician had said the same thing, but Cal was convinced that I was about to squat and push his child out right here and now...or worse, on the side of the road between here and the hospital.

"Do you have my lollipops?" I asked calmly, consulting my list from birthing class.

"Yup. I sure do." He looked nervous—*terrified* might have been a better word—and I found it quite adorable. "Come on, honey, let's go. Baby's coming, don't forget."

I gave him a pointed look. "I'll try to remember, Callahan. What about my pretty bathrobe? My hair's going to be bad enough. At least I can look nice from the neck down." I looked back at the list. "Don't forget the camera, of course."

"Got it, Grace. Come on, sweetheart. Let's not have the baby in the hall here."

"Cal, I've had two contractions. Relax." He made a noise in the back of his throat, which I kindly ignored. "Did you remember the baby clothes? That little blue sleeper with the dog on it?"

"Yes, honey, please, I checked the list already. Think we can leave for the hospital before the kid turns three?"

"Oh, my focal point! Don't forget that." The birthing instructor had said to bring an object to concentrate on during the contractions, something I liked looking at.

"Got it." He reached up over the front door and took down the focal point—my field hockey stick, which Cal had hung up the day we moved in. "Okay, sweetheart. Let's go meet our boy. Want me to carry you? It's faster. I'll do that. Just put your arm around my neck, honey. Come on. Let's go."

Nineteen and a half very impressive and memorable hours later, we learned several things. One, I could be very, very loud when the situation demanded it. Two, while Cal was pretty amazing during labor and delivery, he also tended to cry when his wife was in pain. (Just when you think you can't love a guy any more...) And three, ultrasounds are still wrong once in a while.

Our boy was a girl.

We named her Scarlett.

Scarlett O'Hara O'Shea.

&RIVA™

Live life to the full – give in to temptation

Four new sparkling and sassy romances every month!

Be the first to read this fabulous new series from 1st December 2010 at **millsandboon.co.uk**
In shops from 1st January 2011

Tell us what you think!
Facebook.com/romancehq
Twitter.com/millsandboonuk

Don't miss out!

Available at WHSmith, Tesco, ASDA, Eason and all good bookshops

www.millsandboon.co.uk

Don't miss our **MONTHLY** special offer!

It can be found in the envelope containing your invoice.

YOU WILL BENEFIT FROM:

- FREE books or generous DISCOUNTS
- Most titles sent to you before they are available in the shops
- Free Gifts & Competitions
- Free delivery to your door
- No purchase obligation – 14 day trial
- Easy to order: by phone, post or online

*So what are you waiting for —
take a look* **NOW!**

& MILLS BOON *Book Club*

www.millsandboon.co.uk

Discover Pure Reading Pleasure with

MILLS & BOON

Visit the Mills & Boon website for all the latest in romance

- **Buy** all the latest releases, backlist and eBooks
- **Join** our community and chat to authors and other readers
- **Win** with our fantastic online competitions
- **Tell us** what you think by signing up to our reader panel
- **Find out** more about our authors and their books
- **Free** online reads from your favourite authors
- **Sign** up for our free monthly eNewsletter
- **Rate** and review books with our star system

www.millsandboon.co.uk

Follow us at twitter.com/millsandboonuk

Become a fan at facebook.com/romancehq

How far would you go to protect your sister?

The Lies We Told
Diane Chamberlain

As teenagers, Maya and Rebecca Ward witnessed their parents' murder. Now doctors, Rebecca has become the risk taker whilst her sister Maya lives a quiet life with her husband Adam, unwilling to deal with her secrets from the night her parents died.

When a hurricane hits North Carolina, Maya is feared dead. As hope fades, Adam and Rebecca face unexpected feelings. And Rebecca finds some buried secrets of her own.

Available 19th November 2010
www.mirabooks.co.uk

MIRA

Is the *It* girl losing it?

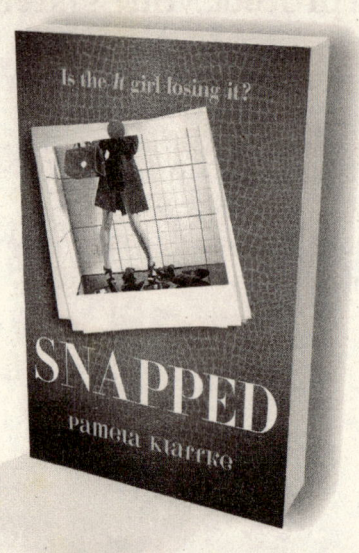

At the helm of must-read *Snap* magazine, veteran style guru Sara B. has had the joy of eviscerating the city's fashion victims in her legendary DOs and DON'Ts photo spread.

But now on the unhip edge of forty, Sara's being spat out like an old Polaroid picture: blurry, undeveloped and obsolete.

After launching into a comic series of blow-ups, Sara realises she's made her living by cutting people down…and somehow she must make amends.

Available 21st January 2011
www.mirabooks.co.uk